KU-167-519

This book is to be returned on or before
the last date stamped below.

THE WEAVER'S APPRENTICE

Michael Brown was born in the Chatham Islands and grew up in rural New Zealand.

From an early age he experienced visions which intensified as time went on until, at the age of 27, he was committed to a psychiatric institution. Later, still plagued by visions, he travelled to South America to search for a secret abbey in the Andes. As a result of this journey, the visions ceased. These experiences were the subject of his first book, *The Weaver and the Abbey.*

Graduating in physics, Michael Brown later gained a diploma of journalism and worked in radio and television. He spent a year in a fishing village where he worked briefly as a fishing-boat deckhand and wrote this novel. Now a television journalist, he is working on a second novel.

by the same author

THE WEAVER AND THE ABBEY

THE WEAVER'S APPRENTICE

MICHAEL BROWN

COLLINS
Auckland   Sydney   London

Cover design by Neysa Moss
Photograph by Geoff Moon

First published 1986
William Collins Publishers Ltd
P.O. Box 1, Auckland

© Michael Brown 1986

ISBN 0 00 222319 8

Typeset by Saba Graphics Ltd
Printed by The Dominion Press-Hedges & Bell, Maryborough 3465

This is a work of fiction. All characters are the products of the author's
imagination and any resemblance to actual persons, living or dead, is
entirely coincidental.

To fellow travellers Sue, Andrew and Sam — in case you need help with the luggage.

ACKNOWLEDGMENTS

The background to life in post-war Waiata was given to me in such rich detail by many residents of Banks Peninsula, Canterbury, New Zealand, that the village lived vividly in my mind before I began to write. The experience has left me with a love of Banks Peninsula that will stay with me. In particular, my thanks to George Brasells, Roland and May Curry, Arthur Erickson, Jack Helps, Lois Holderness, Alex McMaster, Bob Masefield, Joe Narbey, Paul Oliver, Dr Graham Patrick, Gillian Polson, West Shuttleworth, Paddy and Lon Stronach, Lou Walker, Reverend Russell Wells, Constable Gerald Williamson, and Dr Ian Breward of Dunedin — and to D'Arcy.

The brain does not create thought; it is an instrument which thought finds useful.

—Joseph Wood Krutch, *More Lives Than One*

PART ONE

ONE

Matthew Fleming was expelled from the comfort of his mother's womb early in the spring of 1944. His protests at the outrage were vigorous and piercing, turning his already birth-flushed complexion to vivid shades of purple. But then, abruptly, his cries ceased. His eyes opened. And when confronted with his mother's breast, he set about the business of living with snuffling, dogged determination, causing the doctor to observe that this one would lead his parents a merry dance if they neglected the rod. He also noted that Matthew had been born with a short misshapen right thumb, but it would have taken much more than that to dull the shine in Mrs Fleming's countenance.

Outside, where the sun was steaming the last frost off the picket fence, a knot of villagers waited for the news. They didn't have to wait long. The father, a respected fisherman and church elder, flung open his front door and emerged with a grin so broad he needed no words. It was clear. John Fleming's prayers for a son as his first-born had been answered.

The names had already been chosen. Matthew David Fleming. David for the courage that defeated Goliath. Matthew because it meant 'God's gift'.

Twelve hours later, 12 000 miles around the world, in Southampton, England, the passenger liner *Rangitata* set sail via Panama for New Zealand in the South Pacific. On the passenger deck was a tall, upright man whose appearance and manner were so striking that he attracted considerable curiosity from his fellow travellers.

Robert Alexander Fergus McKay was six feet four inches in height, slimly built, with a back as straight as a bricky's drop-line. He was soberly clothed: plain, black leather shoes, grey trousers, and a black serge jacket over a clergyman's collar. The

9

two inches of fully exposed collar in the front and the arrangement of the bib identified him as a minister of the Presbyterian faith. He was handsome in an austere, severe way, the severity accentuated by a thin face, black hair and a carefully trimmed mahogany-brown beard, hinting at red over the cheeks. His black eyebrows grew straight out from the skin, a single hedge across both eyes. There was a resolute set to his shoulders, a firmness to the line of his lips, a purposeful glint to his deep, almost prussian-blue eyes — a magnetism to him that attracted the glances of men and women alike.

He was married. The presence of his family proclaimed the fact. Three small, immaculately groomed, pink-ribboned, pigtailed girls hovered around his legs, wide-eyed with excitement as the ship moved out to sea. His wife Ellen stood amongst them, pleasantly attractive, demure, dutifully attentive, and large with a fourth child.

Even at this stage of the war, there was shipwide apprehension at the prospect of an unescorted Atlantic crossing. Except for the minister. True, he frequently and unnecessarily removed a gold fob-watch from his waistcoat pocket to check the time; but the action was so unruffled, so unconscious, that it was clearly a habit of long standing. Looking at him, it was easy to imagine a quiet, inner certainty that the Almighty had something more in store for him than drowning in mid-Atlantic. And that was a most comforting thought; even before the *Rangitata* cleared the English Channel, Robert McKay was requested, through the Captain, to lead the ship's company in daily prayer for the duration of the voyage. He agreed. He also made it plain that any who wished Holy Communion but were not of the Presbyterian persuasion could expect to be disappointed.

Across the Atlantic, through the Panama Canal, down through the southern seas of the Pacific Ocean, the voyage passed without incident. Neither Presbyterians nor non-Presbyterians were torpedoed, bombed, strafed, or in any way reminded of the world war soon to come to a close. It took six weeks to reach Wellington. It took only another two hours for the McKays to board the ferry to the South Island. And the following morning they were rounding Banks Peninsula in a third vessel: the fortnightly supply boat to the remote village of Waiata, which is pronounced 'Why-uh-tuh'.

10

It was a Sunday. A warm October Sunday.

As the launch steamed in through the heads of Waiata's harbour, the minister and his family came to the rail to watch. The three girls stopped chattering without being told to do so. Ellen McKay forgot herself, placed her hand over her husband's on the rail and gripped it, even though they were in full view of the wheelhouse. He was so absorbed in what he was seeing, he neglected to reprove her. His gaze roamed keenly, recognising detail after detail from all the books and sketches he had been sent in advance.

At several times, millions of years ago, Banks Peninsula had been actively volcanic. Then, after a build-up of pressure and heat to inconceivable proportions, a sickle-shaped segment of earth, six miles long and more than a mile across, had thrown itself into the sky. The ocean had rushed in. And when the steam had followed the last ash into the atmosphere and the lava had cooled, the peninsula possessed what was to become one of the deepest, most sheltered and most beautiful harbours in the world.

Beneath, a small blue penguin flew in the clear water, parallel to the throbbing boat. On the surface, the harbour was smooth silk, with a swell so long and low it was less perceptible by the soles of the feet than by the two inches of wet rock visible at the foot of the eastern cliffs.

High tide.

A shag sunned draggled wings, pterodactyl-like, on a water-bound rock. Another swam away underwater in a straight line, slowly skipping the surface from underneath in some inverted gravity field. All around, a luxuriant green blanket lay in rolls and steep folds that rose to more than three thousand feet. Stately native rimu and kahikatea trees stood out above the spring-tinted foliage, sentinels on the ridges, guardians in the valleys. On the edges of the cliffs that lined the harbour, the roots of manuka trees writhed and groped for purchase. Fat grey-and-white wood pigeons trampled the grey-green foliage or blundered clumsily through the treetops. A small bird, brightly hued in blues and greens, darted out over the water fast and straight, beak held dagger-like before it. A kingfisher. Gulls quarrelled around the rocks and up the cliff faces. High above the bushed hillsides behind the cliffs, crows wheeled in the black cloud, cawing.

As the launch progressed up the harbour, the cliffs began

11

to break into small inlets. A few tiny beaches appeared: tablecloths of coarse, white-grey sand. The beaches widened and deepened. The inlets turned to tiny valleys, and the valleys grew bold and ran from the water to high in the hills.

As the end of the harbour drew nearer, a change began to come over the minister's expression. His lips parted, his eyebrow line shortened, gathering almost imperceptibly towards the centre. Ellen McKay frowned at him, puzzled. She tried to follow his gaze, but it went everywhere, as if he were hunting for something he had overlooked. Surely he could not be having doubts now, she thought. She remembered how quiet he had been back in London when the first letter had arrived. She remembered his growing conviction, as the correspondence with Waiata continued, his absolute certainty that his next charge was to be at the other end of the earth: at a small village so isolated it could only be reached by sea. But the first houses were coming into view around the last point. She removed her arm from his and checked the girls, correcting posture, admonishing for rumpled stockings, disciplining unruly hair.

Then Waiata was before them.

It was the church spire that captured their attention first. It stood proud and very tall, gleaming white against the bush behind, dominating the village from the centre of the waterfront. Below it, the church itself looked as splendid and solid from the outside as they knew it to be on the inside. The grounds were spacious and well tended. And on the edge of the property was another building with a wisp of smoke angling upwards from the chimney. The manse, their new home, had been prepared for their arrival.

Nearly two hundred houses clustered around the steep Waiata basin, pressed unevenly around the waterfront by the aggressive bush. Here and there among them, a grey concrete roof betrayed the war shortage of iron. But mostly the roofs were like angular patches of red paint, set amongst the green dabs of trees. The village trees seemed by their shade and shape to be almost exclusively exotic, further denying the surrounding bush its former domain. The most striking of these was a tree even higher than the church spire, a young sequoia, a Californian redwood: planted, Robert guessed, when the colony was born, nearly a hundred years ago.

The inlet was a harbour within a harbour, with some forty vessels, trawlers and crayfishers, passing the sabbath afternoon over slumped mooring lines and lazy reflections. At the right-hand end of the waterfront milled a great straggle of horses, traps and buggies, amongst a line of nikau palms. Perhaps fifty or sixty horses chewed grass over their reins or stood patiently at the railings of the stores further back. There were just three motor vehicles amongst them. No people.

In front of this restless parking area, the Waiata wharf stretched awkwardly out over the water, with a squat building on piles to one side and scores of rowboats tethered on running lines to the other. On the outer end of the wharf was a solid mass of people, waiting to welcome their new minister.

But before the pale dots resolved into faces, Robert McKay did something that for him was very strange. He took half a step backwards from the launch rail, swallowed, gazed sightlessly about the inlet once more, then returned to his wife's side and laid a trembling hand on her forearm. She and the girls gaped at him, amazed and alarmed by this uncharacteristic, unseemly display.

'Ellen,' he said hoarsely, and stopped. His skin prickled as if his body had been charged with electricity. With fierce dignity he continued. 'Ellen, listen, my love. The Lord has ... the Lord is going to send me a great task here. Do you understand? He's going to send me a test. A great challenge.'

There were speeches on the wharf, presentations to McKay and to his wife, presents for the three girls from the Women's Guild. There were the introductions: first to the church elders, then to the few town councillors who were not elders, then to others of note in the parish. At first, the fishermen and farmers of Waiata found the tall, slim young man's old-world courtesy a strange match with their own abrupt manners. They asked him, as circumspectly as possible, what a Scot was doing without a Scot's accent. He replied that a thick leather strap had persuaded him to leave his accent with an English nanny thirty years earlier. This they understood. And they quickly warmed to him, respecting his ready wit, his direct, forthright glance, and his firm handshake.

It was mid-afternoon now. The sun was descending rapidly

13

down to the hills across the harbour. Many of the crowd had ridden long distances from the bays over winding bush tracks and would have to depart soon. But they were now so intrigued by their new minister they were reluctant to wait for next week's official inauguration service in order to hear him preach. So they approached the elders. Since it was such a fine, warm afternoon, maybe Mr McKay wouldn't say no to giving them a taste of the good word to be going on with. Privately, the elders thought this to be somewhat improper, but they were more than intrigued themselves. They had, after all, gone to unprecedented lengths to secure this man, whose reputation for inspired preaching and for courageous stands against the growing number of modernist apostates had reached them around the world. But did the man measure up to his reputation? They conveyed the request.

So Robert McKay conducted the first service standing on a smelly, upturned diesel drum at the end of the Waiata wharf, with the sun behind him and the gentlest of breezes stirring his Westminster gown. Three hundred people were gathered before him in their drab, twenty-year, Donegal tweeds, their worn serge jackets and faded cotton prints. A hundred more, who didn't count themselves as Presbyterians or church-goers, watched curiously from further on, gradually drifting closer. In all, four-fifths of the entire population of the peninsula stood on the Waiata wharf listening.

Through the invocation, the scripture, the praise and exposition, and the prayer of confession, Robert McKay stood a little apart from himself. He spent that time coming to terms with the revelation that had been granted him before disembarking. He came to terms with his new and strange surroundings. And most of all, he came to terms with the nature of his congregation. With subtle senses extended, he probed the people standing attentively before him, exploring their expressions, their responses to this phrase, to that tone, to this inflexion.

And then there was no longer any doubt. It was going to be very good. In the years to come, he would lead these people on the straight and narrow path to the Lord, and they would follow. He felt himself lifted up on a surge of inspiration as never before, and was riding it when he began the spontaneous sermon.

It was electrifying.

His rich baritone voice ran in torrents, then paused without

14

warning. It flew in rhythms, then turned halting and irregular. One moment it was hard and sharp and grating, then it became soft and mellow, like grass rippling in a summer breeze. He spoke in turn into the eyes of every person he had been introduced to and every person he had not. He spoke of the most heinous, the most nigh-on-unforgivable sins without naming them, and there were many who felt that if they had not actually committed those sins in deed, they must certainly be guilty in spirit.

'... Now you may wonder why our world is rapidly becoming the garden of sin... ' A sudden pause. A raised hand. A tilted eyebrow, daring anyone not to wonder why. '... You may wonder why *alcohol* and *corruption* and *licentiousness* and all manner of pleasures of the flesh and unaccountable other evils are rampant in our world.' The voice dropped to a whisper, easily heard by his furthest listener. 'I will tell you. I will tell you why Satan is even now rapidly consuming the souls of hundreds of thousands of miserable wretches in our so-called civilisation.' Now he thundered. 'It is because we have lost our awareness of sin! We have lost our *sense of sin — more vital to our survival than touch and taste and sight and ....*'

By now, most of the audience were open-mouthed. The elders looked at each other, then back to the minister. The last minister had turned modernist, and they'd got rid of him when he degenerated into the communion wine. It had been a problem finding someone else. With even the General Assembly starting to reek of modernism, they hadn't really liked the sound of any possible New Zealand candidates. And then they'd heard of Robert McKay. They'd written, explaining that they were a god-fearing, straightforward community, untainted by deviation from the scriptures. They'd known, they'd known well, that there was little chance of such a man as this accepting a call from around the world. But they had prayed, and here he was. And his reputation had not done him the shadow of justice. None of them had ever heard his equal for the truth of his words and the power of his delivery and conviction.

'... Theological cuckoos within our own church! Liberals! Attempting to deny that the Garden of Eden ever existed!...' An incredulous pause, as if it were too painful to utter the words. A search of the faces, hoping against hope that there might be some explanation for this stupendous heresy. 'They deny the

15

Flood! The virgin birth! The Atonement! The Resurrection! They deny heaven and hell and the very existence of *Satan*! And in so doing, *they tear out the bottom of the very ship they sail in...*!'

When it was over, a thickset farmer from up Grehan Valley declared loudly that the man could talk a horse into turning over a new leaf. Even Mark Paget from Stony Bay, who wasn't given to talking, was heard to comment that any parson who could make his kids' eyes stick out like this had to be worth his keep. The elders and the welcoming committee were so affected they delivered another set of speeches of thanks and gratitude, this time unrehearsed. And they begged the minister to help them mark this turning point in the spiritual life of Waiata by baptising their newest citizen right there on the wharf.

Fresh water was brought from the general store.

Six-week-old Matthew Fleming had not heard anything of the service. He slept through the preliminaries of his baptism and was still sleeping when John Fleming professed his faith and promised to train his child in the 'nurture and admonition of the Lord'. But once in Robert McKay's arms, Matthew woke. During the sprinkling, and the naming and the uttering of the baptism, he looked directly up at the minister's face. His parents beamed with pride and pleasure, and the crowd breathed audible sighs of delight.

TWO

A small pick-up truck clattered out of Waiata, up Kaik Road, through the bush towards Lookout Ridge. The truck's name was Leaping Lena: somewhere in her long past, she had acquired a speed ratio that made dropping the clutch as hazardous as riding an angry four-inch cannon. Once, she had been a 1923 Chev. Now, war shortages had robbed her even of retirement into the creek behind the crayfish cannery. Her body was a patchwork of old roofing iron, wood, canvas, and baling wire. Her front right tyre was stuffed with grass. Three-quarter-inch flax rope wound in a running hitch through the spokes and round the tyres of the rear wheels, bringing some measure of grip on the greasy clay roads in and around Waiata.

A lone black-backed gull dropped a wing and came to investigate, but Leaping Lena's back tray contained only a kerosene tin and a broken fishing grapnel.

Matthew accentuated the movements of the bush that jolted past the passenger's window by thrusting his sixteen-month-old body up and down, severely testing the device that held him. His nappied and rompered bottom bounced in the end of a fish-crate his father had adapted and wired to the seat. Had he not been strapped into the crate, he would by now have tried most of the knobs and levers in the cab and dropped the ignition key through one of the holes in the floor. A kingfisher flashed through the trees to his left. His back straightened. He snapped a pointing hand through the open window as if to transfix the creature in flight.

'Bird,' he proclaimed in a tone of stern authority. 'Fly.' And seeking praise for this wisdom, he turned to his mother, who was gritting her teeth for a double-declutch down to first gear.

Over the noisy manoeuvre she laughed and willingly fed his insatiable appetitite for approval, glancing across at him with fond

17

pride. What an appealing child he was, with his chestnut-brown hair and forget-me-not-blue eyes, with his determined jaw and his funny squat thumb. He watched the tree shadows and sunlight bars flitting across her face. And when she hummed 'Summertime' from *Porgy and Bess*, he joined in by swaying his upper body from side to side in the fish-crate.

Leaping Lena was just coming to the boil when they came out of the trees at the top of Lookout Ridge. Rachel turned the pick-up as quickly as the front tyres would allow, parked her facing downhill, then pushed rocks under two wheels while steam ticked and hissed in the radiator. She loosed Matthew, felt his nappies and removed them. On impulse she removed his shirt as well, leaving him just in his shoes: he loved to romp without his clothes. But first, she listened for the sound of horses or engines; it would raise an eyebrow or two at the prayer meeting if she was caught letting him run around naked outside.

'We're going to see Daddy soon,' she announced. But Matthew had begun to rip the seedheads off the wild cocksfoot grass and to chortle, sprinkling the breeze with seeds. Rachel smiled and turned away to the lookout fence.

A few paces away, on the other side of the fence, was a pohutukawa tree, flowering brilliant red for Christmas. Bellbirds probed efficiently in the blossoms; their feathers, normally drab green in the dark bush, were almost iridescent in the bright sunlight. Beyond them the grassed shoulder of the ridge curved steeply down towards Purdon's Cliff, named after the farmer who had taken his leave of earth by riding his horse down the slope and off the cliff at full gallop. And beyond the cliff, the harbour. It lay before and on either side of the ridge, dark blue, ruffled by the warm wind to a texture like finely gnarled bark. The trawler would be hard to pick out against the water today. Rachel ran her eye carefully back along the probable route, knowing that John would have the *Phoenix* through the heads by now.

And there it was. Quite close, a lumpy dot at the head of a short white wake. It always made her heart lurch to see how small it was in the harbour and to know how much smaller it must be in the open sea. Every Christmas Eve, the last fishing day of the year, John Fleming would come through the heads as close to mid-afternoon as he could judge. Now, as on other Christmas Eves, the 50-foot side-trawler was heading for the water

18

directly below the lookout. When it drew level, John would sound the brass foghorn and wave from next to the winch. In just three years it had become a ritual, and last year she had held Matthew, then four months old, high in the air for his father to see.

Rachel turned. Matthew's bare little body was standing in the waving grass. He was looking at something.

'Matthew. Come on. Daddy's coming.'

The *Phoenix* drew closer, the cloud of gulls swirling behind the vessel came together and fell upon a spot in the wake. Still cleaning, Rachel thought: another good catch. The fish were coming back all right — and elephant fish fetching one and thruppence a pound now. She felt a glow of wellbeing. Times were improving, the war was over, and soon the days of rationing would be gone. The Lord was good.

Matthew chuckled loudly. He was still standing in the same place.

'Matthew. Daddy's nearly here. Come on, love.'

But Matthew seemed not to hear.

What on earth was he looking at? Rachel began to walk over. At first she thought he was examining something on a pile of fence posts a few paces in front of him. Then she saw that his gaze was directed too high for that. He seemed to be watching a point in mid air, a few feet above the posts. She blinked, looked again. Nothing there. She grinned.

'Daddy's boat is here, come on.'

Matthew's attention wavered for a moment in her direction, but his hand pointed above the pile of posts before him. 'Man,' he declared.

'Silly chump.' Rachel bent to lift him. 'Up you come. Daddy's coming in the —'

Matthew's howl of protest was so sudden and vehement that she hastily set him down. The sound cut off instantly. She stood back with hands on hips, part amused, part annoyed. 'What *is* the matter with you, young man?'

No answer. Matthew's eyes were back at the same spot above the posts. Then his head tilted back slightly and he focused on another spot, this time very close to him. He chuckled, shyly, as he often did with strange adults.

Rachel's smile disappeared.

Then Matthew was turning to her to be picked up. She

hesitated, lifted him, walked towards the lookout fence. The hair on the back of her head prickled and in spite of herself she looked back over her shoulder. Nothing. She laughed, shaking her straight hair about her ears, remembering college lectures on how to deal creatively with a child's imagination: if a child came in and claimed that there was a dragon outside, you were supposed to ask what colour the dragon was. Yes. Imagination. And what a convincing little performance.

'Aren't you a clever little actor then?' she admired. 'I know: you're going to be the next Laurence Olivier.'

Matthew's arm pointed over her shoulder. 'Man,' he repeated.

'Listen,' she exclaimed. 'There's the foghorn. You hear? Parp! Parp! Now Daddy's going to come out and wave. There he is. Wave to Daddy.'

John Fleming's alarm clock jangled next to his ear. 3 a.m. He silenced it, pushed his feet on to the floor and limped stolidly out into the hallway. His leg was always the worst when he got out of bed. It was nearly two years since he'd caught it between the aft davit and the gunwale. It looked as if he was going to be stuck with a gammy leg for life. But the good Lord knew best and no one was going to catch a Fleming moaning about his lot.

In the dark dining room, he cranked the phone and asked for Ken Stewart. Ken had shipped in an army surplus shortwave receiver and had promptly become the local weatherman.

Ken Stewart's wife answered the call. Calm conditions changing to light nor'westers with a two-foot swell, she told him. John grunted his thanks and returned the handpiece to its prongs. He took off his pyjama top without turning on the light. He always dressed in the dark, because his mother Edith was likely to wander through at any time if she couldn't sleep.

He was just feeling for his shirt on the bundle of clothes on the chair when he heard a voice coming from the corridor. Matthew was talking in his sleep: low-toned, nonsense words. John grinned. He was proud of his vigorous, healthy son and took boundless delight in the boy's antics. He limped down the corridor and quietly pushed open a door. There was enough light coming in from the window for him to see that Matthew wasn't lying down; his son was standing against the side of the cot,

20

hands gripping the rail, staring in the direction of the opposite wall.

Then Rachel was beside John. 'What's the matter?'

The slop, slop of slippers came from beyond the kitchen. Edith Fleming was scuffing along the coir mat in the hallway, hugging her gown across her chest. 'Arthur's restless again. I can't sleep when he's restless. What're you doing? What's happening?' John didn't answer. He was self-conscious about the massive carpet of hair on his chest and hated any woman to see it except Rachel.

'Gaaaoonawa. Isanancapaa. Ibidy,' Matthew remarked, as though he were delivering a reasoned, intelligent response to a philosophical point.

'Ohhh,' Edith enthused. 'Isn't that just the loveliest thing? Talking in his sleep.'

'Lots of kids do it,' Rachel followed up quickly. 'It's quite normal. Let's go back to —'

'He's woken up,' Edith broke in. Matthew was glancing over his shoulder at the adults in the doorway.

Then he chuckled at them. It was if they had done something quaint and amusing which had consequently been pointed out to him by someone else. Still chuckling, he turned his gaze back to the direction of the blank wall. Grinning widely, he tilted his head back and refocused on a point in the air close to him. His shoulders jiggled the way they did when an adult touched his head; he waved an arm vigorously, still in the direction of the blank wall. 'Bye-bye,' he said brightly. 'Bye-bye.' Then he folded at the waist, toppled on to his bedclothes in the cot, and was fast asleep.

None of the adults moved.

'What was that?' John Fleming demanded, frowning through the doorway. 'What was that he just did?'

THREE

'Goodbye, Genghis. Be a good boy.' Emily Nisbet blew a kiss towards the bird cage as the budgerigar plinked agitatedly back and forth between two perches.

She picked her umbrella off its nail behind the front door. It would rain, she could feel it in her stiff bones. She stepped into the front porch and closed the door behind her without locking it. She never locked it. Night and day, her cottage remained accessible. It was an almost unconscious gesture, an invitation to the universe to send her some event that would either end her life or smash the invisible bubble that lay in wait for her at the end of the cottage path. Every day now, the bubble closed around her as she stepped through the gate; its wall was made of numbing, touchless ether and every day it was thicker and stronger.

But before facing the gate, she first, as always, inspected and farewelled her family: the random array of shrubs, herbs, flowers and vegetables that took up almost the entire garden. And she began, again as always, at the far end.

'Well done, girls,' she said to her three tomato plants. She patted them lightly, partly to encourage them, partly to get top pollen drifting down each plant. 'Now, now,' she added soothingly, as though part of this morning's blush had been caused by the compliment. She wished good morning to the garlic plants, the horseradish, the French tarragon, and to the begonias growing in the boxes on the garden seat. She acknowledged the best-ever performance from the potatoes, and congratulated the comfrey, growing amongst them, for their part in the success. The cucumber plant accepted an apology for having been fed with over-fresh horse manure; its vines had knotted and twisted around each other in such frenzy that she held grave doubts for the future of the embryo cucumbers.

22

She came to the rosemary bush alongside the cottage, andcommented aloud on how well the subdued daylight broughtout the subtle greens in its foliage. A shout interrupted her.

'Hey! Knucklehead Nisbet!'

Two schoolboys were giggling out on the far side of the road. One of them let forth the moronic sound, 'Duuuuuhhhhh,' and tipped his head back to imitate an imaginary receding forehead. The other rotated a mocking forefinger about his right ear; then they took off down the hill, hooting with laughter, schoolbags beating about them. And in an instant the bubble was no longer waiting at the gate. It was around her. The boys transformed into vague distant splotches and their laughter became mere muffled fluting.

Emily bent down until some of the rosemary bush was inside the bubble. She ran a finger over a sprig of leaves and sniffed, inhaling the sweet, heady aroma. This herb was one of her favourites; it went into her raisin scones, her morning bath water, and her tea. Extraordinary, she thought, that a single herb taken as a cup of tea could lift one and calm one at the same time.

She completed her farewells at the end of the cottage path. There, she stepped through the gate and set off down a hill, a short, dumpy figure, drably dressed, hardly into her late thirties, yet walking with the steady, pace-by-pace effort of the elderly.

A white-haired man, with a gnarled, weather-roughened face, leaned on his gate ahead of her, eyeing the darkening sky and the boats in the harbour. A fisherman, waiting for the weather to come and go. She didn't try to wish him good day, because she knew the sound of the greeting wouldn't reach him. His eyes followed her as she passed.

Images returned to her, unasked. Briefly she was back in London. The party. Reggie, home on leave, drinking and laughing, sporting his D.S.O. and his new moustache. Then the air-raid sirens. The shift, holus bolus, into the shelter in the yard: streamers, balloons, bottles, husband, children and all her friends. 'The present!' she had cried out so gaily. 'Silly me, forgot the present!' She ran back to the house. Then came the searing hammer-blow of the explosion: a direct hit on the shelter. One big hole in the back yard. All of them dead: husband, children, friends. Bang.

She turned on to the waterfront road. Hooves sounded behindher, thudding on the hard clay that waited for the rain. She stepped aside. A horse sauntered by, pulling a red, black-trimmed gig, bearing a woman and two children whose faces she had seen a hundred times but whose names she didn't know. Immediately ahead, the road surface had been impressed with fine, sharp gravel; the sound of the hooves turned crisp and clean and seemed to speed up. The faces of the two children looked back at her curiously, as the gig swayed away between the sea wall and the long line of white picket fences.

Eventually she had attempted to begin again, by emigrating to New Zealand, to this little town far away from the world. But she had not been able to leave the memories behind; the numbness had found her here and was settling around her, sapping her energy, releasing her only to talk with her plants and with Genghis.

In the middle of the bay, she passed the church grounds. She glanced up to the second storey of the manse, through one of the dormer windows. Yes, there he was, seated before his study desk. The minister was there most mornings at this time, a dark slim shape against book-lined walls. He was looking out the window, perhaps at her; but even as Emily pulled her glance away, he was rising from his seat, turning away. The doors of the church were wide open. A shape moved amongst the pews, polishing the floor in preparation for Sunday when people would come from the furthest bays of the peninsula to hear their minister speak.

But she would not be there.

Emily pulled her raincoat tighter against the fast-cooling air. What would they say, these upright church sheep, if she marched into their pen and announced that she had once communed regularly with the spirits of the dead, that she had consorted with a notorious spirit medium? That she had practised the forbidden craft and through it found real solace?

But no, she knew she wouldn't go in there. Another Emily she had once known would have done it. As she walked on, memories of the spiritualist circle returned, sending a wave of longing through her, an aching for impossibilities infinitely far away.

Just past the saddlery, Emily turned off the waterfront, on

24

to the road behind the shops. The southerly clouds were sliding over Lookout Ridge. It would rain very soon now. The brown clay would suck at her shoes.

Just ahead of her, a small boy, about three years old, pattered back and forth across his home lawn. He was gleefully scattering freshly mown grass in the air, and bits of grass were sticking to his chestnut curls. But as Emily drew near, there was a ringing thud, accompanied by a single chirp and a bundle of feathers fell at the foot of the porch-screen, flapping in the dirt below. A song thrush. The boy trotted over to the bird and stood still, head bent, watching it beat at the ground with one wing. Its beak worked open and shut without further sound.

Emily caught a glimpse of the boy's expression. She slowed down, stopped still. That smile... that smile... she had seen it before, somewhere. Where?

Matthew squatted down, not knowing that he was being watched. He held his hands over the struggling bird the way he might have warmed them over a tiny fire. Then he closed his eyes, concentrating on something.

Oh dear God, Emily whispered inside her head.

The thrush stopped flapping for a moment.

'All better now,' Matthew announced happily to the bird and he reached forward with one hand and touched the tiny head. A ritualistic movement.

'Where did you learn that?" Emily's lips moved silently. 'Please, where did you learn that?'

The thrush burst into a frenzy of movement, turning its speckled chest full circle on the soil. There was a dust-covered, dark patch on the side of its head. Matthew frowned; he squatted again, and his face grew puzzled, then anxious, then unhappy.

'All better now!' he shouted petulantly.

Emily's hands writhed near her chest. No. No. Not like that! She took a step nearer the boy. Not like that! A sound gathered shapelessly in her windpipe; then it died as the front door opened violently and a man stormed out. Emily gazed at him, hoping, hoping. The father. Perhaps, even here in Waiata... this family... she could experience it again...

'Stop that!' John Fleming snarled at his son. 'Stop acting stupid!' He hauled the boy to his feet. The boy immediately began to howl, arms stiff by his sides, face screwed up to the

25

sky. The man glared across the fence. 'I'll thank you to be minding your own business, woman!'

Emily's face went slack. Her shoulders sank to their normal roundness. She turned slowly away and continued on up the street. Soon the boy's wails came from inside the house, but she heard them for a long time, because they slipped into the bubble with the first fat, slow drops of rain.

In five minutes Emily was hanging her unopened umbrella in the back foyer of the Banks Peninsula Cottage Hospital. Shortly she was working her mop and bucket on the corridor lino, listening as the day nurse told her to prepare room two for a patient. Emily nodded by way of an answer. The day nurse went away. It was understood: Emily carried out her duties with meticulous care; the hospital staff didn't press her to talk.

8.27 a.m. exactly.

The gold fob-watch had been handed down from Robert McKay's grandfather. It was as accurate as any modern wrist device, and no doubt considerably more reliable. He mused on the intricate workings of Providence: that the craftsman who made the timepiece had been the brother of the engineer who made the mechanism of the Waiata Heads lighthouse. And both exquisite pieces of machinery had been made on the other side of the world in the same town. Edinburgh. The brothers had been Scots, born and bred.

Robert pressed the watch closed, taking pleasure in the firm snick of the catch. A movement in the corner of his vision took his attention out of the study and down on to the road. A horse was tick-tacking by, pulling a familiar red, black-trimmed gig, bearing Margaret Crocker, her boy Jimmy, and the doctor's daughter, Jennifer Pringle. Mrs Crocker came by at this time every school morning, taking the two youngsters to school. She waved, he inclined his head and the gig grew smaller around the bay.

There was that Nisbet woman again, on the way to the hospital. Strange woman. Very strange. The Women's Guild had made several attempts to bring her into the fold, but they could hardly get her to say good day, let alone enter into an intelligent conversation. Still, the woman was known to have dabbled in spiritualism. If the dreadful practice had taken her beyond the reach of grace, then she would not be the first to suffer that fate.

Click. 8.29 a.m. Snick.

He stood, returned Bickersteth's *Commentaries* to its place between *The Westminster Confession of Faith* and Schaff's *History of the Apostolic Age*. Then he went downstairs.

As he entered the dining room, his four dark-headed girls were scurrying across the floor. By the time he closed the door behind him, they were all in line against the scullery hatch. The table had been cleared of breakfast things. Ellen was seated, her hands composed on the table's bare wooden surface; she smiled at him and he noticed how well her blue apron set off her glossy black hair. He placed himself front centre of the line of girls and passed his inspection eye carefully over them all, from biggest to smallest: ribbons, plaits, scrubbed pink faces, ironed white blouses and plain blue frocks, cream stockings and shiny black shoes. He even inspected three-year-old Wendy, who enjoyed lining up with her three big sisters and whose age rendered her immune from the consequences of fault in appearance.

Robert motioned. Four sets of hands came out for fingernail inspection. He nodded, the hands went down and he addressed the oldest girl, eleven-year-old Fiona.

'Fiona. Into what estate did the Fall bring mankind?'

Fiona's nose wrinkled with concentration. 'The Fall brought mankind into an estate of sin and misery,' she recited.

'Correct.' Robert would normally have addressed his second question to the next in line, but the next-to-eldest bore an expression of misery and suffering that was plainly for his benefit. So he made her wait and addressed himself again to Fiona. 'And what is sin?'

'Sin is any want of conformity unto, or transgression of, the law of God.' This too was approved as correct, as Fiona had known it would be. She was doing well in the junior Bible class. Her mouth curled smugly.

'Define pride for me, Fiona.'

The smile vanished.

'Come, come, come.'

'Pride is a sin, Father.'

Robert dryly concurred with this answer also. And only now did he take notice of Bevin. He regarded her expression with an ominous frown, then raised an inquiring eyebrow at his wife. Ellen explained that Bevin was complaining of pains in the abdomen and considered herself too ill to attend school. Robert returned his gaze to his second eldest with his eyes marginally wider than before; where exactly, he demanded to know, were the pains manifesting themselves. Bevin pointed vaguely to her stomach, her shoulders sagging under his gaze.

'Your health is perfect,' stated her father. 'You have something on your mind, and you will tell me what it is.'

'Those girls in Miss Johnstone's class, Father, they all laugh at me.'

'For what reason do they laugh at you?'

'They say I've got a boy's name, Father.'

'Hmmm.' Robert leaned forward. 'And have you informed them that your name means "melodious lady"?'

'But, Father...'

'So. You allowed the ignorance of your fellow pupils to tempt you to the wickedness of lying about your health to us. Am I correct?'

Bevin's freckles stood out against her pallor. Two places away, little Wendy's jaw quivered. She stepped out of line, crying, and was swiftly picked up and shushed by her mother. Robert leaned further forward over Bevin. 'Look at me, girl. Am I correct?'

Bevin's face, distorted against tears, moved back into view, nodding jerkily.

'Bevin McKay. The fact that you have been persecuted by those older and more ignorant than yourself does not excuse you. However, your mother informs me that your teacher has been unable to find fault with your conduct in the classroom and that being so, you will not be thrashed. Instead, your mother will administer a suitable punishment in the kitchen when you return from school. Is that understood?'

'Yes, Father.'

'Children. Children...' The minister spread his hands, a gesture that took in all three girls. 'One day you will be old enough to understand the words of William Wordsworth about the character of the happy warrior: "... even more pure, as tempted more; more able to endure as more exposed to suffering and distress". As you grow older you will face more and more temptation, not less. Satan will beckon you to wickedness at every

28

turn. And do you know what happens to the wicked? Well?'

'They go to hell, Father.'

'Correct. And the details of what happens there are not for such tender ears as yours. Remember that a thrashing from me lasts just one minute; but the punishment of the wicked, after they die, never stops. It goes on forever. And I will do everything in my power to prevent that happening to you. Think on it. Fiona and Lucy, you are not to speak to Bevin on the way to school. She will be praying to Jesus to forgive her for her sin. Clear? Very well. You may kiss your mother goodbye.'

As they went away down the drive, he watched them with such a troubled expression that Ellen came to his side, concerned. When she insisted on an explanation, she found him uncharacteristically hesitant.

'Sometimes... Do you think, Ellen, perhaps I'm overly strict with them?'

'With the children?' With tenderness Ellen took his hand in both hers. 'Robert! Is this my husband? Who preaches that if you put a kitten in an open field it will be lost and terrified, but that if you put it in a room with well-defined boundaries it will play and explore?'

Robert gave an abrupt shake to his head.

'I'm sorry, Ellen. You're right, of course.' Considerably annoyed with himself, he left the room and his wife let him go, knowing that he would not be drawn on the real cause of such lapses. How much longer must he wait, she asked herself, and felt a pang in echo to his. Lord, she prayed, let it be soon. Robert, your servant, is ready. He is ready.

On the front porch, he laced on his riding boots. He wouldn't be riding until this afternoon, but they were so comfortable and so warm on cool days that he had taken to wearing them walking; they had become as much a part of him as his dog collar and black serge jacket. Anyone else seen walking in riding boots would have risked being called an eccentric.

Hands clasped behind his back, he began the morning ritual, the tour of his immediate domain. Except for the manse, the buildings all lay within a square formed by four newly planted young trees: cedars of Lebanon, the trees used to cover Solomon's temple. He inspected the recently built church hall, which still smelled of new-cut timber and putty and fresh paint. He went

29

to the older buildings and peered through the vestry windows and into the Sunday School room.

And then there was the church itself. Robert always touched a corner in passing, feeling, through the weatherboards, something of its solid assurance, its permanence. The entire structure was made of native totara, even the steep shingles; the beams and hidden reinforcing were all of heart-of-totara. Every tree had been logged in Lavericks Bay and hauled over the summit for sawing in Waiata. It had been built more than eighty years ago and built to last; it would be standing long after he had done his work here.

Inside, he walked slowly up the centre aisle, his boots sending sharp echoes around the bare surfaces in spite of his measured tread. His eyes lingered over the stark, austere lines of the spaces, finding only familiar detail, yet extracting new assurance from every part: the raw ten-inch-by-four-inch beams overhead, the plain, unadorned, planked walls, the narrow, ten-foot-high windows, the ranks of varnished pews on either side of the centre aisle, waiting for Sunday. And in the back corner, the steep stairs to the belfry, inside the spire. The presence of both spire and belfry was unusual in a Presbyterian church, a fact Robert McKay ascribed to the influence of those unwilling to let their faith be both seen and heard.

Next to the stairs hung the bellrope. There was a story about the rope, now local history. The previous minister had been woken in the night by two sounds: the bell ringing, and a terrible squealing. Someone had tied a full-grown hog to the bellrope by a hind leg. Robert let a smile rise; some misguided buffoon had apparently thought it the appropriate way to express his opinion of the minister concerned. There had been no such pranks in Robert McKay's three-year ministry, nor serious dissension of any kind.

Quite the reverse. His reputation had already gone well beyond the peninsula. Already, according to presbytery figures, Waiata County boasted more committed Presbyterians, by proportion, than any other presbytery in all of New Zealand. Seventy-five percent of the entire population were now regulars, fifty percent were communicants. Nearly four hundred people answered the Sunday bell these days, packing into the pews, standing around the outer aisles. And now, there was the news that one of Waiata's

30

two remaining pubs was about to close because of falling patronage. In a fishing village.

He should, he supposed, be well pleased.

He went out through the imposing entrance-way and stood on the steps, shoulders braced, weight on the balls of his feet, hands still clasped behind him. The southerly front was pouring over Lookout Ridge. The hills across the harbour were vanishing in dank grey. All the trawlers and crayboats were at their mooring lines, shifting restlessly in the sullen sheen.

Still no sign of what the Lord intended for him. There wasn't a day he didn't relive those minutes before he first stepped on to the Waiata wharf. Some day, some day, the great challenge, the test, would come. And when it came, would that it be a challenge of the order of those faced by the Huguenots, the Argylls, by Knox and Brown.

FOUR

John Fleming trudged home from the wharf, kitbag in one hand and a preserving jar in the other. He was tired, but more than satisfied with the catch. He didn't really care that he'd spiked his new thigh boots on an elephant-fish spine; he was lifting so much gurnard and terakihi out of the big wet paddock these days he could go through a pair of boots a week and hardly notice the difference in the wallet. He whistled 'John Pearce' as he walked, and swung the jar, which contained sea water and a tiny, still angry-red octopus that had come up in the net. Matthew's birthday present.

There were dozens of bees around the driveway and back porch of his home: most in the air, some crawling on the side of the house and shed. He'd never seen so many so early in spring and wondered if they had affected Matthew's birthday party. He hung his jacket and kitbag on a peg, removed his shoes, and hid the preserving jar behind his back. He opened the door, and Rachel was facing him, as he knew she would be, smiling her smile of welcome to the man of the house. They pecked lips cheerfully by the kitchen sink. Rachel looked tired also, but gasped satisfactorily when confronted with the octopus three inches from her face; the little animal, unable to sustain the physiological effects of anger, was returning to its normal hue, a dark mottled brown.

Splashing and swirling sounds came from beyond the bathroom door.

John placed the jar on the table. He crossed to the carpeted side of the kitchen where his easy chair awaited, garnished with slippers, pipe, tobacco, footstool, and a fresh, unopened copy of the *Waiata Weekly*. He slippered his feet and hoisted them on to the footstool, tapped his pipe, pressed tobacco into it with painstaking care, lit it with a series of five matches. And finally he settled back with a sigh. Now the events of the day could be discussed.

'How'd the party go?' he grunted.

'Well.' Rachel's shoulders expressed a mixture of emotions while she scrubbed potatoes at the sink. 'Pretty good, but my ears will never be the same again. We had to keep them inside all the time. Did you notice the bees?'

'Yep. Maybe swarming somewhere near the bush. I'll take a look later.'

'Your son celebrated his third birthday by drumming on Timmy Platt's head with a spoon.'

'Haw,' John guffawed. 'Did you wallop him?'

'Didn't need to. Joan Platt brought him round so quick with her tongue, all the children in the room put their spoons down and sat up straight.' And John laughed again, while more watery sounds came from the bathroom. Matthew was imitating the sound of the *Phoenix* starting up: 'RrrrRRRrrr RRRrrr BuhBuhBuhBuh ...'

'Good crop?' Rachel asked John.

'Not too foul. Not too foul at all,' he said complacently through a cloud of smoke. 'Went out to seventy fathoms. Twenty-six bins of terakihi, eight of gurnard, eight ling.'

Rachel expressed her admiration.

'No! It's my turn,' came Matthew's voice. 'You've had a long, long, *long* turn.'

John removed his pipe. 'Nina again?'

Rachel nodded, smiling lightly.

When Matthew had first started playing with his imaginary friend, Nina, John had been next to impossible. Only with the greatest difficulty had she stopped him laying into Matthew with the flat of his hand. Even when she found a book which said that many children have imaginary friends, he had worried about what people would think. But then very discreet questions among the Guild women had turned up two other children with imaginary friends. One of the women remembered having one herself. That information had brought a truce, at least a temporary one. John grudgingly tolerated the fantasy now, and had even made a joke of it one evening — remarking about his son bathing naked with a woman.

'Anyway, you can't make your nose go like this,' Matthew's

voice challenged. There was a loud bubbling followed by cackles of glee. Rachel dried the potatoes in a fresh tea-towel, popped them in the oven, and damped the air intake to the coal.

Abruptly the sounds from the bathroom ceased. Then Matthew began to cry.

'What's the matter, love?'

The crying grew louder. Rachel, in the midst of working a flour mixture, looked pleadingly at John, apologised for disturbing him and asked if he would mind ... He grunted impatiently and went through the bathroom door.

'Come on, fella. Big boys don't cry, remember? Crying makes you grow smaller.'

Matthew cried harder.

'Tell your dad all about it, there's a good lad.'

The volume swelled. John's brow puckered irritably. The boy always wanted his mother when he was blubbing. Rachel appeared, wiping her hands on the dishcloth.

'What's wrong, love? Got soap in your eyes?'

'Maybe Nina's jilted him,' John offered.

'Nina's not coming to play with me any more,' Matthew sobbed.

'Hah! She *has* jilted him,' his father chortled. 'About time too, if you ask me. All this carry-on in the bathroom.'

Rachel reproached her husband gently, pointing out that Matthew was upset even if it was only his imagination causing it. She held a towel out, wrapped it around her son when he stood, and lifted him on to the floor. She began to dry him and asked why Nina wasn't going to play with him anymore.

'She doesn't like those bees,' he sniffed. ''Cause some bees, they stinged her all over 'til she was dead.' John snorted. Rachel shuddered, and wondered aloud who would tell him such a thing. 'Her mummy couldn't see her any more,' Matthew added.

'Well, don't you worry,' Rachel soothed. 'Maybe she'll come back and play with you when the bees are gone.'

'For the love of Mike, if he wants to forget her, *let* him!' John's exasperated voice came from through the door. He had gone back to his easy chair.

'They're *not* going away.' Matthew was impatient with her for not understanding. 'They just builded a house in the popple tree.'

34

'The what?' John's voice.

'The poplar, down the back.' Rachel handed Matthew his pyjama bottom, and watched him struggle into it.

Suddenly she was apprehensive. She glanced around the door and saw that John had a strange faraway look on his face. She helped Matthew into his top, then cleaned the bath perfunctorily as it drained. It couldn't be. Not a single child had been down the back of the garden all day. When she returned to the kitchen, John had gone through the back door. Matthew saw the tiny octopus in the jar, but being in no mood to show interest, just glared at it and sucked his thumb. In half-panic, Rachel packed him off to the bedroom to play until dinner; this produced more tears, but she overrode them. Then she busied herself at the sink.

John returned. His face was expressionless.

'They're swarming in the hollow in the back of the poplar,' he stated. He waited for a response, but Rachel, though she made a show of surprise, said nothing. 'How did he know?' John added, the words slow with reluctance.

'Two of the children did slip out the back,' Rachel said, light of word and heavy of heart; it was the first time she had ever lied knowingly to her husband. 'They must have told the others.'

John nodded, kept nodding as he looked at her.

'Yeah. I guess they must have.' He went back to his chair. Rachel closed her eyes in pain. John picked up the newspaper and began to read the article about the change of lighthouse-keeper at the heads. Out of the corner of his eye he could see the preserving jar on the table. The octopus was clinging to the underside of the lid.

FIVE

A low murmur penetrated the barn-like gloom of the general store. But Chester Farnsworth ignored the sound and completed the account entry. 'Working trous. Double Knee. 1 pr. 12/-.' The light from the bulb overhead penetrated his prematurely thin hair and reflected off his shiny scalp. He blew on the ink, capped the pen and installed it in the breast pocket of his spotless, pressed, grey apron. He wrapped the trousers in brown paper, tossed and tied the parcel with deft hands, then handed it to his customer with the barest suggestion of a bow. The murmurs swelled, bringing sounds of animal confusion and protest. Bleatings scraped through the open front door, followed by the rattle of hundreds of small hooves on the stony clay. A sheep drive. Chester walked to the front bay window, followed by his customer — Colin Ferris from the lighthouse farm. Both men peered out past the Horlicks tins.

'Agnes!' Chester called back into the depths of the store. 'It's Jack Sullivan's mob.' His wife emerged from the rear offices and clattered towards the front, threading through kerosene drums and casks of tallow, through saddles, collars and hames, sacks of pollard and grit for chickens. Mrs Farnsworth was a keen follower of the post-war 'new look'; the more her heels raised her already impressive height, the noisier became her progress around the store. She shut the front door, frowning at her husband for his lack of foresight, then joined the two men at the window.

The lead sheepdog was abreast of the store, smoky brown with a wide swathe of white hair around the neck and left foreleg. It was a heading dog, a cross between an Australian blue-heeler and a collie; it walked silently, with the sedate pace and dignified air appropriate to its distinguished origins. It constantly turned its head, watching its charges with keen and wary eye. Ten yards behind came the mob, three hundred wether lambs. Romneys.

They followed the dog's authority, but moved in surges, nervous in the unfamiliar surroundings. They cut the clay in the road to fine powder, and the breeze stirred it into a grey-yellow cloud which lifted away behind them. Two black-and-white huntaway dogs ranged noisily on the left and right flanks, their job made easy for a moment by the shops on one side and the waterfront on the other.

At the centre rear, above the dust, rode a man on a bay mare. Jack Sullivan moved with the easy sway of the relaxed and experienced rider. In spite of the cool southerly, he wore just a black singlet on his upper body. He had two days' stubble on his chin and a dead cigarette on his lower lip. Over his dark eyebrows he wore a shapeless green cloth hat. He turned his head just enough to watch his dogs and the mob, and no more. One hand rested on the pommel, holding loose reins, the other rested on his thigh with one thumb in a pocket. And his hands stayed that way, even when he shouted instructions to the dogs. He rode as if the town and all the faces behind all the windows didn't exist. Whenever Jack Sullivan brought his mob down to the boat, the whole town stopped to watch and to talk.

'It's disgraceful,' said Agnes Farnsworth. 'Quite disgraceful.'

'Now, Agnes,' Chester chided. Sometimes Agnes forgot herself. As the keepers of the general store, they had a duty to show restraint when discussing one customer's shortcomings in front of another. Even in the case of Jack Sullivan. Colin Ferris folded thick sunburned arms across his beefy chest and took in the whole outside scene with an appraising eye. Say what you like about Jack Sullivan, he thought to himself, he and his heading dog D'Arcy ran the smoothest, tightest drive on the peninsula.

'A man has to have a bit of backbone to stick it for so long without giving in,' he ventured. 'Even if he is a pacifist, he's got to have a few guts to call his own. Uh, pardon me, Mrs Farnsworth.'

Agnes ignored the crude language. 'If that man had just half a backbone he would have fronted up in court to take his medicine. Instead he ran so fast, he was into the bush before his ballot paper hit the ground. And while he was bolting, there were real men dying just so that he wouldn't have to wake up one morning to find a Nazi and a Slit-eye telling him how to run his farm.' She waved disgustedly at the lambs, a few of which were stamping

37

their feet and gazing wildly into the dark window before being jostled on by the rest. 'Just look at that. It's not right. They should have taken his land from him.'

'Agnes. It's the smallest farm in the district.' Chester was acutely embarrassed that his wife's free tongue was forcing him to defend someone like Sullivan. 'He has to shoot possums to hold it together. And the war's over now...'

'... Doesn't make it right.'

'He kept the military and the police guessing for two years on and off,' Colin said. 'Don't get me wrong; I'm not excusing him, but that has to be worth something in my book.'

'Ptchah.' Agnes flapped her hand at him. 'No credit to Sullivan. It was that dog of his, tipping him off.'

Colin Ferris nodded and peered out to the left, after D'Arcy, now a hundred yards away. 'I spend twenty years trying to breed a dog like that, and Sullivan gets him without even looking.'

Out on the road, a swelling of sheep was showing interest in a boat ramp running down from the waterfront embankment.

'Come out, Tip!' roared Jack Sullivan, the cigarette dancing on his lip. The huntaway on the right flank swung further right. Its body jerked with furious barking, discouraging the wayward members of the flock. 'Come in, Tip!' The dog swung back to position. On the left flank some of the mob were climbing on each other. 'Go back, Glen!' The other huntaway whined and slowed to a half-crouching stalk. Jack checked his mount, dropping back to keep an easier eye on Glen. Cantankerous mongrel! When it wasn't driving the beggars' bums up their throats, it was off loafing in the water-hole.

Up front, the mob reached the intersection with Bedford Road. A fat white tentacle began to grow in that direction. But even as Jack saw it, D'Arcy was wheeling to confront the breakaways. The heading dog pressed them back using only his eyes, then skimmed the edges and returned to his position in the front. In a few more yards he drew level with the grassed foreshore immediately adjacent to the wharf. He turned questioningly.

'Down, D'Arcy!'

D'Arcy crouched, positioned to the inch, eyeing the leading lambs. Those in the centre stamped their front feet and swung their heads. Some, to right and left of centre, allowed themselves to be pushed forward by the mob behind. D'Arcy swung a few

38

feet each way to hold them, then dropped down to his stomach. His head stayed up, his mouth hung ajar. His tongue rolled over his two lower fangs and lolled out, cooling his panting body. The mob stood still. Another yelled command sent both huntaways swinging left. The sheep poured off the road and on to the grass. Tip and Glen danced noisy attendance, darting in and out. D'Arcy circled wide, overseeing until the mob settled.

Jack dismounted, dropping the reins to the ground. His horse snorted and lowered its head to graze. Jack nodded to D'Arcy and then waded into the sheep, with D'Arcy at his heel, and cut out the first third. Tip and Glen took up station on the remainder while Jack and D'Arcy funnelled the cut on to the wharf. This part wasn't difficult. Sheep weren't so bad on the wharf. There had been a time when Jack had run pigs out to the boat, but they tended to leap into the water to swim for it and ended up cutting their own throats with their trotters. But even with the sheep, D'Arcy was careful. As they clattered over the wharf beams, he kept them to the rail side.

Back on the foreshore, the remaining mob began to spread in spite of the best efforts of the huntaways. Outside the store, Colin Ferris looked around. Half a dozen men were within easy reach of lending a hand. No one moved. He tucked his parcel under one arm, then lost his nerve and put his other hand into a pocket as if that had been his original intention. But the sheep on the wharf were quickly inside one compartment of the pen at the far end. The moment the pen gate closed, D'Arcy raced back to the mob on the foreshore, contained the movement, then squatted to wait for Jack who was strolling back along the wharf.

Colin Ferris found Tony Pugh, the butcher, beside him.

'Dog's too good for him,' Tony observed. 'What d'you reckon?'

'Dog in a million, that,' Colin replied.

The second cut went the way of the first. Then the last third went, and this time the two huntaways followed Jack and D'Arcy. When the last pen gate was closed, the two huntaways roamed the wharf, sniffing in nooks and crannies, and investigating an ageing Studebaker waiting to be shipped back to the city for repairs. Two trawlers lay alongside the wharf. Opposite one of them, the *Phoenix*, lay sacks of cocksfoot seed, stacked ready for shipping. Jack climbed up on to the nearest pile and sat down to wait. D'Arcy stood up on hind legs and batted the sack below

Jack, demanding attention. His tail wagged. His tongue slobbered. He was waiting for something. Jack plucked the dead cigarette off his lower lip, inspected it, and felt in his pocket for matches.

'What're you grinning at, yer fleabitten mongrel? Anybody'd think you did a good job.'

'Rrrrrrowf.' D'Arcy leaped into the air off his back legs. He rolled over twice, snuffled his nose through some spilt seed below the sacks, then climbed up beside his owner. He sat on his haunches and gazed at the sights of the wharf, including the *Phoenix* which dipped and swayed a few feet away, tugging gently at its mooring lines.

John Fleming hauled in the bow of the *Phoenix* and swung aboard, ignoring the man on the sacks ten yards away. The crew, Marty Bates, was there already, pumping diesel from the drums they'd rolled on the night before. John hoisted the hold hatch and climbed down to prime the bilge pump. In a few seconds the tic-tac of both hand pumps came from the boat: slow and regular from the deck, fast and light from below.

On the wharf, Rachel and Matthew waited to wave goodbye.

Matthew's version of waiting was more energetic than his mother's. The trip to the wharf was one of his greatest pleasures. The smell of fish and tar and rotted net, the shift and thump of the piles, the mysterious water deep below the cracks in the beams, the coarse textures and the crisp, clean sounds, all combined to make a banquet of sensation so rich that a boy of four and a half couldn't hope to sample it all. But he could try. Today his attention was almost immediately taken by the sheepdogs. Tip and Glen arrived swiftly to sniff him over. They did so under the wary eye of his mother, then lost interest and left him in favour of an interesting smell at the far end of the fish store. But Matthew quickly discovered that the smoky-brown dog with the white markings was a much better prospect.

D'Arcy was shifting about on his rear, looking entreatingly from Jack to the boy, making high-pitched whining sounds. Jack, disgusted at D'Arcy's blatant grovelling for permission for something that didn't need permission, made him wait while he rolled another cigarette between his fingers.

'Yeah, yeah. Go on,' he said finally. With a gulp of excitement, D'Arcy was gone from the sacks and fawning around the boy.

Rachel looked away from the *Phoenix* and eyed D'Arcy doubtfully. Matthew suddenly ran over and climbed the sacks. He patted Jack's pocket where the tobacco tin pressed against the material.

'Can I have this and see if he can find it?'

Rachel spoke sharply, amazed at her son's casual familiarity with a total stranger, annoyed that she should have to reprimand him in front of a man like Sullivan. But Matthew seemed not to hear and the older man didn't look up. At that moment, John Fleming came out on deck. He looked hard at Matthew and Jack, then at Rachel. After a moment's hesitation, he shrugged and disappeared into the wheelhouse. Jack didn't answer, expecting that the boy would be whisked away any second. When it didn't happen, he felt flustered. He took the tobacco tin out, looked at it, then put it back in the pocket.

'D'Arcy doesn't know that game.'

Matthew continued to look at him hopefully.

'He only knows hide-and-seek.' D'Arcy's ears twitched up. He yelped and scrabbled, waiting for the game to begin. Matthew clambered down and looked around for a hiding place. But D'Arcy began to make desperate squeaking sounds. 'He wants to go first,' Jack explained. 'He always has to go first. You've got to close your eyes.' Matthew did so. 'Now you've got to tell him to hide. Like this. Hide, D'Arcy!' D'Arcy bounded past the front of the wharf office towards an empty sack. He burrowed underneath. Matthew opened his eyes too soon and caught the last of the movement.

'I see you! You've got to come out now.'

The sack didn't move.

'He won't come,' Matthew complained.

'Nah. He won't. Watch this . . . Get in behind, D'Arcy!' Jack called in the direction of the sack. The sack stayed motionless. Jack turned to the boy. 'See? He knows it's a game. You have to make him look at you. You have to go and whip the sack off him.'

Matthew trotted chuckling to the sack. Still chuckling, he took a corner gingerly between thumb and forefinger and peeled it back. First D'Arcy's wet nose appeared, then his eyes, then the long mouth, curved upwards over the back teeth. The dog growled. Matthew shrieked with fright and delight. After that he and dog took three turns each. It took that many turns for

Matthew to adjust to the fact that wherever he hid, D'Arcy would be wiping his nose on him in three seconds flat. Then Matthew tired of the game. He clambered up on the sacks and sat beside Jack Sullivan as if he had known the man all his life. Jack didn't look at him.

'Your lights are pretty,' Matthew said.

'What?' Jack glanced at him out of the corner of an eye.

'Your lights are pretty,' Matthew repeated, pointing at Jack's head.

'Yeah?' Jack looked away. 'What're you talking about?' But Matthew was watching D'Arcy and didn't elaborate. After a while, Jack felt an unaccountable urge to put his hand on Matthew's shoulder. He didn't. The slow throb of the *Phoenix*'s 95-horse engine began. A hot, stinging sensation threatened to bring moisture to Jack's eyes. He waited for the boy's mother to hurry up and take the kid away.

SIX

Rachel stripped the last of the skin from the steamed skate wing and began to pull strips of flesh off the cartilage. When fried with beaten, seasoned eggs, it was almost identical in taste and appearance to whitebait. Skittleback: poor man's whitebait, but as good as the real thing. It was a standing family joke to inspect the flesh and demand to know what Rachel had done with all the eyes.

Her parents-in-law came in for breakfast. Arthur, saying nothing, shuffled to his seat at the table. Edith guided his elbow until he was settled, grumbling all the while about another in a series of sleepless nights. But Arthur didn't seem to hear her.

Rachel cocked an ear. Edith poised herself hopefully.

'Is the rascal sleeping in, then? I'll fetch him a hurry-up, shall I?'

Rachel shook her head. 'Let's be thankful for small mercies. We'll be chasing him out of bed aplenty next month when he starts school.'

Edith thought this was precisely the point; soon she'd hardly see her grandson at all. She rattled knives and forks disapprovingly out of the cutlery drawer and suggested that maybe she could just see if Matthew was awake. Rachel stirred the skittleback noisily, pretending not to hear. Edith, in turn, pretended that her suggestion had not been spoken loudly enough and wasn't worth repeating anyway. The two of them had used the system for years. Rachel pursed her lips; if it hadn't been for that geological survey crowd exploding charges in the fishing grounds, she and John would have been in their own home before this. And with half the fish scared off, John was having to stay out longer. Two overnighters this week.

Arthur champed his gums.

'Tchah. He's forgotten his teeth,' Edith said crossly. She

leaned over him. 'You forgot your teeth, dear!' Arthur looked up, startled, confused. 'Never mind, dear, you won't need them this morning. It's skittleback. Skittleback! Never mind, dear.'

Muffled bangs and thumps came from a distant bedroom. Matthew was awake and dressing. A minute later, a deafening combination of banging, scraping and twanging erupted from out of the corridor. Normally, since Matthew couldn't tie his shoes, he wore them loose from the bedroom to the kitchen. Today he dragged his galloping pony along as well.

Arthur's hand trembled.

'Is it someone coming, Edie?'

'It's all right, dear!' Edith turned to Rachel. 'I always think it's the Judgment come when he does that.' The cacophony stopped as Matthew appeared in the doorway. Edith put her hands on her hips, scowling with indulgent severity. 'Well, then. Look who's decided to grace us with 'is presence, then.'

But Matthew wore his own furrowed brow this morning. He ignored his grandmother and clattered to his mother at the sink. He gravely tolerated the morning kiss, but frowned at his mother's head while she tied his shoes. Edith clucked her tongue in reproval, announced that the wee lamb had a black monkey on his shoulder, and told him to say good morning to the grownups. Matthew had something else in mind.

'Mummy, you know that man who always comes into my bedroom?'

Rachel said she didn't, but then looked up sharply, attentive.

'You know,' Matthew insisted. 'That *man*. Well he tells me nice things, but I always forget them when I get out of bed.'

An idea occurred to Rachel. She levelled a warning glance at Edith who was about to speak, then told Matthew that she always forgot her dreams too. Matthew flapped his arms with annoyance.

'No. That *man*. Sometimes even, he talks to me *outside* and I'm not even sleeping!'

'What does he look like? Does he wear clothes like Daddy's?' Rachel rose to cut the toast, sending another sidelong warning to Edith, who was fussing up a cloud of disapproval around the table. Matthew looked incredulous.

'*No*! You know! He's got a big dress like you! And long hair. And big shiny lights right out to here...' He brought his

44

arms back in, astounded by his mother's lack of comprehension. 'You're just tricking me,' he accused.

'I'm not,' Rachel protested. Dress? Lights? For heaven's sake! Did he want her to join in the game, or did he really think she could see this Christmas-tree man of his? Suddenly she was alarmed. After all this time, she still didn't know what was going on inside her son's head. But he was nearly five now, about to go to school. He had to be able to distinguish between imagination and reality before he came into contact with teachers and other children. She lifted a knuckle to her mouth, frightened by the thought that she had let the whole thing get away from her. She bent over to speak to him, wishing that Edith and Arthur were not present.

'I'm not playing tricks, love. I really can't see him. Nobody can. He's really just in your head.'

Matthew's mouth puckered into a tight angry knot. His jaw pushed out. 'You are so tricking me! You are a bad, bad mummy!' He stormed out of the kitchen, and stomped down the corridor. A thumping and bumping sound indicated that he had flung himself under his bed, a favourite sulking place.

The old man clutched at his wife's elbow. 'There's someone coming, Edie, isn't there? Someone's coming.'

Edith said, 'Well! I never in all my born days... Rachel, I know you'll say it's none of my business, but you're not going to get that nonsense out of his head by letting him speak to you like that!'

Rachel rubbed her top teeth with her knuckle. She didn't go after him because she didn't know what to do. She went back to preparing breakfast, ignoring further observations from Edith. Arthur stared dreamily into space. And soon, part of the immediate problem solved itself. Matthew's hunger ate his pride and he appeared shortly after the meal had been served.

'Grace, dear, grace!' Edith jogged Arthur's arm, bowed her head. 'For what we are about to receive may the Lord make us truly thankful.'

'Please can I have an egg?'

'You'll have what's on the table,' Rachel said tersely. 'And you say "please *may* I".'

Matthew ate his skittleback in silence. Then, 'Grumpa, why are your lights gone so little?'

Rachel snapped at him, her patience stretched thin. Later she noticed that Edith's knife and fork were hovering, doing nothing. Edith suddenly looked unwell.

'What's the matter?'

'I don't know.' Edith blinked. 'I just came over all funny. The queerest thing.'

Arthur gripped her arm again.

'There's someone coming Edie. I know. There's someone coming.'

Robert McKay grinned.

The game was so much more interesting in thick fog. He laid the saddle on the gatepost, the reins and pack on the top rail, then banged the gate shut to give warning that the game had begun. Somewhere out in the white mist, Lancer nickered. Hooves thudded on damp ground. Then silence. Where had that last hoof sound come from? Sound was as difficult as sight in fog. The hollow? The hedge perhaps. If he chose wrongly, Lancer would amble quietly back along the opposite fence line and hide against the back of the fire station at the waterfront end of the grazing grounds.

Robert chose. The hollow. He stole forward under the sound cover of a trawler starting up its engine. Yes, there was Lancer's back. The engine sound continued, so the minister crept closer, much closer than would normally be possible without detection. Then he stood up and coughed loudly. With a loud snort and a scramble of hooves, the piebald stallion took off out of the hollow and dissolved into the mist. Robert followed at the run. The field narrowed to a sleeve at this end, but if he didn't move fast there would still be room for Lancer to cut around to one side. There. That would be far enough; both side fences were in view now. Robert checked his lasso as the hoof sounds steadied and Lancer high-stepped to the end of the sleeve. Silence. Another snort. Then the stallion was on his way back at full gallop. Which side would it be? The right. No, a switch to the left. Robert changed stance, walked two paces left, and was poised to throw as Lancer's form coalesced and burst out of the murk. The noose floated out. The stallion ran into it, immediately slowed, obligingly came round on the arc of the rope and frisked to a halt. His lips snaffled at a proffered carrot, then he crunched into it

46

eagerly. He was breathing noisily.

It was the first time Robert had noosed him in fog on the first throw. He slapped a rippling shoulder with pleasure and affection. What beauty there was in God's creatures, what natural innocence and purity in all His works of nature. Only man tarnished the masterpiece; man the spoiler, the defiler. He led the still munching stallion towards the gate.

In ten minutes he was riding through the fog on the road behind the general store: Rue des Arbres. Two months ago, the village councillors had decided to honour the memory of some of the original French settlers by re-naming a few of the roads appropriately. There had been quite some opposition to the change. One resident had expressed his opinion by erecting his own signpost in front of the council office, in full view of women passing in the street. It had three signs: 'Rue Barb' pointed to the market garden, 'Rue Matic' pointed to Doctor Pringle's house, and 'Rue Pee' indicated the urinal next to the wharf. The sign had been removed promptly, of course, and the culprit had been required to tack an open apology to the parish notice board.

As he passed the vacant lot just beyond the general store, he noticed two small moving shapes, partially obscured by fog and tall grass. There was a clack of glass on glass, then an exclamation of accusation. Two boys were playing marbles 'for keeps' on a patch of bare ground. Robert pulled the fob-watch from his waistcoat pocket. Click. 9.06 a.m. Snick. He called the boys to him. A few seconds and a few choice words later, the miscreants were sprinting into the mist in the direction of school.

The minister continued on his way. Childhood was the vital time. Most souls were well on the way to being lost or won before they were fourteen years old, in his reckoning. It was of paramount importance to eliminate tardiness, greed, rudeness, and dirtiness before the child reached the age of spiritual accountability, when those lesser evils would attract the greater and begin to drag the developing soul towards the pit. In the long run, the greatest cruelty one could impose on children was the kindness of lax discipline and overindulgence. But then no one could say that he had neglected to put that message to the parish in the last five years.

Just before the turn off to the track to Flea Bay, Robert saw another youth ahead of him. Young Tim Armitage. He was backing a mare up to a picket fence. The minister could see no more than that because a high macrocarpa hedge blocked his view. But he knew what was happening: the boy had brought the mare to be serviced. Those Catholics, the O'Briens, owned the finest stallion on the peninsula and had taken to putting it out to stud in full view of the road. Mares were backed up to the fence and the stallion would be set to, right over the pickets, regardless of the effect of such a sight on innocent children. Not that the minister was in any way surprised. The O'Briens were known to live their lives with scant regard for common decency and dignity. But what could he do? They were Catholics.

The mare appeared less than enthusiastic. She was shying away from the fence.

'I'm thinkin' she's not ready,' said Patrick O'Brien's voice. 'Tak' 'er away, lad. Tell yer dad she's days too soon.'

From out of sight came the rattling sound of a sash window being flung upwards. Bernadette O'Brien's voice shrilled out. 'Mak' 'er tak' it, Paddy! It's many a good one I've 'ad and didn't want it!'

At that moment, Robert rode into full view of the O'Brien house. He heard a short, sharp expletive that he had seldom heard, and never before from female lips. The sash window rattled down and banged closed. The horses shifted restlessly. Paddy O'Brien and Tim Armitage watched the minister ride by. He didn't return their gaze. He looked neither right nor left, and his back was, if anything, straighter than ever.

Soon, he turned Lancer on to the track to Flea Bay, where Ruth Chapman was ill in bed and Tim and the children in need of help.

Three hundred feet above town, in full sunshine, he reined in. This was his favourite rest point — a small bare shoulder of hillside where the track turned for a new angle of attack on the pass. Below, the mist over Waiata was thinning; here and there were touches of shape and hints of colour. Only two objects stood clear out of the tenacious layer: the gleaming church spire, and the magnificent sequoia tree with its deep green foliage turned almost to black against the white cotton wool below. Behind it, the roof of Ben Clement's two-storey mansion was dark, just under the surface of the mist.

Out over the harbour, the mist was also intact — except for

one small pocket of clear air. A trawler, a symmetric, two-masted double-ender, sat on its own tranquil image. It was as if the vessel escaped gravity by reflecting itself in a horizontal and a vertical mirror. Both its real masts and its image masts cleaved into the mist. As the minister watched this sight, his lips moved with familiar, dearly loved words. ' "... that I, so long a worshipper of Nature, hither came unwearied in that service..." ' Nature, he mused, could take even something made by man, and turn it briefly to a thing of beauty. A pity that Nature could not also redeem the taint of man himself.

Robert heard a distant voice shout. He looked about, but saw nothing.

Five years now. Still no sign of the Lord's intentions. Was it possible that the challenge would involve such as the O'Briens? Some violent act perhaps. Surely not. And no individual held in general contempt could possibly be a threat in any other way. Robert's mind flicked through some of the twenty or so other families still outside the faith. No. Inconceivable. Perhaps someone from outside the peninsula altogether? But no. He was presuming that the test would come by human agency, and he presumed too much. Softly, softly. He would be patient. Even if it were two score years more in coming, he would await the Lord's will. And he would be ready.

'Mr McKay!'

A movement on the track below. A waving arm. The top half of a rider was visible, moving past broad ferns. Then the rider vanished as the track turned him behind trees. Robert waited, and in two minutes, Martin Kean was beside him, the farmer from the land at the bottom of the track.

'Mr McKay. They're asking for you at John Fleming's. Arthur is dead.'

SEVEN

Matthew sat at the pillow end of his bed, scowling. He pushed his back into the corner formed by the bedhead and the wall. Something out of the ordinary was happening, but what it was he didn't know. No one had told him anything. To make matters worse, two strange children had been shut in his bedroom with him. Big children. They were going to school; he could tell. The girl sitting on his dresser was kicking her white-stockinged feet open and closed like scissors. She didn't look at him. The boy on the other end of the bed did, but his expression wasn't the least bit encouraging.

Jimmy Crocker wasn't happy. He was seven years old now; much too big to be shut in a crummy, stupid room with a crummy girl and a crummy little kid. If his mother hadn't stopped to drop off those church papers, he'd be at school now. Why couldn't they have let him walk, anyway? Probably by now Lindsey Bates would have given his chrysalis to someone else. Jimmy's foot hit something under the bed. He rolled off the edge, pulled out a toy box, then rummaged through it, ignoring the glowering face at the other end of the bed. He chose an aeroplane, lounged back on the blankets and turned a wheel by hand so that the propeller moved and the sound strip twanged forlornly.

Matthew came out of his corner. He snatched the toy away, restored it to its box, and returned, latch-jawed, to the corner.

'Well, you're not using it,' Jimmy said, indignantly. Matthew folded his arms. Jimmy shrugged. Normally he would have thumped the little jerk, or found a cow-pat to push him into. But he couldn't do that here, not with Grandpa Fleming dead and all the grownups running round stinky and moody. 'Mr Fleming's your grandad, isn't he?' he accused Matthew, his tone implying that although Matthew probably considered him ignorant, he did, in fact, know all there was to know about the

50

ways of the world. Matthew wasn't speaking.

'Well, he's dead,' Jimmy stated.

Matthew's expression changed almost imperceptibly.

'He is not,' he said cautiously.

'Yaaa,' Jimmy scorned. 'You don't even know what it means.'

'I do so.'

'Go on, what is it then?'

'Not telling you.'

'Dummy,' Jimmy declared witheringly. 'It's when they put you in a big hole in the ground and the maggots eat you. That's how you get flies.'

Seven-year-old Jennifer Pringle swung her copper-brown hair and looked up for the first time. Her legs stopped moving. She rolled a look of cool contempt down her freckled nose. 'You're a rotten liar, Jimmy Crocker. Your tongue is going to swell up and go black and fall out on your porridge.'

'Awww, whadda you know? You're just a girl,' Jimmy's head waggled in disgust. One of the great handicaps of life was the trouble you got into if you thumped a girl.

Jennifer's legs swung again. She watched them, alternately sucking her upper and lower lips. She was bored too. It was all so much fuss. Mrs Crocker had no sooner pulled the gig up outside the Flemings' than the grownups were running around telling her and Jimmy to do this, do that. Then her father had come with his black bag, and told Mrs Crocker to send them in here. The bedroom door had a lock. She hopped off the dresser and put her eye to the keyhole. There was Mr McKay, in a room across the corridor. It looked like a lounge, but the keyhole was too small for her to see more. There was an adult rumble of voices, but she couldn't hear any words.

She darted back to her dresser, hearing the sound of a car engine coming from the near side of the house. The sound grew louder, then stopped. Car doors clicked and clunked, muted, firm. Three men walked past the window. The first was dressed in black, the other two in ordinary tweed suits. And these two carried a long wooden box. Grownups moved through the corridor behind the room. The back door opened.

'See,' Jimmy said triumphantly. 'They're going to put your grandad in that box and then they put him down in a hole.'

'They are not,' Matthew said in a tiny, uncertain voice.

51

Jennifer commented that she had been to a funeral once.

Soon, they heard the back door open again. The three men walked back past the window, returning to the car. This time, the shoes of the two carrying the box crunched heavily into the gravel close to the house.

'Your grandad's in that,' Jimmy offered helpfully.

For a moment, Matthew looked as if he was going to crumble. But almost immediately after the three had passed the window, he sat bolt upright. His face lit up. He bounced to his feet and pressed his cheek to the window glass to gaze in the direction taken by the men. Then he turned loftily to Jimmy, wrinkling his nose in mocking derision.

'Seeee! Grandpa's not even dead. Haaa, haaa!'

Jennifer giggled.

'You're bonkers,' Jimmy said wonderingly. He put his cheek to the window, frowning out. Matthew capitalised on his victory by informing them that he could read books with hard words, and he wasn't even going to school. But Jimmy wasn't listening. He came away from the window furious that Matthew hadn't accepted defeat.

'Awww...! You're nuts in the boko!' His voice was high and loud. 'Your grandad is a stiff! He's dead. The maggots are going to eat him and the —'

The door swung open. Jimmy's mother advanced malevolently into the bedroom. Her eyes took her son by the throat. 'By karracky, boy...' She breathed hoarsely, gulping at rising hysteria. 'You come home with me, boy, and we're going to wait for your dad.'

'But Ma! He's a moron! He says —'

'Not a word! Not one word more!' Mrs Crocker controlled herself enough to tell Jennifer that her father would take her the rest of the way to school. Then she mumbled an apology towards the lounge behind her and passed down the corridor, grim of purpose, holding one of Jimmy's ears. Doctor Pringle came to the bedroom door, eyed his daughter suspiciously and beckoned her away.

Matthew waited. Nothing more happened. No one came.

He went across the corridor and hovered in the lounge doorway, where no one seemed to notice him. His grandmother was hunched forward on the divan, rocking backwards and

52

forwards, her shoulders shaking. His mother was on one side of her, his Great-aunt Wynne on the other. His great-aunt had a fleshy, flabby arm across grandma's shoulders and Matthew hoped he wouldn't have to be hugged this time. There were seven grownups in the room. His father leaned against the mantelpiece, gloomy, drawn. He was listening to Mr McKay, eyes downcast, nodding occasionally. Matthew's grandmother spoke past her knees in a squeaky, high voice.

'He was a good man. He was a good man. He was a good man...' Over and over.

Matthew moved hesitantly across the carpet to his mother's side. Still no one told him off. With more confidence, he squeezed on to the couch beside her.

'Mummy? What's Grandma crying for?'

Rachel put a hand on each of Matthew's shoulders. 'Because Grandpa's gone away, love. For a long, long time.'

Matthew considered this. Then, 'Is he going today?'

'He's gone, love. Hush now. I'll explain it to you later.'

She turned back to comforting Edith. Matthew frowned. He looked up at a spot five and a half feet from the floor, in mid air in front of his grandmother. Then his frown turned to puzzlement. He looked back and forth between his grandmother and the spot in the air. Finally his eyes appeared to follow nothing in particular from that mid-air spot to another, in front of himself.

'Why won't they listen to you?' he asked.

Rachel turned, annoyed. Then she saw how his eyes were focused. Swiftly, trying at the same time to avoid unseemly haste, she picked him up and headed for the door. This was definitely not the time and place for Matthew to air conversations with his imagination.

But Matthew was still puzzled. 'Why isn't everybody listening to Grandpa?' he said over his mother's shoulder. Then he was whisked through the door, and away down the corridor.

Silence. Everyone looked at the now empty doorway. Edith held her sodden handkerchief poised in surprise, then dropped her head again and resumed rocking and moaning softly.

'Odd thing to ask,' Robert McKay mused to John Fleming. He dropped his voice out of deference to Edith. 'He doesn't seem to know what has happened. Did you not show him?'

'No. But, you know how it is, Robert. He's a bright lad.

His imagination . . .'

'Quite. Quite. My point is that at this age it can be a bad mistake to prevent him from viewing the mortal remains. I've seen what happens. In the short term, the child doesn't understand and thinks he's been deserted. In the long term, well, there is a risk of psychological effects.'

'Mmm, maybe you're right.'

'Get Mrs Fleming to bring him to the funeral early, John. I'll arrange for him to see in the casket and explain it to him.'

'Good of you, Robert. I'd be right grateful.'

Rachel took Matthew outside, out the back. She told him she was taking him over to play with Owen Hooper and that maybe Mrs Hooper would take them shopping. Matthew recognised the bribe instantly and accepted. Shopping with Owen's mummy meant gobstoppers, and gobstoppers were exactly his price.

'Who was that shiny lady with Grandpa?' he asked on the way. 'Why does she want Grandpa to go with her?'

'Oh Matthew! What in the world are you talking about?'

Matthew stopped, looked behind in the direction of the back door. Rachel tugged at his arm. He resisted so firmly that she would have had to drag him if she persisted. So she stood back, hands on hips, scowling her worry. His eyes were again looking at a place in the air in front of him. His expression suddenly turned shy. He looked down and scraped a self-conscious foot in the shingle stones.

'Don't want to,' he said. His face rose again, and then he appeared to be looking between two points in the air. 'Are you going away on holiday with that lady?'

Rachel felt tears threatening. She gripped his arm. 'Matthew, you've got to stop all this. You've got to stop making things up. Grandpa's gone with Jesus now . . .'

But Matthew's attention was firmly fixed on one of the two points a few feet above the ground in front of him. His mouth twitched with reluctant humour.

'You're tricking me,' he said, as if he knew there had to be a point to the joke somewhere. But the humour didn't last. His lips drew together in a tight resentful knot. 'You're just tricking me. Mummy can so see you.'

Robert McKay removed the lip of the casket, bowed his head in a respectful silence, then looked at Rachel. He gestured at Matthew, who had never seen the church empty before and was puzzling over the echoing sounds.

Rachel dipped her head in assent. Normally she would not have agreed to confronting her son so bluntly with death. But something had to be done. Matthew had to learn. He had to know the difference between fantasy and real life before he went to school. And yet she was apprehensive, and John, at home helping Edith prepare for the funeral, was even more so. There was a risk. Would Matthew act up in front of Mr McKay?

The minister put his hands around the boy's waist to lift him. 'Now then, Matthew, your mother and I want you to see something.' Matthew, seeing his mother's approving nod, submitted to the handling. He gazed solemnly into the casket, at the formal clothes and the still, wax-like features of the face. 'This is your grandfather's body. God has taken your grandfather away and left his body behind. Do you understand?' Rachel added quickly that God was now looking after Grandpa.

Matthew frowned suspiciously at the contents of the casket. Then he wriggled to get down, jersey pulling around his chest.

'That's not my Grandpa,' he said flatly.

Rachel closed her eyes, seeing, in her mind's eye, two trawlers about to collide head on.

'Good lad,' the minister said. He put Matthew down and patted his shoulder.

Rachel blinked.

'Excellent, Mrs Fleming. I think you'll agree the exercise was well worth while. I must say he shows considerable promise.'

'I'm sorry?' Rachel felt disoriented.

'It's rare for a child of this age to grasp not only the distinction between body and soul, but also the greater importance of the soul. What's more, he doesn't appear unduly grieved.'

At funeral time, only a handful of drinkers remained in the Fishermen's Rest. They were die-hards. They were the ones who shook their heads over the amber-and-white and told the sad tale of how Arthur Fleming had, in fact, been lost to them more than four years ago — plucked from their midst, never again to know the solace of bitter ale and light cheer.

It was back in '45, they said. Arthur had imbibed cheer in sufficient quantity to be pleasantly reminded of a three-foot swell off the heads. He went away to climb the crow's nest and fell over the upper verandah rail, breaking his foot on the road below. Now, they remembered, who should happen along but that overstretched landhog preacher Robert McKay. He stood over Arthur looking down at him like he'd found a mud eel in his bath water.

'How may I help you?' the preacher had said.

'Yer c'n get me a long beer, yer prohibishionish bugger,' replied Arthur.

'By God, I will *not*, sir!' roared the preacher. And he threw Arthur over his shoulder like half a sack of fresh-cut cocksfoot and set off to the hospital — and Arthur with a drinking gut like a scared puffer fish. Arthur groaned and whimpered and begged for mercy. But the preacher just let him down once, for him to resurface the road with the good cheer. Then he continued up the hill, with Arthur moaning and flopping about like he'd been hung out to dry. No, they reminisced, the Fishermen's Rest hadn't seen the like of it since Johnny Wharehinga booked a room for two and rode his horse up the stairs. Poor old Arthur, they said, it took the stuffing right out of him. Went downhill fast after that. Never touched a drop since. Never missed a sermon. But, if a man wanted to knot the last cod-end while he was still in his prime, who were they to stand in his way? Everybody had to square with the Almighty the best they knew how. And here's good luck to 'im.

Arthur Fleming had been amongst the last of those who hunted the great whale schools off the peninsula. Even when the sperm whales became scarce and he turned to fishing, he remained a harpooner at heart. It was said that as recently as ten years ago, Arthur had been known to chase a solitary whale just so that he could put a stone down the blowhole with his slingshot. For that and other exploits, both mentionable and unmentionable at parish tables, Arthur Fleming's name was known to every adult on the peninsula and almost every child.

So nine-tenths of the people of Waiata County were at the church to farewell him. Not that they all went inside. The priestless Roman Catholics waited out the ceremony beyond the church gates. They stood in a small bunch, with umbrellas and collars turned against the bitter easterly drizzle. The handful of Anglicans, also without church or minister, paid their respects from beside the front steps. Jack Sullivan stood alone, also beside the front steps, on the other side of the path. His heading dog, D'Arcy, sat beside him, hair matted, ears drooping and dripping.

Inside, there were three hundred seated and nearly a hundred standing. The three front left pews were allocated for family and relatives of the deceased only. In the centre of the foremost pew was Edith Fleming: in black, veiled, small and still, with her head and shoulders bent far forward. John Fleming supported her on her right; her sister, Great-aunt Wynne, held her on the left. Rachel and Matthew sat directly behind them in the second pew.

Robert McKay was speaking from the exact centre of the pulpit. His hands gripped the rail four feet apart, bracing braced shoulders, anchoring him to the church so as to launch his words more effectively towards the swathe of faces. But he didn't shout, or thunder. He never thundered at a funeral; his subtler tones were more than adequate for such an occasion. Even at half volume, his every word sought out the ears in the far corners and compelled attention.

His voice planed softly upwards: '...The body of man is sown in corruption! And it is raised:..' — a pause, and then the descent — '...in corruption.' He flung his piercing glance across several randomly chosen and widely scattered individuals. Again the rise and fall: 'It is sown in dishonour! And it is raised ... in glory...'

Rachel relaxed as the service continued. Matthew seemed quite happy, unperturbed by the sight of his grandfather's remains. Her son was sitting still, as well behaved as any mother could possibly wish for. In any case, he was always well behaved when Mr McKay spoke; he seemed to like the ebb and flow of the words, though he understood few of them.

'..."Lord, Thou has been our dwelling place in all generations"...'

Rachel suddenly lost the words from the pulpit. Matthew was grinning. She watched him, alarmed. But now he turned to gaze at the minister and his grin faded. A private joke. She relaxed once more.

'..."even from everlasting to everlasting, Thou *art* God"...'

Matthew turned his head to look forward and past his mother. His grin broke out anew, flinging itself broadly across his features. He clutched his mother's arm and hid his face behind it. He was playing peek-a-boo! Rachel looked around, trying not to move her head. No one in the front pew could possibly be playing with him at a time like this. Please let it be a child, in the outer aisle. No. No children there at all. She breathed at him to keep quiet.

'..."Thou turnest a man to destruction; and sayest"...'

Then, Rachel knew where he was looking. Her heart lurched. He was playing imaginary peek-a-boo with the empty space to the left of Great-aunt Wynne. She took hold of his shoulders and gave him a small but very intense shake, hissing at him to keep still and watch the front. He did so.

There was a stir amongst those standing in the outer left aisle. Heads turned. Robert McKay glared in that direction, but continued without pause, speaking the eloquent poetry of the ninetieth psalm.

'..."For a thousand years in Thy sight are"...'

From the outer left aisle a wan, faint-looking woman came forward, supported by her husband. She sank gratefully in the space to the left of Great-aunt Wynne. In an instant, Matthew was on his feet, eyes bulging with indignation.

'Don't you sit there! My Grandpa's sitting there!' Rachel gasped, plucked him off the floor and pushed him back into his seat. The minister had stopped. Matthew, aware of the scores of eyes on him, protested in a child's stage whisper even more penetrating than his normal voice. 'But she made Grandpa stand up! And Grandpa's sick!'

A soundless ripple rolled through the congregation. Edith Fleming swayed against Aunt Wynne. Robert McKay stared down at Matthew, annoyed, puzzled. John Fleming had turned in his seat and was gaping at his son. Heads bobbed and moved together. Clothes rustled. The whispers began: 'What do you make of that?' 'Poor little tyke.' 'Just couldn't accept that 'is Grandad's gone.' Even deaf and blind Tommy Ransley in the back pew sensed that something unusual was happening. A neighbour tried to finger-write an explanation on his palm, but gave it up as too complex. Scores wanted to smile, but didn't dare. Matthew, now

58

feeling the full weight of attention, buried his face in his mother's neck and began to cry. He tried to do it privately and succeeded only in producing a thin, keening wail. Rachel clutched her son to her and stood, looking for the fastest way out. The nearest open door was the main entrance at the far end.

The minister resumed. He raised his voice against the boy's noise and endeavoured to use the rhythm and beauty of the psalm to retrieve the decorum of the service.

'... "Thou carriest them away as with a flood; they are as asleep"...'

A snort of laughter forced its way out of someone's nasal passages. It was contagious. The congregation seethed with strangled gasps, tried to contain its sense of humour within its sense of occasion; and in a community used to providing its own entertainment, this was very difficult. Rachel went swiftly down the aisle, staring wildly and fixedly at the distant doorway. Around her were the bent heads and heaving shoulders of those who were pitting shame against mirth. The people across the back made passage for her. She passed through the main door, coming in sight of the mystified Anglicans outside. Behind her she heard the furious voice of the minister, resorted to its best Sunday thunder, determined to restore the dignity and respect of the funeral service.

'... "In the morning it flourisheth, and groweth up; in the evening it is cut down"...' The voice stopped abruptly.

A gale of laughter propelled Rachel down the steps, and towards the gate. Matthew's wail reached full volume. It continued without pause, even when he raised his head to look at Jack Sullivan and D'Arcy standing sodden by the path. And soon, the small boy and his mother were both crying as they walked home in the freezing August drizzle.

EIGHT

Emily Nisbet peeled the oil-soaked muslin away from her hips. She grimaced at the steaming red skin left behind. The pain was exactly as it had been, like sandpaper fingers pushing and prodding out from the joint. The comfrey poultice hardly ever worked on her hip.

Well, there was always the morning bath. She rearranged her nightgown, joggled felt slippers on to her feet, and shrugged into her long, chocolate-brown dressing gown. She limped towards the bathroom via the kitchen-dining-living room, where Genghis fluttered in bursts, anticipating her appearance. When he saw her, he did two rung-to-rung hops without skip-turning on each rung.

'Good morning to you, Genghis.'

'ChrRrRrRrRrRrRrRrRrRr,' Genghis warbled in tones that throbbed through the half-cottage room.

'Sorry to be a complainer, dear, but the hip is really a touch nasty this morning. Must be weather coming.'

'ChrRrRr,' Genghis replied.

Emily turned on the bath taps and came back to the kerosene heater between the bird cage and the bookshelves. She primed it, lit it, and pumped on the tank. When the heater was hissing and the reflector-bowl glowing cherry red, she stood up in front of the cage. She brought all her waist-length hair over one shoulder in preparation for twirling it on her head. A memory caught her. She let some of the dark, grey-streaked tresses slide off the edge of her hand, reflecting some of the red light from the heater as it fell.

'I'm no Mae West, Genghis. Never have been. But the men couldn't resist my hair, you know. Hah. Archie Smythe — you wouldn't remember him — he used to slip some of my hair through his bow tie and get down on his knees and beg to be taken for a walk. I wonder what happened . . .'

She broke off. A cry heralding imminent disaster came through the kitchen window from the back yard. There was a metallic thud, followed by a snapping of branches and a stifled call of distress and pain. She hurried to the window. A boy lay against the corrugated-iron fence down near the back of the section. It was one of the Pugh boys from next door; he'd fallen off the fence and through a rosebush.

Emily found herself hurrying, limping, down the back path.

'Let's see what's wrong with you. Hold still now. A few scrapes and cuts, eh? No bruises? The ground's not too hard, is it? All right. Upsy daisy then. Come over to the seat and I'll look at it properly.'

Dazed, the youngster allowed himself to be helped to his feet and guided to the garden seat. He kept looking at the grazes on his elbow, and the thorn scratches on his arm and leg. One scratch was bleeding. Emily removed 'potentising' jars and begonia pots from the seat to make way for the boy. She was amazed at herself. She couldn't remember how many months it had been since she spoke so many words to a human being. And suddenly she felt an exultation, an excitement.

'You just sit right there, dear. I've got something that'll have you right as rain in no time. What's your name?'

'Ashley.' A mumble.

As she bustled back to the cottage, the pain returned, slowing her, making her gasp. She tried to ignore it, but by the time she reached the medicine cabinet inside, the sandpaper fingers were searing through her bones and flesh. She leaned on the china cabinet, breathing sharply. The bath! It must be close to overflowing. She hobbled to the taps, rattled them closed. Now, hurry! Hurry!

Outside, Ashley Pugh was collecting his wits. A few days ago he'd had his tenth birthday party. He was, therefore, too old to cry. As he had informed his parents, ten was almost half of twenty-one, so he was almost half a man. On the other hand, though he wasn't so dizzy, he was suffering. So he allowed a few tortured gasps of agony to force their way through, but closed his throat to anything resembling a sob. It wasn't too difficult, because his main worry wasn't really the pain at all — it was being in Mrs Nisbet's garden. Everybody knew Mrs Nisbet was a loonie.

61

Emily scanned the shelves of the medicine cabinet. Nettle juice. Knitbone. Horseradish cream. Arnica pilules. Lavender oil. Where was it? There. Calendula: crushed marigolds in lard. Just the thing for scrapes and cuts. She snatched the pottery jar out, breathless with urgency. But the pain! The pain! She must have something to take the weight off her hip. What? What? She cast about. The broom. She fumbled with it, then found that the cross piece fitted under her arm like a crutch. In a few seconds she was outside, manoeuvring towards the boy, her face distorted, grotesque with pain.

Ashley stiffened. He gripped the end of the seat. His eyes widened and his hair prickled behind his head. Mrs Nisbet was coming towards him fast, lurching down the narrow path on a broom. Her long dark gown flapped and jerked against her body. Her mass of hair lifted up on the morning breeze, some of it flicking about her face and shoulders. Her face was all screwed up like, like . . . like in that story his mother had read him.

Emily saw the boy straighten, mouth open. The poor dear must be in a lot of pain. She waved her pot of calendula and called out reassuringly. 'I've got something for you.'

Ashley bolted. He raced out and around Emily, one terrified eye fixed on her in case she put the broom between her legs. He cut a swathe of trampled herbs and torn stems through her garden in a tight arc of almost geometric precision. He dashed down the side of the cottage, expecting it to yawn and swallow him. He cleared Emily's front fence on an almost flat trajectory, hitting the road at such speed that his next arc took him to the far side of the road before turning him back to his home.

Emily brought her gaze back along the line of distressed plants. She took the broom out from under her arm. While she looked at it, she heard Ashley shouting all the way down his front path. The Pughs' front door slammed. The shouting continued inside. When Emily looked up from the broom, there were faces at the open window overlooking her fence.

The window closed.

NINE

In bad weather, the pupils of Waiata District School were permitted to wait for their teachers inside their classrooms. Early arrivals for the intermediate class stood on their desks to watch the rain slashing at the rugby ground and at the forlorn horses already in the school's grazing patch. Inside, two senior boys were lighting the kindling in the stone fireplace that yawned across the front left corner of the room. The new flames turned faces orange and made grotesque cold shadows dance on the worn plaster. When the fire took, the seniors laid it carefully with coal nuggets, banked it, and iced the arrangement with grey coke. Soon, the heat pushed into the room, waking the smell of the oil the caretaker had laid on the floorboards last summer to keep the dust down. The seniors switched on the lights and left.

With their departure, the intermediate class came to life. Somehow, in weather like this, it was imperative to get the most out of every unsupervised minute. Three boys in front of the fire engaged in a suicidal, fratricidal, three-musketeer act with their rulers. David Clayton fancied himself a giant stepping from island to island, and desk-hopped, attempting to take in all desks on a converging spiral without having to step into the sea. Lily Wharehinga embarked on an attempt to break the record for the number of boys whose hair was pulled before school. But she found this to be a hazardous venture for someone in long pigtails, especially when she dangled them too near an inkwell.

Almost half the class watched Matthew Fleming take on the knuckles champion, Jimmy Crocker. They faced each other across the aisle, each with a fist extended. The fists almost touched, each set of knuckles confronting the other. The defending champion was striker. He passed a few half-inch feints, causing the other fist to be snatched away, then slashed forward and down, cracking his set of knuckles on to those of the challenger.

'Aaaaaaa,' Matthew said, curling his lips back and sucking through his teeth in pain. He massaged his stinging knuckles, then repositioned them for another attempt. If he could make Jimmy miss, he'd become striker. The knuckles wavered at each other; Jimmy's confident and probing, Matthew's nerve-strung, shying at the slightest twitch.

'Come on, Matt!' 'Get 'im, Jims!'

Jimmy's fist blurred again. Matthew groaned and blew on his knuckles.

'Hit his thumb, Jimbo,' Daniel Ferris urged.

'You're horrible.' Rita Stone was disgusted. There was in fact an element of respect for Matthew's misshapen thumb. One day, fed up being teased about it, he had spent an entire playtime brandishing it with clawed fingers, declaring with well-acted menace that it was a murderer's thumb.

'Frostface!' The yell came from the door.

For ten seconds, the noise doubled in volume. Bodies hurtled over and between the desks and down the aisles. Desks and chairs were hustled into line. Desk lids banged. Books slapped on wood, and pens and pencils rocked in their grooves next to the rulers. Rita Stone's eraser bounced to the floor. She rummaged frantically under the desk for it, hearing the click of shoes approaching through the vestibule. The doorhandle squeaked, clicked. Chairs scraped back. The intermediate class rose to their feet.

Miss Julia Sedgewick, L.T.C.L., and senior teacher of Waiata District School, paused, checking that the silence was complete. The door closed behind her, making the leather strap below the glass pane swing from side to side on its hook. Its name was Ginger. Even the boys in the senior class spoke respectfully of Ginger. The teacher laid her handbag on her desk, then crossed to the fire and back, inspecting the lines of humans and furniture for posture and position. The class had already classified her mood. The word *scungy* was in most minds, meaning average-to-foul. They could detect this from the way she arranged her mouth. Normally her lips were thin and straight across, rather like her body, which was thin and straight up and down. But today, the muscles in the centre of her top lip were bunched together the way they were when she suspected Sean O'Brien of planning to break wind.

Miss Sedgewick didn't care for wet Fridays.

From next to the pencil sharpener on her desk, she raised a cork-handled white music baton. Julia Sedgewick had once been considered for second violin in the National Symphony Orchestra; now she was in charge of the church and school choirs. She cocked an ear as a final check on the decibel level, then tapped the pencil sharpener twice, very quickly with the baton.

'Good morning, class.' Every year, at the parish fête, she sang Schumann's 'The Walnut Tree'.

'Good morning, Miss Sedgewick.'

'Remain standing. Six times table. Begin.'

'Six noughts are nought,' thirty-one voices chanted. 'Six ones are six, six twos are twelve . . .' The schoolmistress zigzagged the aisle to her right, checking individual performances, hovering marginally longer by Matthew Fleming's desk. He chanted on confidently, looking straight ahead, and she moved on.

'Stop!' She came to a halt beside Lindsey Bates's desk. She stared at a small black insect scrabbling on Lindsey's arithmetic book. It had just fallen out of his hair. 'Lindsey, go and see Mr Thomas. Then go home for the day.' Mr Thomas, one of the other two teachers, kept kerosene for lice-ridden heads.

'Please, Miss, Sid's got kooties too.'

'Lice, Lindsey. The correct term is lice, the plural of louse.'

A swift inspection confirmed that Sidney's scalp also needed the kerosene. In fact, Sidney was the first of the two boys to go through the door. After inspecting his head, Miss Sedgewick discovered that he was wearing no shoes. Only slimy greenish-brown socks. Every winter, when Sidney lost his socks and shoes, he came to school via fresh warm cow-pats, standing a minute or two in each.

The baton tapped. 'Six sixes . . .'

'. . . Are thirty-six, six sevens are forty . . .'

'Stop!' Miss Sedgewick was poised over Susan Armitage. 'Six sevens are . . . ? *Don't* look at the wall! Six sevens are . . . ?' Susan mumbled something. 'Dunce's table, Susan. Take your book. Write it out twenty times.' Susan moved disconsolately to the table in the back corner. The chant resumed and carried on to the end. The class was instructed to sit. 'Susan, I believe you have forgotten something?' Susan moved her mouth unhappily and put the tall conical black dunce's cap on to her head.

Immediately there was a brief snatch of whispering from the

other side of the room. Not brief enough.

'James Crocker.' Jimmy stood. 'If it's of sufficient interest to whisper it to your neighbour, it is certain to be interesting to the whole class. Be good enough to repeat what you said.'

'It wasn't nothing, Miss Sedgewick.'

'What you mean is that it wasn't anything important. However, though I have every confidence that your assessment is accurate, I require you to repeat what you said to the whole class.'

'I said, "Witchity Nisbet", Miss Sedgewick.'

The teacher sighed with exasperation. 'James Crocker, I will not permit my classroom to be used for the promotion of malicious gossip about senior members of this community, whoever they are. You will write a hundred times "I will not promote idle, malicious gossip" and have it on my desk in the morning.'

Jimmy sat in pale silence. Overnight lines had to be signed by a parent. Every time Jimmy got lines, his father laid into him with a belt until he writhed on the kitchen floor; already he could hear his father's voice shouting, 'You're stupid, Jimmy. You're useless. You're no damn good to anybody.'

Shortly, School Journals were handed out. Friday was comprehension and test day. Miss Sedgewick issued instructions, allocating different stories to different levels, then moved back to her desk. She caught herself looking at Matthew and shifted her eyes elsewhere. Too soon. The time for close scrutiny would be during the test. She would catch him in the act this time.

Matthew flattened out his journal at the beginning of 'They Came to the Gumfields'. He glanced at the picture at the top of the story, then cupped his chin in his hands and let his eyes wander up to the louvre window beside him. There was a sliver of grey sky visible. He stared at it and daydreamed of hot baths and lounge-room fires, and hot roast mutton with mint sauce and gravy.

Irritated, Miss Sedgewick continued to watch him, waiting for him to start his reading. After a long while, he heard pages turning around him. He looked down for just enough time to turn his own page, then wandered back to his daydream.

Well, well. The trickle of irritation in Miss Sedgewick swelled to a stream of annoyance. How very confident of the little upstart. In the last fortnight she'd noticed his daydreaming more and more. And yet his results had not deteriorated. If anything, they had improved. In the last week it had become obvious: he was cheating. Almost certainly he had been cheating for some time. And if there was anything more annoying to Julia Sedgewick than a cheat, it was a successful cheat.

Matthew was now so immersed in his daydream, his eyes had glazed over.

Miss Sedgewick moved into the aisle to her left and passed up and down, changing the angle so as to avoid anyone noticing her scrutiny and warning him. He still hadn't begun the story! If he kept it up, she would have her evidence by the end of the reading. All along, that had been the problem: no evidence. No covert eye action, no wide elbows, no wrong answers identical with those of immediate neighbours. No shiny pencil-cases consistently in the same position on someone else's desk. All of which meant that he had developed a two-step, blind pick-up, note-drop system along the desk braces. Rare, even in the senior classes.

An inspiration came to her. The baton rat-tatted on a desk top, making the occupier jump. 'Class, those of you who have finished may close your journals and head up in your written books for the test.' Two or three journals closed ostentatiously. Then Matthew's closed. He hadn't bothered to read a single line of the story. She had him. Easy as that. The corners of Miss Sedgewick's mouth deepened into crevasses of satisfaction.

She began the test. She read the questions from a piece of paper so that she could keep an eye on her quarry. The conclusion would be even more satisfactory if she could identify his accomplices. But all she noticed was that there was always a long delay between his hearing the question and writing the answer. Sometimes he closed his eyes. She called the last question, waited, the ordered pens and pencils down and returned to her desk.

'Matthew Fleming, bring me your work.'

Matthew did so. While she checked his five answers, he rocked his right heel awkwardly on the front of his left shoe. He was always self-conscious in front of the class.

'I see, Matthew Fleming,' his teacher said brightly, 'that you have all five answers correct.' The class caught the tone and began to pay attention. Entertainment. Matthew blinked several times. The atmosphere didn't seem to promise much in the way of a gold star for good work. 'Be so good as to explain how you achieved this excellent result without reading the story.' The class sat very still. There was going to be a strapping. It was going to be Fleming's first time with Ginger.

Matthew squirmed. 'I don't need to read the story, Miss Sedgewick.'

The teacher swivelled her gaze on the class to see if anyone was smiling. But no one was that stupid. She straightened, managing to loom over Matthew without getting out of her chair. Flippancy, she *hadn't* expected. 'Don't try me further, Matthew Fleming. You are already in serious trouble. I will not tolerate cheating in my classroom.'

'I wasn't cheating, Miss...'

'Don't *dare* contradict me! Tell me whose work you copied.'

'No one's, Miss Sedgewick!'

'But Matthew.' Her voice dropped to a reasonable tone, as if she were sorry for him. 'If you didn't read the story, and you didn't copy from someone, how did you get the answers?'

'I used my head, Miss Sedgewick! Nathaniel —'

'You *what*!' She rose in wrath.

Matthew gulped and stumbled on. '...He showed me how to close my eyes and go up to a special book with everything written in it. So I close my eyes and go up to it on your desk.'

For just a moment, the teacher was taken aback. There was a mental stage in which children believed themselves immune from observation if they closed their eyes. But that was in the *very* young. Nathaniel? There was no one by that name in Waiata. And there was no such answer book, of course. The answers had been written on a piece of paper in her drawer. He was playing her for a fool, stringing her along. The little ratbag had been stringing her along all year, and no doubt boasted about it in the playground.

'You insolent, impudent, deceiving little monkey. You have been cheating and lying, and you show not a farthing's worth of repentance! Go outside.'

Matthew's cheeks went pasty and slack. 'But I wasn't...'

'*Outside*! I'm going to make an example of you!'

He went, shaking. When the door was closed behind him she called the four most likely accomplices out to the front. But her best grilling techniques produced only wounded protestations of innocence from all four. Fuming, she set work for the class, lifted Ginger from his resting place behind the door, and stepped out after Matthew. The class buzzed with excitement. When old Frostface worked herself into a frenzy, she aimed for the fingers every second shot. They debated the number of blows she was likely to deliver, and most agreed that it would be the maximum she gave intermediates: four. When the strapping commenced, they kept up a low-toned count. 'One. Two. Three. Four, that's it. Five! Jeez, she's really in a shitty. It'll be six, betcha. She's making him straighten his hand out. *Six*!' Some of the class weren't grinning any more. A few of the girls and all of the younger boys had gone very quiet.

The teacher returned alone. This usually meant that the victim was blubbing and had been told to stay put until he stopped. But when Miss Sedgewick was really angry, she sometimes made the pupil stay outside anyway so the rest of the class would think he had been crying. So it was hard to tell. While appearing to work with great diligence, the class listened carefully for sobs. They heard nothing, but, of course, he might be one of the silent blubbers. Miss Sedgewick hung Ginger back on his hook. She demanded to know if Jennifer's expression meant that she had something to say. Jennifer turned scarlet; now the other girls would accuse her of going soft on Matthew who was only just out of junior class. She mumbled a denial and hung her head so that only the teacher could see past her long auburn hair.

Matthew entered, holding one set of throbbing fingers in another. He didn't attempt the usual nothing-to-it face. Instead, his whole bearing proclaimed intense resentment. Julia Sedgewick ignored it, confident that it would soon give way to pride at having received six of the best and lived to tell the tale.

But by scripture time, five minutes before the interval bell, he was still glowering at his desk lid, still drawing glances from around the class. And he was still, obviously, unrepentant. Irritation returned to Miss Sedgewick. He was only making life more difficult for himself that way. But, if he wanted to be pig-headed... She called for books closed, brought the two class Bibles out of her drawer, and opened them both to the same page.

'Matthew Fleming. You will do the reading this morning.'

Matthew did nothing.

'Come and get the Bible.'

He did so, sullenly, and took his time going back to his desk. The class watched him, fascinated. If he kept this up, he would get another dose of Ginger, for sure.

'Left-hand page, Matthew. Half way down the right-hand column. Verse eight. Begin at the words "and all". Unless,' she added quickly, catching his glance before it found the place, 'unless you feel inclined to tell us what is written there without looking at it.' Two boys sniggered, only to be silenced with a glance. Matthew gazed at the far wall, his mouth hardening. He shut the book and closed his eyes.

' "And all liars shall have their part in the lake which burn . . . burneth with fire and brimstone . . ." '

There was a buzz of astonishment. He'd got it right; the teacher's face made that clear. Miss Sedgewick silenced the noise with an icy stare. She knew that Sunday School never taught Revelations. John and Rachel Fleming must be teaching him key verses. Not a desirable turn of events, but one easily redirected; she reopened the Bible at random, checked a page quickly for an obscure verse, then tapped with the baton.

'Well done, Matthew,' she said briskly. 'Your memory is excellent. Perhaps you'd be so good as to do the same with Romans chapter one, verse fifteen.' Thirty pupils watched him concentrate. Everyone knew that there was only ever one winner in battles with Miss Sedgewick; but they hoped, they hoped fervently, that he could do it again.

' "So, as much as in me is, I am ready to preach the gospel to you that are at Ro . . . in Rome also." '

The class gasped with delight. Julia Sedgewick froze them with her baton. She thought fast. Obviously she had underestimated his memory, if not his intelligence. His parents must be coaching him constantly. All very commendable; and yet no boy of this age could possibly know every verse in one book, let alone the whole Bible. She had been astoundingly unlucky in her choice of verse. Well, now he needed some wind spilled out of his insolent little sails. And quickly: some of the class were grinning openly. But clearly it would be courting disaster to risk another passage from the gospels. She took one of her own private books from the shelf on the wall. *A Pageant of English Verse.* She didn't open it, but ordered Matthew to come and get it.

70

Matthew was frightened now. He came forward, exchanged books with shaking hands, and returned unsteadily to stand behind his desk. The interval bell clanged dully in the vestibule, but not a single pupil edged pens and pencils closer together. Suppose, just suppose, Matthew Fleming had stumbled on a foolproof way of cheating. What then? They shivered in delicious anticipation.

'Matthew, perhaps your remarkable memory extends to a poem called *Old Age*, by Edmund Waller. The first line will do.'

Matthew felt as though he was surrounded by cotton wool. He had a sour taste in his mouth. He wanted to say that he couldn't do it without looking, to give in, take his medicine and get it over with. But he was in so much trouble already, it couldn't be worse if he kicked her in the shins and spat at her. His eyelids went down, twitching. Julia Sedgewick felt a touch of foreboding. Not since her assistant year had she even come near to being beaten by a pupil. Suddenly, all the strange rumours about the Fleming boy loomed large in her mind. She tried to dismiss them. Of course he can't do it, she thought, it contradicts known scientific principles.

' "The seas are quiet when the winds give... give"... ' Matthew opened his eyes. 'I don't know how to say the next word.'

Miss Sedgewick swallowed. She put her baton down, then she picked it up again. Thirty pairs of eyes followed every movement. 'Class stand. We'll have more from... from... Edmund Waller some... another time. You may leave for interval.'

In the intermediates' play area, the tight press of bodies attracted attention from elsewhere. There were cries of 'scrap, scrap,' and the seniors came running to see the fight. But it wasn't a fight. 'What's happening?' 'Frostface is really going to do him this time.' 'What'd he do?' 'Expelled, I reckon.' 'Who was it got six?' 'You should have seen old Frostface's mush!' 'Go on, tell us how you did it.' 'Bet you can't do it again.'

At first, Matthew tried to push his way out. But he knew that no matter where he went, it wouldn't be far enough to escape what lay in store for him. And anyway, he was beginning to enjoy his celebrity status. He put his hand into his pocket nonchalantly.

'It's easy,' he declared. 'You just make a special book in your head, and it's on the teacher's desk with all the answers in it.' Only a few heard him in all the noise, and they just looked puzzled. A small blue notebook on the end of Jimmy Crocker's arm was thrust before him. Jimmy urged him to see if he could work out what was written on the third page.

Matthew shrugged, concentrated.

'What's he doing?' 'You watch this.' 'Shh. He's going to do it.' 'Do what?' 'Shhh.'

' "I love Alan Westlake because he is really beaut." '

Hoots of raucous laughter erupted. But in the midst of it all, there was one piercing wail of distress. Penny Parker burst into tears of fury and clawed her way to the centre. She snatched the book away from a startled Matthew.

'You bloody, bloody bugger! That's private. It's not fair,' she sobbed. 'It's not fair.'

Someone cried out a teacher warning, only to be dumped in the nearest puddle for giving a false alarm. But the crowd was beginning to break up anyway. In half a minute, only a small group of boys was around Matthew. Nearby, half a dozen girls clustered around Penny Parker. Jennifer Pringle was amongst them, urging Penny to 'go and tell'. Throughout interval, Jennifer had been beset with taunts about her and Matthew. So she formed a deputation to Miss Sedgewick. Its members shouted their intention to Matthew's group and left for the teachers' room, with Jennifer conspicuously to the fore.

Miss Sedgewick wasn't in the teachers' room. She was still in the classroom, hunting distractedly through the Bible. 'Yes, yes. What is it, girls?'

'Miss Sedgewick, you know what Matthew Fleming was doing before...? Well he just did it in Penny's private diary!' 'And he didn't even ask her.' 'He told everyone what was in it. The whole school almost!' 'It was so embarrassing too,' Lily Wharehinga added, because Penny was weeping too hard to say it for herself.

'Is this true, Penny?'

Penny sobbed a heart-broken affirmative.

'Did you lend your diary to him?'

'No, Miss Sedgewick! He must have taken it out of my bag. It's not fair. It's private. Now everybody...'

72

'All right, girls.' The teacher's mouth thinned down to two pale wafers. 'Thank you for letting me know.'

By the end of interval, Miss Sedgewick had found the passage she wanted. But she said nothing about it during class. The children waited expectantly for the retribution that must fall on the boy who sat with arms hugging his chest and with head leaning against a wall. At lunchtime they filed out of the classroom, mystified. Obviously something very drastic was going to happen to Matthew. But it was puzzling that his parents hadn't been summoned to school.

Jennifer Pringle was among the last to leave the room. She saw Miss Sedgewick place one of the class Bibles in her handbag. She saw the teacher leave the grounds and head briskly down towards the waterfront. Jennifer didn't eat her lunch. She left the grounds also, and walked home holding her hand across her stomach.

Rachel and John Fleming sat on the sofa, saying nothing. Rachel gazed into the empty fireplace. John stared sightlessly at the family Bible on the coffee table in front of them. Robert McKay stood before them, speaking thoughtfully, reflectively, his eyes directed out the lounge window.

'Four years ago I conducted a funeral that turned into a cheap sideshow. At the time, I thought it to be the result of chance and the ramblings of an overwrought child. But, I am forced to reconsider...' He indicated a chair inquiringly, pulled it over and sat facing them both. 'John, I'm not forgetting that you are a ruling elder. But I would rather speak to you both now as friends; I am so concerned for the safety of your son's soul, I must speak bluntly. Will you let me risk imposing on our friendship?'

'Yes. Yes, go on.' John's voice was dry.

'I have been making inquiries. Were you aware that for some time after the funeral, Matthew was observed, alone, talking to what he believed to be his grandfather?' Neither parent responded. 'Were you aware that very recently he has been observed, again alone, talking to one he calls his friend, Nathaniel?'

Rachel's head sank. John's gaze swung like a scythe towards his wife.

The minister continued. 'Were you aware that he has been

seen attempting to heal injured and sick animals, using what can only be a ritual commonly used by spiritualists?'

Both John and Rachel paled. Rachel tried to hold ground. 'I know his behaviour is unusual at times. But I know him as a mother, Mr McKay. I know how rich his imagination is. He's so bright, he makes things up all the time. That's all it is.'

'Mrs Fleming, forgive me, but I don't think you believe that yourself. Especially after what he did today at school.'

Rachel's shoulders slumped. John turned his head very slowly to look at her, his expression bleak with new understanding. 'You and I are going to have a wee talk, later,' he said slowly.

'It could be argued,' the minister pressed, 'that Matthew is suffering from some mental aberration. But I think not. In my opinion it is much worse than that.' He nodded at the open Bible. 'I think you'll agree that the verse exactly describes the situation.' John dropped his head to read it silently yet again. The minister paraphrased it aloud. ' "There shall not be found amongst you one that useth divination, or a consulter with familiar spirits." But there is more. You must understand the nature of the danger your son is in. Matthew believes he spoke with his grandfather. He believes he speaks to one Nathaniel.' John's face was losing more of its colour all the time. 'One Timothy, chapter four, verse one: "...In the latter times some shall depart from the faith, giving heed to seducing spirits and the doctrines of devils." '

For a heart-racing moment it occurred to the minister that this might somehow be connected with his mission. The challenge. But it was a surge of hope that promptly drowned in its own absurdity. When the great task came it would hardly be in the form of a small, impressionable boy.

John ran his fingers through his hair repeatedly. Faster each time.

'No,' Rachel protested brokenly. 'It can't be that. There's no harm in Matthew. He's only a boy. Just a small boy!'

The minister nodded, then stood and paced before the fireplace. 'Let me tell you something. In England, some of my time was spent with refugees from the occult, people who had been tempted into spiritualism and then learned its true nature the hard way. A few of them, I might add, in spite of our best efforts to repair the damage, were fit only for a psychiatric hospital.'

'Holy Father forbid...' John began to stand.

74

'However...' Robert held up a reassuring hand. 'Matthew is young. He can have made no conscious decision to embrace evil. He is so young, he can't be held spiritually accountable. In my opinion you have nothing to fear; he will come out of this unscathed, *provided*...' He turned intently on them both. '...*Provided* he is taught to allow those dark forces that assail him no further part in his life. He must be shown the error of his ways so effectively that he loses his susceptibility.' John's head was nodding slowly, balefully, purposefully. 'John, I believe he'll still do you both proud. Firm, decisive action now will put him out of danger, and shortly this unpleasant day will be just a memory.' He spoke to both. 'You'll want to be alone, now. If you need me, don't hesitate to call, whatever the hour.'

When he had gone, John went into the backyard and returned with a stick of green willow two feet long and half an inch across. He tramped into the lounge and glared at his wife. He made a guttural sound in his throat before speaking. 'May God forgive me for letting you sweet-talk me out of showing the boy what's right and wrong. And may the Lord forgive you, woman, for keeping half the boy's devilments from me.'

Rachel was looking at the stick; if she heard him, she didn't respond. She cradled the Bible to her, and began to sob deep down. When she looked up next, John was opening the door to Matthew's room. She ran down the corridor to their bedroom, lay on her bed and put her hands over her ears.

Not long afterwards, on a weekend day when his father was fishing, young Matthew Fleming began the first of many solitary wanderings in the bush around the village. And it was on one such day that he stumbled on what was to become a priceless possession.

It was a very small clearing. A magical glade furnished with soft grass and a tiny stream, well off the beaten tracks and high above the harbour. And it would become his haven, his hideaway, his special and private place.

Here, he passed his time imagining faraway places and people. One day he would be a pirate, swinging his cutlass in the rigging of a treasure ship. On another he would be a Red Indian sending fire arrows arching into a waggon train. He would singlehandedly round up a notorious kidnapping gang disguised as a police squad,

75

captain a liner around Cape Horn and through the Northwest Passage, both in the same day, or pilot a fighter jet through the first-ever breaking of the sound barrier. So adept did his imagination become that at times his retreat from Waiata was total: for brief intervals he could make the forest clearing disappear until he seemed really to live in the adventures conjured by his schoolboy mind.

Gradually, imperceptibly, the emphasis of these flights of fancy changed: more and more they took place in the past. Sometimes the remote past. They became less grandiose in their drama, dwelt more on the detail of human interaction. This didn't puzzle him, however. Nor did it puzzle him that his fancies took him to places he had never heard of and turned up details he had never known, because no small boy questions the power of his own imagination.

But the hideaway in the forest was not to remain his alone.

After many months, he came across evidence that someone else was using his glade: disturbed grass, a stick or stone in a different place, even parts of a footprint, always from the same shoe sole. Not that the discovery upset him. Far from it. He saw it as a sign that there must be someone else in the world who also needed what he needed, someone else like him, perhaps as lonely as he. He considered leaving a message under a rock, a message containing a secret password, code names and a rendezvous time, but fits of shyness always prevented him from beginning it.

PART TWO

ONE

In bed, night after night, he dreamed the same dream.

He was crawling on stones, small angular stones that cut into his knees and into the palms of his hands. Keep moving: left palm forward, right knee, right palm, left knee... Where each knee came down there was already a delicate tracery of blood from the palm that had gone before. His ugly squat thumb left its own unique pattern and he studied this with meticulous care, hoping that it might tell him what he was looking for. Fear forced him on... thoowhoomp... thoowhoomp... thoowhoomp... and he knew it was driven by the pulse of his own heart.

He raised his head.

But above the stones there was only fog: a grey, seamless void that robbed his gaze even of the relief of focus. His sense of direction, a thin and brittle shaft, collapsed. He didn't know which way was up, which way down, which way forward. There was only the asynchronous lock-step of hands and knees on the cruel carpet of stones. Beyond the rasp of his own breath the only sound was the sibilance of a faraway sea.

He crawled on into the freezing fog, searching, trying to escape.

On each contact, the feet rolled, heel to toe, heel to toe, with fluid strength and easy reserve. The sandshoes padded almost silently on the clay, which was firm, resilient from breathing the overnight dew, but not clinging. There were two paths. Dray wheels had worn twin lines on either side of hoof-chopped ground. The track lifted up through the bush with gentle pitch and easy camber. The stream alongside slid daintily back down the valley. Undergrowth muted its sound and the water was still dark in the dawn light. Tall kahikatea reached for each other overhead, sometimes leaving glimpses of sky and the surrounding hillsides waiting for sunrise, sometimes enclosing the runner in a tunnel.

The track steepened. Soon Matthew was taking just two steps for each breath. He lifted his jersey over his head as he ran, and tied it round his waist. Even so, sweat continued to slide over his forehead and temples; sweat residues tingled around his eyes. At this rate, he'd be there in twenty minutes. He leaned into the pace, welcoming the effort that helped to distract him from thinking. Three years of work on the *Phoenix* had seen him through most of his physical growth and brought him to the peak of physical fitness. He was nineteen and a quarter of an inch over six feet tall. Sun and salt had layered his skin bronze, and lightened his chestnut hair almost to amber. His expression was open, pleasantly innocent, but his eyes were intense and betrayed vulnerability. His face was deftly proportioned in firm clear lines. He knew girls found him attractive. Of course, he would have preferred to be so devastatingly handsome that girls would faint with pleasure at the sight of him, but he knew he couldn't complain that he'd been short-changed. At least not as far as his body went.

The track rose towards the foot of a vertical bluff, rock columns known as the Pillars, guarding the upper valley. On top of the bluff, lying like the Sphinx of Egypt, was the dog; a smoky-brown dog with white markings. It appeared not to notice Matthew jogging by below. Nor did Matthew make any sign that he had seen the dog. And that was part of the game: no acknowledgment, no sign of recognition. The dog watched, then left the bluff and slipped into the bush.

Matthew knew what D'Arcy was doing. He was weaving through the trees beside him, going ahead, lying in wait, hidden, then loping on to lie in wait again. Normally, Matthew would try to spot him, looking about for a moving shadow, a gleaming eye, or a wet nose through the leaves of a shrub. But not today. Matthew's heart wasn't in it today. He ran on, without slackening the pace.

But then he saw something odd, up ahead. He blinked through the sweat. He rubbed his eyes and halted, panting. Through the trees, on the next bend of the track, were half a dozen small bobbing shapes. He bounded off the track and hid behind a bush. Shortly, six blue-grey penguins waddled busily into view. Their squat legs lurched along on the clay as fast as their awkward bodies could manage and white-trimmed flippers probed the air, extended for balance. The birds moved downhill almost soundlessly, with such an air of impending important business that Matthew pictured them waddling into the Waiata Bank to make a withdrawal.

A dark shape streaked out of the undergrowth and down towards the penguins. In an instant, they were off the track and half running, half sliding down the bank to the stream. Their bodies were almost parallel to the ground, and their flippers beat at the twigs and leaves on the bush floor.

'D'Arcy !'

The sheepdog skidded to a halt at the edge of the track. He looked back at Matthew in bewilderment, then swung his head again in time to see the last little body flash away down the stream. He whined in frantic, pleading falsetto.

'Please yourself.' Matthew resumed his run.

D'Arcy did. In a moment, he and Matthew were rolling on the track, wrestling in a squall of barking. But, too soon, Matthew patted his combatant, stood up, and continued to run. D'Arcy yipped, puzzled. He feinted for another assault. No response. So he settled into a trot beside the running feet, subdued.

The track straightened and levelled off. The two came to a gate across the track. It was a poorman's gate, no more than a length of ordinary fencing tied across the track, sagging in the middle. Man and dog hurdled it easily. And a few seconds later, they came out of the bush and into the upper basin. Jack Sullivan's farm. It was known as Pudding Flat: so named the previous century because the summer thistledown had reminded someone of rice pudding. But the thistles had gone now. Pudding Flat had become pasture land, sprinkled with walnuts and oaks. It was a gently sloping shelf, surrounded by steep, bush-covered hillsides. A few cattle, astonished by the two runners, stared uncertainly at a safe distance. There were no sheep in sight today, but Matthew wasn't surprised. It had been a dry spring: the lambs would have been weaned early and the whole mob rounded up for dipping.

The first shaft of sun lanced down from the ridge directly ahead. Matthew, now in the centre of Pudding Flat, wondered if he could make the sun set in the east by running faster. He tried briefly, failed, and jogged on towards the cluster of buildings at the top end of the farm where enthusiastic barking was already heralding their arrival. There had been a time when Pudding Flat had been envied for more than its beauty. The land was good, and on most of its borders the dense bush formed a natural fenceline. But nowadays it was no longer an economic unit; three hundred acres and a base of six hundred sheep was scratch living. And it showed: the faded red lead on the rooves had seen too many seasons. One corner of the shearing shed sagged over dry, rotted weatherboards and supports. The stables leaned on the hayshed, both made feeble by age and years of nor'westers.

The hut door was open. D'Arcy went in. Matthew knocked, even though the kennelled huntaways behind him were still declaring his presence.

'Shut up yer noise!' a voice roared from inside the hut. The dogs eased down on their larynxes. Matthew stood in the doorway. Jack Sullivan was crouching in front of the fireplace, looking up from under the shapeless green hat that only ever left his head when he slept. He was eyeing Matthew's shorts and bare legs. He said, 'Get in here and shut the door. That flamin' rooster'll sink 'is spurs into the back of your knee as soon as look at you.' A White Leghorn rooster was circling, craning his neck and scratching testily in the dirt. Matthew closed the door and Jack went back to laying twigs on the fire in preparation for cooking. D'Arcy was already comfortable beside him, head resting between paws, eyes following the flames.

Pudding Flat farmhouse had never been built. Jack's home had been thrown together as a temporary accommodation, and had stayed. It was no more than a single room. No electricity. No phone. Lighting was by candle, and by a Tilly lamp now quiet on the warped wooden table in the centre of the hut. There was no ceiling. Some boards had been laid loosely across the beams, holding cardboard boxes, kapok mattresses, and an ammunition box. A .22 rifle, and a Lee Enfield .303 hung untidily on railway spikes projecting from the central beam. A swathe of crockery and cooking paraphernalia swept up from the sink bench and across the wall on nails and makeshift shelves. Next, against the same wall, was the bed: sacks across a wooden frame. Opposite, on the wall near the door, another random array of nails kept Jack's clothing off the bareboard floor. One nail held a sombrero and poncho which had never changed their position since Matthew first saw them. Piles of magazines lay along the wall near the clothing. And against the end of the hut, taking up the entire lower half of the wall was a bookcase of thick eight-inch planks, crammed with books.

Jack asked what the weather was going to do to him. Matthew, who only came when the fishing was off, informed him that a stiff nor'wester was due in the afternoon. The older man grunted. He tipped water from a bucket into a soot-blackened billy, selected an S-shaped wire hanging from the chimney and suspended the billy over the burning twigs. The flames silhouetted the stubble on his chin and the lines on his cheeks and round his eyes. He moved to the makeshift sink to prepare tortilla, his usual breakfast. Matthew sat at the table and fiddled with the wire handle of the Tilly lamp.

'I saw penguins going down the hill from here.'

'Roosting under the shearing shed.'

'Long way to the sea.'

'Nope. Seen 'em at fifteen hundred feet and fishing every day.'

Matthew walked to the bookcase. Most of the books were on travel of one form or another. Exploration. People and places. But one shelf contained a string of writers such as Camus, Priestley, Goethe, Kafka and Kant. He removed a book by Sartre, sat back against the wall on Jack's bed and opened it at a place marked with a scrap of paper. For a minute or two he read, then he looked up.

'What's "inference"?'

'Means something you've figured out from something else.' Jack moved back to the fire. He heated the frypan on the wood-coals, poured in the tortilla base, then scattered pieces of chopped boiled potatoes across it. When it was cooked underneath, he flipped it, guiding it through a half somersault with a fish slice.

'What's "neo-Darwinism"?'

'Take monkeys. Darwin knew each one was born different, right...? But he didn't know why. Now scientists reckon it's because of genes and chromosomes. New idea to stop Darwin fretting in his grave...neo-Darwinism.'

Matthew went back to reading, but couldn't concentrate. After a while, he laid the book aside, but stayed where he was, with hands in his pockets. Jack brought the first tortilla to the table, rolled it into an enamel plate and jerked his head at it. Matthew sat at the table and started to eat, slowly, methodically.

'Out with it,' Jack said from over the pan. 'You haven't got ticks on your belly. Must be something on your chest.'

'I feel funny,' Matthew said immediately. 'Like I'm scared.'

'What of?'

'I don't know exactly. Except I always get this dream.' Steam from his tortilla wafted on his face, but he looked right through it. 'The same dream over and over. And I always wake up thinking something's going to happen.'

'Try me.'

'It sounds stupid,' Matthew warned defensively. He related the elements of the dream self-consciously, half afraid the older man would call it a load of nonsense, half hoping he would know some reason for there being nothing to fear. But Jack only grunted and tossed the second tortilla.

A clamour of barking started up outside. D'Arcy, asleep by the fire, raised his head with a jerk. Jack swung the door and looked out. The rooster was strutting around the huntaways, cackling, taunting them just beyond the range of their chains. Jack picked up a stick of firewood from outside the door and hurled it. It twirled through the air and whumped into the ground a foot from the rooster, which squawked an obscenity and trotted away round the corner. Jack went out, yelling at the dogs to shut their faces. The safe door clashed, and he came back inside with a jug of milk. Then he brought the second tortilla to the table and started in on it with gusto.

With his mouth full: 'You think your dream is something to do with Nathaniel coming back, don't yer?'

Matthew toyed with his plate.

Jack's fork hovered half way to his mouth, then lowered. 'By heck. You'd better know what you're doing. Last time, it all came down on you like a ton of bricks. How long's it been?'

'Nine years.'

'Yeah. Well, you're sitting pretty the way you are. You got it made: they reckon you know the front end of a fish from the back end, top try-scorer for the fishermen's rugby team . . . what I hear, your ma and dad and the preacher reckon you're the next best thing to Christmas . . .'

'But they don't know I still think about these things. They think I just come here to help out. If they knew what we — '

'So? You've got your faith, right? You're confirmed, baptised . . . the works. You're in, cosy with everybody, including the Almighty. You don't want Nathaniel to come back and upset that, do you? I mean, that Bible of yours says he's evil, one of Satan's devils in disguise —'

'But he's not! He's not!' Matthew slapped his hand on the table in frustration and uncertainty. 'And I *do* want him to come back.'

'Sure now?' Jack said with his mouth full.

'You —' Matthew snorted with disgust at being so easily trapped.

'Say it. I'm a crafty old bugger.' The billy lid danced frantically in steam. Jack rescued the billy from the flames, threw in tea leaves and brought it back to the table. He ladled sugar into his mug, then stabbed the spoon in Matthew's direction.

'Look. You're going to have to sort yourself out. It's eating you up. You'll go loopier than a can of worms. Two years you've been coming up here, grubbying up my books, picking my brains. One minute you're mooning about Nathaniel and about healing and giving me demos of telepathy; next thing you're ripping me to shreds for even mentioning the subject, parsonising about how fast I'm headed for the brimstone. You're trying to play two hands to the round. You can't do it. You have to choose one hand and play it right out. Give it everything you've got. Then you're in control.'

Matthew was taken aback. It was the longest speech he had ever heard from Jack. 'I can't choose. Not just like that.'

'You have to. Before your screws fall out.'

'So which hand do I play?'

'Don't ask me! You think *I* know what this Nathaniel is?'

'You want him to come back yourself,' Matthew accused. 'The same way you like to see me do the telepathy and get those pictures from your tobacco tin.'

Jack shrugged. 'Sure. You got me. I never met anyone could do those things, and this Nathaniel joker seems to be behind it all. But it's your life . . .'

Enraged barking erupted from the kennels. The dogs were choking against their chains. D'Arcy leapt up and made vicious sounds in his throat and Jack pushed his chair back. 'By jeez, that flamin' bird has got to come down a peg or two.' He flung open the door. 'Hold 'im, D'Arcy !' With a woof of joy, D'Arcy scrabbled across the floor and out the door. The rooster saw him coming and took off, emitting a long cry of terror. It thrashed the air with its clipped wings, hovering at six feet, knowing that wherever it came down, D'Arcy would be there. In fact, D'Arcy didn't wait that long. When the exhausted rooster sank to an altitude of three feet, the dog plucked it out of the sky and pinned it to the ground with two front paws crossed over its back. The bird murmured weakly, knowing what fate had in store for it. D'Arcy glanced back to the hut door to check on his audience, then closed his teeth around one of the rooster's more magnificent tail feathers and plucked it out. The rooster screeched. D'Arcy released it, and it sprinted away, shrieking its pain and humiliation.

'God help the hens,' Jack commented. They returned to the table. Matthew's mood had lifted markedly and by unspoken agreement they kept off the subject of Nathaniel.

After breakfast, in good spirits, they released the dogs and set out for the stream that separated the hut from the holding pens. They crossed it, then walked uphill to where a corrugated-iron water chute lay on the bank. Jack manoeuvred one end of the crude device on to the top of a concrete channel, Matthew dropped the other end into the water, and half the stream took off down the channel to the dipping trough near the pens. They followed.

Jack emptied a packet of yellow arsenic powder into the trough. A shrill squawking rose from the woolshed, above the sound of the tumbling water. The penguin chicks. Matthew pointed in the direction of the shearing shed and declared that he could get more peace and quiet back in town. Jack grunted that he hadn't heard anything yet; that when the adults got back after dark, the noise would make him think Dracula was his fairy godmother.

'Pull the other one,' Matthew grinned.

'Fair go. It sounds like human kids being done in with a knife. The shed magnifies the sound somehow. Gets the wind right up anyone who doesn't know. Had a government joker here a couple of weeks back about the new dipping chemicals . . . didn't know whether to load up the .303 or hide under the bed . . . Told him next morning.'

The trough filled and the water chute was hauled out of the

stream. The dogs brought the first of the mob into the trough pen. D'Arcy pressed the leaders into the race, and Jack began to push them into the water. Even with dogs running over their backs, some of the old ewes with good memories had to be wrestled down the ramp. Once in, however, they had no choice but to swim the trough. Matthew walked with them, shoving their heads twice under the yellow liquid with a dipping crutch. Then they swam on, snorting through their noses. One ewe, terrified witless, kept trying to swim upside down and had to be hauled along by hand. At the other end, she wouldn't climb the steps until D'Arcy nipped her ear.

But the lambs, kept until last, were a different story. They seemed almost eager for the experience. D'Arcy set them in the general direction of the ramp, then sat down to scratch. Jack took over the dipping crutch. Matthew sat down on top of the pen rail and watched, whistling, his good humour fully restored. Idly, he whittled shavings off the rail with his miniature pocket knife, a beautifully made instrument with fine steel and a puma engraved into the bone handle. Jack had sent to Chile for it, and it had been on Matthew's belt since his last birthday.

After a while, Matthew looked up. 'What made you become a pacifist?'

Jack shrugged. 'Hard to say, really.'

Matthew pondered the evasion. It wasn't like Jack to sidestep like that. He either answered straight or he told Matthew to mind his own business. Another time, Matthew thought. He snapped his knife shut and returned it to its pouch.

'Let me try your tobacco tin again,' he said to Jack.

Jack hesitated. In the last few months, Matthew had developed the uncanny knack of getting mental images of Jack's life, past and present, just by holding the tobacco tin and closing his eyes. He was getting better at it all the time, a trick, if that's what it was, that Jack never tired of seeing. But was it wise now, with the boy so worried about things? And yet Matthew was his normal self at the moment. So why not? Jack fished in his pocket and tossed the tin across the trough.

Matthew caught it neatly, shut his eyes and concentrated. The last bunch of lambs leapt into the water. Jack dunked them rhythmically, the crutch lifting, setting on a woolly neck, plunging, then lifting again. When the last one was stroking towards the steps at the far end, he leaned on the crutch and looked at Matthew. Matthew had turned red with embarrassment and suppressed laughter.

'Let's have it,' Jack said.

'It's rude. You're sitting on a board with no clothes on — '

Jack froze. 'Here,' he said quickly. 'Give us the tin back.'

But it was too late. Matthew's expression pulled back into one of unbelieving horror. He leaped off the pen rail with a sharp cry, throwing the tin down as if it were red hot. It splashed into the yellow scum in the dip, splayed open, and sank. And Matthew panted as if he had been running.

'They were right. It's evil. It's a vision from Satan — '

'Leave it alone, Matt. Forget it. It's all right.'

'It was a thin board,' Matthew babbled on. 'You were on the edge with your feet tied underneath and your hands tied behind your back, and there were men — '

'That's enough — '

'The one with the pistol — '

'Stop it! You'll make yourself sick! Leave it — '

'It's Satan!' Matthew gabbled on. 'Filling my mind with falsehoods and evil. I should never have listened to you. Satan is using you! Holy Father, forgive me...'

Jack jumped the trough and shook Matthew's shoulders, hard. 'Listen to me! It's not false. It's true. It's real. It really happened to me.'

Matthew stopped. He gaped at Jack, his features distorted with distress and suspicion. Jack turned around and pulled up the back of his black singlet. The move exposed a mass of weals and pockmarks, dappling the skin over his lower back and kidneys. 'Look. Look. They did that in South America. In Chile. I used to be a communist, and the police caught me with communists over there. They thought...' He broke off; plainly written on Matthew's face was the suspicion that anything could have caused the marks.

'Bloody hell,' Jack said quietly. He undid his belt, turned around on the edge of the sheep dip to face Matthew, then lowered his trousers and his underpants. Matthew stared, went white, then turned away and vomited over the pen rail into the dust. Jack did up his trousers, took the boy's arm then led him to the stream. He made him clean his face in the cold water, then sat beside him on the edge, while D'Arcy watched them both from the top of the bank.

'Don't you see? You wanted to know what made me become a pacifist. You got your answer. That's what made me start trying to work out what it's all about. Why do you think I read all those books? Why do you think I let a kid with a jinky brain come up here and gab at me for two years? . . .'

'You can't have kids. That's why you're not married.'

Jack sighed. 'Look. Maybe I was wrong showing you. But you had to know what you've got in your head isn't telling you lies. You've got something real there, kid. Something important. And it's not put there by Satan. That Satan stuff is even worse bullshit than —'

'Don't say that!'

'Cripes. You still haven't got it, have you?' Jack shook his head and sat back. Beyond the far end of Pudding Flat, the harbour water was visible. Behind him, the penguins had quietened; a temporary lull.

After a while, 'I ruined your tobacco tin.'

Jack looked at him, then away. 'Never did protect it against ticks and fleas.'

TWO

The fifty-foot trawler had no forward speed. She pitched and lurched in the unpredictable nor'west swell that chopped at her starboard beam. In the windward water beside her floated a shapeless, pale mass of fish. In the air above, grey and black wings wheeled impatiently; and on the stern rail, a row of pearl-clean, preening, keen-eyed bodies waited. The winch groaned, forward of the wheelhouse. The snatch block squealed on the aft mast. The floating mass of fish gathered itself together and lifted from the water, becoming a seething lump of white, grey, silver and red. It scraped across the gunwale and slumped heavily against the mast, gushing water. Underneath, a slip-knot jerked free and the catch slopped on to the boards of the sorting pond like a great drop of crude oil.

The net rasped back over the side. It sank, its mouth yawning as the lower jaw dropped faster than the floated upper. The side-trawler's engine engaged. The propeller chewed dead water and the vessel gathered way. The extension cables followed the net under the waves: they would shortly skip along the bottom like great swirling whiskers, sweeping food into the net mouth. The trawl doors fell away — underwater planes that would strain outwards, keeping the mouth wide and the whiskers under tension. Pulleys rattled on the starboard-mounted cranes; the two tow cables freewheeled out along the side and stopped at the 120-fathom marker. The wheel spun; the bow edged to port, and the stern sidled up to the two cables. Obligingly, the rear, pin-mounted crane swung the cables high up above the deck with a resounding crash of steel; and out over the stern, the cables began to spread like long arms, widening to embrace the propeller-churned water. The *Phoenix* settled to a forward speed of three knots and the tow was under way.

John Fleming eyed the froth on the tops of the swells. The

90

nor'wester was freshening too quickly, and he didn't like the way the sky was lining up. This had better be the last run. He turned the tow gradually through half the compass until it headed northeast towards the distant lumpy grey mass of the peninsula. He stretched loop-stays over the wheel spokes and made his way aft along the agitated deck. Matthew was in the sorting pond, knee-deep in fish, working with the gaff. He spiked some into other ponds, some straight into bins, and non-commercial species were whisked over the side. Not too many flat fish, John saw, a good proportion of cod and elephants with a few rig sharks and skate thrown in for good measure. He unrolled his thigh boots up from the knees, lifted his own gaff from behind the smokestack, and stepped into the sorting pond.

'Not bad,' he commented.

A carpet shark swished close to his face on the way over the rail. He fell back, sitting down in the catch. 'Thunderation! Take it easy, boy.'

'Sorry,' Matthew muttered.

'Go and check the warps.'

Matthew didn't answer, but clomped away to measure the angle between the tow cables. John grumbled to himself. Lord alone knew what was wrong with the boy these last few days. He was jittery: jumped a fathom if a cod so much as slapped a tail behind him. Unreliable. Unsafe. Now that John was in his late forties and feeling the twinges of fisherman's back, he had to be able to count on Matthew's taking over from him. But this sort of carry-on didn't do much to boost his confidence. And not a word of explanation from the boy. Not that Matthew opened his mouth much at the best of times.

Half way through the sorting, a seventy-foot stern trawler up from the south coast slowed off the port beam. Glass glinted in the afternoon sun. John glowered. Thieving sods. Raiding other people's waters. Spying on a man's catch instead of calling him up and asking him straight like men. They deserved to have their cables cut. He considered bringing out the bolt-cutters to wave at them, but the stern trawler soon moved away to deeper waters.

A school of porpoises found them and played briefly, rolling lazily out of the sides of the swells, expelling air with their wet rush of breath. A female casually inspected one side of the vessel's kauri hull, all the while nudging her two-foot baby to the surface for air. John looked at Matthew, hoping for some reaction to the sight, but the boy worked on, tense and drawn.

Two albatross chicks swept down on them, turned upwind and settled in the water. The rising swell thrust and sucked their bodies in and out of sight; and on each crest, their stern faces regarded the *Phoenix* with the same grave dignity. Whenever the *Phoenix* drew too far away, they paddled into the air, set their wings and skimmed the tops in graceful, effortless pursuit. Then they touched lightly into the water off the bows to wait once more for the feast.

The wind rose steadily.

The two fishermen swept shells, octopi, and undersized skate out of the scuppers. They touched up their heavy knives on wet-stones and set to gutting and cleaning the catch. The heads, fins, tails and guts swept around their feet to the increasingly erratic movements of the *Phoenix*, while blood escaped under the pond dividers and washed out through the drain hole. The waiting gulls swirled into a restless cloud, skirling their impatience to the wind. The albatross chicks half flew, half walked the water, and settled even closer to the bows. John paused. He stared aghast at the tense, slashing speed of Matthew's knife. The blade stabbed sideways through the body of an elephant fish, ripped down and out, and tore too hard and fast through the dorsal fin and tail.

'Here. You'll be a fat lot of use to me without a hand.'

Matthew looked at him, breathing hard, then resumed at the same pace.

'Enough's enough. I'd rather sort fish with a white pointer. What's on your mind, son?'

'It's nothing.'

'Son. If you've got a burden on your conscience and you don't want to tell me, you know what to do. No sin is so bad it can't be confessed to Jesus.'

Matthew nodded, though the movement was no more than a jerk of the head. He kept working. John wished, as he had wished many times, that he could have had a son more willing to share his problems with his father. A thought came to him.

'Matt. Hark here, lad. If it's a girl, maybe you'd be better off asking my advice. Between you and me, I got around a bit before I met your mother. I could...'

But Matthew had no chance to respond. An unusually large

swell lifted the stern of the fishing boat and swung it hard to port. The rear crane dropped back to its original net-drop position with a loud crash.

'You forgot to chock the davit!' John shouted, annoyed. But Matthew wasn't listening. He had dropped his knife amongst the fish and was half crouched, facing the crane, trembling violently. Another oversized swell rolled under the vessel. The waves were beginning to crack on the tops. Spume swirled out of the froth and into the air. Overhead, the high cirrus had set into cloud bands radiating out of the northwest like sky waves. John's attention wavered between the weather and his son.

'Take it easy!' he shouted. 'Just take it easy, will you? Leave the crane alone. I'm going to check the radio. I think we'll be getting the gear up right away.' He left the sorting pond and went forward.

Overhead the gulls screeched, waiting for the sludge of fish guts to be unloaded from the bottom of the pond.

In the wheelhouse, the old army surplus radio was chattering. '. . . Nothin' but flats anyway.' 'You packing it in?' 'Reckon so. Might as well lay along the lee side of bum island for a while, whaddya say?' John turned the volume down angrily. Godless lot! Not content with poaching in Waiata waters, they had to foul the air with their unclean mouths. No, it wasn't what went into a mouth that made a man unclean . . . He waited a few moments, then raised the volume. Clear air. He identified himself into the handset and called for anyone who'd heard a forecast.

'Yeah,' a voice answered. 'Hammer here, John. Bring in your washing, boyo. She's going up to fifty knots to please the weatherman. Everyone's away home.' Hammer Keegan had earned his nickname with a tall claim that he had once dropped a hammer over the side and picked it up in a cray pot the same day. John thanked him and replaced the handset. He leaned out the wheelhouse door to signal Matthew, only to find his son right in front of him.

'We've got to get the gear up,' Matthew demanded, his teeth chattering in spite of the warmth of the nor'wester.

'Swift off the mark, aren't you?' John shouted irritably against the wind. 'You've seen a lot worse than this. What's the matter with you? . . .' But Matthew was already moving aft.

The *Phoenix* swung her starboard beam against the wind her

93

engine throbbing in neutral. At once, she lost way and began to plunge and toss, rolling to the gunwales. Gulls swept close over the sorting pond, calling angrily against the delay. John Fleming, out of temper, clambered forward to the winch, while Matthew manned the rear crane. The winch hummed. The tow cables thrummed in, drawing lines of spume out of the waves. The trawl doors threw themselves out of the water, clashed on the cranes and were bolted down. The extensions came in. John and Matthew left the cranes, met amidships and began to haul in the first few feet of net by hand. They jammed hard-won mesh against the gunwale with their knees, partly to prevent the sea from snatching it back, partly to avoid being thrown into the water.

Then the catch wallowed before them. A big one, in spite of the short run. A bit too big in this weather, John thought. But it would be all right if he timed the snatch. Clean and no jerk. He returned to the winch and waited while Matthew looped a hemp strop around the neck of the net. Matthew reached behind him for the snatch-hook, slipped it through the strop and signalled. John engaged the winch, took up slack, then slipped the clutch while he waited for the right moment.

Then he snatched.

He regretted the decision almost immediately. Even before it left the water, the catch was clearly going to be the biggest he'd had in a month. O.K. in good weather, but asking a lot of the gear in this sea. Still, it was spare seconds from being safely aboard. He went ahead. He noticed Matthew step a long way clear as the bulging load swung across the gunwale. It whumped on the mast and John felt the tremor under his feet and through the winch controls. They'd got away with it. He braked the winch and lurched aft, bracing himself all the way. Difficult going. They'd better be under way fast.

Half a dozen steps from the net, he saw that they hadn't got away with it entirely. One of the three strands on the strop had parted and was unwinding. Matthew was under the net, reaching for the pull rope of the cod-end slip-knot.

'Look out!' John screamed above the wind. 'Get out! It's going...'

But the next awkward wave was already under the rail. The *Phoenix* jolted heavily. Matthew looked up as the two remaining

94

strands parted with the sound of two small-bore rifles fired in quick succession. His legs straightened desperately as the loaded net slumped. It threw him off balance, with a glancing blow to the shoulder, then caught his legs and smashed him to the deck so that his head hit the side of the sorting pond on the way down. His head lay sideways, seeping more blood into the offal and slime that swirled with the motion of the boat.

Jack Sullivan missed with his hammer, and came close to swallowing the nails between his lips. He carefully removed them before saying anything.

'Christ, dog! You trying to give me a heart condition?'

But D'Arcy's attention was elsewhere. One moment he had been daydreaming with his chin on the warm summer grass between his paws, the next he had shot to his feet with a piercing bark. Now he was rigid, his ears rotated and strained forward into the wind. His tail tip curled sideways, taut. Jack scanned the grass ahead but saw nothing. Must be a rabbit. Or a possum.

'Hold 'im, D'Arcy,' he urged.

D'Arcy moved just ten feet, forward and slightly sideways, tense as a coiled spring. He barked again, this time at Jack, then took up the same stance as before.

THREE

'Mrs Nisbet!' Staff Nurse Purdy pulled a watch from the top pocket of her crisp white uniform and help up a hand, stopping Emily in mid-corridor. 'It's 5.20! In the morning!' She knew there was nothing wrong with the woman's hearing, so resisted an impulse to hold the watch in front of Emily's face. Emily met her eyes impassively and the nurse sighed. It was always the same. That unwavering, expressionless, dumb gaze. It made you want to reach inside her and give her a thorough shaking. Now there would have to be a question, and questions never got verbal answers. As far as anyone knew, Emily Nisbet hadn't uttered a single word for years. Except to her garden. 'What are you doing here, Mrs Nisbet? You're three and a half hours early!'

Emily broke her gaze and hobbled up the corridor, her hips rotating with the gait of advanced arthritis, her rubber-tipped cane tapping on the green hospital linoleum that she worked to a high polish every weekday. Her shoulders were rounded well beyond her fifty-two years and her hair was rolled into a grey bun at the back of her head.

The nurse fumed. Really, it was too, too ridiculous. The woman was long overdue for psychological help. Maybe she did have a good record for reliability, but whoever heard of a hospital board continuing to employ someone who couldn't answer the simplest question? Why was it that a government employee had to be caught with fingers in the till in order to be sacked? Perhaps the Board should hear about Emily carrying non-registered medicines around with her inside the hospital. Now this erratic, unpunctual behaviour: nearly half a shift early this morning. And late last night, according to the sister, loitering in the corridor for heaven knew what reason. Really, she was sorry for the poor creature to be sure, but charity could be stretched beyond the limit.

Emily reached the broom cupboard at the far end of the shining linoleum. She pulled out a bucket and mop.

The nurse clipped hotly up the corridor. 'Mrs Nisbet. You absolutely cannot start work now. You'll disturb the routine. It's *not* fair on the patients. And we've got poor Mrs Fleming sleeping in room three. You'll have to wait until the usual time.' Time, she thought, for another few words to the sister about Emily.

Emily swung the mop and bucket back into the cupboard, and made her way down the corridor. She turned off at the visitors' seats in the front foyer and heard a sound of exasperation behind her. She sat, waiting until she heard the nurse go into the staff lounge. Then, quietly, she walked the few steps past the front door and, even more quietly, stole into room two.

Matthew Fleming lay on his back, his upper body slightly raised on pillows. If it hadn't been for the heavy bandage around his head and above eye level, he might have been peacefully asleep. But he'd been in a coma since coming in early last evening. Emily had unobtrusively followed everything since his arrival; she had been listening close by when Doctor Pringle said he couldn't rule out possible brain haemorrhage, and that if Matthew wasn't out of coma by morning, they'd have to call the city for a helicopter to lift him out.

Emily hadn't slept last night.

She gazed at him, standing as still on the floor as he lay on the bed. She also kept an eye on the time. At 5.42, she slipped back to the visitors' seats in the foyer. At 5.45, the staff nurse came past and disappeared into room two. Emily knew what the nurse would be doing: pressure, pulse, temperature checks, and the penlight probe into the eyes. Doctor Pringle was to be called immediately if Matthew Fleming's pupils didn't react to the light, or dilated, or if there was any sign of fluid in the ears and nose.

The check completed, the nurse stepped back the other way.

Emily returned to Matthew's bedside. She looked at him again, searching his face. Over and over she saw him as a small boy, a small boy with a thrush that had flown into the porch glass. Throughout all those years she had seen him, from her distance, growing from a boy to a young man. In all that time, she had not been able to approach him. How long? How many years? The horror of all those lost years lay inside her like a bitter, wasted vine. What had she done? What had she done to herself?

97

One of Matthew's eyelids twitched.

Emily willed him to keep going, to come to life. Minutes went by. Small movements started in his facial muscles, including the eyelids. His lips twitched, parted, closed. Emily knew she should call the nurse, but she didn't. His throat worked. He made a rasping sound. His lips parted again, and he pushed out a loud, formless vowel sound.

Bedsprings creaked in the next room. Stockinged feet padded swiftly in the corridor. Rachel Fleming came to a halt beside Emily, her face filled with hope. She approached the bed slowly. Matthew's throat tightened and his vocal cords scraped out a series of sounds.

Rachel put a hand on his shoulder.

'Complete,' Matthew said, the sounds slow and slurred, his eyes still closed. Rachel burst into tears, then tried to reassure him. She asked if he could hear her. 'Extreme,' he said. 'Change. Niceties. Odd ... ' Each word came out with slow deliberation, through thick consonants and flat vowels. But his voice was surprisingly strong, Emily thought, for someone coming out of unconsciousness. And low-pitched. She noticed that his right hand flexed twice as he spoke. The words continued...

Rachel was alarmed. She decided that he was delirious and told Emily that they had better call the nurse. But even as she spoke, the regulation shoes pattered towards them down the corridor. The nurse listened to the string of disconnected words without obvious concern. She ran swiftly through the pulse and penlight checks and took his right hand, asking him to squeeze if he could hear her. After a pause, the hand tightened. The nurse nodded, satisfied. The words kept coming, clearer now, and closer to normal speed. The nurse muttered about chatterboxes, warned Rachel not to jump to conclusions before the doctor came and left to call him. On the way out she glared at Emily, who then moved out to the corridor but stayed in sight of Matthew.

'Discover,' said the voice from the bed. 'Ordinary. Retrieve. Cupboard ... ' The pitch of his voice was dropping even further. Something stirred in Emily. A small sharp twist of excitement, deep down.

The nurse returned. 'The doctor will be here at nine in the morning, Mrs Fleming.' She cut across an anxious question with professional ease. 'That's not for me to say. But you can be sure that if there was anything urgent, Doctor Pringle wouldn't wait until nine. Now, I expect you'd like me to call Mr Fleming.' She allowed the smallest of encouraging smiles, brushed aside Rachel's profuse thanks, and moved around the bed, smoothing out creases. Then she swept efficiently away.

Emily slowly came back to the bedside.

'Basement.' Matthew's lips moved with the word, but the sound seemed to come up from deep in his chest. Rich, and resonant.

Rachel looked around, frowning, puzzled. 'His voice doesn't sound right. Do you suppose his throat is hurt?'

Jennifer Pringle swished back and forth in the pear-tree swing. She scissored her lower legs as she swung, and bubbled with good humour. She looked towards the house, then tossed her head back, sending peals of laughter ringing up through the ripening pears. It was so funny. She looked down again, laughter-tears rolling down her cheeks. Her black poodle Candy was dashing towards her across the back lawn, carrying her doll Amanda in its mouth. Without slowing the swing, she reached down and lifted Amanda up beside her and they swung higher. Each time the swing rose, Amanda spoke to her. Something important, something urgent; but Jennifer was laughing too much to hear what her doll was saying.

Then she woke up.

She was in bed, glowing with the mirth of the dream. Her cheeks were still moist on the pillow. Her eyes were fixed on the top of the bookshelf where Amanda sat resignedly against the wall, looking much as she had looked on Jennifer's third birthday. Seventeen years ago. To the left of Amanda, in order of decreasing size, were the eleven other dolls of her childhood, all projecting straight legs off the top of the bookshelf. The room had not changed while she had been away at boarding school and secretarial college. Nor had she changed it in the three months she had been back in Waiata. And yet it didn't feel like her room any more. It didn't seem connected to her — even though the photographs of her and her pony still hung on the same picture hooks; there were still the same green chintz curtains with pink roses to match the bedspread, the same thick pile carpet, the scalloped china bedlamp.

She turned to the window. The curtains were half drawn, leaving only the muslin to veil the waterfront road. A single car hissed along the wet surface.

Sleepy, isolated, backward little Waiata. But how lucky its inhabitants were. How much fun for them to have Jennifer Pringle to gossip about. How delicious that the fallen one was the high and mighty doctor's daughter. She worked as her father's receptionist, and she could see it all in the eyes of everyone who came to the surgery — especially in the middle-aged scorpions that masqueraded as women. Those smiles that never quite covered the condescension, the not-quite-as-holy-as-thou-thought expressions, the smug satisfaction, as if her sin had somehow enriched their lives.

It had opened her eyes, really. There was that consolation. It had shown her the masks people wore, the elaborate, deceitful games people played to hide their own selfishness, stupidity and weakness. How could such people understand the way her whole body ached for her baby? How could they know what it was to have your newborn baby taken away while you were still pushing out the placenta? Then to feel the new embryo of doubt, growing too fast, too late. How could such people know the cold tentacles of emptiness that had sucked at her body every day for six months? Jennifer plucked Amanda from the shelf. With deliberate cruelty, she tipped the doll forward. 'Mama,' Amanda cried. 'Mamaaaaaa...'

After a while, Jennifer dressed. She ignored her make-up bottles, donned her flat-heeled work shoes and her faded-blue print dress, then went down to breakfast.

The others had already started. She apologised perfunctorily and sat. Doctor Pringle nodded pleasantly and continued the business of buttering his toast. Diane, her younger sister, looked at her briefly, then went back to her apricot halves and her dreams of tennis stardom. Mrs Pringle's mouth said that Jennifer's lateness was quite all right.

Hypocrite, Jennifer thought. You hate me being late. You hate me sullying your spotless, hygienic kitchen with my presence.

To Jennifer, every adult she knew was a hypocrite. They pulled mental wires to twist their faces into masks and words into screens. They said one thing, meaning another, so often that it seemed to her to be the conventional reflex to all human encounters.

100

' . . . It's a bit much,' Mrs Pringle was saying. 'I don't see how they can expect other people to help them if they bring it on themselves. Nine children, and counting, by the looks of Maureen Reilly. I mean, she is a dear, really, a dear, but there comes a time. . . . '

'That's not right,' Jennifer said heavily. Mrs Pringle broke· off. Diane stopped eating and looked apprehensive. She hated family quarrels. Doctor Pringle chewed his toast, watching Jennifer dourly as she ploughed on. 'What difference does it make if they're Catholic? If our church wasn't so loaded with hypocrites, there'd be twenty Presbyterians on the Reillys' doorstep right now, with stuff to tide them over.'

'Of all the colossal nerve.' Mrs Pringle's mouth turned into a cold arch. 'You. Of all people. Daring to sit there and criticise people who never did you any harm. You'll be calling me and your father hypocrites next. You seem to forget who took you back!'

'You don't really think Mrs Reilly is a dear,' Jennifer went on doggedly. 'You can't *stand* people with red faces and sties around their eyes.'

Mrs Pringle turned to her husband aghast. But, knowing that his policy was not to fight her battles for her, she stood. 'Well. Since my eldest has the years of an adult, I can't send her away from the table for the ungrateful, spoilt child she is. And seeing the conversation is likely to remain uncivilised while she is present, I'll eat elsewhere.' She scooped up her toast and coffee and departed in high dudgeon for the lounge room. Diane looked from Jennifer to her father, muttered 'excuse me' and departed also. Doctor Pringle leaned back in his chair, cradling his coffee in both hands.

'That was rough,' he observed.

'I just can't stand all the sham and the lies any more. All the hypocrisy.'

'So you've discovered honesty, then. Seems to me you've learned how to use it like a truncheon.'

Jennifer toyed with her cereal. She just wasn't hungry some mornings. She put an elbow on the table and covered her face with her hand. She didn't cry. She supposed that was because she had done so much crying before. Instead, she mumbled through her hand, 'Everything is so rotten and futile.'

Doctor Pringle put his coffee down. He reached across the table and patted her arm, even though he found such physical contact difficult. He said something about it taking time. Jennifer didn't respond outwardly, but she felt a surge of gratitude. He wasn't much help, really, but he was all right. Sometimes. Maybe it was his experiences in the German prison camps or something. The doctor stood. He looked gloomily in the direction of the lounge room, then at his watch.

'I'm off to do an early hospital round. Matthew Fleming seems to be coming round. Do you want to come? As my receptionist, of course.'

Jennifer looked up. He really did try hard. She took a deep breath and nodded, tried to look brighter and said that she'd pick some flowers for the hospital foyer. Her father told her with exaggerated gruffness that if she picked any of her mother's prize roses, he'd put her across his knee the way he used to. She smiled.

Jack and D'Arcy, both bedraggled by the summer drizzle, climbed the front steps of the hospital. They passed Nurse Purdy going down, on her way home. At the bottom of the steps she turned to glare at them. Her nose made it clear that nothing in the world smelled quite as bad as a wet dog, and the rest of her expression threatened dire consequences for someone if D'Arcy were allowed inside.

'Sorry, fella,' Jack said to the dog. 'We're in the spit-and-polish country. Members only. Stay.' D'Arcy, who had his front paws up on the window ledge of the room nearest the front door, protested. Jack pointed firmly to a spot near the edge of the verandah and repeated the command. D'Arcy moved and sat on his haunches, huffing his displeasure. The nurse stayed where she was, openly suspicious. Jack plucked a sodden cigarette off his lower lip, crouched down and placed it carefully between two toes of D'Arcy's right front paw. He asked the dog to look after it for him; he said he didn't mind if D'Arcy took a drag or two, but that if he finished the lot, he would be taken for a run through the mincer. Having made this clear, Jack turned to Staff Nurse Purdy and doffed his dripping hat half an inch. The nurse humphed, turned on her heel and went away down the path, raising her umbrella.

D'Arcy batted his violated paw up and down on the verandah.

He growled menacingly at the limp cigarette and cuffed it with his other front paw.

Jack tossed his oilskin across the verandah rail, wiped his boots and walked into the visitors' foyer. At that moment, Doctor Pringle, Sister Thomas and the day nurse walked into view on their way down the corridor. The day nurse came to listen to Jack's inquiry, then waved him towards the lounge chairs. Would he mind making a seat? The doctor was about to examine Matthew. Jack eyed a clean lounge chair doubtfully, brushed his hand across the seat of his trousers and sat. The doctor and nurses disappeared into the room nearest the foyer.

Almost immediately, John and Rachel Fleming came out of the same room. They looked taken aback by Jack's presence, but nodded distractedly and took seats themselves. Jennifer Pringle came from the other end of the corridor with a bunch of irises and a jug of water. She arranged the flowers in the foyer vase, took the jug away, returned, then she too took a seat.

Somewhere out of sight, a mop worked the corridor. The swish-click sound muted each time the operator moved into a room, then grew distinct again, slightly louder than before.

Soon the doctor emerged from Matthew's room, with the two nurses.

'Nothing wrong with him,' he announced to John and Rachel. He smiled. 'I'll be surprised if he goes away from here with anything worse than a sore head and an oversized vocabulary.' Rachel's shoulders slumped with relief.

'What about that funny voice?' John asked. 'And all those words he's gabbling?'

'He's not any more. He's out of coma. But . . . hold your horses . . . he's asleep.'

'Asleep?' John and Rachel grinned at each other.

'Good thing too. If you ask me, it's because he's over-exercised his jaw! But nothing to worry about. We all talk nonsense on our beds, and it's not uncommon for vocal cords to relax during unconsciousness. A politician's voice, I think. Or perhaps Waiata's first international opera singer. Just joking, John, just joking. Well now. He's almost certain to stay asleep for a while. Why don't you pop home and get some rest? I'm sure Sister won't mind calling you when he looks like waking . . . !' With the help of repeated assurances, the Flemings allowed themselves to be ushered out the front door. Doctor Pringle and the two nurses departed for the maternity end of the corridor, where the unprecedented number of two babies had been born inside twenty-four hours.

Jennifer stayed behind to look in on Matthew. She took a handful of stems from the foyer vase. No one had told Jack to remove his dirty boots, or himself, so he interpreted this as permission to see Matthew. Emily, having completed the corridor as far as Matthew's door, hobbled in with her bucket and mop. Since it was her habit to begin behind the door, she was just closing it when Jennifer and Jack walked in. She partially closed it behind them.

The three visitors all knew each other by sight, but had never met. So they stared at Matthew's face without speaking to each other. Without shifting her gaze, Jennifer dropped half a dozen irises amongst the flowers in Matthew's bedside vase. Jack leaned on the tall iron bed-end and crossed his legs and Emily leaned on her mop handle.

Matthew's room didn't get mopped that day. As they looked at him, a smile grew on his face. It was so wide, so warm and humour-filled, so unexpected, that it was catching. Jennifer and Jack glanced at each other and grinned. Emily gripped her mop tightly, forgetting the pain in her hips. In spite of her smile, a shiver ran up her spine.

'Emily,' said the voice from the bed. 'Jack.' The eyes were still closed. 'Jennifer.'

Jennifer blinked several times. She looked hard at the closed eyes. She turned to the other two; but when she saw their expressions, the words died on her lips. As she turned back to Matthew, his eyes opened. Her frown deepened. There was something wrong with his eyes. It was like looking at someone else. She blinked again. Looked again. And it was still different. The eyes were dark, piercingly acute, and glinting with dry humour.

'Good morning,' the voice said. 'I have looked forward to this meeting.'

'What...? Jennifer, bewildered, saw that Jack was now nodding.

'It's...' Jack swallowed, flicked a glance at the other two. 'It's ... ah ... Nathaniel, isn't it?'

'It is.'

'What are you doing?' Jennifer's voice rose slightly. She looked from Matthew to Jack, to the deeply happy face of Emily, who was still clutching her mop. Jennifer laughed stiffly. 'This is some kind of elaborate joke.'

'This is not a joke,' the voice said. The head rolled on the pillow and the dark eyes focused on her. 'Nor is it any kind of deceit. But it will be a shock, Jennifer, because you accepted no advance warning into your consciousness.' Jennifer's stiff grin stretched out in frozen incredulity. But the eyes in the head on the pillow crinkled with the humour of the situation. 'Absurd though it seems, you are not all in this room together by chance. And you came with a purpose much more significant than you suppose. A common purpose. Impossible though it may seem, this is not Matthew speaking to you but another personality, speaking with the help of his body.'

'I don't like this.' Jennifer took half a step backwards. 'What's wrong with you all? I'd better get my father.'

'Jennifer.'

She stopped.

'When you came through the door, you were puzzled by a feeling that the situation was somehow familiar.'

She stood quite still, her eyes wide, holding the question.

'I knew,' the voice continued gently. 'In the same way I know that a small part of you has already accepted the truth of what I say. This face I use now could truly be called a mask. And yet, although my language is similar to that of conservative members of your society, I hope you will discover that I am not a hypocrite. I hope to show you that life is not as empty and futile and meaningless as you suppose.'

'Oh God,' Jennifer whispered. 'Oh God.' Her jaw sank through the words. Her legs felt like jelly.

'Come closer. Do you see Matthew in these eyes?'

Jennifer made herself bend forward. She steadied herself with one hand on the bedside locker. It could not be. It could not.

They were not Matthew's eyes.

She stood back, shut her own eyes tightly for a moment and breathed again, 'Oh God.'

Jack shook himself abruptly, as if to wake himself. 'What about Matthew?'

'He is here, in this room, listening to us. He is not too surprised by this meeting. But he is no less shocked than Jennifer; he is not accustomed to lending his body the way he might lend a lawnmower. However, he is well. As you will see when he wakes shortly thinking that he has been dreaming.'

'I think that's what I'm doing,' Jennifer murmured to herself.

'Wha...' Emily struggled to force words out against the weight of the presence of other people. The walls of her private bubble were beginning to move ... She came closer to the bed. 'Wha ... what ... do you want us to do?'

'First, I must tell you all that you have difficulties ahead. It will not be easy. So, in the meantime, you should keep this to yourselves. Second, if Emily remembered all her dreams, she would not be surprised to know that our next meeting takes place at her cottage. Today week. 7.30 in the evening.'

'All...all...,' Emily stammered. 'All those words. This morning. I knew!'

'Yes. I had to familiarise myself with parts of Matthew's body. It is somewhat more complex than the lawnmower.'

Jennifer's face was tormented. 'Who are you? *What* are you? I don't get this.'

'I am a person, just as you are a person. But my existence has a base frequency different from that of your world. Your physical senses are attuned to the things of your plane. You cannot see me, or touch me, but I am as real as the bedside locker under your hand, and as real as this body which helps us to communicate.'

'A spirit,' Emily blurted. 'A great spirit.'

'Many in your world would call me a spirit, yes. But as to my worth, make no hasty decisions. Now ... ' The dark eyes softened. ' ... I must return what I borrowed, and leave your will to make peace with your thoughts.'

The eyes closed. The head relaxed subtly on the pillow.

None of the three moved. After a while, Jack looked through the window and saw D'Arcy looking back at him from the verandah. When he next looked back to the bed, Matthew's eyelids were lifting. The eyes had returned to their normal light blue and they focused, slowly, painfully, on the familiar face at the end of the bed.

'My head hurts,' Matthew whispered. His voice was thin and hoarse. 'I've been dreaming about this room.'

FOUR

Robert McKay took his usual place at the window end of the vestry table. He lifted the water jug over the mirror-like kauri surface to the glass on the clean white doily before him. A glass of clear water, he thought, was the perfect refreshment for Session, a reminder that cleanliness and purity could be found in this sordid and impure world.

Conversations tailed off. The seven black-suited church elders around the room began to move. One returned a book to the vestry shelves. Two let the window curtains fall on the soft summer evening outside. Another closed the minutes book of the Session of Elders of the Congregation of the Waiata Presbyterian Church and placed it next to the jug on the table. They all took their places and passed the jug. Here and there a drop spilled on the table. The session clerk moved around unobtrusively with a felt cloth, mopping up the drops to prevent the water spoiling the polished surface. This done, she sat at her desk, which was separate from the main table, and prepared her pen and pad.

'Good evening, gentlemen, Mrs Hughes,' the minister said, laying his forearms on the table and clasping his hands. 'Before we constitute this first kirk session of the year, a couple of items of interest.' He nodded to John Fleming, seated on his immediate right. 'I'm sure you'll all be as pleased as I am at the news of young Matthew's discharge from hospital.' Heads nodded, voices murmured ready agreement. The minister added, 'I think we all know how diligently Matthew has applied himself to growing in Christ since his earlier difficulties. It's surely fitting that the good Lord has chosen to bless him with a speedy recovery.' More murmurs. John Fleming blinked and nodded, delighted by the minister's gracious remark.

'...And I'm sure you'll also want to join me in asking Gordon...' Robert indicated Gordon Crocker, church elder, town councillor, contractor and businessman, '...to convey our felicitations to young James on his engagement to be married.' Another murmur of assent rumbled quietly around the table. Gordon Crocker's weatherbeaten countenance acknowledged the pleasantries with a smile. It would have been an ear-to-ear beam had he been anywhere else. He was a happy man. It had undoubtedly been the best new year he could remember. A good-looking city girl had, for some reason best known to herself, said 'yes' to Jimmy. Why anyone would want to marry a lad with the world's worst case of facial acne was a mystery to Gordon, but it was about to happen. And the girl's family was wealthy. Very wealthy.

On top of that, Gordon had finally been granted the rights to quarry a huge seam of decorative fossilised wood out of the cliffs across the harbour.

'If there's nothing else,' the minister was saying, 'I will constitute Session.' The heads bowed. The minister prayed that the elders would be granted guidance in the management of the spiritual affairs of the parish and the wisdom to cope with the difficulties of the coming year. This last was a reference to the fact that the road from the plains was expected to be completed within a year, opening Waiata up to the direct influence of the outside world.

The secretary, Mrs Hughes, lifted her eyes the instant after the Amen. She was trying to settle a recent dispute with a friend as to whether or not the minister's height hid a thinning scalp. But if it was thinning, she couldn't detect it. He was in his early fifties now. He showed only the first signs of a receding hairline, and his temples had turned steel-grey — an effect which only added to his distinguished looks. His back was as straight and almost as strong as ever, his jawline as severe as when he had first stepped on to the wharf all those years ago. His expression betrayed not a feather's whisk of self-satisfaction, even though most would agree that he had earned it: the latest National Council of Churches survey showed that more than eighty percent of the total population of Waiata and the surrounding bays were now committed to the Presbyterian Church on at least a regular-attendance basis.

The minister asked for, and received, acceptance of the minutes. He made Mrs Hughes blush by complimenting her on reversing the tendency for the minutes-book handwriting to deteriorate over the decades.

'Matters arising from the minutes?'

There were none.

'Then to the first item.' Robert ignored the handwritten agenda at his elbow. He looked straight at Chester Farnsworth, who was scratching self-consciously at part of his bare scalp. 'Chester, if I understand your proposal, you would like to see us inviting members of other denominations to participate in Holy Communion. You have the floor.'

'Well,' Chester sipped from his glass. 'I haven't really made up my own mind about this. But I heard that a few of the parishes up in the Wairarapa are inviting members of other churches to the Lord's Supper as a gesture ... of ... ah ... unity.'

Heads were already shaking. 'Don't see it,' John Fleming said.

'Quite inappropriate,' said Sam Clement, who was the mayor of Waiata.

'Doesn't surprise me, frankly,' said Norman White who, everyone knew, would become mayor as soon as old Sam had the grace to retire.

'Due respect to Chester,' Gordon Crocker said. 'But isn't this exactly what we've just been hearing from Robert? Deterioration of standards. We all know it's affecting the church. It's been creeping into the northern parishes for the last five years. Now this ... ' He waved his hand at the top of the agenda. ' ... Holy Communion! The Supper of our Lord! It's hard to credit.'

The minister waited. Then, 'Chester? Do you wish to put the proposal as a motion?'

'No. Not really. As I say, I'm not for or against it as such; I just thought it might be interesting to throw it in for discussion.'

Gordon Crocker assured him that they'd be a sorry lot if they weren't open to discussing new ideas.

Robert McKay said, 'I'd only add that I commend the intention to extend the hand of friendship and help to the misguided in other churches...' Norman White suppressed a grin. He never ceased to admire the way Robert McKay dealt with half-cocked ideas. First, let the other elders do the spade work on the grave. Second, anaesthetise the contributor with a

109

graceful compliment. Third, surgically remove the idea and place it in its coffin. '...However,' Robert continued. 'In this instance, the gesture would require us to lower the standards of entry to the Lord's Supper. Gentlemen, if we lower our standards in an area at the very core of the faith, we are lost. Nothing but the highest standards will do, for there are no grades or degrees of salvation. Such a proposal would be fatal to ourselves and worthless to others.'

'Hear, hear.' 'Well said.'

'Which brings me to a much more difficult problem. If you'd permit me to depart from the agenda for a moment...?' All nodded, except for Chester, who was gazing absently at the opposite wall.

Robert allowed a few seconds of silence, partly for effect, partly to marshal his thoughts: it had been eighteen years now. Eighteen years of preparation without any sign of the Lord's will with him. Now that the outside world was about to reach them, it was tempting to think that the great test would be brought from the outside. But he must not presume. At all costs he must not presume, or he could be blind to the challenge when it came. No. He must be ready on *all* fronts. More than that, the parish must be ready, strong, stalwart, able to face anything. And the imminent arrival of the road could be used as the means to prepare the parish. He looked around at all of them.

'...The deterioration in other parishes is only a small reflection of the general spiritual decline of our so-called civilisation which, as you know, is pressing towards us from the plains.'

Emphatic nods.

'We can't stop the road. But we can prepare for its arrival. It is my contention that we must work towards building up our spiritual defences. Starting now.'

'Hear, hear.'

'I will arrange my sermons to suit, of course. But just as important, each of you, as ruling elders, must redouble your guard on the spiritual values of the families in your section. And don't be blinded by the fact that the road will bring material goods. Civilisation is a stranger bearing material gifts, but the danger is not in the gifts themselves. It is in the ideas that lie behind them. If I may give an example: the tobacconist who sells pornography is not nearly as dangerous as the man who has a plausible theory that tells you it's all right to buy. Ideas. Theories. Rationalisations. They will be our greatest challenge, gentlemen. Be watchful. Be vigilant.'

FIVE

'Midnight blue?' asked Mrs Drury, the draper's wife.
Emily Nisbet shook her head.

'Forest green?' Elaine Drury avoided looking at her husband,
who was frowning at her from behind the pyjama shelf. She
pointed out yet another dark, sombre colour to Emily. 'Now this
one would suit you down to the ground. Charcoal. No? Are you
sure? It is for you, isn't it?'

Emily nodded.

'What about the straight black then? That would be spell-
binding on you.' Out of the corner of her eye, Mrs Drury saw
that her husband was refolding freshly stacked pyjamas that were
already perfectly folded. In front of her, Emily pointed firmly to
a roll of lilac seersucker in the rack. Mrs Drury's eyebrows rose with
surprise. 'This one? That's a *very* gay colour. Oh well, as long
as you're sure it's suitable. How much do you want then,
Mrs Nisbet?'

Emily pointed to the bench measure and held up three fingers.
While the cloth shears hissed across the roll, she went to the
cotton stand near the front window. But before she could select
a reel to match the lilac, she saw a figure walk by on the pavement
outside. It was Jennifer Pringle. Emily hurried back to the counter
without the cotton. She fumbled quickly in her purse and handed
over a pound note, looking back and forth to the door. Her face
contorted with effort. 'P . . . please. Hurry.'

Mrs Drury paused for another show of surprise. Then she
resumed wrapping at the same pace as before. And when Emily
finally took the parcel and hobbled towards the door, the draper's
wife watched derisively, hands on hips.

'Well. It speaks,' she said as the door closed.

Nigel Drury returned to the counter angrily. 'Why do you do
that? What do you have to treat the poor woman like that for?'

112

'Poor woman? Poor woman, my great Aunt Fanny! When she first came here she could toff down to us just as good as any pom with a plum in her Lady Muck cheek. You saw her just then. She can speak all right when she wants to give one of the natives the hurry-up. Oh yes.'

Jennifer heard steps and panting behind her. She turned, then slowed. Emily drew level, making heavy use of her stick as she regained breath. The younger woman was taken aback by the encounter and said no more than a 'good afternoon'. But she slowed down. The two walked around the waterfront, while the high tide licked at the concrete retainer wall under them. The harbour was still almost empty of fishing vessels; dinghies clung to the mooring buoys instead, rocking in the angular easterly chop. The sun was on the western hills now, and the women's profiles shone as they walked.

'Please,' Emily said soon. 'I want ... to talk.'

Jennifer sighed. 'I still don't know what to make of it myself, Mrs Nisbet. I've hardly ... ' She broke off, seeing alarm on Emily's face.

'No,' pleaded the older woman. 'Not that. Yes, that too. But ... more ... about ... More.'

Jennifer stopped, aghast at the open desperation, uncomfortably aware of the proximity of too many houses. How the town gossips would relish this public emotion between two of their favourite subjects! A wash of cold anger passed through her.

She looked around. Further along the sea wall was a bench, set into the concrete, out in full view of the world. She touched Emily's shoulder, wondering at the shrinking that simple action produced. 'Come on,' she said. 'Why don't we take the weight off our feet?'

High up behind them, isolated showers tumbled on to the summit ridge in columns, brightly lit by the sun.

SIX

Matthew might have gone all the way to Emily Nisbet's cottage oblivious to all but his own turbulent thoughts. But as he neared the end of the sea wall, a startled cry and an indignant oath brought him back to awareness of his surroundings. A figure sprawled heavily on to the road ahead of him, near a road works ditch that had been dug across the bottom end of Rue Lafayette. It was Tommy Ransley: totally blind since his thirtieth birthday more than fifteen years ago, and next to stone deaf for almost as long. He had missed the marker drums and stumbled across the ditch. He lay where he had fallen, emitting a shrill, petulant stream of blasphemies, many of which Matthew had never heard before. The angry man then scrabbled around on his hands and knees, casting about for his white-tipped cane and flicking painfully skinned knuckles in the air — all without a break in his commentary.

Matthew scooped up the cane and touched Tommy on the forearm. Tommy's body jerked with fright, and froze. His tongue ceased its commotion and his hand reached out, clawing hopefully for the cane. It was placed in his fingers. His free hand darted to the boy's arm and shoulders, locating him. Matthew took the hand and finger-wrote on the palm; 'road', then 'works'.

'I ain't fuckin' stupid,' Tommy answered in his unnaturally high voice. But Matthew was gazing at the white clouding in the unseeing eyes before him. He'd seen Tommy hundreds of times before, but never this close. Suddenly Matthew felt gauche, helpless, and bitter.

It always happened; whenever he came across sickness or physical affliction he was gripped by an urge to put out his hands and somehow take away the suffering. Where the urge came from, he didn't know. He couldn't remember, and in spite of what they said had happened in the hospital, Nathaniel still wasn't

114

around to tell him. But what was the point anyway? Healing didn't work. It had never worked. And ever since that beating nine years ago, he hadn't had the courage to try it again on animals, let alone humans.

Tommy's hand found Matthew's face, quested deftly over the cheekbones, the chin, nose and eyelids. It wasn't one of the faces his hand knew. He repeated the sequence. Then he grunted. The white stick rose to point obliquely across the road.

'Where's the railing?' he demanded. 'This way?' His free hand found Matthew's chin again, and clutched it, waiting. Matthew, who had seen this happen before, nodded his head vigorously. He watched the almost shapeless man set out for the sea wall. The fleshy chin was pushed aggressively forward, the shoulders were stooped, the cane tapping in careful arcs. Every night, Tommy Ransley went to the local saddler's semi-public poolroom, where he remained until it closed late at night. He had once been the unofficial peninsula pool champion. It was said that there was just one sound in the world that Tommy could still hear: the sound of two pool balls colliding. For this reason, few in the church tried to reprove him for associating with drinkers, although Matthew had seen one enraged deacon attempt to correct Tommy's blasphemies by finger-writing entire Bible verses on his hand. Lay opinion was divided between those who maintained that Tommy's double affliction was punishment for his own sins, and those who said that his suffering was the visitation upon him of the sins of his forebears. The latter view held sway: Tommy's grandfather had indulged in systematic sheep-stealing with a dog specially trained for the purpose.

Matthew continued up Rue Lafayette with a sour lump of failure in his throat.

Big Jimmy Crocker walked out the front door of his parents' home. And because his lovely bride-to-be, Angela Croyden-Platt, was with him, it was more like floating than walking. They stepped off the porch. Angela slipped a hand through his arms and he was almost surprised that gravity had sufficient hold on him to bring his feet down to the driveway stones.

As they wafted towards the road, he stole a wondering sideways glance at the slender, tightly-jeaned, silk-bloused girl on his arm. He asked himself, for the sixth time that day, why this glorious,

115

sophisticated, golden-haired creature from the city would want to share her life with him. It wasn't for his brains. He had left school early and was ignorant. He knew that. She had been to university and knew everything about the world, and he spent half his time thinking up things to say that would interest her. Nor was it for his money; even when he inherited the quarry, he wouldn't have half the money her parents had. And it certainly wasn't his looks. He was too big for a start. His size and strength had scared off half the girls in his past; and his acne scars had scared off the rest. The acne was the worst. 'How're you expecting to pass on the family name with a dial like that, Jimmy boy?' his father used to joke. Or after too many beers: 'Take the mask off, Jimmy. You trying to frighten the girls or some'at?' Not any more. No such jokes now that this exquisite creature had chosen him. When they were married just let anyone try to tell him he was stupid and worthless.

Angela caught his stolen look, smiled and squeezed his arm. No other woman had ever rubbed his muscles, no other woman had told him he was a real man and that he had 'earth wisdom'. Whatever that was. Soon he would be placing the ring on her finger to begin a lifetime of happiness. Yes, that was what God wanted for him, Jimmy Crocker; why else would He have sent him this angel?

As they turned out of the driveway on to Rue Lafayette, Jimmy saw Matthew Fleming on Nisbet's front porch across the way. He stopped, intrigued, in spite of the call of love. Now Matthew Fleming at the witch's door, of all people. What was *he* doing with that lot? Jimmy seized the opportunity, and Angela's arm. 'You wouldn't believe the bunch of weirdos in that place,' he said.

Angela laughed, as always delighted by his forcefulness and by the explosive abruptness of his movements. He talked, and they sauntered down Lafayette Hill, happy, laughing, in love.

'Nothing at all,' Matthew said. 'I don't feel any different at all.'

The four were in Emily's kitchen-dining-sitting room. Jennifer was reclined so deeply in the armchair that her legs stuck out over the circular rug and her body was almost straight. Emily perched, hands in lap. Jack lounged cross-legged on an old, home-made settee. And all three were looking at Matthew. The initial

116

awkwardness of the atmosphere had vanished: they had quickly discovered that they were comfortable in each other's company. But in spite of that, Matthew wasn't happy; he sat tense and restless, unable to forget the unseeing eyes of Tommy Ransley, not knowing what he was meant to do now to get Nathaniel back.

Jack began to look doubtful. 'If you're not feeling up to it, maybe ... '

'No. It's not that. Something on my mind. It's nothing.'

'Should you lie down? The way you were in hospital?'

Matthew shrugged gloomily.

Emily took a breath and concentrated. Words still had to be forced past reluctant lips. 'You've got to ... to be relaxed. Or it doesn't work. Shall I make some rosemary tea? That helps. I used ... I used to make some for a circle in London.' Jennifer moved to help, but the kettle had been filled long ago, and was sighing on the range, ready. The two women smiled at each other in shy wellbeing.

'What's a circle?' Jack asked.

'Circle of people,' Emily replied, clinking cups, breathless with anticipation of the evening. 'They talk ... to people who have passed on.'

'They *what*?'

'Emily used to be a spiritualist,' Jennifer explained. 'She knows how to do this.'

When Emily returned with the tea, she was pressed into a long explanation of spiritualism, mediums, and what she thought spirits really were. Throughout, she held her cup close to her face, looking through the sweet-smelling steam at Jennifer, so that she could answer more easily. Jack asked what her circle did before the spirits talked, and he hesitated on the word 'spirits', as if he was compromising himself by uttering it. Was there any procedure? he asked. Emily replied that there was, but protested that this was a different situation: Nathaniel didn't seem to be like any other spirits that she'd heard.

'I'm not sure I go for this ghost business,' Jack said thoughtfully. 'But I don't hear Nathaniel speaking up. Maybe we should give it a go, Emily. What do you do?'

Emily looked anxious. 'It's a prayer. Then everyone sits back ... with their eyes closed. But it was always the medium who said the prayer. And I don't remember any of the words.'

'I don't want to do it.' Matthew cut in quickly. Jack said flatly that he wasn't the praying sort, that he wouldn't know where to begin, and made his point even plainer by going to hush D'Arcy who was sulking noisily out on the back porch. Jennifer directed a knowing look at Emily.

'All right, all right, I'll try,' Emily squeaked unhappily. She stood, pulled the curtains and turned on the bedroom light so that some cross-light came through the doorway. She took a box out from the bottom of the bookshelf, rummaged through it and lifted out an ancient pencil and a dusty booklet of blank pages. These she handed to Jennifer. 'When it's a really evolved spirit, you're supposed to write down what it says.' Jennifer accepted the equipment without a comment. If there was any recording to be done, her shorthand made her the obvious choice.

Now Emily instructed Matthew: 'When you close your eyes, don't try ... don't try to do anything. Just let your mind go. Let it drift. If thoughts come into your mind ... just ... just .. stand back ... and watch them go by. That's how you do it.'

Emily bowed her head, her face creased with tension and concentration. With a roomful of people, leading a prayer was much more difficult than ordinary talking. 'Holy Father ... hear us ... ah ... please help us to ... ah ... look down ... I mean, grace us this evening with wisdom and enlightenment from the spirit world. I hope this is enough. Amen!

They settled back to wait. For ten minutes there was hardly a sound. The range cooled slowly, its metal ticking, the dying coals shuffling in the grate. Genghis, the budgerigar, obligingly stayed on one perch. The small amount of outside light creeping around the blinds was fading for the evening, leaving the room to the side-light from the bedroom. Jennifer was glad of the low light; the thought that they were trying to have a chat with a spook kept a nervous giggle close to the surface. But then the ticking of the range seemed to become regular and somehow her sense of inanity faded away. She listened to the metallic tick, tick, tick, and remembered a time when she had watched a metronome for more than an hour, sitting perfectly motionless until she thought that with the slightest whim of will she might float.

118

Matthew's head was nodding. His chin sank slowly to his chest. When it touched, it rose immediately. His eyelids flickered, then lifted. His body sat upright on the chair.

'Good evening to you.' The voice was the same as it had been in the hospital: rich of timbre, filled with warmth and dry humour. The eyes were penetrating, ageless in the youthful face, dark in features already darkened by half-shadow.

'Good evening,' Emily replied formally, now on familiar territory. 'Are you Nathaniel?'

'I am.'

Jennifer found herself breathing shallowly, nervously. That was Matthew's face, and yet it wasn't. They were Matthew's features, but they somehow reflected the expression in those strange, powerful eyes. She glanced around at Emily, and then down at her pad. Take it down? She looked up to find the eyes on her. Her heart thudded, her pulse quickened.

'This room is like the centre of a very large pond, Jennifer. It will be helpful if one of the ripples is an accurate record of what is said.'

Jennifer stood abruptly, breathing shakily. She walked to the far end of the room and leaned on the bench, standing side on to the others, biting her lip.

'There's nothing to be scared of,' Emily said.

'I'm not scared,' Jennifer said too quickly, annoyed at herself. 'I'm sorry. It's just that it's hard to take. I still don't know that this isn't some kind of fancy leg-pull.' Emily shook her head vigorously. Jack commented that the only way they were going to find out was to listen to what Nathaniel had to say. Jennifer went back to her seat.

'I'm sorry,' she said tersely.

The face nodded. The eyes twinkled. 'This is certainly the worst possible time for me to suggest that you avoid losing touch with the sense of wellbeing that you have found in the last five days.'

Jennifer gasped and went rigid for a moment. But her absurd giggle broke through, so that she laughed outright and threw her hands up in mock surrender. 'All right, you win for now. Whatever you are.'

Still the eyes hinted at a chuckle. 'You will have to forgive me, I was unable to resist the temptation. But before you assume

119

that I can plunder the contents of your mind at will, I should point out that your every thought and emotion is known, at some level, to every person you meet.

'Now.' He looked around them, the eyes moving, but the head almost still. 'I ask you to accept nothing at face value.' He turned to Emily, who was smiling hugely and happily. 'The fact that I am what you call a spirit should lend no authority to my words. If you must judge me at all, then let it be by what I say and do rather than by what I claim to be.'

Emily contrived a look more serious and objective. A slow smile pulled into Jack's cheeks, a smile of amusement and grudging admiration.

A whining sound penetrated the back door.

'At the risk of offending your sense of reason in the first minute,' Nathaniel said, 'I will tell you that Jack's impatient friend outside is aware of my presence. If he were allowed in with us, he would not be disruptive.'

Jack looked inquiringly at Emily, who acquiesced immediately. With the door open, D'Arcy loped in. He took a fast sniff at everybody in passing, then settled on the floor between Emily's chair and the settee, laid his chin on the rug between his paws and rolled his eyes around the circle. Jack returned to his seat. Emily and Jennifer gazed at D'Arcy, then Jennifer shook her head wonderingly and looked up.

'Excuse me,' she said. 'But what's it all about? Why are we here? Why are *you* here?'

'I am here because of your desire to make sense of a painful existence.'

He paused, inviting comment. Jack struggled to pick one question from many. 'Look. I'd like some proof. What's there to say we're not just listening to some part of Matthew's subconscious? Part of his mind?'

Jennifer looked up from her pad and blew air out through her teeth.

'I am as distinct from Matthew as you are.' A smile. 'I am also part of your friend's greater mind. There is no paradox when you understand there is no limit to Mind.'

Jennifer groaned. Jack said, 'I'm sorry I asked.'

Emily sat up firmly, speaking without her normal hesitancy. 'There is something I have to ask you. When I was in a circle

120

in London, the guides always said we should check on whoever came through. We had to ask them if they came in the name of Jesus. Do you?'

'No, I do not. You are referring to the belief that if the spirit does not come with that authority, he will depart in undignified haste on hearing the name. You were misled. You will notice that I am still here.'

'Oh.' Emily blinked, taken aback.

'Know me by my works,' Nathaniel repeated softly. 'Not by who or what I claim to be.' He paused. 'Now. Matthew is present and pressing so strongly with questions that I will speak up immediately in case he expels me like a naughty schoolboy. First: he wants to know why I don't talk with him alone. The answer is that for the difficult times ahead it is important that he develop his own resources, his own ability to choose a course of action and carry it through.

'Second: he came here distressed and asking why he is plagued by persistent impulses to heal with his hands ... ' Jennifer stole a look of surprise at Jack and Emily who seemed unperturbed. ' ... I don't reveal that of him lightly. The answer vitally affects all four of you. Nothing is predestined. Much depends on the choices you make in the near future. But continue to make the right choices and I promise that not just Matthew, but all four of you, will know the joy of the power of healing.'

SEVEN

Chester wrapped the kitset Lancaster bomber with a tube of model cement, then pushed the parcel across the counter. 'Seventeen and thruppence,' he said and winked. 'That's the third in a week. When are you going to join the air force?'

'Stops my head from exploding and flying off in different directions,' Matthew said humourlessly. The doctor had told him to rest for a fortnight before returning to work on the *Phoenix*, and his old hobby kept his mind from churning.

'Still hurts, eh?' Chester was sympathetic.

'No,' Matthew replied flatly, rudely. He ignored Chester's bafflement and walked out of the general store to the waterfront. He stood on the sea wall, watching the Saturday morning shoppers weaving through the nikau palms, trying to shake the feeling that he had somehow entered a strange, foreign town.

It was one of those soft, clear, midsummer mornings that made winter no more than a wisp of memory. The few boats still in harbour were set in warm glass. A duck with half a dozen ducklings meandered out from the sea wall, their wake fading into the still water like ripples in oil. The supply boat was in, nestled against the wharf, the sounds of the unloading crisp and clear across the water. It came every week these days. A black-topped car brooded on its afterdeck, waiting to be driven off. Now that the road from the plains was only six months away, a few of the more affluent locals were spending their savings and shipping in motor vehicles. This morning there were half a dozen motor cars parked amongst the gigs and traps by the sea wall. It was said that the Council was considering marking off parking spaces for Saturday mornings, a rumour which caused most locals to shake their heads and cluck their tongues and ask what the world was coming to. The stock answer was that it was coming to Waiata.

A car horn pamped behind Matthew. Brakes squealed. A large, open Studebaker pulled up beside him, stopping so abruptly that its wheels skidded, dragging sharp stones out of the clay. Inside were five of his old school friends, their faces creased with the laughter of a joke just shared. It was the Westlakes' car. Alan Westlake was at the wheel, looking as nonchalant as is possible for a young man in a Studebaker.

'Hey, Matt! We're burnin' over Takamatua way. Come on.' Cigarettes slid out of packets held in casual wrists. Lighters clicked and flashed. Heads dipped stylishly to suck flames into white tubes in the manner of men of the world. In every direction, adult faces turned, covered with hoar frost.

'Well, uh ... '

'Come *on*, Matt.' Alan revved impatiently.

Matthew jumped on to the running board and plumped down into the back seat. He accepted a proferred cigarette, even though he had only ever smoked once, behind the toilets at school. He began to bask in the noisy, boisterous atmosphere. He'd been too wrapped up in himself. He had to let himself go a bit. The car took off, skittering loose stones behind and changing from first to second gear only when the engine screamed for mercy. Matthew accepted a light.

'What's that?' Alan called back, jerking his head at Matthew's parcel.

'Model aeroplane,' Matthew answered artlessly, and he groaned mentally at his stupidity. The others looked at each other aghast, then shrugged with the easy-going manner of men who have encountered every possible vagary of life and still found living passably pleasant.

'Those Takamatua dames are pretty classy,' Daniel Ferris informed Matthew, nudging him with an elbow. 'They've got the fast eye over there, know what I'm sayin'. That Sheila Wilkie, you only need to show her the bush behind her place and she starts rubbing her legs together. Know what I'm sayin'?'

'And *man*!!' Owen Hooper shouted above the noise of the engine. 'Does she go off like a rocket!' Matthew joined in the laughter, hoping they weren't going to Sheila Wilkie's place. From the way everyone talked, most boys of his age seemed to have done it with a girl already. He hated being inexperienced about as much as he hated the thought of his present companions being around when he came across a willing girl. The car built up speed around the waterfront. He wondered if it was true about Sheila.

'We're going to Sheila's?' he asked Daniel casually.

'Hey!' Daniel removed his cigarette. 'Fleming can't wait to get into Wilkie!'

Matthew swallowed, Daniel tapped Sidney Irwin on the shoulder. 'Show Matt, Sid.' But Sid smiled a secret smile and pretended to be absorbed in the view ahead. Daniel's hand came over the seat back and dived into Sid's pocket. He came up with a tiny cardboard packet and thrust it under Matthew's nose. Matthew fought down an impulse to gain marginally on experience by looking inside to see what they looked like. He hesitated, then handed the packet back, saying that he didn't bother with them himself. But he had hesitated too long. A chorus of jeers demanded to know who Matthew thought he was trying to fool. Now he was certain: he didn't want to wait around to find out the truth about Sheila Wilkie. The only problem remaining was how to get out of the car without a catastrophic loss of mana.

The Studebaker neared the other end of the waterfront where Waiata's short strip of beach held the water away from the sea wall. There were already half a dozen bodies toasting on the coarse sand. Sidney Irwin yelled and pointed: two of the women were wearing two-piece costumes. Alan Westlake stabbed repeatedly on the horn button, and all but Matthew rose to their feet to yell and wave as the car swept past. Matthew sat lower in the back seat, but not so low that he missed a familiar female shape further along the sand. Jennifer Pringle.

He watched his arm reach out to slap Westlake's shoulder. 'Stop! Stop! I just saw someone who owes me some dough.'

He didn't fool anyone. 'Chicken, man!' 'Can't take the pace, Fleming!' 'What are ya, Fleming?' The car skidded to a halt, released him and accelerated frantically. As the jeers and hoots faded, he carefully raised two obscene fingers, masked from all but the speeding car. It occurred to him that no one in the car had ever made it with Sheila Wilkie.

When he was level with the beach and saw Jennifer again, he stopped. He stared down at the kitset in his hands, then placed it on the ground by the sea wall. His feet edged it hard against the wall.

Jennifer was alone, the sand around deserted since her arrival. Heads rose, shifted, as Matthew trod towards her into no-man's-land. She lay face down, eyes closed.

'Hi.' He sat beside her.

'Hullo.' She looked up in surprise.

'Do you mind? Me sitting here, I mean.'

'No.' She looked doubtful. 'You sure you want to be seen with me?'

'Nobody knows. They can't possibly guess.'

'I don't mean that. I'm a fallen woman. I should be ringing the bell to warn people I'm coming.' Under her breath she mocked, 'Unclean! Unclean!'

Matthew dropped his eyes. He pushed his toes into the warm sand, scooped up a handful and let it fall through his fingers. He said, 'I don't care about that.'

Jennifer watched him for a second longer, then lay on her back and closed her eyes. Matthew was suddenly, and acutely, aware of her body. The sleekness of the dark-blue one-piece made him think about the curves and surfaces that undulated beneath. He thought about it some more. Then he sat upright and looked at the tiny wash of water combing the edge of the sand. He unclipped his miniature pocket knife and whittled self-consciously at a piece of bone-dry driftwood. Jennifer, hearing the sound, looked at him sideways. A small muscle in her cheek twitched.

'Are you *sure* you don't mind?' he pressed.

Jennifer rolled onto her side and looked at him with amusement. 'It's your funeral. But I don't mind: usually the only guys who talk to me in public are the ones who think I can't wait to take off my pants for them.'

Matthew looked away quickly as the crimson tide rose, seemingly from as far down as his toes. He hoped fervently that his tan would hide the colour. But when he turned, he saw that she had lain back and closed her eyes again.

'You talk pretty direct,' he commented.

'Anything else is hypocrisy. I hate hypocrites.'

'Hmmm, yes.' Matthew said vaguely. He picked up a driftwood twig and traced random shapes in the sand. One of the shapes turned out like a heart, so he quickly erased it. Change the subject. 'I was wondering what you thought of Wednesday night.' Jennifer looked straight up at the sky where thistledown

125

clouds wafted high above. But before she could answer, there was a commotion on the road above. Heads lifted off the sand along the beach. The Studebaker was back, U-turning in a cloud of fine clay dust. It revved high, then pulled up almost on the sea wall itself, directly above Matthew and Jennifer. Sidney Irwin stood up in the front and looked down at them. The others in the car were watching with expectant smirks.

'Hey, Fleming,' Sidney shouted as if he were a full hundred yards away. 'Going to have a wee ride on the town bike, are ya?' The car began to pull away. Sidney raised his voice even louder. 'Don't forget to pump up the tyres!'

Matthew went white with fury. He raced to the sea wall, but could only stand helplessly on it, as the Studebaker gathered speed and the mocking laughter floated back. His two fingers twitched to be used, but the gesture didn't seem adequate for the situation. He did nothing but tread his wrath back to Jennifer. She was looking at the water, her face an impassive mask. He shouted at her. 'They're filthy rotten animals! I thought they were my friends!' She didn't move. He squatted beside her and mused incredulously. 'They've all been confirmed.'

'Hah!' Jennifer laughed out loud. 'Boy, have *you* got a lot to learn!' To cover his hurt, Matthew stood to take another look down the road. Still she watched the water. 'For God's sake, don't make all this fuss. You're giving our audience exactly what they want. The only other thing we could do for them now is burst into tears and run home to Mother. Pull yourself together.'

Matthew sat, fury and shame churning.

Jennifer continued, in a tone of quiet detachment that denied her own words. 'I hate this miserable dump of a town. I'm only staying for one reason now — for what comes out of your mouth. Hah. That's me: staying in a hole to listen to a spook.' Now she turned to him. 'I'm telling you, Fleming: the moment your Nathaniel turns out to be a phony, I'll be gone from here faster than you can spit at a spat.'

'Good morning, Matthew.' It was Mrs Crocker, with Jimmy. Matthew returned the greeting with minimum grace and tried to continue on his way. 'Oh Matthew...' He stopped. '... I do hope you'll be able to come to the reception.'

'Wouldn't miss it, Mrs Crocker.' He nodded to Jimmy,

knowing that if his parents didn't get on so well with Jimmy's parents, he might not have been invited. 'Congrats and all that, Jimbo. She's really nice, they reckon.' Jimmy grinned self-consciously. His eyes glowed.

'Matthew.' Mrs Crocker's voice was concerned. 'We couldn't help but wonder if Mrs Nisbet is all right. I mean, with three of you visiting her . . .'

'She's all right,' Matthew replied steadily.

'Oh. I'm so relieved. It's always best to be sure, that's what I say. You see, we thought she might be unwell, because well, we couldn't think what you might all be going there for?'

Matthew spoke through tight, thin lips. 'We're making gunpowder. We're planning to blow up Parliament.'

He had to be alone. He had to get as far away from humanity as he could before he started tipping people off the end of the wharf. Instead of going home, he turned up past the hospital into Aylmers Valley and on up through the farmland. After the last farm, he turned on to a cart track. The cart track became a narrow foot track as it climbed the valley side. Soon he left even that and pressed into the bush, weaving a way he had taken many times before, holding tears down by breathing harder and sharper than the demands of the terrain made necessary.

At his secluded forest glade high above the harbour and the village, he stopped. And before he allowed himself to see his refuge, he stood in its very centre, with his hand clutched to the sides of his head, eyes tightly closed. He moaned aloud through clenched teeth, expelling sound and air and pain, until his lungs were empty to the point of collapse. This done, his hands fell, his shoulders relaxed, his chin dropped and only now did he allow his senses to feast on the subtle banquet this special place always provided.

Matthew Fleming's hideaway was a tiny natural haven. A streamlet entered down a sloped rock-face, sliding almost soundlessly into a pool hardly bigger than a wash tub, then slipped mirror-flat across the glade, tipping quietly away under the branches of an old-man walnut.

Before anything else, he scanned the ground for evidence of his anonymous shadow, the unknown companion who had shared his retreat with him over the years. He found it in the gravel and clay by the stream: again the imprint of a shoe, perhaps only two days old. He stood over it, recognising the outline as one recognises a friend. It scarcely seemed possible that the two of them had not encountered each other in all that time, nor found evidence of identity. Once, he had tried to spot the familiar outline amongst the hundreds of feet at the annual bazaar, but the translation from effect to cause had been impossible. Even now, he could not have said with conviction whether his kindred spirit was a man or a woman.

When his breathing quietened, he sat on the rock by the pool, with elbows on knees, and made himself perfectly still.

At first there was only the sun, drenching the small space with its warmth and turning the broad green leaves of the walnut to emerald. But then came the fantails: mustard, white and brown. Chubby, inquisitive acrobats without trapezes, they twisted and darted after insects stirred up by his presence. Later came rustlings and murmurings. A tiny shape dashed across the roots of a young lancewood across the glade: a field mouse, so fear-driven that its body vibrated in the air between leaps. A lithe brown body flashed after it. A stoat. Somewhere out of sight there was a thin squeak. Afterwards, in the stillness, he could hear leaf caressing leaf, water sighing on granite, even the effervescence of soil exhaling moisture into the sun-warmed grass.

But the pleasure of all of this did not in itself account for Matthew Fleming's presence here. It was what was to happen next that he always savoured in anticipation in the weeks between visits.

Over the years, his schoolboy fantasies had changed beyond recognition. No longer just pictures: now his daydreams conjured moving images, sounds, tastes, smells, feelings, as seemingly real as the glade — of times and places far removed from the people and village of Waiata.

He began to hear strange sounds. Then, equally strange images emerged in the glade. At first he saw them in glimpses, as if through a curtained window. But the frame would shiver and ripple away outwards, and the shapes would flow towards him, like mirages out of the desert, until he found himself walking among them.

He heard the grit of sandals on sand, the scrape of earthenware

128

on wood.

His eyes closed.

And this time he was walking towards a well with two pitchers swinging from a yoke. He was indignant that he, Kassim, now fully twelve years of age, had been sent to do the work of women. And he groaned inwardly as he recognised the one girl standing among the women at the well side. Why did Shabnan have to be there, of all people? He maintained an air of lofty disdain while he waited his turn. Listen to them, he thought scornfully, listen to their prattling voices running in and out and around like reeds in a mat.

The women who lowered and raised the great water skins for him looked at each other with knowing amusement. Since he was on the threshold of manhood, they stopped short of openly laughing; and because he had not yet crossed that tantalising threshold, he didn't dare lash them with his tongue. Which they richly deserved. Particularly Shabnan, who now with pot on shoulder walked right around the well to where he could no longer pretend not to have noticed her impudent face.

Strange, he thought. She reminded him of someone.

Facing him, Shabnan made a blatant mockery of downcast eyes and smirked infuriatingly. How he ached to trip her up and rub goat dung in her face the way he used to.

His pitchers filled, he attempted to move away with the required dignity. But he stumbled and precious liquid silver slopped to the sand, splashing his djellaba. Shabnan's laughter tinkled above the giggles behind him and he bore his load away with ears hotter than the sand he walked on. Let her laugh now. But he would show her. He wouldn't be an apprentice for ever, sent hither and thither like a stupid woman. One day he would be a master weaver and *that* would take the smirk off her face.

A kingfisher's wings thrummed overhead.

Matthew opened his eyes.

Swiftly, the child's resentment faded away into the trees. He blinked, adjusting to the change. Then he broke into a smile, laughed aloud and slapped his thigh with delight. This one had been unusually entertaining. And also unusual in taking him back to an age younger than his present nineteen years.

But, as always, there had been that odd feeling of recognition.

Unresolved recognition. It happened every time.

No matter whether he found himself hunting fur seal with a bone-tipped spear or reading love sonnets written with a goose quill. No matter if he watched a race run by naked men in an arena, boiled maize in a windowless cob hut, wheel-danced in a cobbled square, or cast wolf bones into a fire to study the cracks for meaning. Invariably, in every new reverie there would be someone with whom he seemed to share a powerful bond. This time Shabnan. The time before, Wladek. Before that, the mongoose keeper, Urs. Sa'pang. Iwako's baby. Giovanni... each one was different.

And yet, in some indefinable way, all seemed to be linked, like separate beads belonging to the same necklace. All reminded him of a single personality. As if each was a mask worn by an actor of such exceptional talents that his real identity could not be guessed.

Another kingfisher. Flying in the same direction.

Still in high spirits, he leapt to his feet to go. But first, he stood again over the shoe print by the stream. He bent to run his fingers over the depression, and as he did so, his miniature puma knife came off his belt and fell unnoticed into the grass.

He left the glade then, not knowing that it would be many years before he returned.

EIGHT

'Brethren. I know there are some amongst us who picture Satan as a black, man-like beast with horns and cloven feet, with barbed tail and a voice of doom.' McKay paused, allowing time for uncertainty to register amongst the scores in church who pictured the devil in precisely the way described. He inclined over the pulpit and dropped his voice to an almost conspiratorial tone; and many in his four-hundred-strong congregation leaned an inch further forward, without realising that they had done so.

'But do you imagine that Almighty God would, for one second, be seriously challenged by a beast with a pitchfork or black imps behind lamp posts and under beds? I say to you that such imagery blinds you to the creeping subtlety of Satan and his loathsome legions.' His gaze roamed the pews, singling out groups and individuals for momentary transfixion.

'A voice of doom? Oh, no. No, my friends. Satan has ten thousand voices, all of them different. And I say to you that many of them are as sweet as honey. Some of them, moreover, are the dulcet-toned voices of apparent reason ... !' His gaze passed across the Fleming family, six rows back to the left, stopped, flicked back over Matthew. The boy was unwell. Still feeling the effects of the accident, perhaps. '... And the beguiling voices of apparent reason are the deadliest voices of all, because their detection requires a keen sense of sin.

'For salvation's sake, I implore you to hold fast to your sense of sin, because without it you cannot hope to recognise that moment when beguiling evil pulls you from the path, stupefying the soul to unconsciousness of its own spiritual death!'

There was an appreciative murmur from the congregation. If only, the minister thought, it were possible to avoid words altogether and express vital truths by thought in an undistorted

131

state. He found his glance drawn back to Matthew, to something odd about the lad's expression. He continued.

'Make no mistake. You may be saved. Not because you are fit to be saved, not because you have any claim whatsoever on heaven's reward, but because your human frailty is in constant need of His mercy. Be convinced of your state of sin. Know that you wallow in depravity. Admit that you may only be saved by donning the armour of God's word!'

Another murmur of approbation. He dropped his voice to a low and carrying tone.

'And believe me, brethren, we in Waiata are shortly going to need our strongest armour.' Again his glance returned to Matthew. The expression was shifting only in minute ways, but Robert was well used to reading faces that had something to hide. He went on, a pin-point of disquiet tucked into a corner of his mind.

'Even as I speak, a road is being built towards us through the hills. And poised on it are all the trappings of so-called civilisation: material luxuries, alcohol, drugs, sexual licence, loose, godless ways ... But beware, beware; they are *not* the real danger. Shall I tell you where the real danger lies?'

He had them intrigued: whatever was more dangerous than anything in that list had to be at least interesting.

'The real danger is in words. Words, concepts, ideas. They are the devil's most powerful tool.'

Another subtle change in Matthew. Robert's memory flicked the years back like a single page. Disquiet.

'The unfortunate wretch who offers the whisky bottle or invites you to indulge in debauchery is not nearly so dangerous as the one who distorts such concepts as "tolerance" and "personal and social freedom" to persuade you that such activities are acceptable. The worshippers of false gods and the followers of erroneous paths are not as dangerous as he who uses sugar-coated theories to persuade you to do the same.' On impulse, Robert added another example. 'Those deluded and damned souls who dabble in spiritualism are *not* so dangerous as the one who can produce a plausible reason why you, too, should communicate directly with the henchmen of Satan.'

Matthew's face set abruptly into pale immobility. For a single moment McKay was aware of nothing but that waxen image.

Swiftly, he recovered the smooth flow of the service.

Afterwards, the minister greeted every parishioner as he or she passed out the main entrance. This was done every week. he could not hope to shake every adult hand, but it was his duty to make at least some contact with each of his flock, be it only a glance or a nod. Today, the praise for his sermon was even more forthcoming than usual. Margaret Crocker told him that it was nothing less than inspired, to which he replied that she was too generous, but allowed that the subject might perhaps have been timely.

Not long after the Crockers came the Flemings. Edith simply thanked him. John grasped his hand and pumped it briefly, but enthusiastically, while Rachel smiled her agreement with her husband's feelings.

Matthew pushed roughly past them all and walked swiftly towards the gate without so much as a nod to the minister. Rachel gasped at the rudeness. She apologised loudly, John fumed, and the line of parishioners came to a halt.

Matthew squeezed acrid-smelling model cement on to the Lancaster bomber's wing. Carefully, he spread the transparent substance with a matchstick until it glistened evenly around the base. He hovered over the fuselage and was about to insert the wing when he heard a familiar voice rumbling quietly in the house. Swiftly, he went to the wall and switched off the electric light, plunging the old stable into darkness. After a few moments, when his eyes adjusted, he could make out a few of his models around the walls, and the Vulcan bomber mounted on the old saddle tree. He returned to his stool and sat in the gloom doing nothing, while the wasted glue dried on the base of the Lancaster's wing.

Ten minutes later, he heard the back door of the house. Footsteps clipped briskly on the concrete path.

'Matthew?' A head peered through the stable doorway, and saw him.

Matthew went to the switch and flooded the workshed with light. He stood stolidly at the wall near the switch, resentful, then somehow glad, that the minister had found him with his childhood hobby. The minister bent at the waist to avoid scraping his head on the door frame, entered, and advanced to within six feet of the workbench. He cast his eyes around the cluttered space, at the broken old fishbins and rusty grapnels, the empty boxes, an old saddle, and at the dozens of model aircraft.

'I hear you're back to work on the *Phoenix* next week.'

'Yes.'

'Nothing like a bit of hard work to swing the keel to centre.'

'Yes.' One part of Matthew clamoured to confide in this old family friend who was so knowledgeable abbout the ways and wiles of life. But then he resented feeling like some kind of criminal. He stood slowly, faced the minister squarely.

'Well, Matthew, I'll not beat about the bush. I think you know why I'm here. I was hoping that you would come to see me first. Or, at least, that you would confide in your father.' Matthew's face tightened cynically. The minister regarded him gravely. 'Your behaviour today, Matthew: it doesn't offend me, but the thought of what might have caused it makes me fear for you.'

'I wasn't feeling well.'

Robert shook his head irritably. 'My boy. Neither of us is stupid. You are obviously under great mental stress. Wouldn't it be easier if you unburdened your thoughts?'

'It's nothing.' Matthew leaned back against the wall, attempting to conceal his surprise. Surely Mr McKay couldn't know.

The minister sighed. 'Then I will be direct. I believe your troubles relate to the inner voices and visions you heard as a child.'

Matthew swallowed, blinked.

'Do you see or hear what appears to be your grandfather?'

'No.' Tersely, but emphatically.

'And what of the one you used to call Nathaniel?'

'No.'

'Tell me.' The concerned gaze bored down at Matthew.

'No!' Matthew protested. 'I can't tell you anything, Mr McKay. Leave me alone.'

'Matthew, Matthew.' Robert shook his head slowly. He roughened his voice. 'Look at me, boy. Look at me. It is obvious that you are trying to stand on the edge of a very sharp knife. Am I correct?' Matthew swallowed again. He nodded, reluctantly, cautiously, and the minister went on. 'Don't you remember what lies on the wrong side of the blade? Surely you can't have forgotten the disharmony that evil influence sowed into your family, into your school, into the congregation?'

'Don't. It's not like that!'

'You cannot turn your back on it,' Robert snapped. 'By the Lord Almighty, sir, you cannot hide your head under a blanket for such as this! You of all people. Could you look Jesus in the eye right now and tell Him what you're contemplating?'

'I don't know. I can't talk about it!' Matthew groaned. He screwed his eyes shut and moved his head as if the electric light were too bright. Moths had come in out of the night and were pinging against the bulb.

The minister fell to silence. Nothing would be gained by making the boy feel cornered. He turned and looked out through the doorway to the street where a horse was clopping by, its rider wrapped to anonymity against the evening chill. Something had to be done. He spoke again, this time in a reflective voice, still looking outside.

'You're a boy trying to grapple with a problem that has destroyed mature adults. I dislike scaring you, but your situation is too serious for me to risk mincing words.' He turned on Matthew suddenly with soft but urgent tone. 'Do you have any idea what happens to some who practise conversing with spirits? I'll tell you. I have seen mature, normally responsible adults committed to a mental asylum, foaming at the mouth after inviting spirits to speak through them. Possession! And that's only what you risk here on earth. What can happen to your soul when you die is unimaginable!' He watched Matthew narrowly, and knew that he had hit something on the mark.

'It's not like that.'

'Not *yet*,' Robert rejoined. He put his hands behind him and paced back and forth once. Time to press the advantage. Think. Think. He stopped. 'I know you, Matthew. Your motives are good. You would not be tempted by anything transparently false. If I am not mistaken, this Nathaniel behaves like a wise being. He speaks to you with words of great wisdom. Am I correct?'

For a moment, Robert thought he had succeeded. Matthew's expression filled with a desire to blurt out everything, to get it over with, but the words were checked by the lips and the mouth clamped firmly shut. Now the minister was deeply worried.

135

Normally, Matthew would have responded long ago to reasoned argument. What to do? Leave him now? But the prospect of this bright, promising young man, young friend — he wanted to say — making a terrible, irreversible commitment of the heart filled the minister with deep dismay. No. He must give it one more try. For a brief moment longer, Robert prayed inwardly for guidance. Then he turned to Matthew.

'Have you forgotten so soon? There are only two supernatural sources of guidance: God, and Satan. And since man's only path to God's wisdom is through scripture and prayer, any other supernatural path *must therefore be of Satan*, the master of lies and deceit!' He gave Matthew no time to answer. 'Or perhaps you have already begun to doubt the infallibility of the word of God as revealed in the gospel!'

There! The youthful face had turned bleak, stricken by the further loss of certainty. Now there was hope, Robert knew. He would have savoured its warmth, but was too distressed at the pain he was causing the young man. Too young. Too young. But it had to be done. The minister strode to the door and turned for the last word.

'Deuteronomy, Matthew. Chapter eighteen, verses ten to twelve: "There shall not be found among you . . . a consulter with familiar spirits . . . For *all that do these things are an object of disgust and horror to the Lord*"!'

An hour later, Rachel Fleming looked nervously at her husband and took a steaming mug of hot chocolate out of the kitchen and down the corridor. She knocked timidly on Matthew's bedroom door, and hearing an indecipherable sound she went in. He was on the bed, on his back with a hand over his face. She offered him the drink without speaking and hovered while he took it, anxious to comfort him. But as she stood there, she realised for the first time, that she was not only afraid for her son: she was afraid *of* him.

'Mum?' Matthew's hand gripped her elbow. When she looked down, she saw that his eyes were close to tears. When had she last seen him cry? Her little boy, years ago. 'Mum, why did it happen to me?'

'I don't know, Matthew.' She didn't know what to say to him. She wanted to sit and cuddle him. Suddenly she mourned,

'It's my fault. I'm to blame for encouraging you when you were small.'

'Mum? Nathaniel says —'

'Stop!' Rachel's whole body shook in a swift spasm. 'I don't want to hear about it. Not ever again.' She sat quickly beside him and took his hands. 'Matthew, it's evil. It's wrong. You've got to cast it out of you. You've got to confess your sin before God and cleanse —'

'Mum! Listen —'

'No!' Rachel was on her feet. 'I won't hear it! You mustn't ever speak such things in this house.'

NINE

Margaret Crocker's spoon returned, full, to its place. She pointed out the window across the road, to where Jennifer Pringle was opening Emily Nisbet's gate.

'There she is. That's all of them...' Without faltering, or changing her voice in any way, she cracked a hand down on the fingers of her ten-year-old son Colin, who was reaching for an after-dinner mint. '... Same day as last week, same time.'

'Can't see what they'd have in common,' Jimmy said, diverted for a moment from his daydreams of wedded bliss with Angela.

'Beats me,' Gordon grunted without interest. He glared at Colin, silently promising terrible wrath if there was another attempt on the mints. While he was at it, he also spared a warning frown for his two daughters, Sonia and Stephanie, who then pouted with downcast eyes.

'They're all misfits, that's what!' Margaret said tartly. 'No, don't get me wrong; I'd be the last to deny that Matthew's a fine boy. But you know what he used to be like, and you know how strange he's been lately. But what are they up to? That's what I want to know.' Gordon said that other people's doings were other people's business. Margaret hurrumphed and resumed eating her brandy trifle. But ten minutes later, she detected something else.

'There! I told you! They're drawing the curtains. And the sun hardly set!'

'Curiosity killed the cat,' muttered Gordon impatiently.

'I want to get down,' Colin said.

'Say *please*!' thundered his father, making everyone wince. 'Little guttersnipe. Manners of a hog.'

'Please, then.' Colin left for the hallway.

Jimmy was looking at his father with concern. 'You wouldn't shout like that when Angela's here, would you?'

138

'Blue blazes!' Gordon slapped his hand on the table, making the coffee cups bounce on their saucers. 'He's ashamed of his own father. Now you're engaged to Angela, suddenly your own father's not good enough for you, eh? Just you watch your step, sonny boy. You're still living under my roof.' He slurped at his coffee, scowling into the cup.

'It's his secrecy that annoys me,' said Margaret.

'Whose?'

'Matthew's. I mean, that silly nonsense about blowing up Parliament. And that funny business at church. He's up to something. Silk to a sack, they're up to something.' Gordon told her to leave the subject alone. Sonia and Stephanie began to clear away dishes. And shortly, Stephanie spoke from in front of the kitchen in a loud, aggrieved tone.

'Mum, Colin's gone out. Why aren't we allowed out?'

'Oh, drat the boy. He's more trouble than the rest of you put together. Where's he gone?'

'*I* don't know,' Stephanie said sulkily.

'You told us what you are, but *who* are you? What do you look like, if you look like anything at all? What do you do?'

Nathaniel smiled. Tonight, the expressions conveyed by the eyes found their way into the rest of Matthew's face. The face was considerably more mobile, reflecting subtler shades of feeling, emphasis and humour. The smile showed in the wrinkles at the corners of the eyes, and pulled into the cheek muscles. He moved his head at will now, and could lean forward or backwards with ease.

'Let me tell you first what I do *not* do. I do not rap on walls and tables. I do not normally open creaking doors in musty corridors. Nor do I make a habit of moaning and rattling in old cellars.'

'We get the picture,' Jack grinned.

'Excellent. Now. Describing my existence in your words is something like trying to make a tree out of pebbles from the shore, but I will try. I have no one shape to describe to you. The word "spirit" is a good one because it does convey the idea of an essence capable of assuming a variety of forms. However, I appeared to the child Matthew in one form only and became recognisable to him by that form: robe, sandals, long hair... all

139

of which you associate with biblical times.'

D'Arcy raised his head from the mat and held it poised. He snorted and stood, looking at the back wall.

'Siddown,' Jack growled.

'It'll be a possum,' Emily said. 'They get into the garden.'

'Siddown, D'Arcy!' The sheepdog blew through his nostrils and lay down, head between paws, reproachful eyes on Nathaniel.

'I am Matthew's greater self. He is one of my aspects: a part of me, yet with his own independent existence . . .' He looked around at the puzzled faces. '. . . The tree is part of the mountain, but has its own separate identity. The mountain is greater than the sum of its trees, rocks and earth, yet has no existence without them. It *is* all its parts. And *I* am not a nebulous mist swirling in nothingness! I am my various forms. There is no separation between me and my creations!'

Abruptly, Jennifer stopped taking notes. She, Jack and Emily looked at each other in consternation. Jack eyed Nathaniel with suspicion. But Nathaniel continued cheerfully. 'You think I am about to claim that I am God. Not so. Instead, I claim a fundamental property of the universe. Creation permeates all existence. It is not the property of a remote deity or a jealous god.'

He paused. There was little softening in the expressions of his audience. He shifted an arm, the first time they had seen this happen. A hand came up for emphasis. Four pairs of eyes watched the hand, three human, one canine.

'You, too, though you are not aware of it, are creators. The earth that you know is like a classroom in which you are the creators of your experience. Before birth you *choose* which corner of the classroom you will occupy, you *choose* your classmates and, with their cooperation, create your own lessons. Listen. You are responsible for everything that physical world does to you.'

Jennifer slapped her pencil down. 'Just hang on a minute. That's . . . that's . . . You can't mean that literally!'

'I do.'

'But . . .' The patent absurdity of it annoyed her. '*I'm* responsible if a horse runs me down in the road? *Emily* is responsible for her arthritis? That's callous!'

'It would be callous if I were allocating blame. But I am not. What I do is direct your attention to both cause and effect

140

by pointing to one place: your self. Of course you do not say, "Today I'll look for a horse to trample me." Nor did Emily get out of bed one morning and say, "I think this morning I'll develop arthritis." All the same, experience does begin in the self. Let me point out that it is no coincidence that Emily is now recovering from her arthritis at a time when she feels better able to manoeuvre socially.'

Emily frowned at her hip.

Jennifer said tartly, 'Are you sure you weren't a middle-class Anglo-Saxon male in your last life?'

For the first time, Nathaniel grinned widely. He straightened and said simply, 'Watch.'

They did. Nathaniel's eyes didn't seem focused on anything. For a few seconds, nothing. While they waited, D'Arcy's chin came off the floor and he whined. Jack growled at him. Then Matthew's face began to change yet again. No one feature altered; it was more a subtle shifting of muscle lines and demeanor. The cheeks hollowed, the mouth and lips seemed to thicken, the eyebrow line softened, the eyes grew large and luminous and were downcast in humility. For perhaps half a minute she was there, glancing up once, twice, at Emily and Jennifer, unable to raise her gaze to meet Jack's. Then she faded, dissolved away, and Nathaniel returned.

'Who was she?' breathed Emily.

'Me. In one of my most recent lives.'

'Yes. I get the point,' Jennifer mumbled.

'In your world you have entered into a self-induced trance. In this trance, your skin seems to be a border between "you" and "not you". You feel disconnected from your environment.'

A twanging sound penetrated from the back yard. The dog's ears stood straight up. Emily said, 'They get through the fence.' The ears came down.

Nathaniel spoke to Jennifer. 'Think of it this way. You are like walking movie projectors, projecting your internal dramas on to the environment so that they play about you. The trick is to learn how to consciously direct your own movie.'

When the interruption came, Jimmy was deeply immersed in thoughts of Angela. He was on his bed, gazing at one of his numerous photographs of her, with the future laid out quite clearly in his mind: the cloudless skies on the day of the wedding, the glances of admiration and respect at the ceremony itself, and some day a baby. Yes, a baby girl just as beautiful as her mother. His daughter would be born in the village hospital while the bellbirds sang in the porch honeysuckle. That was how it was going to be. God wanted that for him because only God knew what Jimmy Crocker was really worth.

Someone tapped on the window behind him. He jumped, startled, then glared at the small figure outside in the dark. He wrenched the sash up, ready to whop his brother over the ear. But Colin had his fingers to his lips and looked excited and mysterious.

'Let me in,' he demanded. 'If you let me come in through your room, I'll tell you what I saw in the witch's place. It was real weird... spooky!'

'Big deal,' Jimmy grunted. There were times when he imagined his fingers around his little brother's neck. The little sod seemed to exist just to give the family a bad name. Like the time Colin combined his fascination with practical jokes and with fires by putting pig manure into a paper bag and setting it alight on the neighbour's front porch. The thought that Colin might one day try such a stunt in Angela's presence was almost unendurable. Really, strangling was too good for him.

'Honest. I saw them through a curtain.'

'Typical,' sneered Jimmy. 'Tell that one to Dad and see how fast he whips his belt off. All right, come in. But if you're pushing a slide, I'll wipe you out, boy. I'll nail your feet to the garage wall.'

Colin clambered in.

A few minutes later he left and sneaked down to his bedroom.

Another two minutes and Jimmy went through to the lounge. He told his parents he was going for a walk, then left via the front door so as to avoid going past Colin's window. He went immediately to the empty ground three doors down from the Nisbet place, walked through to the bush, and shortly he was at the fence along Emily Nisbet's back yard.

Nathaniel gestured earnestly. 'Satan does not exist, there is no such place as hell and the universe does not revolve around a struggle between good and evil. There *is* no evil. In spite of your

142

wars, your genocides, your traders in human suffering, your rapists and strangers, there is no such thing as a force whose motivation is to oppose good. Dig down to the root of all evil and you will find nothing there.'

D'Arcy's eyes opened slowly. He sniffed at the air, curious.

'Creation progresses along a one-way path. If you like, call those ahead of you "evil" and those behind "good", but both are moving in the same direction; they are not opposites.'

Jack said dryly, 'If you strangle little old ladies for their money, seems to me that's going to put your progress back aways.'

'Not so. In the eye-blink that is a single lifetime, you can only, by such actions, automatically sow the seeds of progress for both persecutor and victim.'

'So it's *all right* to strangle little old ladies?' Jennifer said hotly.

The dark eyes glinted.

But then D'Arcy was on his feet, a single bark shattering the intimacy of the room. He leapt to the back door, body tensed, throat rumbling. Jack swore, but in the silence that followed, it became clear that no one was thinking of possums. He levered himself to his feet. 'Heel,' he ordered, and opened the door. Nothing. D'Arcy whined. Jack went out into the near dark of the late evening, the dog coiled and twisting eagerly in his wake, pining to be set free. In a few minutes they returned. The dog lay by the door, restless. Jack shook his head at the unspoken questions of the two women, but he was frowning as he lowered himself into his seat.

'What was that?' Jennifer demanded of Nathaniel, who had watched impassively throughout. 'Was there someone out there?'

'Yes.'

Emily's breathing quickened. Memory rushed in: all those years of leaving the door unlocked, half-hoping . . . She went to the window, and though somehow afraid to disturb the curtains, closed the gap between them.

Jack was looking at Nathaniel. After a while he spoke softly, almost as if musing to himself: 'You didn't warn us.' Nathaniel nodded, saying nothing. Jack thought about that for long seconds. He turned to the others and spoke in much the same tone. 'Matthew said his parents and the minister have guessed that Nathaniel is back, so it's just a matter of time before they know exactly what we're up to in here.'

'What do you suggest?' Nathaniel asked in reasonable tone.

They looked at him for some time, as if he were newly a stranger.

'What about Matthew?' Jennifer asked, a pulse of distrust sharpening her voice. 'How is he?'

'He is even more distressed than last time. He asks himself if I am good or evil. He wants me to be a perfect, all-wise being, but is tortured by the possibility that I am really a resourceful deceiver.'

There was silence. The three sat before him, wary, hoping for reassurance, finding none. They eyed each other, weighing doubts. D'Arcy rose and padded backwards and forwards in front of the door.

'My place,' Jack heard himself say. 'Next week.'

Briefly, a smile touched one corner of Nathaniel's mouth. He gathered the slow assent of the two women into the sweep of his gaze, first Emily, and a long breath later, Jennifer. He said, 'Beware the belief in evil. It can be a useful orientation for those seeking the first spiritual signposts, but it quickly becomes a liability.'

TEN

This time the dream went further and he moaned in his sleep.

Out in the chill fog, a light appeared, a patch of incandescent gold, sown in the fathomless grey shroud. It flooded him with warmth, filled his mind with an irresistible promise, seduced and won his promise in return. His pulse quickened the internal tides... thwoomp... thwoomp... thwoomp... He strained towards the siren light. He cried out to his hands and knees to crawl faster; but they would not be hurried. They padded methodically on, scraping on the rough stones.

He studied the pattern of blood left by his misshapen thumb but still it would not tell if he was ascending or descending.

Jennifer Pringle appeared off to one side. She was naked. With one hand she held a doll to her breast and he thought it curious that the doll was not suckling. With the other hand she beckoned him, beckoned him, eyes wide, lips parted in mute pleading. Her skin was silken, her nipples dark and swollen, her pubic hair glistening. And he saw then that he himself was dressed in a flour sack which was unravelling as he moved on, exposing more and more of his body. He tried to call out to her that he couldn't stop, but found that he was unable to make sounds come from his throat.

Soon, still beckoning, she passed from his sight as he crawled on towards the light.

ELEVEN

Peter Newberry owned and ran Waiata's grocery and tea rooms. He was forty and very fat. He had decided early in life that the only way to be very fat and to enjoy any kind of social acceptance was to behave in a way which convinced everyone else of their own normality. Carefully managed, such behaviour was a community service, and he had developed this undeclared social work to a fine art. When he was angry, for instance, he was able to make his face look remarkably like a dried-up and dangerous lemon, or, and this was the closest he dared come to eccentricity, he would burst into a rendition of the 'Song of the Volga Boatmen'. No one dared laugh, not if they hoped to continue patronising the tea rooms.

He kept alive a century-old Waiata custom of serving Devonshire tea in the late afternoon. And he was very good at it: so good that he earned the valuable support of those Women's Guild ladies who could trace their lineage back through the first four colonising ships. He had never married. He gave his love, instead, to the tribe of cats that roamed his home and the tea rooms — fourteen of them and counting. He loved children. That is, he loved them until they turned into adolescents. He then hated them. As he told them repeatedly, if baboons had money, he'd prefer to serve baboons. And Waiata's young folk hated him with equal enthusiasm, while continuing to use the tea rooms as the centre of town. The arrangement was dynamic, on some days very dynamic, but on the whole stable enough. 'Dumpling' Newberry always had the last say.

Before Jennifer Pringle came in, Peter was in a particularly irascible mood. School always got out early on Wednesday, for sport, which invariably meant that a dozen of the adolescent beasts would slither away and play hookey in his tea rooms. Half of his tables had gone to them already. To cap it all, Peter fumed, that no-good, shiftless bum Sidney Irwin and his crowd were feeding at another table. Only one table had real people — three farmers' wives from Le Bons Bay. But his mood improved the moment Jennifer appeared. It wasn't that he liked Jennifer any more than the other teenagers, it was just that he enjoyed the perversity of making one of their outcasts welcome.

Jennifer sat at the remaining table, facing the sea. She placed a full shopping basket on the floor beside the chair, ignoring the hush that entered with her. Already, she regretted the impulse to stop and rest at her old haunt. But she was committed now. Behind her, the three farmers' wives stood and left and she resisted the impulse to turn and check on the level of the tea in their cups.

Peter affectionately cuffed a cat stalking the cream bowl, then came out from behind the counter and waddled right up to Jennifer's table. This unheard-of courtesy prolonged the hush. In a loud and cheerful voice he inquired about her health, and whether or not she'd like a spot of Devonshire. Jennifer, disconcerted, said yes though she had been thinking about a milkshake. Peter departed, grandly ignoring the catcalls and the hand-shielded smirks. In the buzz, she heard Sidney Irwin's voice and groaned inwardly.

Sidney sniffed the air. He said, 'Bad smell in here.'

Smirks and giggles. Doggedly, Jennifer admired the view.

The door opened. Matthew Fleming walked in and headed for the counter. But he caught sight of Jennifer, changed course half way, and plonked himself down in the chair opposite her.

'Hi. D'you mind?' His face was tired and strained.

Jennifer spoke under her breath, without changing her expression. 'Go away. You'll just make it worse.' Matthew looked around, then understood. A muscle on his upper lip twitched. Jennifer spoke with more intensity. 'If you make a fuss again, I'll get up and leave.'

That had the desired effect: Matthew's expression eased reluctantly into neutral.

Peter swayed out from the counter again, bearing a tray of tea and scones and bowls of cream and jam. He talked to Matthew with another display of boundless empathy and brought an extra cup and saucer for him. Then he went back behind the counter looking smug.

147

'Christ, Peter.' Sidney Irwin's voice. 'What'd you want to leave a dirty mattress in here for? Can't you keep the place clean and tidy?'

Matthew's nostrils flared. He began to stand. Jennifer hissed at him. But then a sound from behind the counter halted them both. All eyes turned to Peter as a moan of loathing and disgust quivered from his mouth. He started to wheeze. His hand went behind him and reappeared with a wooden spoon. Then he waded out from the counter and advanced on Irwin, swishing the spoon through the air and bellowing.

'You oiking swine! You noisome little snod-gurk! This place was clean until you brought your filthy blaspheming mouth into it! Get out! *Get out!* . . .'

Sidney went out backwards, amazed at the results of his miscalculation. He attempted to retain some dignity in front of his friends and the schoolgirls by advising Peter not to expect to unload any more of his putrid food on him or his friends from now on, or on anyone else once the word got out. But the effort wasn't very successful, partly because most of it was delivered from the road and partly because his sandals came flying out after him, one of them hitting his shoulder. His friends came shortly after.

Inside, Peter shouted truculently at his remaining customers. 'Anyone else? Anyone else want to blaspheme? Anyone else want to tell me how to run my place?' He gave his spoon another couple of swishes at the grinning faces and the overemphatic shaking heads, then returned to his place behind the counter. Soon he began to hum, a sure sign that 'Dumpling' Newberry was pleased with himself and with the way the world was going round.

As Sidney's group moved away past the window, one of them shouted to attract attention. He mimed flying a toy plane in the air, made childish engine noises, and called out to enquire when Daddy was going to buy Matthikins a teddy. Then they were gone, and with them much of the hostile atmosphere. The tea rooms chatter returned to normal.

'You think I'm a child too?' Matthew muttered, still smarting.

'Don't be so self-centred,' Jennifer said crossly. But as Matthew's face emptied of expression, she laid a hand on his forearm. 'I'm sorry. That was nasty of me. I'm only feeling sorry for myself. It's really great of you to sit with me, even if you are asking for trouble.' Matthew looked down at her hand and she took it away. They ate their scones and drank their tea in silence. After a while, Jennifer said, 'Has McKay had another go at you?'

He nodded. 'They're putting the pressure on. But they don't know about Wednesday nights.' He tried to make it sound like a mildly amusing game of wit and deception, but tension thinned his voice.

'Just ignore them,' Jennifer said indignantly. 'It's your life. It's not —'

'You think I don't know that!' Matthew's voice, though almost down to a whisper, turned fierce. 'But what if they're right! The Bible can't be wrong, can it? If it's wrong, it can't be God's word, so there wouldn't be any point to Christianity! What if Nathaniel really is from the devil?' Suddenly there was moisture threatening to show in his eyes. 'And I get this dream.... I keep getting this dream —'

'Stop it,' she hissed, alarmed. 'Not here! Control yourself.'

They sipped the last of their tea while he calmed. Behind the counter, Peter Newberry was laying out saucers to feed his cats. He poured milk into each, dropped a dollop of cream into the milk, then laid the saucers out on the floor. One moment there was only a single cat in sight, the next there were at least a dozen converging on the plates.

In a few minutes Jennifer and Matthew were outside. They stood awkwardly. Matthew turned to go.

'Just hang on, O.K.?' Jennifer said.

'Yeah.' Matthew was disgusted with himself.

'Thanks for sitting with me. That was nice of you.'

Their glances crossed as Matthew shrugged. In the same moment, a strong picture of the two of them with their arms round each other passed through Jennifer's mind. She was astonished at herself. She was supposed to be finished with men, and Matthew barely made that category anyway. He was so immature. But the image was there: so vividly in place that she knew she was going to blush. She turned away, furious, speaking with clipped words.

'See you tonight.' She began to walk away. 'Eight o'clock. Past the last farm, right?'

'Yeah,' Matthew said bleakly. 'Right.'

Early afternoon. A launch pulled away from the wharf. It whined a mile and a quarter across the harbour, then slowed to an idle under the lava cliffs that rose out of the far side. At the helm, Gordon Crocker surveyed the work that was fast turning the cliffs into a quarry. Soon, he glanced impatiently at Jimmy beside him.

'Well. What do you think?'

'Not bad,' Jimmy said. But his tone masked distraction.

Gordon was irritated. This scheme, after all, was going to put them on the map. The name Crocker Quarries would be known from Cape Reinga to Stewart Island. They would be wealthy. Jimmy would be wealthy. He'd be able to buy Angela another silver spoon to go in her pert little mouth. But he was so starry-eyed these days, he didn't seem to bother about mere earthly things. Well, marriage would cure him of that.

Gordon soothed his ruffled pride by pointing out the details and explaining them, though Jimmy had seen the plans a dozen times. Undulating near the top of the almost three-hundred-foot cliffs, was a layer of fossilised wood. Ninety million years ago it had been dense bush, until the moment of inundation by superheated lava. The red, black and yellow tints in the wood-stone were so richly intermingled that a geologist, brought out especially, had declared the stone to be the finest ever found in the country. It was, Gordon felt, the next thing to owning a gold mine. Definite orders were already in the in-tray, from jewellery chains, craft shops, craftsmen who normally worked only with greenstone jade, and even from builders, who had in mind luxury fireplaces for wealthy clients.

At the foot of the cliffs was a half-mile-long ledge of even older lava, which had once been under water, but now formed a natural road a few feet above the high-water mark. A bulldozer squealed along the strip, clearing it of loose rocks. In the water off the right-hand end of the ledge, sixty black manuka piles bristled — the beginnings of a loading jetty. A dozen men clambered over them; and a crane waved above, swinging the next rough-hewn cross-beam drunkenly towards its place. The foundations for the office-lunchroom-bunkhouse had already been laid, twenty yards back from the half-built jetty. The work was about on schedule. By the time the diamond saw sank into its first fossilised rock, Gordon would be in hock up to his ears.

But he knew it would all come back, a hundred times over.

Jimmy wasn't listening.

'Look,' Gordon demanded. 'You see that shoulder between the pier and the cliff? Well, when we're ready for another load, we trundle all the machinery behind the shoulder, let rip with the jelly, and the stone just drops down on to the strip for us. Child's play. What doesn't come down, we push over with the dozer. Course all the rubbish comes down with —'

'Dad.'

'. . . the good stuff. What?'

'I've got something to tell you.'

'Oh yeah?' Gordon jogged his son's arm in sudden amusement. 'About the wedding night? Thought you were supposed to ask me, not tell me. But I guess you know all about it already, eh?' He winked. Man to man.

'Don't talk like that,' Jimmy said hotly. 'Angela's not like that!'

'All right, all right. Just ribbing,' Gordon said hastily. Incredible how Jimmy couldn't see Angela for the brilliance of her halo. It seemed to Gordon that the girl only went to church because Jimmy did. 'Well, what's so all-fire important?'

Jimmy began. He had known for days that it was his duty to tell the church elders. Not an easy duty, since it involved confessing that he had peered through a neighbour's window. The morning after, he had threatened to rip Colin's ears off if anyone found out. But really there was no choice. Hadn't Mr McKay told him that he must not go into marriage with sinful blemishes on his mind and heart? No, there would be no blemishes. No faults. Nothing could be allowed to mar the perfection of the wedding day.

A few seconds later, Gordon Crocker switched off the launch engine and gave Jimmy his complete and, at first, unbelieving attention. He didn't interrupt, not even when Jimmy came to how the discovery was made. Then he questioned his son tersely on several points, especially on what had been overheard, and finally fell silent. Jimmy waited, relieved at first, but then increasingly nervous. What if his father had to tell the other elders who supplied the information? It might get back to Angela.

'What are you going to do?'

'Shut up. Let me think.' Gordon started the launch and idled it parallel to the cliffs, holding an acknowledging hand up to men who waved from the shore. 'Right across the road. Right under our noses,' he muttered.

Jimmy said nothing.

'This is Wednesday,' Gordon snapped suddenly. 'They'll be doing it *tonight*. It's taken you all week to find me?'

Jimmy's regret was mingled with pride at having overcome the temptation to cowardice.

Gordon leaned his thigh against the throttle and swung the launch towards the distant sprinkle of colour that was Waiata. He shouted above the noise of the motor. 'You're a bloody fool, Jimmy, but you've got guts, I'll give you that. You did right to tell me.'

The wheel spoke of the *Phoenix* passed swiftly under John Fleming's hands, left to right. The trawler nosed to starboard, pointing its bow at pile after pile of the wharf. His left hand swept the reverse bar into gear, his right spun the wheel back the other way. White water thrashed and rumbled under the stern, frothed back into the piles, then the trawler was nestling gently against the wharf opposite the diesel pump. The fisherman had taken to halting the *Phoenix* so that the fuel-tank inlet was as close as possible to being exactly under the nozzle of the town's new fuel pump. It was a quiet, but favourite, piece of showmanship.

Two inches out, the best yet.

Above him, the fish-store manager eyed the nozzle and the inlet, shook his head and suggested, straight-faced, that John have another run at it. John grinned to himself. He and his temporary hand winched the catch on to the wharf. Twenty-five bins, mostly preferred species. Not bad. Not good. After refuelling, the deckhand and the fish-store manager walked the mooring lines as he slid the *Phoenix* forward to an overnight berth against the wharf. An early start tomorrow. He paid the hand for the last time and saw him off the boat with mixed feelings. The farmer's son had not had Matthew's experience, but then Matthew was an unknown quantity himself these days. He might be physically O.K. to start tomorrow, but there was no saying what his mental state would be. John loosed both lines and went below to shut down.

When he emerged, Gordon Crocker was on the wharf above. 'Can I come aboard?'

'Hah!' John waved him down, then took a second look at his expression. 'Something wrong?'

'Very. Sorry to bring you this, John, but I've got some bad news for you.' He looked up at the wharf. 'Can we go below or into the wheelhouse?' They went to the wheelhouse.

Ten minutes later, Gordon left the wharf alone. A few minutes after that, John Fleming set out for home. His face was like cold granite and he ignored anyone who spoke to him.

Matthew was at the kitchen table, reading. So for the first time, John neglected to kiss his wife. He stood in the doorway with gaze fixed furiously and fearfully at his son. Rachel froze, a dish mop in one hand and a dripping plate in the other. Matthew stood slowly. There was no doubt in his mind. His father had found out about the meetings. How much did he know? Rachel asked a question but her words were lost. John trod slowly forward, until only the table separated him from Matthew. He spoke in a hoarse whisper.

'Go to your room, boy. Until I've decided what to do with you.'

Matthew felt as though his feet were fastened to the floor.

'Go to your room.' Softer, more menacing.

Matthew backed slowly to the kitchen door.

'John? What is it? It's not him talking to the Pringle girl, is it?'

'Hah!' John swung on her with an almost falsetto laugh. 'That! That's not the half of it. That's nothing to what ...' His mouth closed and opened as more and more of the implications occurred to him. He turned his gaze back to Matthew, who had stopped in the doorway, and this time his voice shook. 'You can forget about going to the Nisbet woman's place tonight. You'll be staying under this roof until it's sorted out. Now, if you're still my son, get — to — your — room!'

Matthew took a long look at both his parents. Then he turned away down the corridor. His movements were drawn out, not defiant, but curiously like slow motion.

Rachel saw that her husband was close to panic. She took herself in hand and lent all her powers to calming him sufficiently for an explanation. And after she had it, they talked on — he

153

explosively, she with forced calm — trying to see a way out. But whichever way they looked at it, nothing was going to prevent the town finding out. Nothing was a secret in Waiata. And this one would already be sliding over the fences. Then the same thought occurred to them both at the same time. John sent a chair flying and ran down the corridor. Rachel heard him fling open Matthew's door. Silence. He came back slowly. He looked drained. His voice was flat and colourless.

'He's gone.' He leaned on the table, staring down sightlessly at Matthew's aeroplane album. After a while, his face grew flushed and his eyes went small and hard. 'You know what this means, don't you? It's not just him. It's us he's ruining as well. If we don't do something, life won't be worth living in this town.' He began to breathe like a man who has been jogging steadily for some distance. He picked up the aeroplane album and flung it against the wall.

'John, it won't do any good to —'

Without even a glance at her, he went out the back door. She watched fearfully through the window until she saw that he was hacking a length of stick off the willow tree. She ran out to meet him as he came back, fastened her hands on his arm and sobbed at him.

'It's too late, John! He's too big. It won't work any more.'

But he threw her off with one sweep of his muscular arms and she stumbled weeping into the house. With stick in hand, he strode down the drive and turned on to the road towards the waterfront and Emily Nisbet's cottage.

TWELVE

The full moon rose out of the summit ahead. The shimmering disc cast shafts of fine gold through the bush foliage, penetrating at times to the inky black of the stream. Tilda, the hack between the shafts, plodded steadily up the track to Pudding Flat and the buggy's Tilly lantern swayed in the still warm air, unlit, unneeded.

Matthew seethed with impatience. He moved from side to side on the padded leather of the rear seat, nervous, uncommunicative until they reached D'Arcy's rock at the beginning of the upper valley. There, the black silhouette of the waiting dog led him to explain the game to Jennifer and Emily. After that, he talked endlessly with excitable good humour, finding will and wit for jokes that had the women breathless with laughter. When Jennifer asked if he was all right, he only cracked a joke about his health. She let the matter drop because the memory of the end of their meeting earlier in the day was too fresh in her mind.

Once on Pudding Flat, they stopped for D'Arcy to frisk around them and eventually jump on board. Then they urged Tilda to a trot. They swayed across the flats and through the oaks and walnuts towards a bright orange spark that grew bigger as they approached and began to pulse and flick.

'What's that, D'Arcy?' Matthew asked. 'Has Jack lit a fire for us?'

D'Arcy acknowledged his name with a single bark. He stood with his hind legs on the back seat and forelegs on the front between Emily and Jennifer, allowing the breeze to lift the long hair in the white ruff around his neck. Occasionally he tried to lick Jennifer's face, or sniffed after a stick of dried rosemary in Emily's handbag. When they pulled up by the hut and put Tilda on to a long tether, D'Arcy raced about in high delight, in and out between the buggy wheels, around his kennel, and once over

155

the top of the other kennels to reassert his authority.

Jack had lit a fire down by the stream. By the time they arrived, he had a stack of wood waiting beside it, along with four log seats, each with its own sack for comfort. Delighted exclamations greeted this arrangement for the evening, and Jack hid his pleasure behind gruffness.

Before long, they were seated and quiet, while Matthew prepared. D'Arcy, too, settled to gaze at the fire, while the other sheepdogs yapped their final frustrations at not being loosed, then lay down to watch from their kennels. Twenty yards behind the semi-circle of humans, their eyes reflected the flames. The firewood, macrocarpa, had been cut in the late spring, and every now and then pockets of sap would set the fire to crackling and spitting.

Matthew was still alert when they heard splashing and thumping in the stream on the other side of the fire. Small, dark bodies wavered uncertainly at the water's edge, blinking at the flames. Jennifer looked swiftly at Jack.

'Penguins,' he explained quickly. 'They roost under the shearing shed. And you'd better brace yourselves. When they get back to the chicks, there'll be a hell of a din.'

The penguins detoured the fire and the log seats, waddling in a wide arc, stopping every few paces to look at the flames and wave their white-edged flippers at each other in surprise. In anticipation of their arrival, cheeping sounds started up from under the shearing shed. Half a minute later, the sound swelled and burst into a chorus of blood-curdling shrieks. At the fire Matthew and Jack grinned at the expressions of the two women.

'That's them?' Jennifer was aghast. 'It's like someone torturing little children. You sure they're not killing the chicks instead of feeding them?'

'Nope. They're enjoying themselves. And it'll be even better when the adults join in the sing-song a bit later.'

Matthew put his mind to relaxing. It was much more difficult tonight. The disquiet of the other three was almost palpable. The day's events clamoured at him, demanding some screening mental or physical action. But he was better practised now, more familiar with the mental side-step necessary to make way for Nathaniel. It wasn't concentration, as much as letting the mind drift in a controlled direction. If a thought comes in, don't worry,

156

stand back from it, watch it pass by. Stand back, watch it pass by. Wait for the right one...

'I'm ready,' he said.

Emily prayed briefly, focusing all attention. And shortly Nathaniel was with them.

High above Waiata and above Pudding Flat, just below the summit of the central ridge of Banks Peninsula, were two very tired and disgruntled men. Tom and Alan Glubb had spent the day in the backblocks, bagging protected wood pigeons. But in the mid afternoon they had lost their bearings in thick bush. They'd climbed trees without success. They'd gone downhill, only to find themselves in a remote bay on the wrong side of the peninsula. Then they'd climbed again, knowing that they'd have to find a patch of bare summit to regain their bearings. Only now, on the other side of the summit and with the moon behind them, could they make out Pudding Flat below and the harbour below that.

'Quickest way,' Alan grunted, nodding down at the flat. 'Marge is going to be calling out a search party if we're not home mighty quick.'

'She wouldn't call Lou Crawford, would she?' Tom said, referring to Waiata's policeman. He eyed the full pigeon bag.

'She ain't *that* stupid.' Alan hoisted the bag irritably. 'Let's go. I could eat one of these raw.'

By the time John Fleming reached the foot of Rue Lafayette, there were half a dozen children following him at a very respectful distance. Phones warbled and front doors opened as people came out to watch him pass. Even though gripped by his unerring purpose, he was aware of the attention he was attracting. He flicked his stick once. So be it. Justice would be seen to be done. And he might yet snatch his boy back. His boy. His only son. Every minute, bitter purpose pulled the corners of his mouth further downwards.

The moon was well up when he reached Emily's cottage. There appeared to be no lights on inside, but he had been told that they worked their foul practice in near darkness. So he turned up the path, on to the front porch, and burst straight in through the front door.

157

Gone.

Moonlight came in the far window on a long slant, bouncing off the patch of empty floor and illuminating a cage in the adjacent window. A small bird flurried frantically in a wire cage, then tic-tacked swiftly, rung to rung. John clumped the length of the room and looked out the back.

Nothing but shrubs.

He swung the stick twice as he recrossed the room, cracking it uselessly against a wall, and then toppling a coffee table. When he reached the front porch, Gordon Crocker was there, awed and fascinated by the intensity of John's rage.

'There's no one home, John.'

Where are they?!' John smashed the stick against the weatherboards.

'I don't know. The Nisbet woman went out a while ago. I thought you had Matthew at home.'

'He got away. He's with them! Where are they?!' The stick smashed again into the weatherboards, its end starting to splay. There were a dozen adults watching from the road now, and as many boys on push bikes. Jimmy, among the nearest group, called out that they might have gone to Jack Sullivan's farm.

'Get your car, Gordon,' John demanded.

'No, John. We don't know what powers we're up against. First we've got to get Robert.'

It wasn't right. Something wasn't right. The more Jennifer thought about it, the more unsettled she became. Of course it was to be expected that the open spaces and the firelight would make a difference to the atmosphere — but it was more than that. And she had felt it from the moment Nathaniel first opened his dark eyes to the flames and spoke. Also, Jack and Emily were unusually withdrawn, listening to the resonant voice roll around the fire, responding with scarcely more than an occasional word. Even D'Arcy wasn't himself; his liquid eyes shifted from one human face to another.

'You don't look so much like Matthew tonight,' Emily observed to Nathaniel. 'Maybe it's the firelight.'

'Also because I have more control over his body.'

'Something's wrong,' Jennifer said, making her heart thump.

'Tell us what you sense.'

158

'It's like this is going to be our last meeting.'

'It is. The last for some time.'

There was a stunned silence. Nathaniel's eyes were pools of shadow.

'My words may help you in one direction, but they are bars in another. It's time to remove the bars for a while.'

'Until when?'

'Until the next stage.'

'What next stage?' An unexpected sense of loss came to Jenny, catching her off balance. It made no sense to miss someone she didn't trust and had never really seen.

'If it could be adequately described in words, you would have no need of the experiences ahead of you.'

'What exp — ?' Jennifer began, but lapsed into silence.

No one spoke. The only voices were those of the fire and the stream, each speaking to the night in its own way. Occasionally, a farm animal moved somewhere out in the dark. The warm air stirred for the first time, slipping between them to lean for a moment on the fire, the first hint of a coming breeze. Emily's gaze fell on her handbag. She remembered her stick of rosemary and welcomed the chance to try to lift the atmosphere.

'What about some dried rosemary on the fire?' she asked, deliberately inviting indulgence. 'The fragrance is lovely.'

'By all means,' Nathaniel said. Jennifer and Jack were expressionless. Behind, the eyes of the dogs glowed blood-red in the firelight, and blinked: off, on, off, on.

At that moment, the penguins started up their full chorus.

Tom and Alan Glubb froze in their tracks in the darkness of the bush. Chills rippled up their spines and prickled around their scalps. They waited for the piercing sound to stop, but it grew louder.

'Jesus Christ A'mighty,' Alan quavered. 'What is *that*?'

'Kids,' Tom breathed shakily. 'Little 'uns. Some fucking bastard — ' He wrenched movement into arms and fingers, fumbled a cartridge into his .22 and slid the bolt home. With Alan breathing almost on his neck, he stole, very carefully, the last few yards of bush between them and Pudding Flat. From behind a screen of low scrub, they looked across at the fire, their gaze darting fearfully to either side in search of the cause of the sound. There was an echoing quality to the screeching that màde it almost impossible to locate by ear. Then they saw the pin-points of light up in the darkness behind the fire: three pairs of red eyes looking down on the four motionless figures around the flames.

'Oh Lord A'mighty,' Alan whimpered. 'Let's get out of here.'

'Shut up. Look, there's Sullivan. And — my *God*...' Tom's free hand gripped his brother's upper arm. '... That's Matthew Fleming. Look at his face, will yer? *Look* at it!'

The two men crawled backwards, deeper into the scrub, unable to take their eyes off the scene until the last possible moment. They saw Emily Nisbet stand over the flames, making sprinkling motions while the fire crackled and spat. Tom and Alan wasted no more breath. They abandoned the bag of dead wood pigeons and ran away around the edge of Pudding Flat between the scrub and the trees. At the far end of the flat they jumped the sagging gate without slowing. Then, under the bright full moon, they pounded down the track towards Waiata.

Robert McKay stood on the steps of the manse and held up his hand for silence. Gradually, the arguments and chatter died, though John Fleming, beside himself with frustration, had to be hushed by the men around him. The minister waited until he had every ear, then turned to the young man in police uniform beside him.

'With your permission, Lou?'

Waiata's new policeman, Lou Crawford, nodded uncomfortably, envious of the minister's commanding presence. Robert now spoke to Gordon Crocker in the crowd. 'You understand, Gordon, that on a matter as serious as this, we cannot act on hearsay. We must hear first from Emily's accuser.'

Gordon shifted uncomfortably. Beside him, Jimmy shut his eyes.

'We're wasting time!' John Fleming shouted. There were uncertain mutterings in the crowd.

'It was me.' Jimmy's voice was quiet but calm in the sure knowledge of duty.

'Right.' Lou Crawford tried again to recover control of the situation. 'Tell us what you saw. Emily Nisbet's place, was it?' Lou followed this by glaring at the crowd. But having already failed at getting them to disperse, he succeeded only in showing his anxiety and inexperience.

Jimmy told them. He told them in detail what he had seen with his own eyes and heard with his own ears. And by degrees, the astonishment grew noisier, then turned to anger, directed mainly at the two older and supposedly more responsible of the four — Nisbet and Sullivan.

'What's the law say?' someone called out.

'How would I know,' the policeman responded hotly. 'Never met it before. I'll have to go and look it up. You'd best leave it to — '

'We can't wait for that!' shouted John Fleming. 'Every second we waste time here, there's less chance of saving my boy.'

'Let's go,' growled Peter Thorn, a young farmer from Aylmers Valley. There was a rumble of agreement. Doctor Pringle was on the edge of the crowd now, questioning people anxiously. He pressed his way to the front as a group of men around John Fleming began to push towards the cars. But then there was a commotion at the gate. Two men, one carrying a rifle, staggered towards the policeman. For a few seconds, neither of the Glubbs could speak. Then they gasped out the first words.

'Witchcraft!'

'Jack Sullivan's.'

'The Fleming boy — he's possessed!'

'Screaming! Little kids! Someone cutting their throats or somethin'!'

Two women fainted on the spot. Others paled and leaned on equally pale husbands and someone retched in the shadows. Children searched their parents' faces for some clue as to what it was all about. Then, with a rumble of decision and determination, there was a concerted move for the motor vehicles. But over the top of it all came the powerful voice of the minister.

'*Be still!*' he roared.

They came to a halt. Looked back at him.

Lord, Lord, he whispered to himself. Could this be it? Could this be Your task chosen for me? The possibility lent his presence such an aura of power and purpose that the crowd seemed transfixed in awe of him.

'Did you think you could overcome such forces by *physical* means? There's only one way. There's only one weapon powerful enough to protect us and to save the souls in peril. Wait here.'

He turned his back on the crowd, knowing that they would wait, and disappeared into the manse. John Fleming, now next to one of the cars, laid his head on the roof and groaned. But the minister returned in less than a minute. His Westminster gown flowed from his shoulders; he carried a torch, a Bible and a second, leather-bound book in his hands. He strode to Gordon Crocker's car, reading a page in the second book by torchlight even before the car pulled away. All nine cars parked outside the church grounds filled with men and followed. A few buggies came on behind, the horses protesting as they were urged on.

The policeman dithered, then went home to call City Central for advice.

The last stack of wood had been fed to the fire. The flames burned lower, quietening as Nathaniel talked. D'Arcy rose, stretched, sniffed at something by the stream, then lay down again closer to the warmth. The breeze was steady now, pressing the flames away from them, fanning the burning sticks to cherry red. The moon was higher and smaller.

Emily's distrust had been submerged by a wave of sorrow. It rose inside her, reminding her of the years of solitude, and the sorrow became grief. 'I'm going to miss you,' she said to Nathaniel.

'And I you,' Nathaniel said.

'How can we be certain you'll speak to us again?'

'You cannot. It is probable, but no future is certain.'

'I thought you could see what was going to happen.'

'So I can. But the future does not remain static, waiting to become your present. Imagine that the stream below us represents time. The entire stream exists, from beginning to end, but it constantly changes along its course and the agent of that change is your free will. Much depends on the way you recover, in the next few years, from what is about to happen.'

All three went very still.

Nathaniel took a slow breath and spoke as if to the embers of the fire. 'Now, it is almost time to go.'

As one, D'Arcy and the three other dogs leapt to their feet in a flurry of barking. After a moment, Jack yelled at them. And when they quietened, a faint humming sound hung in the air.

162

There was little surprise around the fire.

'They've found out,' Jack said. A statement of fact.

'They have.'

'What's going to happen?' Jennifer seemed only idly curious.

The humming was louder, more clearly defined. Jennifer pulled her cardigan closer around her, even though the breeze was warm. 'Hard to... remember all that stuff... you said... when you're... when it's happening,' she murmured.

'Soon you will also remember that the reins of your experience are in your hands.'

Lights twinkled and slashed in the trees at the far end of Pudding Flat. The humming dispersed, resolving into the individual sounds of motor vehicles. 'I must give Matthew a moment to return to the physical. Now, I leave you.' His eyes closed, his head sank forward.

As the first car broke out of the far trees and halted for the gate, Matthew opened his eyes. He raised his head, immediately bursting into violent trembling. He stood, but his back was bent, his shoulders slumped like those of an exhausted man, his arms hugging himself. Beside him, D'Arcy faced the approaching lights, his lips drawn back in silent snarl.

'I'm cold, cold,' Matthew muttered. He walked away from the fire, then came back and stood close to it. But the trembling didn't stop. Jack took his arm and guided him to his seat. He spoke brusquely, urgently to Matthew, trying to instil some self-control in him before the cars arrived, more alarmed by Matthew's state than the approaching cars. Jennifer and Emily watched, not trusting themselves to speak. Briefly the two women clasped hands.

'I just... I just...' Matthew clamped down on his rattling teeth. 'I just wish... I could be sure... before they get here. In my own mind.'

The headlights swept across them once, twice, dazzling them, then died as the cars stopped. Doors slammed. Many feet moved on the grass, coming closer. Jennifer's hand sought Emily's again, frantically, and stayed. D'Arcy's throat rumbled, but Jack silenced him with a word. The sounds of the feet slowed and stopped. Sight returned to the four around the fire.

Ten paces away stood Robert McKay, tall, thinned by the moonlight, Bible in hand, gown stirring about him in the freshening breeze. A few paces behind him was a tight bunch of grim, silent men. In the distance, more lights were coming — swaying this time, to the faint crisp tattoo of hooves.

'Almighty God.' The minister's voice was clear and carrying. 'Grant, we beseech Thee, Thy protection. Grant that we are not too late; grant us the strength to win back Thy precious souls.' His voice rang out. 'Matthew Fleming. Are you able to speak?'

'Wha ... what?' Matthew rose, still hugging his shaking body.

'Answer me clearly, boy. I beg you to summon all your strength.'

'What do you want?'

'Listen carefully. The evil within you cannot be cast out unless you wish it so. I call on you to cast your mind back. Remember, Matthew, remember: four souls hang in the balance: what did the evil one bribe you with?'

Matthew shook his head erratically, as if the question didn't make sense. He seemed to be losing control of his body. His thigh muscles jerked spasmodically against their moorings on his bones.

'What special powers did he dangle in front of you? Think! Think!'

Suddenly Matthew's body went quite still.

'Tell us!' roared the minister. 'Tell us the price of your soul!'

Emily and Jennifer let their clasped hands fall away and shut their eyes. Jack bent down and took a grip of D'Arcy's neck ruff.

'The power of spiritual healing.' Matthew's voice was hardly more than a whisper.

The minister dropped his voice to match. ' "*Now* know we the stink of the pit." ' His hand shot forward as if to transfix. '*You*! You, the spirit! I speak to you and not to the boy. In Jesu's name, and by the Blood of the Lamb, I command you to release this boy and come out!'

Matthew opened his mouth wide and screamed up into the night in agony and despair. Then he fell to the ground, unconscious.

THIRTEEN

The first reporters were hurrying along the wharf in less than twenty-four hours. By the weekend, the town teemed with newsmen from every major newspaper and radio station in New Zealand, and a few from Australia. The timing of the event gave the greatest advantage to the Sunday newspapers, and brought a new festive season to their newsrooms.

The headlines read:

Satanic Rites in Banks Peninsula Hills
Sounds of Children Being Tortured

and

Vigilante Villagers Storm Satanists' Lair
on Isolated Farm

and

Mystery Disappearances after Black Magic
in Remote Hills.

Some reporters discovered that there were a few locals who held doubts about the torture of small children and who pointed out that there weren't any small children missing. But there was better copy to be had at the Glubbs' farm —the two brothers were nothing less than journalists' gold. Only one reporter, a hunting enthusiast from the Waikato, came away vaguely dissatisfied. He decided in the end that anyone who went hunting pigs with a .22-calibre pop gun and without pig dogs was either mentally retarded or had developed the sport to unprecedented heights of artistry and courage.

Radio reporters found another bonanza at the Presbyterian manse. While the minister didn't rave about lakes of fire and brimstone, as hoped, he was, as they put it, great talent. He behaved as if the microphone and the large box of attached machinery didn't exist; he was so dynamic that the reporters knew the story was going to put a booster behind the current upsurge

165

of religious orthodoxy and fundamentalism.

The local policeman was little use to them. He refused all radio interviews out of hand and only grudgingly supplied basic facts. No, no complaints had been made to the police. No, witchcraft wasn't against the law. Yes, there had been violence on the farm, but there was no evidence to implicate particular individuals.

Not a single reporter interviewed any of the four alleged members of the satanic circle. Emily Nisbet's house was empty, with front door swinging in the wind, windows broken, and a budgerigar dead on the floor. The woman was barricaded with Sullivan inside the hut on Pudding Flat. Occasionally, reporters glimpsed them through the window and noticed that the man was limping and had a bruised face. The men from the Sunday papers shouted offers of large sums of money, without approaching the door. No one approached the door. It was guarded by a ferocious brown-and-white dog which lunged, snarling, at anyone who came near.

The Fleming boy and the Pringle girl had disappeared. Great copy. But on the other hand, the more thorough reporters discovered that both had been glimpsed separately since the event. A private launch had anchored in the harbour the following day and, in the evening, the local publican had seen the doctor row his daughter out into the harbour and return alone. As for the boy at the centre of it all, he had been seen on the old stock route to the plains. And in the weeks that followed, all inquiries at the other end of the route, and in the city, failed to locate him.

PART THREE

ONE

The day was clear, cold and still, the sky mid-winter pale. A light blanket of snow lay on the roofs and ground and along the beach. It had fallen in almost windless conditions, so it lay evenly before every wall and fence. And this morning, though it was almost midday, the surface was still brittle with the night's frost.

Over the white hills to the north of the harbour appeared a small, single-engined aeroplane. It was travelling west, hardly more than a metallic dot, though the air was so still that a few people fancied they could hear the drone. Not that many stopped to watch at first: every fine day, for the last three months now, similar aircraft had been flying that same route. But this morning, the plane turned aside from the usual course and headed directly for Waiata.

Inside the Cherokee 160 trainer, the instructor took the controls, changing attitude for a shallow descent, adjusting revs and resetting trim. Then he grinned at his impatient trainee, a lawyer from the city.

'Sorry, Peter, something I've got to look at. Don't worry about the extra time. This little excursion's on me.'

The lawyer grunted, glanced at his slide-rule computer to draw attention to the wasted calculations, but made no further comment. Antagonising the chief instructor and club owner before the flight test made about as much sense as insulting the jury before the verdict. In fact, he quite liked Bill Sanders; the man couldn't be more than thirty, but had the strength and assurance of someone considerably older. With a touch of envy, the lawyer briefly pictured his instructor arguing a legal point before the jury: dark chestnut hair in slight disarray, a strongly lined, tanned face, hand movements that were over-controlled but firm. He had a poise and presence that was startling in a young man.

169

The Cherokee descended until there was just sufficient height to clear Takamatua Saddle. Then the saddle was sweeping under them at 120 knots; the line of poplars to their right wheeled as they passed, a formation of grey winter wraiths guarding the village. Waiata lay before them. The instructor tucked in two notches of flap and slowed the craft for a crawl over the rooftops.

The village was vividly clear in the crisp morning. It might have been a model, brilliantly constructed, the cars, the horses and buggies, and the upturned faces. Nothing seemed to be moving; it was as if the model was waiting for a breath to bring it to life.

Soon, the lawyer realised that his instructor wasn't just sightseeing. He was looking at specific things: a particular boat, a house behind the shops, another on a hillside. 'You know this place?' he asked, looking down at his route map.

The instructor appeared not to have heard. Below, the town was a tapestry of fine detail and rough texture that passed as remembered Braille under searching fingers. A wry smile creased his face, broadened, and he began to laugh as he pushed the throttle forward and released the flaps.

The lawyer looked at him askance as the Cherokee gathered speed out over the harbour.

'You all right, Bill?'

The instructor laughed again. 'Bill Sanders just bailed out, Peter. Without a chute.'

The lawyer's eyebrows rose. But an explanation was not forthcoming.

'Right,' the instructor said. 'Let's get back on course. You have the controls. Take her up to five thousand feet. No, let the air speed build up before you bring the nose up. That's it.' The craft settled into the climb. 'This is your last lesson with me, Peter. We'll jack you up with a new instructor when we get back. Know anyone who wants to buy a fleet of Cherokees?'

TWO

The bus whined on to the crest of Takamatua Saddle just as the sun lowered on to the frozen hills on the far side of the harbour. For a moment, the light glared coldly through the windscreen, casting a harsh beam the full length of the aisle. The windscreen dipped away for the last downgrade, and the bus clattered down the bends to Waiata.

Matthew knew the other passenger. Elaine Drury, the draper's wife, was sitting at the far front of the bus, opposite the driver. She had boarded at the last town on the plains and, after the initial shock of recognition, pretended she didn't know him. Throughout the journey she took covert glances, as if afraid that he might disappear. For his own part, though he had been well prepared, the first sight of a Waiata face had pumped unasked-for adrenalin into his veins.

The coach rattled through the first houses, nearing the junction of the road up Lafayette Hill and the beginning of Waterfront Road. Mrs Drury tapped the driver's shoulder and pointed. The bus pulled into the side of the road, the driver hauled on the door lever, and Mrs Drury climbed down the steps with a last glance down the bus. Matthew, taken by an impulse to walk the rest of the way along the sea wall, signalled the driver and manoeuvred his suitcases along the aisle and down the steps.

Mrs Drury was moving up Rue Lafayette at a fast clip.

Matthew picked his way through the slush on the road, placed his bags by the sea-wall railing and looked about him, drawing his sheepskin coat more snugly against the cold. The harbour was almost black against the white hills. Half the boats were out for the night: the fish must be scarce. A pleasure boat rode at the visitors' mooring. The beach, even in this light, seemed to have less sand and more mud; which meant that someone had cleared a lot of bush. On the waterfront, two cars waited for the milky air to bring the frost. A new house was going up by the reservoir, its ribs half clothed against the night. Nothing moved except the thin dark plumes of chimney smoke. The sun had set. House lights were already on, some curtains already drawn around floral settees and coal fires and mantel radios.

Shoes scraped on gravelled clay, the sound accompanied by an uneven tapping. An awkward figure shuffled into view down Rue Lafayette, its white-tipped cane tapping and sweeping, tapping and sweeping, as it had done for two and a half decades. The deaf and blind man came across the road, his stick reaching for and finding the railing pipes a few paces along from Matthew. But instead of continuing along the sea wall, Tommy Ransley suddenly faltered. His shoulders thrust further forward and the white tip on his cane waved in agitation. He turned his head about, as if looking for something with seeing eyes, and for a moment his face was turned in Matthew's direction. He made a high-pitched sound with an upward inflection of questioning. A pause. Then, with a puzzled and exasperated grunt, he turned away and continued towards the poolroom.

Matthew, smiling a small, fierce smile, watched him go.

In a while, a phone burred. In the still air, Matthew heard it quite clearly. He picked up his bags and began to walk along the wall, recognising individual marks on the posts of the railing. He had made some of them himself as a boy. The light was fading. A curtain twitched in a window opposite. A silhouetted head. Two heads. Another phone rang. A door opened, then shut. Dark figures stood on a front porch.

They saw that he was dressed casually but well. His coat was fashionably rough-cut, and expensive. His jeans were new. His shoes were ankle-length and of soft leather with the seams turned out in the same style as the coat. Even in the poor light, it was obvious that whatever Matthew Fleming had done to keep himself alive, it had paid well. But it wasn't his clothing they looked at as much as his bearing.

This was not the Matthew Fleming they remembered. The diffidence and the youthful mix of brashness and uncertain intensity were gone. There were some who had claimed after that night twelve years ago that a misty vapour had been seen issuing from his mouth during the exorcism. They were the ones who maintained that the Fleming boy had been cured for good

172

at that moment. Looking at him now, it was tempting to believe that they were right. But appearances can often deceive. And why, if he had been cured, had he never sent word to his parents? What was he doing here now anyway? Visiting or staying? Matthew grinned to himself, anticipating the manner in which some of their questions would shortly be answered.

He passed the church. The hall was lit and he wondered if it was still the young men's Bible class at this time. The manse curtains were drawn against the evening and, though a shadow moved behind a curtain, no one looked out.

Just past the church, he crossed the road and stopped by a gate with broken, faded, white pickets. He looked through the shrubbery behind the rickety fence and surveyed what lay behind. A hundred and fifty yards back was the run-down, two-storey, colonial mansion, imposing, in the last moments of nightfall. He and his friends had once referred to it as the 'giant's house', though Sam Clement had been no giant. In front, the long stretch of lawn was overgrown, littered and tangled with debris from the oaks and pines, and the silver birches that lined the driveway.

In the centre of the grounds, the sequoia stood quietly against the stars.

In his coat pocket, Matthew's hand gripped tightly around a key. Then he pulled the 'For Sale' sign off the gate and took it and his bags up the drive.

The same evening, he left his new home and walked the quarter of a mile to his parents' house. Word had reached them already, and they were waiting. His mother allowed him to kiss her cheek at the door, but he felt the tension through her flesh. She was much thinner than he remembered. Her features were sharper, sour creases pulled deeply between mouth and cheek, and her hair was short and swept severely behind her head.

She stood aside for him to enter and indicated the way to the lounge. His father stood, nodded to him and sat, without releasing his copy of the *Waiata Mail*, but his stiffness was in part because of his gammy leg. He was in pain, Matthew saw immediately. The Bible lay beside his father on the armrest — the family Bible with Matthew's birth recorded in the front.

The conversation was clumsy and painful. His parents, in spite of having anticipated this meeting for so long, were afraid

173

to come to the most important question. Instead, they told him that his grandmother had passed on, that the summer had been a warm one and that Jimmy Crocker's wife had presented him with a daughter and then run away and abandoned them both. John and Rachel asked nothing about how Matthew had lived his life or earned his money, or how he had arranged to buy the old Clements' place. Rachel said that the fish had mostly gone, and that John's back and leg had stopped him fishing anyway. Gordon Crocker had bought the ageing *Phoenix* from them to use as a ferry for the quarry. They said nothing about what they were going to live on when the sale money ran out.

'Are you ... well?' Rachel said finally.

'I'm well, Mum. I was never unwell.'

In the silence that followed, Matthew was struck by the seeming distortion in his memory. As a young man he had somehow thought of his parents as being physically much larger than himself, but now it was as if they had shrunk. He wanted to grip his father's hand, to embrace his mother and melt all the cold springs coiling inside her.

'It's still inside you,' she said finally, more a statement than a question. His expression more than answered her, and her last hope vanished, to be replaced with dread. 'You brought it here, again. You're going to do it again,' she said, wonderingly. She searched his eyes, and couldn't find words for what more she saw there. She looked then at her husband and Matthew understood that they had worked out their answer long ago. She turned back, the creases round her mouth twisted into bitter knots. 'How can you do this to us?'

John laid his hand on the Bible. 'We no longer have a son. You're not welcome here. You're not welcome in Waiata.'

Matthew stood. He was not surprised, except by how much more it hurt than he had expected. He told them he hoped that one day they would understand why he had to do what he was going to do. He bent to kiss his mother goodbye, but she was rigid. He walked across the worn, familiar carpet towards the corridor and the front door.

'Filth,' his father's voice snarled behind him. 'Scum! Get out! No one in this town will have anything to do with you. No one. You're not fit ...'

But Matthew didn't look back.

Next morning, a Saturday morning, Margaret Crocker lounged in the deck-chair making grandmotherly, admiring noises as golden-haired, six-year-old Amelia propelled herself around the hopscotch squares. Margaret's purpose was twofold. She was also out front keeping watch against the possibility that young Fleming might pay a visit to his old crony Emily Nisbet. And sure enough, at ten o'clock, he was walking up her path. He spent an hour and a half inside before making a conducted tour of the woman's garden and then leaving.

A further possibility occurred to Mrs Crocker. Just before midday, she called up a friend who worked at the telephone exchange and invited her for lunch. Her friend came and, in the course of a carefully managed conversation, declared that Margaret couldn't possibly guess who Emily Nisbet had been talking to on tolls to Wanganui. Margaret agreed that she couldn't possibly, and was gratifyingly astonished when told, in strict confidence, that Emily had been talking to Jennifer Pringle.

That afternoon, Matthew walked the waterfront again. A dozen boys on push bikes rode fearlessly past him and back, scrutinising the young man who was already a heavyweight in the verbal histories of Waiata. But as the safety of town was left behind, the boys dropped further and further back.

Only two brave souls, the proud possessors of bikes with three-speed gears, followed him as far as the rock columns short of Pudding Flat. There, the adventure came to an end. There, they came across proof of the black magic they'd heard about. The bikes about-faced so fast they came close to somersaulting backwards and each owner was standing on the forward pedal as the front wheel touched dirt. The faster they flew down the hill, the more incontrovertible their proof seemed to be and the more certain they became that Matthew Fleming was springing down the track after them. Finally, they skidded to an impressive halt at the edge of town where the others were waiting.

'Sullivan and his dog were standing on the Pillars waiting for Fleming,' they panted, astride their bikes. And this was indeed proof, because, as everyone knew, Jack Sullivan didn't have the phone on.

Late Monday morning, a furniture van and a freight truck drove into Waiata and up the sweeping drive to Matthew Fleming's new home. A great deal of building equipment was unloaded:

timber, tools, many two-gallon cans of paint. There was a sit-on, motorised lawnmower of the type used for parks. There were large bolts of a velvety, deep green cloth. Scores of padded kitchen chairs came off in four-foot stacks and were taken through creaking French doors to the old ballroom.

On Tuesday, a journalist drove in from the city and walked on to the property, clutching a clippings file. He talked to Matthew on the porch for less than a minute, then was on his way out again. He spent another two hours discovering that everyone else in town wanted to know what he had learned and knew nothing themselves. He drove back over the hills in disgust.

Every morning Emily Nisbet walked in, a work bag slung over one shoulder and carrying a basket. The contents of the basket were always covered with a cloth. 'Typical of her,' said Mavis Hendry, one of Matthew Fleming's new neighbours. 'She always was the sly, secretive sort.'

Jack Sullivan came on his new motorbike, with his old heading dog, D'Arcy, squatting in the back tray. Sullivan had turned a small profit the last two years, since he'd got rid of his Romneys and restocked with Drysdales for the wool trade. It wasn't so much the profit that rankled; it was the fact that he had made it by bucking the local system. Peninsula sheep farms were Romney farms — had been so since the turn of the century. Trust Sullivan to stand out like a sore thumb.

Fleming, Sullivan and Nisbet began the task of restoring the old, run-down property. It took Sullivan half a day just to reduce the overgrown lawns to a manageable state, and another two days to work the worst of the weeds out of the shrubbery borders. They began scraping and cleaning the weatherboards of the rambling old place, breaking the huge job occasionally by working on the renovation of an old buggy in the shed. D'Arcy spent much of his time dozing on the front porch or dragging his ancient bones through the shrubbery after winter-sluggish hedgehogs.

Jennifer Pringle arrived on the bus and moved her bags into Emily's cottage. She paid a visit to her parents' home, and the same afternoon was wire-brushing old paint on the mansion roof.

One day, more than three weeks after he had arrived, Matthew Fleming came down the driveway with a piece of wall-board, three feet square. It had words printed on it. He nailed it to the gate and went back to the house. A few minutes later, the

Hendrys sent along a boy to read it. It said:

WAIATA HEALING SANCTUARY
Healing of Mind and Body
Wednesdays 7.30 p.m.

THREE

Robert McKay patted the grey mare regretfully as they moved into Waiata off the dirt road from Goughs Bay. After all these years, the visits to outlying farms were as satisfying as ever. The swaying ride through the rugged bush was, to him, one of the true natural pleasures. To refresh one's spirit with His works on a clear weekday was to enrich communion with Him on Sunday.

Cars drove past him with respectful care. Often buggies and traps went by, the drivers raising hands in cheerful and comradely greeting. It occurred to him that the buggies were all drawn by single horses these days, and that it had been some time since he'd clapped eyes on the most handsome and comely of all transports: the buggy and pair. A sign of the times, of course. But then he could hardly complain: it was only through his example and influence that there still was some horse traffic on peninsula roads. It was said fondly of him that the day the minister grew too old to ride his horse over the summit was the day half the nags in the district would be retired. Those who said so, usually followed with the thought that the way he was riding now, at the age of sixty-five, they wouldn't have to wait more than another fifty years.

He always knew what people said of him.

On his way to the grazing field, he rode past the church grounds. Ellen came out on the porch to wave. She was, he knew, as proud as ever of the figure he cut on horseback, perhaps even more so now that his hair was iron grey and the creases were deepening on his face. He, equally, was proud of her graceful, increasingly stately carriage. She too, fifty-five now, was as upright as ever; pretty testimony, he thought with a smile, to an upright life. Some days just the sight of her brought him a glow of warmth and thankfulness. God grant that he continue to be worthy of her. She was as fine a marriage partner as a man had any right to expect.

He had not gone more than thirty yards when he heard a call and reined in. His second eldest daughter, Bevin, walked quickly to catch up. She brought a request. Would he mind calling into the drapery on his way back to pick up the damask for the new tablecloth? He agreed readily and watched her approvingly as she walked away. What blind fools the young men of Waiata were not to see the quality and soundness behind the girl's plain face. He flicked the reins and the mare plodded on. Bevin had not been as favoured in looks as her sisters. There was every prospect that his thirty-eight-year-old daughter would be looking after her parents in their old age. Not that either he or Ellen would ever ask her to do so; but it was, he had to admit, a comforting notion.

The sign proclaiming 'WAIATA HEALING SANCTUARY' passed in the corner of his vision. He didn't turn his head or even redirect his eyes. He would not miss out on the developments; everything that happened would be reported to him. Once he might have believed that Matthew Fleming was at the forefront of the challenge to come. But the impressionable boy had been too easily beaten, too easily corrected. Even if the exorcism had not left a deep impression on Matthew Fleming's psyche, it certainly had on the psyche of the village. Apart from a couple of oddballs, the villagers simply wouldn't take the boy seriously any more. His name was, after all, still held in contempt.

Robert's mind went back to the handsome, likable little boy Matthew used to be, whose company he had enjoyed so much. Thinking about it now, he realised that having had only daughters himself, Matthew had been something of a son to him. A pang of sorrow curled through him. He overcame it by lifting his chin more firmly to the passing street.

Yes, it would be a mistake to overestimate the importance of the affair. Once again, it would turn out to be an empty, if smelly, molehill. An interesting, diverting molehill if the truth be known. And there were few enough of those to liven the long years of waiting for the Lord to show His hand. Thirty years now. Almost half a lifetime.

At the gate beside the fire station he dismounted, though Bonny, the mare, was easily capable of sidling up to the latch.

179

He always walked with her through the gate and across the field, an acknowledgment of the day's effort. It was one of his favourite sayings that a mark of respect was never lost on an animal's instinct. Bonny was a shepherd's hack basically, not as spirited as Lancer had been; but she was strong, willing and reliable. He took her across to the stable that had been built for her by the parish, rubbed her down, watered her and watched her dispose of a bucket of chaff.

A few minutes later, he was at the counter of the drapery, waiting while Elaine Drury folded the damask for the new altar cloth. Her practised wrists flipped the material over and over into a neat, creaseless, flat roll. She stroked a palm across the result respectfully and asked if Mr McKay wouldn't prefer her to deliver it directly to Alice Fee, who was doing the embroidery. But he declined, saying that much of the design had yet to be drawn.

The drapery door opened, causing the bell to leap into a frantic dance. Elaine Drury glanced in that direction. Her expression changed so strangely that Robert somehow knew who had just come in. He didn't turn around. He indicated the cloth, returning Mrs Drury's attention to wrapping it. She did so as a figure appeared at the counter a few feet along and leaned on it sideways, facing them. Robert gave Mrs Drury a civil word of thanks and turned.

'Good afternoon, Mr McKay,' Matthew said.

The minister didn't reply. The moment his gaze locked with Matthew's it was obvious that there would be little need of civility. No need even for questions; the answers were right there, in the boy's face and eyes. Boy? No, a man now, with strength and sure purpose. And ... and something else. So, it had been reversed after all. Nathaniel was back. He would be the force behind the so-called Sanctuary. Healing. Teaching. Two doors from the church.

In the heart of the parish.

Then Robert knew. A chill enveloped his stomach and ran up his spine within the space of a breath. The suddenness and the certainty of the knowledge made him dizzy. He swayed briefly but forced himself not to look away.

'Mr McKay! Are you all right?' Elaine Drury, alarmed.

So this was it. After all these years, revealed at last. For this

180

that the Lord had brought him to these distant shores and prepared him for so long. His mind recalled the time, three decades ago, when he had stood on the wharf, baptising this creature into the Lord's community... the personal interest he had taken in this once so promising boy... the careful training he had given him in the word of God. The viper had grown well in the bosom of the church. Your ways are mysterious, Lord, so mysterious. Yet I thank You now with all my heart that You have lifted the scales from my eyes. The task is clear. Through Your grace, I will, I will, be worthy of You.

In that moment, the chill was gone from him, replaced by a welling of sheer joy — so strong that it was all he could do not to laugh out loud. He broke gaze with Matthew, having held it, seemingly, for minutes. He turned to the draper's wife, who was looking from one to the other, hand hovering at her mouth.

'I'm well, Mrs Drury. I promise you I have never been better. I'll be bidding you good day.' He went, his proud glance raking across Matthew with contempt only slightly tempered by respect for a dangerous foe. After some time, Matthew faced the counter. Mrs Drury drew back. He asked for ten dozen curtain rings. She pressed her lips together, shook her head, and told him that he wouldn't get any satisfaction in her shop.

In ones and twos, seven elders entered the minister's study for the special informal session. He was immersed in a book, *The Abingdon Bible Commentary*, and paused only to greet briefly each person entering the room. So they sat on the circle of chairs provided and murmured quietly, catching up on the latest developments. The most recent news was only hours old. The four had been seen moving around inside the Sanctuary buildings wearing biblical-style robes.

Ellen McKay came and went, leaving a tray of glasses and water. They sipped and waited. John Fleming sat dourly, looking at the floor. Outside, a cold easterly rain hissed relentlessly onto the lawns and drummed on the road.

The minister closed his book.

'Gentlemen. Before we begin, John has asked me to tell you that he is willing, if asked by you, to formally offer his resignation.' The response was immediate and unanimous: no one thought John needed to resign. Robert turned to him. 'None of us is in any doubt that Matthew is long past the age when a boy's responsibility for his actions moves from his father's shoulders on to his own. However, this is a distressing time for you, and for Rachel; I'm sure no one is going to object if you are absent for this particular session.' There was a chorus of agreement.

John Fleming expelled air softly, grateful for the warmth of the support. But then he straightened in his chair. 'No. If it doesn't bother you — me being here — I'll stay ... try to undo some of the damage ...'

But Robert declared flatly that no damage had been done yet, his tone carrying approval for the courage of John's decision. He bowed his head and led them in informal prayer, then clasped his hands together and looked around resolutely. Norman White, the mayor, was intrigued by the elderly minister's underlying animation. In spite of the grim expression, there was an eagerness about Robert McKay, an anticipation. Well, Robert had always risen to a challenge.

'This is the position,' Robert McKay began. 'In the twelve years since the coming of the road, we have successfully combated its spiritually damaging effects, so much so that our parish is regarded as a beacon of hope by the unpolluted. But! Drunk with success, flushed with self-satisfaction and complacency, we are suddenly confronted with the fact that our greatest test lies ahead of us. You all know what is involved. I welcome your suggestions.'

Voices tangled. The first to make himself heard was Peter Thorn, town councillor, sheep farmer. He was in his late thirties, the most recently ordained elder and the youngest for some time. He was a stocky, ruddy-faced man with a blustery manner and with a sharp tongue to back the bluster. He'd left school at the minimum age, and was proud to be self-made and self-educated. He worked his own farm, but was never seen out of doors without a neck-tie of some description. He was fond of quoting his favourite recipe for a good upbringing: liberal applications of the Bible and the belt ... for some, an uncomfortable reminder of the excesses of the old backblocks Presbyterianism. All the same, Peter Thorn was a shrewd and respected member of Session; somehow he had the ear of both the youngest and the oldest adult sections of the community. Not an easy alliance. As early as his late teens, Peter Thorn had been one of Robert's most enthusiastic supporters. For the last ten years he had worn his black hair and beard cut in the same style as the minister. Now, he was particularly irate about the fact that those in the Sanctuary had been seen wearing biblical-style robes.

'They're an affront,' he grated. 'A direct, blatant insult. It can't be tolerated.'

'What are they for? That's what I want to know.' Alan Bailey.

'Some kind of ritual opening night, maybe.'

'*Healing Sanctuary*,' Peter Thorn sneered. 'Fleming's Pit, more like!'

Grins sprang up in delight; but, out of respect for John's feelings, no one laughed out loud. McKay nodded, pleased. 'Fleming's Pit,' he repeated.

'What kind of healing is it supposed to be? Faith healing?'

'Emily Nisbet makes ointments and things,' Gordon Crocker offered.

'A gimmick, to get people in to listen to their occultist poison.'

Robert raised a hand. 'Don't forget that the original bribe offered Matthew was the ability to give spiritual healing.' He paused to let that sink in. 'Even if that only means advice aimed in the direction of the soul, we are in difficulties — it only takes one of our people to be talked out of a psychosomatic symptom and our job becomes a hundred times harder. And I'm afraid it's going to be worse than that. We must not deceive ourselves. Matthew is no weakling or fool, by anyone's standards. We must face the fact that he has been won by a clever deceiver, a persuasive and powerful being, quite capable of delivering the promised bribe. I saw Matthew today, as you know. I have seen this... this *thing* he calls Nathaniel coiling in his eyes. I tell you that we are dealing with no ordinary power. The devil has a great deal of power to grant his own if the prize is worthy, and I think you'll agree that Waiata is a worthy prize. A *key* prize.'

Silence, as the implication of the last comment sank in.

'Can't you exorcise it again?'

McKay shook his head. 'Too late. It only worked then because Matthew still desperately wanted deliverance.

'Aren't we..?' Chester Farnsworth faltered into silence, realising that his intended quiet aside to Paul Marsen had everyone's attention. He cleared his throat, suddenly conscious of his shiny, almost completely bald pate. 'Uh, I was only going to say, aren't we overemphasising the danger of this? I mean, spiritualism, in other places...' Even at the best of times, Chester hated speaking to a group. Now he grew uncomfortable and frustrated. So much so that he blurted out the next thing that came into his head. 'I'm not even convinced that this spirit business is possible. It seems a bit much to think of Satan walking around inside Matthew Fleming.' He flushed as he said it.

'I object!' Peter Thorn said hotly. 'Chester's tone implies naiveté on our part. Under the circumstances —'

'I doubt,' the minister offered dryly, 'that the Lord would bother to forbid something that wasn't possible, Chester. I had thought we were all aware that the decline of faith in every area of the Western world, *without exception*, was preceded by increasing *dis*belief in the reality of Satan. Perhaps you could clarify your position?'

'I, uh...' Chester was in a sorry state. 'I didn't mean to imply... No, of course I believe in Satan. I mean if there's good, there must be evil.'

There were pained looks from those who considered the last remark unnecessary.

'How did he get all the money to buy the place?'

'Investigate his background,' Norman White said. 'If he's done anything at all...'

'Starve him out,' growled Peter Thorn. 'It would only take the retailers to refuse to serve him and his bunch of nasties, and he'd have to give up.' Faces shifted quickly into neutral. Session was hardly the place to advocate actions of borderline legality, whatever their merits. Robert watched impassively.

'Wouldn't work,' Paul Marsen said. 'They're getting most of their stuff in on the bus anyway. And they've already winter-planted down the back. Got the seeds from somewhere.' Carefully, he avoided looking at Chester, who owned the only seed outlet on the peninsula.

'There are other ways,' Peter Thorn said darkly and vaguely. 'Our people won't tolerate this snake pit for long. There's going to be more than a few will act in righteous anger.' Attention switched to Robert.

'You may well be right,' he said, his inflexions implying only that Peter had made an accurate and helpful analysis of the community. 'However, if we do *our* job well, it won't get to

184

that stage. We must promote such unity that not a single person, no matter how weak or physically affected will indulge their curiosity.... We cannot risk anyone coming away from ...' — he inclined his head to Peter — '... Fleming's Pit with a single symptom alleviated or illness cured. *No* one, I repeat, *no* one must attend. Do you agree that that must be our objective?'

Unanimous agreement. Peter Thorn perked up. This was more like it.

'You'll be dealing with it in your sermons?' It was the first time John Fleming had spoken since Session began.

'I think not.'

Blank faces.

'I must mention it, of course, since Waiata talks of little else. But I must not run the risk of distorting its significance so as to make it perversely attractive to some minds. My teaching part must be low key. Indirect. Though, I concede that if we are going to prevent *every*one from attending, we must have *some* kind of unified strategy ...?'

Inwardly, Norman White chuckled. Admirable. As always. Who would rise first? Paul? Odds on Paul.

'Robert,' Paul was struck by an idea. 'If you can't deal with it in your sermons, why don't we all deal with it individually with each of our charges. And we play it cool, right? We wait for the subject to come up, then we give them what the gospel says and ...' Another thought came to him. '... Also, we all act as if we don't think anyone is actually stupid enough to turn up. Nobody is going to risk being the odd man out, are they?' He beamed at the general rumble of agreement. Norman White rubbed an eye carefully, though he had to admit the sense of the suggestion; in small-town Waiata, that was very sound, practical psychology.

Robert nodded at Paul gratefully. 'Well, if I read your reactions correctly, Paul has given us the crux of our strategy. However, perhaps you'll agree that it is not sufficient on its own ...?'

'We should keep an eye on the place, just in case,' Peter Thorn said.

'The neighbours are doing that already. And Kay Hooper's got a clear view —'

'I mean...' Peter pressed, '... get the Hoopers and the Hendrys to organise themselves so we can be sure of knowing immediately if any of our people go in.'

Seven faces turned to Robert. In a moment he nodded. 'A sensible precaution, though we must hope it turns out to be unnecessary. And don't forget — we must stress to one and all that this is a matter on which *all* Christians are united. Not just our people.' He straightened, giving an all-embracing inclination of the head. 'Well, gentlemen, the critical day is this first Wednesday. We have five days in which to make sure this so-called Sanctuary gets a nil attendance. If we succeed, then we are well on the way to rendering Fleming's Pit impotent before it claims a single victim.'

FOUR

'Another one?' Margaret Crocker was so appalled, she didn't notice a glob of batter falling from the wooden spoon to the floor. She shook her head in disgust at her son. 'Jimmy Crocker, you're spoiling that child rotten.'

But she might as well have saved her breath. Jimmy was half-bent over the table, watching Amelia open a present, anticipating the reaction. The scarlet ribbon came away, followed by the first layer of wrapping paper, which was covered with pictures of Jumbo, the flying elephant. Jimmy always gave Amelia's presents two complete gift wrappings because that made her squeak with excitement and shake her head so that waves pulsed down her long, golden hair.

The second wrapping was flung aside, and fell to the floor. Amelia gave a gasp, jerked the lid off the cardboard box before her, and stood biting her lower lip with abashed joy. A real china, forty-five-piece tea set.

'Well?' Jimmy demanded eagerly. 'What have you got to say to your Dad?'

'Thank you,' Amelia said in a small, thrilled voice. She put her slender arms up, pulled him down to her and planted a smacking kiss on his scarred and pitted cheek.

Margaret Crocker snorted and returned to the kitchen. There would be no sense out of either of them now. She didn't know which one of them doted on the other more. The wonder of it was that Amelia wasn't manipulating him. Only a matter of time, really. Sure, fathers were supposed to dote on their children, but this much? It wasn't healthy. Perhaps Gordon should get Robert to try to talk sense into her son. Jimmy didn't appear to be living for any reason except Amelia; he seemed only to continue working at the quarry so he could buy her endless presents, each bigger and better than the one before. Margaret called out from the kitchen bench.

'I suppose you realise, Jimmy Crocker, that you're just encouraging her to grow up like that mother of hers?'

In four bounds, the big man was behind her, his face contorted. 'I told you! Don't mention that slut in front of Amelia! Amelia's different! She's not like that! She's *different!*' He rocked from one foot to the other, twisting the fingers of his massive hands. Margaret nearly dropped the bowl.

'Of course she's different. I'm not defending Angela —'

'Don't talk about that slut! That whore! God is going to punish her. He's going to strike her down! Don't talk about her, or He'll strike you down where you stand!'

FIVE

The entranceway was a small, carpeted alcove, containing a low bench, a burning candle, a basin of clear water and a white towel. Curtains opened into the main room, the old mansion ballroom — a space big enough for echoes to pause in the returning. But there was no sound now, save the fire hissing in the great stone hearth at the far end. The flames shed soft orange on to the grains of the native kauri lining the walls and on to the deep green floor-to-ceiling drapes. Six dozen candles burned in carved sticks mounted in the timbers; a standard lamp glowed in each corner. Dozens of padded kitchen chairs lined the edges of the space and, in front of them, russet-coloured cushions lay scattered about the varnished floor.

An old sheepdog lay dozing next to the fire. His smoky-brown hair had grown long, especially in the white of the neck ruff. The once glossy pelt had dulled. The hair was coarse and dry, and stiff as his bones were stiff. His skin was scarred by countless fights and his face sagged towards the floor, which supported the chin and jowls. But he wasn't discontented in old age: even though his physical adventures were now restricted to persecuting hedgehogs, his memories were vivid and served him very well. Sometimes he slept, the skin on his forehead and eyelids flickering to the tune of a dream. He lay at such an angle that when he woke, he could see most of the room without having to raise his head. His eyes would simply rotate in their sockets, lazily, from the flames in the hearth to the four humans seated in a circle of straight-backed chairs in the centre of the huge room.

The four were clad in rough-textured, bone-coloured, cotton robes, tied with macramé belts of similar shade. They wore no jewellery, nor footwear, nor anything on their heads. They sat perfectly still, eyes closed. Not a movement of finger or toe, nor stirring of limb. The only muscles under constant control were

189

those holding the back straight and the head level. The four had been like this since 7.30, the time referred to on the notice at the gate. They were meditating, though it was not entirely possible for them to free their minds of questioning wisps of thought. How many would come? Would anyone come?

Emily's body had changed in twelve years. The dumpy, awkward bulges had gone, leaving her with the thinness that suggests fragile bones. Her long hair was grey and white, tied in a loose, low-hanging bun. In spite of her robe, she was unmistakably grandmotherly in appearance. Her face showed all of her sixty-four years, but serenity had some time ago given her the looks that are never dulled by age and wrinkles.

Jack's face was grizzled with lines. The ironic twist to his mouth had deepened. Even now, while meditating, he gave the impression that he was thinking of a risqué joke unsuitable for present company. His scalp was freed at last from the enduring, shapeless cloth hat, exposing a thin straggle of wiry grey hair. He had, at first, refused to remove his hat, declaring that it would be like amputating a limb. The others had removed it for him at the cost of a round torrent of abuse. By contrast, his language on seeing himself dressed in the robe for the first time had been relatively polite and came nowhere near to cracking the mirror.

In the last few years, each of them had taken up meditation independently. Jennifer had adopted a cross-legged position and, by way of compromise with the others, she sat that way now on a cushion on her chair. Though she had not practised yoga, her limbs were arranged in the eastern half-lotus, with her hands resting in her lap and cupped upwards round her navel. The relaxed nature of the pose wasn't entirely reflected in her face: even though she was calm now, there was an underlying pain, the result of a series of disastrous relationships with men. If asked, she would have said that she had felt middle-aged for the last five years, though it would have been an exaggeration of her own feelings. For all that, she had taken good care of her body: her figure had kept to youthful proportions, slender, lithe and supple from a long interest in free dance. Her complexion had darkened, as had her coppered hair. The girlish prettiness had gone, exchanged for the stronger lines of maturity.

Matthew was the most at ease, the most assured. The years of stress, of forks endlessly dividing the paths ahead, had ended.

Even without physical movement of any sort, his body expressed certainty, purpose and determination. He gave the impression of belonging to the place and situation in which he found himself. Of the four, he wore the robe most comfortably.

Now, after half an hour of meditation, his head slowly dropped forward, a movement of less than an inch. Then it came back. The eyelids rose, and he was no longer there. The eyes he left behind were dark, almost black in the flickering light.

'Through meditation,' Nathaniel said, 'you have prepared for healing in the way you might develop a long-forgotten muscle. The healing hand of your orthodox churches atrophied as they lost touch with such attunement and you are living in the age when that hand is to be revitalised.'

'I don't see how what *we* do is going to make physical changes to someone's body.'

'You do not make the physical changes as such. The physical world is only that tiny portion of the spiritual that you perceive. If the healing works, the physical changes follow as a precise reflection of the broader changes.'

'If?'

'If!' Firmly.

Eight o'clock. No one had yet come. Jennifer unhooked her legs and went to one of the drapes on the west wall. She pulled it aside and gazed out the window, pressing her face close to the glass to avoid reflections from inside the room. She looked out under the mass of trees, through the dark trunks across the lawns to the street. The gate, some of the shrubbery and the end of the driveway were illuminated by an upside-down cone of yellow street light. The frosty air hung softly in the cone as if left there by a single giant breath. Above the mass of trees stood the sequoia, a massive blot, a black place in the sky.

Apprehensive, she asked aloud if the others thought anyone would come. Then, when they all arched eyebrows at her, she put her fingers to her nose and waggled them rudely. Jack said something to D'Arcy, who peeled back his eyelids, frowning reproachfully at the intrusion of his dreams.

At 8.30, the neighbours saw a figure cross from the sea wall, step across the gate and walk briskly up the drive. It was hatted, coated and scarved up to the nose, but there was no mistaking

191

the build and the distinctive, loose-limbed walk. It was Peter Platt, the bank teller, one of the eight Anglicans in Waiata. The neighbours' phones were off their hooks before he was beyond the range of the street light.

He was inside for just quarter of an hour. When he came out, he wasn't so carefully hidden. He walked away down the waterfront with an expression of contempt and scorn clear for the world to see. In less than an hour, the grapevine had more: Platt claimed he had gone there for a bit of a laugh, that he had pretended to be sick just to see what they did. And he'd seen enough, he said, to know that the outfit was a fake and a fraud, pushing hocus-pocus that wouldn't impress a moron. Just what Peter was suffering from, the grapevine never established.

When Peter Thorn brought the news, the minister was in the vestry, conducting his monthly meeting with the home prayer- and study-group leaders. The story caused more than a little amusement at Platt's expense in particular and Anglicans in general. 'Anglicans,' said the minister, 'have that knack of hiding the right hand behind the back where it can't see the left hand trying to remove cheese from a rat trap.' The group laughed appreciatively. Then, the meeting over anyway, the home-group leaders departed. As the door closed, the faces of the two men left in the vestry lost all humour.

'An isolated case,' Peter Thorn declared. 'And to our advantage.'

'Pray God you're right,' the minister said quietly.

It wasn't a Wednesday, so no one expected it. In any case, Fleming was known to be the only one in the Sanctuary at the time, so the gate watchers were caught flat-footed. The night was cloudy, pitch black away from the street lights. The thin young woman who slipped over the dark end of the fence would have made it unobserved but for the boy on his way home from the Sea Scouts' den, riding a bike without lights.

The phones were chattering within minutes.

Kay Cameron was healthy enough, as far as anyone knew. She was inclined to be tautly strung; but common knowledge attributed that to her being lumbered with a husband whose personality resembled the underbelly of a fresh cod. In fact in some quarters it was suggested that Dave Cameron be watched very carefully while his wife was getting her ailments healed, in case he vanished. But marriage handicap aside, what really mattered to Presbyterian Waiata was that Kay Cameron was a communicant of the church.

When she returned to her home an hour later, Chester Farnsworth and Paul Marsen were waiting with her husband. Dave Cameron's pale jowls were rolling with each nervous swallow and his pink-rimmed eyes blinked in bewilderment.

'I'm going to divorce you,' she said to him with supreme poise. Dave's jaw foundered and the elders' eyebrows shot towards their hairlines.

'I'm leaving now,' she added.

The elders fled to find the minister.

But Kay Cameron's cocoon of self-assurance lasted only as far as the bedroom and the first suitcase. She stopped in mid-stride, dropped the still-empty suitcase and moaned as if in great pain. Then she went to bed fully clothed and no one, not even the minister, could persuade her to emerge.

Much later, she stood at the window and declared, though it was the dead of night, that she could see a black slime creeping across the peninsula, down the hills and valleys into the Sanctuary grounds. After that she washed her hands. Thoroughly. And from then on she alternated between the window and the washbasin until she fell into an exhausted sleep.

In the morning, six men stood in the Camerons' tiny kitchen: Dave Cameron, the minister and the four elders, who murmured appropriate comforts to Dave in spite of irritation at the man's inability to stiffen his spine for the occasion. Indecisive at the best of times, Cameron had now entered a state remarkably akin to a coma. While he waited for God or His nearest deputy to solve the problem, the only sign of life on his gloomy face was the slow blink of his moist eyes.

The men fell silent at the sound of tap water in a basin. Old plumbing shuddered in the cottage walls and a muscle twitched on Dave Cameron's cheek. Kay was washing her hands again.

'Evil bastards,' muttered Gordon Crocker, bunching his fist.

'What have they done to the poor woman?' Peter Thorn said fiercely. It occurred to him that much use would be made of a breakdown in the Camerons' marriage at this point. If the Sanctuary was seen to have put asunder those whom God had joined in holy matrimony...

'Guilt,' Robert McKay said thoughtfully, a look of compassion coming over him. 'It's guilt that's doing this to her. She's consumed by it.'

Abruptly, he strode through to the lounge, where Kay was seated with her face in her hands. The others milled uncertainly behind him as he seated himself opposite her and laid his tattered travelling Bible squarely in front. It remained closed as he clasped his hands.

'Mrs Cameron, we're here to help you.'

The bleary eyes slid reluctantly into view behind the fingers.

'I want you to tell me what you see out the window.'

Kay Cameron described the black slime in a flat monotone.

'Tell me again. I didn't quite hear you.' This produced some puzzlement behind him. What was he up to? But Kay went through it again, and this time she added such picturesque objects to the slime as human heads and rotting eyeballs. This time, her voice was sharp-edged with tension.

'Again. Tell me again.'

Chester Farnsworth mumbled uncertainly, 'She's under a lot of strain, Robert. Don't you think —'

'Tell me!'

On the fourth telling, Kay Cameron broke. She dropped to the cold floor boards, curled up and wailed, while her husband wrung his hands by the kitchen door. Robert took the woman's hands and made her sit up.

Did she want to ask Jesus to forgive her and cleanse her?

'Yes, yes!' she sobbed.

'Then...' McKay's voice was instantly gentle. '... He knows already. Can't you feel His forgiveness. Can't you feel Him wanting to come into your heart?'

An expression of wonder, of amazement, gradually dawned on Kay Cameron's face. The sobs became sporadic, but then broke out afresh as joy superseded all else. The minister put a hand on her shoulder, commanding her to remember the joy felt in heaven over one repented sinner. He then directed her dumbfounded husband to take his place and departed with the ecstatic elders.

But he didn't share their delight.

'It's one battle only,' he replied grimly when they proffered their congratulations. 'It's by no means the whole war.'

That night, at the manse evening meal, Robert was withdrawn to the point of rudeness. Eventually, he apologised to his wife and her guest from the embroidery circle and withdrew to his study. There he searched the bookshelves until he found an old address book, brought with him from England so many years ago. Methodically, he turned the pages, scanning them until he found the address he wanted. Then, with fountain pen freshly filled, he began to write a letter.

From time to time, he glanced up to look out into the night. A hundred yards away, a street light glowed dimly over the front of the Sanctuary grounds. A little shrubbery, the gate and part of the fence, even a portion of the driveway, were visible in the dingy, rain-drenched patch of light.

SIX

In the old, rambling building, Matthew slept.

He was close. So close that his downturned face was flooded with the brilliant gold light. It was so intense it shone right through his body and individual cells seemed to dance with a will of their own. But still he could not see what caused the light. He had to determine its source. He came even closer, his face nearly scraping the cruel stones.

But he knew he was only inches away. Close, close, closer. His heart was a drum. Pain seared his head, hands, knees and every intervening fibre. But soon, he knew, it would be gone.

As he continued looking straight down, he became aware of the tides of radiance pouring up towards him. The source had been among the stones all the time.

The source was itself a stone.

For an instant, he felt he was in the presence of something infinitely wise and knowing. Each of the stone's countless facets was a different shape and glowed with a different colour, each part of an exquisite whole. The colours seemed to come from fires writhing in its centre, as if to promise that the object of his search was near.

But I've found you, he protested. I'm here.

Not yet, the fires answered him and they faded away, leaving the stone lifeless. He himself was left blind and bereft. When his sight returned he saw that the fog still enshrouded him. Fear returned. The dead stone began to swell threateningly, crushing the stones around it. Fear became paralysing terror. And a hand appeared out of the fog with fingers curled like talons.

SEVEN

The harbour was at its brilliant best. The water was clear and deep at the edges, and bonnet-blue all the way to the quarry cliffs on the far side. Elderly folk sunned themselves on the benches above the beach, and games of draughts waited contentedly on the pleasure of the men who sat to either side. Kingfishers preened on the overhead wires, denying winter with the brilliance of their blues and greens, balancing themselves with precise strokes of their tails. Occasionally, one would swoop away, frightening little children who had heard that a kingfisher is so fast and its beak so sharp it can fly in one ear and out the other without slowing down. The air was so unseasonably warm that shirt-sleeved strollers on the sea wall talked with each other about the possibility of an early spring. Traps swayed behind the languid clopping feet of their horses. Cars purred behind.

It was a Sunday afternoon.

A pick-up truck came to a halt in front of the house between the church and the Sanctuary. The distinctive four-wheel-drive flat-back was recognisable anywhere as belonging to Trevor and Beryl Digby of Okains Bay. The Digbys had been seen departing for the long ride home straight after church; a few of the passers-by were surprised to see them back, but only mildly so. They must have forgotten something. And no one thought there was anything amiss when Trevor Digby switched off the engine and just sat where he was, glowering straight ahead. After all, he was moody at the best of times, and so cantankerous at others that some wondered how Beryl had ever seen enough in him to say yes at the altar.

Beryl clambered down from the passenger seat and lurched straight into the Sanctuary driveway. Within moments, a dozen strollers had stopped to watch. Before she was half way down the drive, people were coming from within a radius of hundreds

197

of yards. This time, there was no doubt as to the ailment involved. For five years, she had suffered from a progressive scoliosis — a lateral curvature of the lower spine. For the last year, the compensating curve at the top of the spine had been insufficient to keep her shoulders level. The result was a grotesque, uneven, S-shaped displacement of her upper body to the left.

She mounted the front steps and knocked. Knocked again. No answer, so she sat down to wait. Many of those watching from the street could have told her there was no one home. But they stayed to watch anyway; Fleming and Pringle had been seen at the bus depot, collecting their groceries and would be along shortly.

In less than five minutes, Gordon Crocker and Peter Thorn were moving briskly through the Sanctuary gate. When they were standing before the woman, a book opened in Peter Thorn's hand and with his other arm he began to gesticulate. But Beryl Digby just sat there, hugging her knees. Out in the street, her husband continued to glower through the windscreen. Two men went to speak to him, but the only words they got out of him were 'Silly cow'.

Matthew and Jennifer approached, carrying a large carton. The group of onlookers at the gate made way for the pair, but sullenly, giving them only just enough room to squeeze through. A youth remarked that Matthew had forgotten his dress. Another ran a leering eye up and down Jennifer, commenting that she was probably so worn by now that it would be like rolling around in a barrel. He miscalculated — a few voices around him told him to shut his filthy mouth. He shrugged.

In a few moments, there were five on the front steps of the Sanctuary. Even from the street, it was obvious that while the elders were doing most of the talking, they were making no headway at all. After a while, the woman went into the building with Matthew and Jennifer, and the elders came back to the street shaking their heads.

Peter Thorn declared loudly and angrily that standing around watching was just encouraging wickedness. At this, some of the older onlookers went, knowing that the news would catch up with them shortly anyway. The younger ones moved to the railings opposite, still within sight. A carload of overnighters from the city approached them to ask what was going on. But being outsiders, they got cryptic answers.

Ten minutes later, Emily Nisbet was given silent passage and appeared not to notice the crowd's hostility, nor its curiosity, as it closed in behind her as far as the gate. She was even thinner now, near gaunt. Her cardigan hung in loose black folds. As she went up the driveway, one of the Tomlinson brothers from a farm at the far end of the peninsula spat carefully on the ground and wiped his mouth with a tweed sleeve.

'If you took the clothes off the old bag you'd find the Devil's mark on 'er. That's what I say.'

Daniel Ferris tucked gum into an opposite cheek, nodded, then jerked his head at the Sanctuary. 'What about that thumb on Fleming, then?'

The crowd waited.

An hour later, Beryl Digby came out. She stood on the entrance steps for a while, then came slowly towards the gate. It took some seconds for the crowd to work out what was different about her. Normally, her shoulders tilted left.

Now, they tilted to the right.

But even as she approached the waterfront, she stopped compensating for a condition that no longer existed; her shoulders levelled off. Her husband leapt out of the Landrover and gaped as she came towards him. She walked delicately, fragilely, unaccustomed to the straight spine. The shoulders heaved occasionally and a tear squeezed out of half-closed eyes.

She said nothing to anyone, just climbed into the truck. Trevor Digby stood out on the road a moment longer, blinking at her and at the open mouths. Then he jumped in behind the wheel. The pick-up U-turned on the waterfront and headed towards the road to Okains Bay.

According to the crop farmers, the earth-circuit, single-wire telephone lines were bad news for earthworms in the immediate vicinity. If so, then the worms along the way to Okains Bay went into a state of continuous shock the following day. Scores of people found one reason or another to call the Digbys' neighbours. And since the neighbours all had one reason or another to be frequently within eyeshot of the Digbys' farmhouse, they were reasonably well informed. Their observations, once in Waiata, were distributed with a speed and efficiency surpassing any conventional medical information service. Every known nuance of Beryl Digby's health crackled over the fences and over the hills faster than a bush fire in the height of the dry. And it all boiled down to the fact that Beryl's spine was as straight as a die, and she had taken to singing as she hung out her husband's underthings on the line.

The session elders gathered in the minister's study.

Peter Thorn, the Digby's elder, was seen driving towards Okains Bay. He was back in less than two hours.

A formal extraordinary session was held in the vestry.

At the doctor's surgery, patients pressed Alan Pringle for a medical explanation, only to have him reply curtly that he would have to examine Mrs Digby for himself. A few days later, Beryl Digby did come to his rooms, but for an entirely different matter. As she put it, now that her back was straight, her husband was finding her more... well, he wanted to... uh, and she would like to take some precautions please. Naturally, the doctor took the opportunity to run his eyes and fingers along her spine and over the associated muscles. He told her that there did appear to have been a certain amount of straightening, almost certainly through a redistribution of muscular tension. It simply wasn't possible for the discs to change their structure so quickly, he said, and she would be well advised to go to the city for an X-ray before she jumped to false conclusions. Mrs Digby, never having been off the peninsula, felt no urgency to leave now. She asked if it would be all right, instead, if she just let him know if she ever felt any more pain.

Thereafter, Doctor Pringle answered other patients' curiosity by using such words as 'spontaneous remission'. He said that the emotional atmosphere created by faith healers was a deliberate device to induce psychological change in suggestible people. He hinted darkly that once the emotional atmosphere was removed, the previous physiological equilibrium would re-establish itself. If there was some temporary relief, he said, then it certainly wasn't anything miraculous. Just the natural work of the body. And the body, after all, he was fond of saying, is the best of all healers.

Many days later, Beryl Digby was still singing.

Seconds before Robert McKay opened his mouth, the congregation knew that this was going to be no ordinary sermon. He surveyed the filled pews and crowded aisles in silence, as was usual; but this time, the silence was extended. And the striking thing was that he didn't do it for effect. He didn't raise his shoulders dramatically as he breathed in. He didn't flare his nostrils, as he loved to do, or tense the corners of his mouth.

He just looked at them.

Then, as he began to speak, many felt the hair on the backs of their necks prickle in delicious anticipation. The elaborate vocal gymnastics were gone. The extraordinary range of tonal inflections simply wasn't there. No frills. No prepared notes. The minister delivered his message as a man who talks from the deepest place he can reach in his own heart.

'My brothers and sisters. If Satan can offer kingdoms, would he have the slightest difficulty in granting the power of healing to one who serves him well?'

Sidelong glances in the pews. This was Robert McKay as no one had ever seen him.

'A sister is not with us, this morning.' No one looked around. Everyone knew that both Beryl and Trevor Digby were not in church. 'I must speak now to those of you amongst us who are tempted as our sister was tempted. I plead with you to listen to me with your innermost heart. Listen, or you are in great peril.

'Know Satan's purpose. Everything he does has one ultimate end point: he wants as many as possible to share his fate with him. In hell. But in order to do that he must absorb... no, he must *devour* your personality. And there are two ways to do this: he can win you with honey-coated teachings...'

Emphatic nods. Everyone knew where one might find such teachings.

'... or he can bind you with the chains of a bribe. A bribe! Think! Think! We are known as the most god-fearing community in the nation. Think! What is the most alluring bribe the master of sweet falsity could offer any of you who have ever been sick or broken a bone or been in pain?'

No one needed to think.

Yet the minister felt a discontent in his audience as if it were an animal he could sense in the dark. '"For wrestle not against flesh and blood,"' he quoted from Ephesians, '"but against principalities, against powers, against the rulers of the darkness of this world..."' He gave them verse after verse, teaching that if any were so foolish as to attend the Sanctuary, they would be actively *soliciting* the fellowship and leadership of Satan.

The great majority of the congregation were with him. He could see it. They were stronger with every minute. And yet the nightshade poison doubt was still out there, unbanished. The whisper of restlessness was like a vehicle poised ready to move.

There was no choice, then. The last card would have to be played now.

'Perhaps you doubt the risk involved. Perhaps now that you've seen our sister apparently healed, you think to yourself, "How can this be bad?" You think, "Surely, this is a good deed?" You think, "If it is a good thing, how can it be of Satan? Surely God must approve!"'

Heads stirred. Peter Thorn and Norman White, frowning. Dangerous ground.

He drew a piece of paper from his waistcoat pocket, unfolded it, and laid it on the pulpit. 'I have received this letter from a fellow minister in London, whose particular expertise is in helping souls shattered by spiritualism. I'm afraid you will not find the contents pleasant.

'Dear Brother in Christ,
I have received your letter and pray that I may be of assistance. Your news is indeed alarming, and your fears more than justified. I thank the Lord that you have written now, and not waited for your flock to be tempted. Believe me, experience shows that invariably there are a weak few who will be tempted. I implore you to convey to your charge that in twenty years of working in a community riddled with spiritualism, I have found the following to be associated with the vile practice:'

The minister read from a list, looking up after each item.

'Unexplained accidents. Family discord. Vile and blasphemous thoughts. Personality dislocation. Marked resistance to biblical truth. Criminal behaviour. Fits of uncontrollable temper. Severe depression, sometimes leading to manic depressive psychosis. And, as if those were not enough, even suicide.'

He pressed on, despite growing signs of discomfort in his audience.

Elderly hands were wavering and feet were shuffling.

'My brother, these are just labels. They cannot convey the agony endured by some who have succumbed. Let me tell you of one of our number, a young woman who was cured of cancer at a healing ceremony, immediately after a seance. For a while she was happy, then she drifted into severe depression and finally threw herself under a train. But the tragedy is not just that she lost her life, or just that she left two children motherless — it is that she died never understanding that *in accepting a healthy body from a supernatural source other than God, she had in fact accepted Satan's bribe.* In dying in that state therefore, her soul was finally and irrevocably lost...'

He stopped. Many of the congregation were now openly distressed. Immediately in front of him old Mrs Irwin was fumbling with her walking stick, her hands trembling. There was no need to continue, he knew. It was done. The hearts of the Lord's children had returned to Him. 'There is more,' he said gesturing grimly at the letter. 'But I think there is no need to continue.'

Yes. It was done. But there remained one more matter to be taken care of. His task would not be complete until success was irreversible.

Eventually, the service ended. The long line of congratulatory hands passed and the congregation collected in animated groups on the lawns. The minister stood on the front steps and looked about for a particular face. Paul Marsen. Yes, there he was, standing near the spire with his wife Kate. Robert chose a path through the clusters and the chatter. A moment later he brushed Paul's elbow as he walked by.

'I beg your pardon,' he apologised.

'Robert.' In his enthusiasm, Paul came close to plucking at the minister's sleeve. 'I've got to say it again: tremendous! Just tremendous. You really ran out the wide gear with that one. You've finished Fleming's little cesspool for sure...' He looked to his wife for agreement. Kate Marsen nodded shyly, abashed by her husband's boyish fervour. But Robert himself appeared doubtful.

'Hmmm. Kind of you, but I don't think so.'

'What? You can't doubt it, surely.' Paul flapped a hand at the people around. 'I mean, look at them all. Never more united.'

But Robert wasn't happy. 'Perhaps we've gained something this morning, but you know how many Sunday-faithful we carry, Paul. I'm concerned that there's no collective reference point outside the church grounds and outside the sabbath.'

'Pardon?' Paul said.

'There's been no expression of *public* feeling. Something that lets *every* individual know where his peers stand on the matter.'

'Yes. Yes, yes. I see.' Paul looked worried.

'Still. I'm not sure anything can be done in that line...'

'I don't see why not.' Paul crossed his arms and scowled at the grass, concentrating. He came from a line of pioneering fishermen who counted themselves as ideas men. He looked up eagerly. 'Why not call a public meeting?'

Robert looked surprised. Considered the idea. 'Would it work?'

'Sure it would. Let everyone speak. You know, make it open. In the rugby ground maybe. It's floodlit.'

'We'd have to choose the right evening. To have the maximum effect...'

'Ahah! What about Wednesday, 7.30? That would *really* make the point!'

'Hmmm.' Robert appeared to be warming to the idea reluctantly. 'That timing would certainly be effective. But if everyone's away round in the rugby ground, someone might take the opportunity to slip into —'

'Wait! I have it!' Paul was excited. 'Why not hold it on the waterfront, smack bang in front of Fleming's Pit! Then it'll show those four what the town thinks of them as well.'

Robert's face cleared. He appeared to be impressed. But then his features clouded. 'I still see a difficulty. If it's organised by the clergy then it's not really a *spontaneous* expression of public anger, is it?'

Paul's arms waved about. 'Then we don't have to organise it. There's any number of people who'd jump at the chance of organising a spontaneous demonstration against Fleming's Pit. It doesn't have to come from us at all!'

'You mean placards, verses on banners, and so on?... You certainly come up with some ideas, Paul. It would be unprecedented on the peninsula.'

'There's got to be a first time for everything, Robert. That's

204

what I say. If we're going to remain an example to the rest of the country, then we have to think for ourselves. Now you just leave it to me to have a word in the right ear.'

EIGHT

Her nostrils flared in eloquent disgust, Margaret Crocker placed bowls of steaming porridge before Gordon and Jimmy. One of the drawbacks of winter mornings was having to brew that abominable grey glue. The other was having to watch them salt it and shovel it down, and to listen to the inevitable remark about that soft, modern generation that ate it with sugar. Gordon held a dripping spoonful above her plate and suggested, straight-faced, that she was bound to enjoy it if she put it on toast with garlic and tomato sauce. She shuddered, pulled her cardigan more tightly around her and sighed heavily. Money or no money, the Crockers were not yet ready to sup with the Queen.

'Where's Amelia?' Jimmy hated Amelia's being absent for grace. Even though he had given up going to work in order to devote all his time to her, he was never comfortable when separated from her, even briefly.

Mrs Crocker went to the dining-room door.

'Amelia! Amelia! Breakfast's up, love.'

She went out and came back in a minute, wearing a forced smile. 'She's tired again. She'll take her breakfast a bit later.' She sat, bowed her head. 'For what we are about to receive, may the Lord make us truly thankful.'

But instead of eating, she exchanged an uneasy glance with her husband. He nodded apprehensively.

'Jimmy lad, we've been thinking...'

Jimmy's porridge spoon stopped half way to his mouth.

'... Amelia's been looking a bit peaky for some time now and... we thought... well, that it wouldn't do any harm if—'

'I told you. Amelia's not sick.' A warning. The spoon hovered.

Margaret took a breath.

'What your dad means is that we think... just in case she needs some vitamins —'

206

'No!' The spoon crashed down as the big man surged to his feet. The milk jug fell off the table and smashed in a white tide on the crocheted rug. He snarled, looming over them, 'There's nothing wrong with her. She doesn't get sick. You're making it up. You're trying to take her away from me, aren't you. You think I'm not good enough for her. You think I can't look after her.'

'Nobody looks after her like you do, Jimmy.' Margaret said forcefully. Then more softly, 'Amelia couldn't have a better dad than you.' The pupils of Jimmy's eyes widened perceptibly as he subsided. White-faced, Margaret Crocker righted a tea cup without taking her eyes off him.

NINE

The soft springs had never been designed for anything rougher than the main street. So when they left the houses behind and paced up the uneven, narrow Aylmers Valley Road, the buggy swayed and bounced drunkenly. But Matthew only grinned and flicked the traces and called out to the mare. The horse broke wind, unloaded fresh manure between the shafts and sped up. They flashed past the bushes, the hedgerows and the farm gates. Sheep beyond the fences scrambled. Cattle raised their heads swiftly and wheeled in the paddocks. Outraged geese with clipped wings flapped away from the road.

Matthew's hair flowed behind his head. Jennifer hung on to her sunhat, crying out that he was an irresponsible delinquent. The hat was part of their agreement that the picnic would be conducted from beginning to end as if it were the height of summer. The only exception granted had been warm clothing. The week-long spell of mild weather, however, still wrapped the peninsula and it was so warm today that nature seemed to be a party to the deal. Much of their heavier clothing had already been discarded, leaving both with bare arms, jeans and shirts. Jennifer kicked off her shoes, placed feet to either side of the picnic basket and clamped it tightly in place.

'Now will you tell me where you're abducting me?' she shouted across the wind.

'No!'

'Kidnapping is a capital offence,' she shouted. 'And besides, we don't have a chaperone. What will people think?'

'Hah!' Matthew shouted in devilish glee and with a phantom whip lashed a phantom team of black stallions. 'Huyahh! Hah!' Jennifer's face was turned into the wind with sheer enjoyment. Since Beryl Digby's healing, Jennifer had had many such moments — times when it was almost impossible to see in her the reserve,

208

the cynical caution, the determination that no one was going to put one across her. She was so very beautiful like this. How could he have missed how beautiful she was?

At the end of the last farm, they turned on to a track that led away towards the side of the valley. The mare's flanks were gleaming with sweat now, so they slowed to an easy walk. At the end of the track, they unhitched her, put her on a long grazing tether, then set out with blanket and basket up the valley side on foot. Higher still they padded through the bush, on a floor that was sometimes grassed, sometimes brown with earth and fine twigs. The occasional deciduous tree sunned bare wood. The evergreens released fragrances into the unaccustomed warmth.

Matthew stopped just outside his forest glade. He looked intently at Jennifer, but could determine nothing of significance in her expression. He tried then to usher her in first with a gentleman-at-large wave of his arm; but in mid-flourish he hesitated, as long-forgotten reverence for his childhood hideaway welled up. Abruptly, he walked in first.

Jennifer, taken aback somewhat, came to the entrance under the old-man walnut. Then she gazed about in delight at the soft deep grass, the tiny stream and the clear rock pool.

In the years since Matthew had been here, the edges had blurred with new growth so that it was no longer clear where the glade ended and the surrounding bush began. New seedlings had taken root. The once young lancewood tickled the bush canopy, another grew at its feet and silvereyes bobbed for insects in the outermost branches. There was a new backdrop now: a thick tree trunk lay aslant nearby, felled just clear of the glade by a past storm.

With scrupulous care, Matthew was inspecting the ground. But there were no obvious signs of human visitation, no depressions in the grass, no shoe prints by the stream. He kept up the search for some time, every now and then darting a speculative glance in Jennifer's direction.

After a while, she became irritated and wondered why she felt as if she was trespassing.

'What in the world are you —?' She broke off.

Matthew was staring at something behind the main rock by the pool. A second later he leapt over it and came up with a small preserving jar, still sealed, with a badly rusted screw cap.

Inside was a miniature pocket knife. It took a few moments for Matthew's hands to wrestle off the cap and force the seal. Then he was warming his old knife in his hands. He picked the blade out and it came smoothly. It had been cleaned and oiled and left for him.

'Jesus. Twelve years,' he muttered.

He took a final hopeful glance at her then. She saw his elation dull with disappointment, as his eyes returned to the knife. She was the one who now hesitated. Clearly there was more to this place than Matthew had chosen to explain. She retreated to the edge of the glade and sat near the basket and blanket with her back against the walnut tree. There she let herself absorb the atmosphere of the place, all the time keeping an eye on him. He kept opening and closing the blade and she could see an engraving on the bone handle: a cat of some sort. Finally he looked up at her, blinking, not knowing what to say.

'You want me to wait outside?' she asked dryly, waving at the bush.

'Damn. Damn.' He came to crouch before her. 'I'm sorry, Jen. I've got some explaining to do, haven't I?'

'If you want me to stay,' she smiled.

His humour suddenly returned.

'Stay!' he ordered with a finger pointing to the ground.

'Talk,' she countermanded firmly.

And he did. They spread the blanket on the grass, lay side by side and gazed into the rock pool. Matthew told her how he had come across the glade for the first time as a small boy and been entranced by it. He told her how he had used his schoolboy fantasies here to escape from Waiata, and he reduced her to helpless laughter with exaggerated tales of his earliest and most swashbuckling adventures. But the fantasies had changed, he said. They had become more lifelike and dwelt exclusively in the past. In the end, he had been forced to use all his wits to impose some influence on their course.

'Self-propelled daydreams,' Jennifer observed with deliberate ambiguity.

Then there was still the unresolved enigma, the tantalising invisible thread that ran through every one of his historical jaunts. Hidden within them all was a single personality — someone he wished he could recall; someone who would not, despite all his efforts, ever come into focus.

'It's as if some actor was following me around in a series of historical plays, adopting a different role in each.'

For some time, he said nothing more.

Their arrival had cast a disturbance into the bush, a ripple of silence that had sped out from their intrusion. Now it returned: soundlessness shrinking back on itself, sounds on the back of silence, running one on another like water droplets on new crystal.

Jennifer prompted Matthew to continue by picking up the miniature knife and turning it over and over so that it flashed in the sun. He completed the story, from the first time he had found the imprint of a stranger in the glade and seen this as evidence of a soul mate, to the present and the return of the knife.

'Ah.' Slowly. 'You thought it was me.'

He nodded cautiously.

'You're disappointed.'

This time her ambiguity flummoxed him. And he was further robbed of adequate reply by the sardonic twist in her expression.

For a while she studied obscure minutiae of the glade. Then, avoiding his eyes, she went to the rock pool where she knelt with great care so as not to disturb the surface of the water.

There was no enigmatic element in those waterborne eyes that she could see, no tantalising fathomless depths. No surprises. How very clear the significance of her failure to be Matthew's alter ego of the forest. Second best. Second place. Once again. She had seen too much of life to expect the terrain of love to be anything but precipitous, but was she forever to be denied its peaks? And — most cruel denial of all — when this one was so close?

She felt his gaze. A bitter-sweet longing swept through her. She countered it by picking up a pebble between thumb and forefinger and dropping it with precision between the eyes in the water. Swiftly she scooped up the broken pieces and splashed them on her face. The shocking contrast of the cold water and the liquid warmth in her thighs acted on her like a switch. She gave a laugh. And when she returned to Matthew on the blanket, it was with a glint in her eye, and with a spurious French accent on her tongue.

'*Sacré bleu,* Inspector Clousseau! Eet appears that we 'ave not only a mysterious Meester X lurking in your daydreams, but also ...' — she raised a declamatory finger — '... a mysterious Meester Y, who, you claim, is *not* in your daydr —' She shrieked in best *femme fatale* fashion as a much-relieved Matthew aimed a mock blow in her direction.

'That's about it,' he admitted, grinning. 'Only in both cases I don't know about the "Mister".'

'Ahah,' she commented dryly.

They lay silent for a while, close together.

A fantail in the black phase appeared at the edge of the glade and attached itself upside down to a branch over the pool, probing the bark for six-legged delicacies and observing the two humans.

Then, in one of those effortless moments that does not ask or answer, Matthew and Jennifer came together, her head in the crook of his arm. Soon, wanting to speak, but reluctant to disturb the glade, Jennifer whispered.

'Suppose this whole life is just another of those times you see in these daydreams. What then?' When he didn't answer, she turned his face to her and saw that the thought had already occurred to him. She said wonderingly, 'You're afraid. You don't know what's going to happen to us any more than I do.'

After a while, he touched her cheek with the tips of his fingers and she held his fingers there while they searched each other's eyes. With exquisitely slow motion they brought their lips together and brushed them so lightly they scarcely touched. In an instant, they were clinging, tightly, breathlessly. Had they kept their eyes open, each would have seen the contortion of both pain and pleasure in the other. They stayed that way for some time, rocking minutely, while newly discovered spaces filled with delight.

Piece by piece, they removed each other's clothing and lay back on the sun-drenched blanket. Then, slowly, they came together and made love, while the silvereyes chattered, astonished, in the lancewood.

Every Thursday morning, the minister visited hospital patients, and this week, the rooms were all occupied.

'Good morning, Mr McKay,' the day nurse breezed. 'A fine crop of sinners for you this week: bronchial infection in room one, an appendix in two, and a broken ankle in three. Right sorry for himself he is, too.' Robert smiled politely and turned towards the nearest room.

Then he slowed and came to a halt. He stood, frowning, looking at nothing in particular. He blinked, turned again and faced the nurse. 'What was that you said?'

'Oh, goodness.' The nurse tried to think if she had said anything out of the ordinary. The list of ailments? 'About sinners? I was joking. Really.'

'Of course, of course,' Robert said distractedly. His hand moved vaguely in the air, as if trying to locate something. 'Who were they again, these sinners?'

'Bronchial infection,' she repeated uncertainly. 'Appendix ... broken ankle ... Is something wrong?'

'No, no. Just a thought,' he replied absently.

TEN

There were three hundred people on the waterfront, and more were arriving all the time. The banners were already aloft, facing the Sanctuary. The biggest was fully eight feet long, and it read: 'Because of These Abominations, the Lord Thy God Doth Drive Them Out From Before Thee. Deuteronomy 18:12.'

Not a single person present had ever before taken part in a demonstration of any kind. There were countless jokes bandied around, about student hippies and communist agitators. Respectable men told respectable elderly parents to get their hair cut, but assured them that the first charge of disorderly conduct didn't always lead to prison. A retired seaman waved a scrap of paper which he gleefully claimed was a telegram from the Prime Minister acknowledging that the country was on its knees and asking when they would like to take over.

It was better than the annual fête.

Almost every boy who owned a bike was showing off with it at the edges of the crowd. Adults held their banners high and laughed and joked, while children played chasing games amongst them. A few boys even played football until a Landrover turned up with more loose sheepdogs on the back than there were people inside. The dogs immediately monopolised the game, raising the carnival atmosphere to such a pitch that the ball was confiscated.

Elaine Drury arrived with a banner that was nothing short of a work of art: a cloth-on-cloth depiction of Christ crucified. Jimmy Crocker paraded here and there with Amelia high on his massive shoulders, beaming hugely as adults fondly greeted his beautiful daughter. In all the excitement she tired quickly and sometimes didn't answer. The entire Richardson family arrived and every one of its eight members lined up with his or her own placard on a stick. Even two-year-old Amy, still in nappies, bore a tiny piece of cardboard. It exhorted: 'Do Not Defile

Yourselves. Lev. 19:31.' She kept it only as long as it took her father to work out why it provoked witticisms about pots and kettles. Tommy Ransley came by on his way to the pool room, and he stayed in spite of the commotion about him. He held on to the sea-wall railing, while someone finger-wrote an explanation on his hand.

What everyone knew and discreetly didn't mention to each other was that 'Bluebottle' Crawford had been called away to investigate a report of strange boats dynamiting fish in Le Bons Bay. No one knew if the report was genuine. No one wanted to know.

It was after eight o'clock when a boy threw the first stone across the Sanctuary fence. It was hardly more than a pebble and he just lobbed it through the shrubbery. He looked around for a reaction, but no one seemed to have noticed. Another boy picked up a larger stone and threw it high, so that it thumped down on to the lawns. Soon, boys were crisscrossing the road, fetching rocks from below the sea wall, hurling them as far as possible into the grounds. Town councillors, in easy evidence earlier, could now be found only at the rear of the crowd where it was difficult to see. The elders weren't to be found at all, nor were they sought: the word was that the clergy felt their presence would make no positive contribution to a spontaneous demonstration of lay unity.

Dozens of teenagers joined in the stone-throwing. A competition developed to see who could throw far enough to hit the sequoia tree in the centre of the grounds. Claims of success were invariably jeered at because the only evidence of a hit was by sound: projectiles were thrown from near a street lamp, but fell in darkness.

A hundred and fifty yards back, the rambling building was also in darkness, except for the light over the front porch and a faint, curtain-screened glow on the ground floor at the north end. The porch light only accentuated the black bulk of the old structure, making the demonstrators speculate on what manner of vile practices were being planned inside. The elder Tomlinson brother extracted a pipe from his jacket. He remarked, while stuffing it with tobacco, that it wasn't so long ago that they used to burn witches. And no one denied that. The night air made the flame of his match dance, so that his orange-lit face seemed to shift ominously.

215

The only elder not in his home was Norman White, the mayor. He and his wife had arranged some time ago to dine with the McKays this evening. And since there was an excellent view of the demonstration from the minister's study, there had seemed no reason to cancel the engagement. The meal had been disposed of early. The women were clearing the table and preparing to bring cups of tea up the stairs. Robert and Norman were already at the study's south window, watching.

'Maybe they'll go on to the grounds,' Norman said with neutral tone.

'I doubt it,' Robert replied evenly.

'Why don't I get votes of confidence like that?' Norman growled in mock envy, jerking his head at the throng on the waterfront. 'You've got cause to be well satisfied, Robert.'

'A vote for Him is not a vote for me,' the minister said dryly.

'All the same. You've disposed of the Pit, Robert. I don't see the placards doing a great deal for yon Fleming's salvation, but you've finished off his Sanctuary.'

'Perhaps.' Robert went from the window, then returned. He couldn't shake off the feeling that something was amiss. He was humbly grateful that his efforts had borne such fruit as this. But it had been so easy! Was a challenge thirty years in the making to be so quickly won? Yet the evidence of success was before him now. No one but an idiot would brave the stones; and, more importantly, no one in his right mind would go near the place in the future — not if he valued living on the peninsula. In a community like this, fear of peer disapproval dictated even the most trivial of activities. Fear of becoming a social outcast would, for many, be an even more effective deterrent than the prospect of losing their souls. And it was a fear that was no respecter of faith. A sad fact, but a fact nonetheless.

'Wait a minute.' Norman frowned through the window. 'Something's happening.'

Tommy Ransley let go the sea-wall railing and meandered on to the road. A running child jostled him, checked him, but he recovered and tapped his way further into the confusion. He walked into the back of a long banner, ignoring the helpful hands trying to set him back in the direction of the poolroom. He detoured round one banner, then round another, somehow ending up out front where the boys were launching their missiles. Some

216

good-natured laughter suddenly went up. Poor old Tommy; the commotion had unhinged his sense of direction. Colin Richards handed his placard to his nearest son, took hold of Tommy's hand and finger-traced 'wrong way' on his palm.

As he did so, the questing, white-tipped cane located the fence. Tommy pulled his hand away, tapped the pickets carefully, then set off in the direction of the poolroom. After a few paces he stopped and came back, still tapping the pickets. The laughter increased. Then it ceased abruptly as Tommy's stick found the gate latch. He fumbled with it. In a moment, the gate opened and Tommy was heading up the Sanctuary driveway.

There was a gasp from the crowd, a single intake of breath. Colin Richardson, Sidney Irwin and Alan Glubb leapt forward and took Tommy Ransley firmly by the arms and elbows. But they had not counted on his determination.

'Gerrof, ya buggers! Piss off, the lot o' yous,' he shouted in a high, querulous voice. He flung his arms free, then lashed out with the cane, striking one man on the upper arm and another on a wrist. They fell back, sore and angry, but disconcerted by his fury and unwilling to overwhelm the afflicted man physically. When the cane found no further target, Tommy continued along the driveway, his stick fanning expertly, locating rocks on the gravel.

Behind him, a few of the older boys hefted rocks in their hands and looked questioningly at their parents. Heads were shaken. One eager lad complained, frustrated, but was skelped over the ear for his trouble. Nothing could justify throwing stones at a deaf and blind man. There was a buzz of conversation; arguments unresolved. More heads were shaken and all the crowd could do was watch the bent figure's slow progress into the darkness between the road and the Sanctuary.

The flames licked the back of the fireplace. The candles were glowing on the walls. The drapes, chairs, cushions and wooden floor were warm in the flickering light. The old sheepdog raised his head from the hearth mat. His ears stood up, alert. His eyes were fixed, unblinking, on the silent group in the centre of the room.

In the middle sat Tommy. He was on a stool, front on to the fire, but with his head bent so far forward that the whites of his eyes showed themselves only to the floor. He was pale, but made no sound. Around him, the four healers were straight-backed and still, three seated normally, one cross-legged on her chair. The prayer for attunement had been given some time ago and the meditation that followed was coming to an end. The man with the shoulder-length chestnut hair opened his eyes first, and one by one, responding to some unconscious signal, the other three opened theirs. They stood.

Tommy, sensing the movement around him, made a small mewing sound. His hands trembled.

A glance, a smile, passed between the four in robes. Swiftly they placed their hands to Tommy's hands, to his shoulders, over his ears and, from behind, directly across his eyes. Tommy's indrawn breath was almost a cry. His cane dropped from his hand to the floor with a clatter and a shudder passed through him. For a few seconds he settled, remaining quite still under the hands. Then he began to pant, sharp and fast.

'It tingles,' his voice crackled. 'It's hot!'

'There he is. Sullivan's with him.'

No stones had been thrown in the intervening time. Of their own accord, the boys had ceased bringing ammunition from the foot of the sea wall. They had also ceased doing wheelies on their bikes and chasing each other through the throng of grownups. The adults still held their banners, but not aloft. The jokes had died. The festive air had vanished and the anger that had taken its place had also gone, both replaced by a detached fascination, a compulsion to see the outcome. Many had been staring for a long time at the Sanctuary's distant front steps. The organisers, recognising the danger, had tried to persuade the crowd to break up and go home. But few had gone.

The two figures came down the far steps. Jack Sullivan appeared to be holding Tommy Ransley's elbow as they walked forward into the darkness of the grounds. They became only occasional black outlines that stopped moving every now and then for a reason that wasn't apparent from the road. Children edged forward through the crowd, to be in a good position to see.

Twenty yards from the gate, Jack left Tommy and turned back. No one thought to shout at him, even though he was still in his robe. Tommy emerged into the light, his cane wavering in front of him as it had always done. He tapped obstacles carefully, as he had always done. His walk was the same hesitant shuffle it had always been.

Then he giggled. That was the only sound on the waterfront, because the sea was flat calm in the still night. It was as if he possessed a particularly juicy piece of gossip that he would impart in his own good time. Small boys drew back, as he shuffled, still giggling, through the gate. He stopped and moved his head about, screwing up his face as if trying to see something. He moved towards one of the men closest to him, chin thrust forward, and spoke in his high pitched voice.

'By jeez, if it isn't Len Taylor. Whatcher done with all yer hair, Len? I didn't know you wuz a baldy.'

On Sunday, there was an unprecedented interruption to the church service. The moment the minister finished the sermon, Mrs Irwin, in the front row, stood up, glared at the congregation behind her, then began to clap. And within seconds more than half the congregation was standing also, applauding Robert McKay, ignoring urgent signals from the deacons. Before today, most would have argued that last week's sermon had been far and away the finest in Robert McKay's distinguished career. Yet now he seemed to have surpassed even that. A more heartfelt, urgent, passionate, yet intelligent plea to the human spirit could hardly be imagined. And there were many who didn't stand and applaud who would gladly have done so, if such behaviour were not improper inside the church.

Applauders and non-applauders alike waited for the rebuke.

But though it came, it was delayed. For the first time in his adult life, Robert McKay was afraid. In the midst of what many would remember as his finest hour, he was certain he was looking at the beginnings of his failure: thirty or more faces, scattered amongst those who were seated, detached, sceptical, cynical. At the beginning he had detected in many of these a desire to be convinced again, in some, a desperation to be brought to the end of doubt and uncertainty. And for a few minutes he had even believed that he might be able to win them back. But he had failed; in just twenty minutes, Satan's thoughts had taken root and grown monstrously well in the soil of his congregation. It was as clear as if a shadowed black cross had

219

been painted on each of their masks. The applause faded. People sat. When the rebuke came, most of the congregation were amazed at its mildness.

'In God's house, the merit of my words is only measured by the extent to which I am a vehicle for His word. Therefore it is inappropriate that you applaud me. Let us pray.' But in the brief pause before the prayer, his own thoughts rose up as if to mock his gloom. In all the years of waiting he had never once contemplated the possibility of failing the challenge. No. He must not ever use the word failure. This was a temporary set-back. Lord, he whispered fiercely to himself. Show me what I must do. Show me.

He began the prayer.

The following Wednesday night, the spontaneous demonstration was bigger than that of the week before. But the very act of gathering precipitated its own failure. No sooner had Tommy Ransley and Beryl and Trevor Digby pushed through to the gate, than twenty from the front ranks of the crowd looked at each other, then followed. A few from further back pushed through to join them. The shock, to the majority, was so great that not a single stone was hurled after the defectors.

That night, the healing session was followed by teaching.

The following week, more than forty walked through the gate. And this time there were two newsmen amongst them: a reporter and a photographer from a Sunday newspaper based in the city. The photographer was asked not to use his flashgun inside, so he stayed outside and took shots of the protesters. Afterwards, in response to insistent hand signals from the reporter, he aimed his camera at Tommy Ransley as he left the Sanctuary. But when Tommy realised what was going on, he shielded his face.

When the two newsmen returned to the city and handed in the story and the photographs, the chief reporter called for a glass of milk for his ulcer. There was no way to headline a photograph of a man hiding his face from the camera with 'Deaf and Blind Man Claims Miracle Cure'. Why, why, why was the editor hiring cub reporters who didn't understand that a 'no' meant a demand for more money? It was tempting to revive the original Satanist angle, but there wasn't a shred of evidence to support it. Never had been. No, the Sunday papers were taking a thrashing in defamation cases these days. So much for the guts of the story. The chief reporter finished his glass of milk and took the story to the chief sub. The sub commiserated, chopped the story to ten pars under 'Sect Evil, Say Villagers', and consigned it to the bottom left-hand corner of page eight.

Even so, it was enough. A few people began to travel to Waiata from the city.

They were amazed to find demonstrations going on so far from a main centre. In such a remote village, they seemed out of place, even quaint. Visitors smiled at the unsmiling faces behind the placards and at the impressive array of Bible quotations. When the occasional half-hearted stone whisked through the trees nearby and thudded harmlessly to the Sanctuary lawns, many of the visitors laughed.

The teacher took Robert McKay out on to the playground, where most of the junior boys were playing 'bar-the-door'. He quickly recognised Steven Slater amongst them, but couldn't see the boy's features in detail. So the teacher called the five-year-old over on the pretext of asking if he'd lost his raincoat. He hadn't. He was in front of the minister for only a few seconds, but that was long enough. Steven Slater had lumps on his scalp, swelling over one temple, a purple-black eye, and bruises where there shouldn't have been bruises: in the hollows between the bones.

'When I ask him about it, he just says he's a wicked boy and he keeps bumping into things,' the teacher explained. In the distance, Steven stood near the front of the 'runners', waiting to be picked by the 'catchers'. The teacher continued. 'But he's no more wicked than any other small boy. Or at least he wasn't until *now*. He's starting to get aggressive, picking fights. And I must say it's hard to blame him when he gets this treatment!' Robert agreed.

That afternoon, he rode up Aylmers Valley to the Slater farm. Wayne Slater was in the east paddock, forking new potatoes; he waved cheerfully, stuck his fork in the ground and cut across the paddock to meet his visitor. He was a short, thickset man, rough-mannered, but one of the hardest workers in the district and a stalwart of the church. He was surprised to see Robert, but pleasantly so, and asked if Mr McKay would care to step over to the house for a cuppa with him and the missus.

On the way, Robert mentioned that he'd come for a word about Steven. Wayne Slater's face fell and an underlying concern surfaced. He shook his head, worried. He said frankly that he was sorry Mr McKay had found out about Steven's problem, but now that it was out, he and the missus would be right thankful for a bit of advice about the boy. In the house, Daphne Slater hustled a dog, two cats and two small children out of the dining room, filled a kettle and unwrapped scones from a tea towel. Wayne and the minister seated themselves at the table.

'Fact is,' Wayne said gloomily, 'me and Daph are worried sick about the boy. Aren't we, Daph? Thing is, Stevie just don't know when 'e's doin' wrong.'

Robert frowned. 'I'll not deny that boys need correcting, Wayne. But Steven's too young for what you're doing to him.'

'But you don't understand, Mr McKay. Stevie don't *know* when he's sinnin'. Lord knows, I've tried to whop it into 'im, but he still ain't got no *sense of sin*!'

Daphne brought the freshly buttered scones over. She looked at the minister with sudden concern. ''Ere. You feelin' all right, Mr McKay? You're lookin' a shade peaky.'

ELEVEN

The clock on the waiting room wall said 7.35.

More than a hundred from both peninsula and plain sat on the waiting-room chairs. Most were silent, attempting to follow at least part of the instructions on the wall. For a while, a group of young men and women wearing university scarves told jokes in undertones and sniggered. But unspoken scorn pressed in on them until they looked abashed at the floor and thought their own thoughts. This capitulation unnerved two teenage farm-workers from Aylmers Valley. Already uncomfortable with the disability and suffering around them, they left with red faces and self-conscious, aggressive shoulders. Tommy Ransley was there, on the same bench as Trevor and Beryl Digby. There was a paraplegic in a wheelchair, a young man in callipers, a small boy with his left foot turned sharply inward, who gazed solemnly about from the safety of his mother's lap. There were relatively few with obvious disabilities. But, all the same, the three dozen or so who had come for healing were easy to identify. In them there was hope: in some cases, masked and tempered by refusal to hope, in others, iced over with self-mocking cynicism.

The rest, about two-thirds of the gathering, had come for many different reasons: all the shades and textures of curiosity. Some nursed a private wish to witness an out-and-out, twenty-four-carat miracle. Others had responded to the animosity on the faces of the crowd in the newspaper photograph: if the establishment church was so upset about it, it had to be worth at least a look. Still more had been attracted by the mystical connotations of the article, some having spent years nibbling samples from the shelves of the fast-expanding spiritual supermarket.

Many could not have explained what prompted them to come. 7.40. They filed across the porch, past the box which said

223

'Donations', and into the Sanctuary room itself. There were four people in robes on a dais, meditating. And there was something about their stillness that compelled even the most casual of visitors to tread with care. The crowd settled, thinly distributed across the cushions on the floor and around the seats against three walls.

They waited. They scrutinised the faces of the meditators and studied the space around them with detailed attention: the drapes, the candles and carved sticks, the fire, an empty chair in the centre of the circle, another on the two-foot-high dais against the fourth wall... and the old dog, who looked back at them all without lifting his grizzled head off the mat. One of the arrivals, who appeared to have a regular spot near the fire, took small logs off the stacks at the end of the hearth and carefully placed them in the line of flames. The small boy with the inward-turning foot remained standing when his mother settled on a cushion. He gazed solemnly at D'Arcy, then bent to speak in his mother's ear. She shook her head and pointed firmly to the nearest cushion.

At some signal invisible to the audience, the four in robes opened their eyes. There were glances within the circle, affirmative dips of the head. The elderly woman looked around and into the audience. Her gaze went from one to another until a thin, wiry-looking man against the wall nodded eagerly. He took a deep breath, blinked heavily, squeezed hands with the woman beside him, then weaved his way forward through the people on cushions. He seated himself in the middle of the circle, facing the younger man. The conversation that ensued was carried on in such low tones that the words were lost against the background hiss of the fire and subtle shifting of limbs. But anyone who had been in that central seat before knew that he was responding to just two questions: what was his name? what were his symptoms?

He pointed to a bent, stiff wrist and to hooked fingers, and painfully flexed the elbow of the same arm. The four in robes rearranged themselves around him. Then, in quick succession, they laid on their hands: the two older ones put their palms to the head, the younger woman lightly grasped the elbow. The younger man took hold of the wrist and hand; his lips moved. For a few moments nothing seemed to be happening. Then the patient's breathing sharpened. The two younger healers began to flex the joints under their control, exploring, seeking limits. And it was over in less than two minutes. The hands came away. The patient's eyes, from being tightly closed, flew open. His same hand was taken again and the elbow straightened freely as he came to his feet. He gaped, flexing his wrist and elbow. He mouthed 'thank you' several times, and set out shakily for his seat. Sixty people watched him go and took in every wrinkle of his dazed expression, grinning at the continued, unbelieving elbow-flexing.

The three-year-old with the deformed foot stood to whisper to his mother. 'Are those ladies going to make my foot better?' Nearby, giggles were suppressed. But his mother didn't hesitate. 'Yes,' she whispered in return.

In a few seconds, an elderly woman was seated inside the circle. She, like the previous patient, was in pain, but it was a deep, enduring pain that had sharpened her features and sallowed her complexion. No one could identify her condition by looking at her, but whatever she told the group caused all four sets of hands to go to her head. When it was over, she sat where she was, rocking backwards and forwards, reluctant to move. Clearly, some of the pain had lifted. But it was just as clear, as she returned to her seat, that she was disappointed.

Locals in the audience were easily identifiable by their clothes, Trevor Digby by his tweed jacket. A neighbour touched his elbow and pointed. 'Who *is* that?' The neighbour being a townie, Trevor told him in two words. 'Matthew Fleming.' The neighbour shrugged.

The third patient hugged his chest as though he was cold, in spite of the warmth of the room. He went forward with such determination and desperation that somehow no one was surprised when he returned with his hands relaxed beside him, smiling broadly. But the smile was itself partly of desperation, masking even from himself the knowledge that the healing had been incomplete. Several onlookers who counted themselves as old hands already, looked at each other significantly as if to say, he'll be back.

And so it went. Without exception, all who came forward found at least temporary relief from pain and discomfort. A few, perhaps half a dozen, appeared to be cured completely, next to instantaneously. The majority were partially healed; they would slowly improve to full health by themselves, or come back for more treatments, or slowly deteriorate to their original state. Over a period of time, one in seven would gain no significant improvement at all.

Spectacular recovery or crushing disappointment, the atmosphere became so charged that emotions flowed. Tearful joy, or sobs or bitter defeat — both seemed in place. When the three-year-old came back from the circle walking normally beside his mother, he pointed a hand at D'Arcy and declared that his foot was 'all better now', so he could take the doggy outside and play with him. D'Arcy's eyelids peeled way back to regard the pointing hand and his ears stood straight up, for a moment or two. Mirth poured around them both and the woman's cheeks were suddenly wet, reflecting the firelight.

After an hour and a half, the healing circle ended. Three of the healers found cushions among the audience; Matthew moved to the chair in the centre of the dais. And it was less then a minute before his head tipped forward.

Nathaniel's head lifted.

He remained seated, palms on thighs, and looked at the audience. In the soft light, his eye sockets were fathomless black pools. He began, his rich, resonant voice echoing in the old ballroom. He introduced himself. He described his own nature and the way it related to Matthew's. He said he hoped that movie-film scenes of seances had not led them to be disappointed that he did not speak like a wolf with chronic laryngitis. And as he spoke, he occasionally turned his palms up and tilted them forward for emphasis, a gesture no one had seen in Matthew.

'One way or another, at some time or another, you all ask the question, "Who am I?" Some even set out to discover their own self as if a complete one were lying around somewhere, mislaid.'

Laughter rippled softly.

'It's not that I mean to be flippant, because there is immense value in such a quest for the soul: somewhere inside each of you is an awareness that the you that you know is only a tiny fragment of your complete self. Let me call it your *greater* self.'

'Be my guest,' a voice said in generous sarcasm. There was a smattering of laughter, but most faces were annoyed. A smart-aleck student.

Nathaniel regarded the young man soberly, considered the invitation.

'Are you *sure* you want me in there?' he asked. The laughter swelled as the student betrayed sudden nervousness. D'Arcy's chin came up off the floor. He looked crossly at the crowd, shook his jowls and resumed his dreams.

'You and your greater self are the makers of your body at all times. If you imagine that you have a box of tools for building and maintaining your body, then a large section in it would be marked "Beliefs". Each belief is one tool.' He raised a hand. 'For example, do you believe that as you approach the end of this life you will become frail and lose your faculties?'

No one would be drawn. But back against the wall, a distinguished middle-aged man leaned forward as if listening more intently. He was in a pin-striped suit, appearing out of place even for such a mixed gathering.

'Most of you will be thinking something like this: "Of course. Everyone knows that old people do!" And the trap is in the word "know": knowledge is the innocent name for belief. But knowledge, of itself, is impotent. A belief is powerful. Now. Here is the sting in the tail of a false belief: believe strongly enough, and you will make it happen — *you will make the belief appear to prove itself!* It will be self-fulfilling. And without knowing it, you collect such beliefs more easily and in greater numbers than the most ardent stamp-collector. You can't see or touch them, but they have more power over you than a war or a hurricane.'

The conservatively dressed gentleman was frowning.

'If you feel angry,' Nathaniel said to the audience, 'I urge you to consider that some deeply entrenched false beliefs will kick and scream and hang on by their fingernails at the first sign of threat. And what I really threaten tonight is that comforting and most deadly of all beliefs... — he softened his voice and slowed his words for emphasis — '... that you are not the director of your own health and life.'

The distinguished gentleman stood. Something about his bearing gave him the floor, in spite of the number pressing to speak.

He rasped, 'In fairness to these people I should like to point out that you are simply putting a plausible fancy dress on the old "think positive" routine. Furthermore, by giving people the

227

illusion that they are cured, you are encouraging them not to go to their doctors.'

Near him, a student miming the action of a hypodermic, mouthed the words, 'Establishment prick'.

The doctor turned an angry red and set his jaw firmly at Nathaniel. 'I've seen terrible harm done by faith healers like you. I've seen patients die — I'm not exaggerating — die, because they put their trust in a faith healer and delayed going to a doctor for something that could have been easily dealt with at an early stage. That is what I wanted to say.'

He sat. All attention turned to Nathaniel.

'Spirit healing is not faith healing. But faith, or rather belief in its effectiveness, *is* an important factor. And precisely the same is true of orthodox medicine. If, for example, you are elderly and believe that you could die in the next round of Asian 'flu unless you are immunised, then an appointment with the doctor's hypodermic is more than advisable. However, while the doctor tells you that the illness is caused by a virus, I will tell you that such organisms are the means by which your body carries out your instructions.'

The doctor was on his feet again, his face dark. 'If it's a question of belief, how can you justify making these people lose faith in modern medical science? You talk glibly enough about viruses, but how can you justify condemning in these people's minds a health system built on millions of hours of exacting, scientific method?'

Heads turned again. The audience was enjoying the unex-pected volleying. Clearly the doctor was regretting trotting on to a public court with a faith healer, but was unable to restrain himself.

'I do not condemn it. Nor would I cut down an apple tree because the fruit is not yet ripe. Orthodox medicine and science will mature when they see that the world and its people are more than physical mechanisms. It is a matter of perspective. Let me give you an example. Your scientists have long maintained that a fundamental law of the universe is: "Energy can be neither created nor destroyed, but may change its form". Recently the perspective has widened, so that the law is stated "Matter and energy are interchangeable". But soon, when science looks over the wall, it will make a leap in perspective. The fundamental law will be restated: *"All is consciousness, which can be neither created nor destroyed. Ever seeking greater self-expression, consciousness changes its forms."'*

For a moment the doctor didn't react. But under the silent pressure of the audience, he said slowly. 'By what authority do you claim these things?'

Nathaniel's answer brought a mutter of surprise and disapproval. 'There is no God to authenticate my words. The truth of what I say must be decided by you and no other.'

TWELVE

Instead of sending in the next patient, the receptionist came into the surgery. She shut the door behind her.

'It's Jimmy next, doctor.'

Doctor Pringle grunted gloomily. There were times, he thought, when this was the most difficult job in the world. He pictured again the sample of blood between the slides, the chilling profusion of white corpuscles in the clinical light of the microscope. Absurdly, briefly, he envied the city doctors who didn't know one patient from the next without reading the cards.

'I'll put the kettle on for him,' the receptionist said.

'Yes. Yes, thank you. And I think we'd better have some phenobarb. on hand.'

'Thirty milligrams?'

'Sixty.' She nodded, understanding, and left.

The moment Jimmy Crocker saw the doctor's face, all colour drained from his own. He wandered further into the room, then stood trembling in the middle of the floor, gaping fearfully at the man who had delivered both him and his daughter into the world. For the moment, Jimmy — the big man — seemed to have been replaced by a small boy who was silently begging not to be hurt. Doctor Pringle wished the receptionist would hurry with the phenobarb. He guided Jimmy to the patient's chair, somehow afraid to touch the hulking shoulders.

'I'm sorry, Jimmy, but I've got some bad news for you.' He glanced at the hatch to the reception room, but Jimmy seemed quite docile, expression vacant, lips parted. The doctor decided to take the risk. 'It's best I give it to you straight,' the doctor lied. 'Amelia has a serious disorder of the blood. I'm going to have to send her to a base hospital for specialist analysis and treatment.'

THIRTEEN

Boarding the *Sea Nymph* wasn't easy. The forty-six-foot trawler was berthed down behind the wharf fish-store. She'd been there for three days and nights, apart from fishing time, the indefinite berth only tolerated because no one else wanted a spot with such poor access. The one way on to the vessel was down steps to a loading platform just above the high-tide mark and then along makeshift planks fastened to the inside of the outer piles. It was a blustery, southerly afternoon when Robert McKay and Peter Thorn went aboard. The planks were slippery in the rain and only inches above the petulant water. The gusts came side on, without warning, demanding full concentration on footwork and balance.

As they climbed over the gunwale, grateful to be aboard, the wheelhouse door swung open. Alex and Karen Drury were inside, standing back in mute, passive invitation. But it was quickly clear that the tiny space was much too cramped for the strained atmosphere; reluctantly, the Drurys conducted their half-expected guests down the deck hatch to the sleeping compartment in the bows.

It was a cluttered, dingy place. The small, battery-powered bulb threw shadows rather than light. All around, in the gloom, were the paraphernalia of living: clothes on raised slats and on nails in the exposed ribs of the hull, pots and pans and dishes at their feet, a kerosene cooker against the bulkhead, blankets and pillows on the sleeping ledges. The air was heavy with smells of fish, cooking, and diesel oil. Last Wednesday, the Drurys had attended the Sanctuary. Later that same night, Alex's mother had given them a choice: promise never to go again, or get out of her house.

The young couple sat close together on one sleeping ledge, facing the two bearded men on the other. Karen apologised that the fresh water had just run out and she couldn't offer a cup of tea. The small talk was brief and awkward.

Peter Thorn began; since he was the Drurys' elder, it was only proper that he should initiate proceedings. He set to with a will, his words rattling and his hands providing emphatic punctuation. The couple listened, but said little. Alex Drury's mass of tightly curled hair nodded minutely on occasion, but his mouth was already set to stubbornness. Karen was as attentive and moved even less, keeping her hands lightly over a belly beginning to swell with child. For the first while, Robert kept his peace, watched and listened. So much had changed since he had married these two, he thought. Just last summer. This scene would have been unthinkable then. Unthinkable in autumn, unthinkable even in the first winter weeks of the Sanctuary. But now... now... He wondered how long Karen could put up with these conditions. It was no place for a pregnant woman; even, he thought dryly, a pregnant woman in a boiler suit. But he doubted that their material discomfort would be a significant factor in the problem to hand; the Drurys would not be easy. However, they must be won. They were key personalities in the parish: poorly educated and quiet to be sure, but well liked and well respected, especially in their own age group. Influential. An important prize. And one he could scarce afford to let slip: of a dozen such confrontations this week, fully ten had produced only vague promises or nothing at all. And tomorrow, he must face the congregation.

Peter Thorn made no headway, and grew steadily more annoyed.

The minister took over. But it was like duelling with feather mattresses: the best of his arguments were neutralised by sheer lack of resistance. The couple were scrupulously polite. They were sorry to have brought such shame and unhappiness to Elaine Drury, sorry there had been so much trouble to Waiata since the Sanctuary opened. Yes, the Bible did seem expressly and clearly to forbid contact with all forms of occultism and spiritualism. But no, they were not going to change their minds.

There was a pause. The only sound came from the weather outside: the wind and the lapping of water, the creaking and shifting of piles. Inside, the air was cloying, but the hatch had been closed against the rain. It would help, Robert thought distractedly, if there were at least a porthole to let in some decent light.

'Tell me,' he asked, 'what is so attractive about these so-called teachings?' He felt Peter Thorn's sharp disapproval and knew what the elder was thinking: dangerous to invite further entrenchment of a false doctrine. Alex Drury shrugged. He was weary and so was Karen, but long years of respect for the minister held him back from saying so.

'They make sense,' he said. 'We understand things. Like, it's not blind faith any more.'

'Blind faith?' Peter Thorn snapped. 'It's you that's blind, Drury. Can't you get it into your thick head... anything that can give healing on demand can dazzle the likes of us with false teachings!'

'No! That's not right, Mr Thorn. They're not false. They're true! We knew the minute Nathaniel started talking.'

'Sinful pride!' the elder accused. 'Puff-headed conceit! If we could work that sort of thing out for ourselves we wouldn't need the Bible to tell us!'

'So it's wrong to use the brains God gave us, is it? What the flaming —'

'Alex!' Karen warned, alarmed.

'Yeah,' Alex muttered, subsiding.

Karen frowned, thinking. She pressed a fingernail in and out of a space between two top teeth. Then she looked at the minister who had let the argument come close to the boil without saying anything. She said, 'It's got nothin' to do with brains, Mr McKay. Those teachings, they make us feel good right inside, see? We can't explain it like you can, but we don't need to, see? 'Cause we don't even have to tell *ourselves* in our heads...' She tailed off, convinced she'd made a mess of it.

Peter Thorn was disgusted. He glanced at Robert, anticipating a swift rejoinder. But the minister was staring at a spot on the bulkhead, the shadow of a smile showing through his beard. When the smile was gone, he faced the two on the opposite ledge.

'You've admitted that the Bible forbids what you're doing. So, really, it all boils down to one thing, Karen, Alex: do you, or do you not, believe that the Bible is the revealed word of God?'

'It's not as simple as that,' Alex objected.

Then the minister was leaning forward. 'But it *is* as simple as that, young man. It is *precisely* as simple as that. Either the Bible is God's word inspired in man, or it is not. Do you seriously imagine the Almighty would give His only Son to die in agony redeeming our sins, and then give us a book containing only bits and pieces of His word? Oh no...' He patted his black serge jacket, over the pocket where he kept what he called his 'walkabout' Bible. '...This *is* His word. And since souls are not saved by parking them on fences, you must accept it, or reject it.'

But they did neither. They refused, point-blank, to make the choice.

And shortly, all four were on the deck, tightening clothes against the freezing wind. The minister and the ruling elder trod carefully back along the planks, on to the platform, and back up the steps to the top of the wharf. Peter Thorn, fuming, stopped by the end of the fish store above the bow of the *Sea Nymph*. The Drurys were looking up at him, unhappily, an arm around each other's waist.

'What about the child?' he barked down to them. 'Have you thought of that?'

The couple glanced at each other. Karen called back. 'Don't get us wrong, Mr Thorn. We still want to keep coming to church. Then the baby can make up its own mind when it grows up.' She looked anxious. 'That's all right, isn't it?'

Peter Thorn was speechless. Of all the colossal gall. They weren't sitting on the fence, they were trying to graze both sides at once. If they thought that that was the way to protect the child from the sins of the fathers... He framed a rejoinder to the effect that maybe they should split forces, or go turn-about, or toss a coin. But before he could deliver it, there was a snort of amusement beside him. He looked sideways, horrified.

Robert McKay looked as if someone had played a clever joke at his expense. 'Come, and welcome,' he called roughly and wryly into the wind. 'Just make sure you bring those foolish young hearts with you, and we'll repair the damage yet.'

After the third hymn, he led the congregation in a special intercessionary prayer for Amelia Crocker. He called on everyone present to unite in this petition to the Lord to look down upon her with tender pity. And they did. That, at least, was safe from the undercurrents of dissension: there was a universal fondness

234

for the bright-eyed angel of a child. Even elderly folk of the old school, who still maintained that children should be seen and not heard, admitted that the Crocker girl did seem to be the exception that proved the rule. Even before the exact nature of the illness was known, the Women's Guild was arranging for a huge carton of toys and books to be bussed through to the city hospital. Her school class had been organised to write letters to her. These were checked before posting: despite stern lectures to the contrary, several of her little classmates still tried to include the suggestion that her daddy should bring her back to Waiata and take her to the Sanctuary.

The minister followed immediately with a second prayer of intercession, this time for all the tempted and all who had gone astray. Some did not join in the amen.

Then, missing out both the praise and the prayer for illumination, he went straight to the sermon, a departure from the established order that raised many eyebrows. He began in a reflective tone.

'There is much doubt amongst us. It has become *fashionable* to doubt. As if we didn't carry enough in the way of natural doubts, some people, it seems, seek to bear more!

'But on the day the trumpet sounds,' the minister continued, 'I say to you that doubt simply will not exist. Doubt will wither and vanish in an instant. All of the millions of this unfortunate world, the followers of the lord *and* the fallers by the wayside, all, all will stand amazed, looking at the heavens. There will be great rejoicing. There will be weeping and fear. But *no* one will be in doubt. So I say to you, brethren, that whosoever would know the boundless love of Almighty God on the great day —'

'In a pig's eye!'

The shout so stunned the congregation that for a heartskip there wasn't a breath of sound. Then a moan of outrage tossed around the walls. Halfway back, a young man was on his feet, pushing towards the aisle, his face a mask of fury directed at the gowned figure behind the pulpit. 'In a pig's eye!' he repeated, yelling at all the goggle-eyed faces. 'Don't you see? All these years he's been selling you a load of dried-up horse-shit! He talks...' His voice ascended, pitching above the tumult. '...He talks about God's love. Hah! There's no love in *his* God. It's frigid where his God is!'

It was young Bill Paget, known to have attended the Sanctuary from the first night of the defections. He was a wiry little rake of a man, with unkempt hair falling about his face. Perverse, fiery, swollen-headed. On the other side of the church his parents' faces were chalk white. His two sisters were weeping. His younger brother was on his feet, his face suffused with rage. Half a dozen men were bearing down on Bill Paget, the two duty deacons to the fore. They grasped him by arms and elbows and trundled him back towards the main doors. He didn't struggle, but he yelled his last effort even more piercingly.

'Why does the old bastard sound off about the Sanctuary when he hasn't even set foot in the place? Don't you see? He tells you the teachings are evil and he hasn't heard one word! Not a single word! Ask him why! Ask him why!' Then he was whisked out the doors and down the front steps. Lou Crawford manoeuvred to an aisle and followed. Voices were heard, some shouting, some arguing, Lou Crawford's warning. Warning again. Then they all returned, without Bill Paget. Very slowly, order returned. More and more faces turned back to the pulpit where the minister waited impassively. The sounds of crying faded.

Complete silence.

'A good question,' the minister said, mildly.

More whispers. He never acknowledged any sort of inter-ruption, let alone sacrilege like this. What was wrong with him? At the rear of the church, Norman White was openly frowning in consternation. Peter Thorn leaned across his wife and said something. The mayor nodded, worried.

'However,' the minister continued, 'I doubt that I need to put my head into a crocodile's mouth to check that it has teeth.'

FOURTEEN

'There is no death,' Nathaniel said.

The audience was bigger tonight: a hundred people watched from the chairs and the cushions. For the first time, the robed figure on the dais was standing. From the beginning of the teaching he had stood in the same spot in front of his chair. Although he attempted no steps, he was obviously at ease; his head, hands, arms, torso, all relaxed and mobile. Every week he had better control of his host's body.

'Your scientists have another fundamental law which they state as, "All matter tends to randomness and disorder", meaning that the ultimate fate of organisation, cellular or otherwise, is decay. When the change in perspective comes, that law also will be restated. *"All is consciousness, part within part within part. Each part progresses to new form, leaving simpler parts behind. Each simpler part is free to join a new whole. Thus it journeys until it, too, progresses to new form, leaving even simpler parts behind."*

'Within your bodies, for example, each cell is "aware" of its function and its relationship to the whole. Within the cell each molecular strand, within the molecule the atom, within the atom, each subatomic particle and beyond: all are "aware". Consciousness *is* all its myriad forms. And in the magical metamorphosis of form, there is no death. Ever.'

There was a long silence before the first of the questions. Then the self-appointed fire-stoker raised a hand, looked around, stood. His question produced such a rumble of agreement, it was clear he spoke for many.

'What happens when we pass on then?'

'I hope you'll pardon me if I continue to use the word "die". Your...'

He smiled at the laughter.

'Your experience when you die will be different for every

237

one of you — depending on the box of beliefs you carry over with you. But you can be certain of two things. First: you will meet and recognise those who can only be described as your travelling companions, people who have known you for many lives. Second: no one will add water to your spirit and stir — you do not become a great wise soul if you were not so already. Of course, having entered the new type of existence, your perspective changes — and dramatically. *Provided* you agree that you have died.'

This time the laughter was a roar.

'That was not entirely a joke. If you could see some of the arguments that occur between the guides and the recently dead . . . some people are very difficult to convince.'

On the tail of the mirth was a series of sharp, oddly toned giggles from a fair-haired woman a few feet back from the dais. She was in her early thirties and her face bore the scars of extensive surgery. Briefly, Nathaniel's eyes rested on her.

'An example. Let us suppose you are in a car with faulty brakes which crashes into a ditch . . .' The woman now gazed at him with startled, fraught concentration. '. . . Immediately you begin to go through strange experiences. You may, for instance, move through a long tunnel and hear loud buzzing sounds, at the end of which you find yourself behind the crowd of bystanders watching your body being pulled from the wreck and laid out on the ground.' A pause. 'However, there is a problem with this . . .'

The understatement appealed.

'Exactly. There is now one body where you think you are and another where you think you should be.'

The audience rocked with enjoyment. Nathaniel feigned surprise that anyone could find such a tragic subject amusing. The scarred woman was giggling again and at such a pitch that her friend nearby looked at her with puzzlement and embarrassment.

'The ambulance arrives. The men with the stretcher check your pulse. They shake their heads gravely and pull the sheet over your face. Now this is, as it were, beyond the pale; you turn to the nearest bystander, tap him on the shoulder and say, "Here I am. It's me. I'm not dead." But he ignores you. And, what is more, you realise that your finger sank into his shoulder without resistance. So you begin to perform antics worthy of a circus act in front of the crowd, in your effort to get someone to notice you. But they all ignore you. Totally. This is too much. Impressive or not, this hallucination has got to go.' Nathaniel raised two questioning palms.

'Now I ask you. In this frame of mind, how are you going to feel about a guide coming to your side and saying, "Excuse me, but you're dead, you know"?'

The hilarity lasted nearly a minute. As it subsided, it became increasingly apparent that the giggling woman was, in fact, hysterical. So hysterical that it touched off another, separate wave of humour. Nathaniel looked directly at her for the first time.

'I fear that if I put this young woman's body under any further strain, she will be giving us a practical demonstration.'

The roar was short-lived. Nathaniel continued to look directly at the woman, and the twinkle seemed to have gone from his eye. In an instant, her laughter switched to weeping. Her companion, amazed and confused, put a hand on her elbow, then an arm about her shoulders. The weeping mixed with sobs, which gradually faded until her body wracked silently. The old ballroom grew very quiet as more and more realised what Nathaniel had done.

'Those whose bodies cannot be returned to must be helped to make the transition and the guides have many ways of doing so. They are equipped with an ability to manipulate the environment in a much more direct fashion than you do now; in fact the abilities of the guides would arouse the admiration of your greatest movie directors — let me return you to the previous example to make one change to the ending. Suppose that you have been a committed Christian, fervently believing that when you die, Jesus will come for you . . .'

There was a shocked hush as the audience realised what he was going to say. But the scarred woman closed her eyes, lay down and put her head in her friend's lap.

'. . . Suppose that when you have given up trying to make the bystanders notice you, you look over your shoulder. There, with His hand held towards you, smiling, surrounded by a great radiant light, will be the Christ: more powerful, more wise, more compassionate and gentle than you had ever imagined.'

Consternation.

Nathaniel let it ride, then raised a hand. 'Before you rise in wrath and stone me for heresy, let me say that such a performance owes nothing whatsoever to marked cards. The guides do not don the appearance of a great being the way an actor slips on a false mask. The props of the guides are the *living* energies of the universe. If *your belief* creates the need to meet Jesus in order to make the transition through what you call death, then *you will indeed encounter the Christ Spirit!*'

A few slow nods. Bafflement. On many faces, frowns of suspicion.

'Now. Understand. There are still many who are prepared to wait quite literally by their gravesides for the Archangel Gabriel to blow the trumpet. No amount of logic will budge them, but only sound the trumpet and the slow process of orientation can begin. Believe strongly enough that the ferryman must take you across the Styx and it *will* happen so that you can make the transition. Believe, for example, that your sins are so terrible that you must go to hell, and a lake of fire may have to be created for you.' He grinned. 'If this should happen to you, I advise you to look around for someone who appears not to be affected by the heat. He knows the way out and is waiting to show you . . .'

The loudest guffaws came from the city people. But a wit called out, 'Robert McKay!' And someone else commented loudly that the minister probably wouldn't even remove his jacket.

FIFTEEN

The Crockers' Mercedes Benz rolled to a slow, smooth stop on their driveway. The ambulance halted quietly behind. In a few moments, Margaret and Gordon Crocker were close to the front steps as the ambulance men brought the stretcher towards the house. Amelia's head was rocking slightly with the movement. Her face was pale, waxen pale; the skin seemed close to becoming transparent, and showed clearly the blue-black shadows of internal haemorrhaging. But the skin and the shadows were not ugly: they gave her a fragility which only made the seven-year-old child more delicately beautiful than ever. She wasn't in pain, or even unhappy. She was serious, thoughtful, perfectly aware of where she was and the people nearby.

'Am I going to die soon, Gran?' she had asked in the hospital, when Jimmy was out of the room.

'Of course not, darling,' Margaret had replied indignantly, summoning all her wits. 'What a silly idea. Whatever put such a thing in your head?

But, later Amelia had asked, 'Is Jesus going to come and take me away soon?'

Then Margaret had known that whatever was said, her granddaughter would see through it. Amelia knew. Almost unendurable to think that this innocent child was aware of her own impending death. About six months. Possibly longer with good care in familiar home surroundings, according to the specialist. Well, Margaret determined, no one had ever had the loving care and attention that her grandchild was going to get in her last weeks.

The stretcher-bearers halted on the porch, waiting for instructions. Margaret led them inside and down the hallway to the bedroom that had been meticulously prepared for Amelia's homecoming. Gordon went to the back of the ambulance. Jimmy

241

was still there, sitting upright, gazing sightlessly at the frosted glass of the opposite window.

'Come on, lad,' Gordon said. 'Let's go get a cuppa, eh?'

But Jimmy didn't move. The ambulance men came out of the house and slid the stretcher back into its frame. They watched silently. The younger of the two was showing an unprofessional pallor, so the senior man indicated the cab with a jerk of his head and his colleague promptly disappeared. The senior spoke to Jimmy in a kindly, patient tone. But Jimmy didn't seem to hear.

'Come on, Jimmy,' Gordon said again. 'Come on inside lad.' He put out a hand just as Jimmy's head turned sluggishly. Gordon pulled his hand back quickly, even though the malevolence in his son's eyes did not seem to be directed at him.

The big man came out of the ambulance and stood by the driveway, blinking slowly in the bright sunlight. He didn't hear the ambulance drive away.

SIXTEEN

The first of Waiata's four guest houses changed its admission rules. On Wednesdays they had been telling strangers that all beds were taken. But when one proprietor's daughter came home from the Sanctuary without her eczema, he experienced a change of heart and began to admit Wednesday townies. The other three guest houses followed suit immediately. It became a matter of principle that no discrimination should be allowed to mar the long tradition of Waiata hospitality. It had nothing at all to do with the fact that the takings from Wednesday nights alone would soon be enough to wipe out the winter overdraft.

All of these recent events were well timed. On Wednesday night every available commercial bed in Waiata — in the hotel and in all the guest houses — was taken. As far as anyone could remember, that hadn't happened since the whalers last came, before the turn of the century.

Half a dozen tents blossomed in the rugby ground. Within minutes, the mayor was there with Lou Crawford. The tents came down, and went up again by the side of the road, just out of town.

A farmer on the main road put up a sign which offered beds at a quarter of the guest house rate. A few of the townies were glad enough to sleep on sacks in his woodshed, though some were discouraged when they heard that their host had once tracked down a firewood thief by plugging dynamite into manuka logs and waiting to see whose fireplace exploded. The same evening, he put up a 'No Smoking' sign in his woodshed. No one smoked.

Sean O'Brien, who had taken over his father's stud business, downed the first of his two nightly jugs in the Fishermen's Rest, then held forth loudly against both Protestant heathens and Satan-worshipping heathens. There were very few hotel patrons these days, and certainly no one of the size or will necessary to tell

Sean to keep his opinions to himself. Well into his second jug, he announced that he had a foolproof plan for helping God to wipe out Protestants. He would give free accommodation and a free meal to all Protestants, he said, and all they had to do to take advantage of this offer was promise to go to the Sanctuary.

Nearly two hundred people filed into the old ballroom at 7.30. Alex and Karen Drury passed the word that anyone who didn't mind roughing it would be welcome to sleep in the hold of the *Sea Nymph*. It was a late session because so many had come for healing; but when they emerged, after eleven o'clock, the core of protesters was still there, cold, tired, grim-faced, but inwardly strong in the knowledge that their action was for good and right. An exuberant middle-aged man walked out past them, looking at his newly redundant walking stick. He stopped in front of the placards and banners. With a great deal of effort, he snapped his cane into a splintered dog-leg, threw it down in front of the protesters and told them to go and show that to their Bible. City people walking out with him grinned and laughed. Locals walking with them did not, and many walked by without looking at either the placards or the people holding them.

The next morning, Matthew pulled down the sign on the fence and replaced it with a new one.

WAIATA HEALING SANCTUARY
New Timetable
Healing only: Mon. Fri. 8 p.m.
Teaching and Healing as usual: Wed. 7.30 p.m.

Then he fetched a half can of white paint, left over from the mansion's window sills. He started on a new coat for the front fence, beginning at the end where someone had painted a skull and crossbones and a black ace of spades on the pickets. Jennifer arrived when he was halfway through. She admired the new sign, climbed into the lowest branch of a gnarled rata tree behind the fence and pretended amazement at Matthew's industry. She remarked that it looked as if the devil was never going to let *his* hands go idle. He held up the paint can and offered to whitewash her sins free of charge if she'd care to step down from the tree. She didn't care to. He painted on. His hair slipped forward over his shoulders, obscuring his vision, so he divided

244

it into two thick strands and tied it in a granny knot on the back of his head. This brought down more wit from above.

Occasionally, the two exchanged glances. His paint brush would hover, then slap on to a picket. When the sun came out from behind the scudding clouds, Jennifer swung her legs back and forth. He was suddenly struck by a childhood memory of her sitting on a dresser in his room. So long ago. He remembered himself in the corner of the bed. It was like remembering a different person.

Suddenly he grinned. He dipped his brush and cleared the excess.

'Has it occurred to you that the four of us have a distribution problem?'

Jennifer looked down coyly. 'Speak for yourself.'

'Really. People are beginning to talk.'

'Heavens to Betsy! No!' Horrified.

'Take Jack and Emily for instance: he lives on Pudding Flat, she lives on Lafayette Hill. Two healthy, normal, unattached people...' He shook his head sadly, then waved his brush in evangelistic fervour. '...We are starving the grapevine, depriving the gossips of their natural rights. Where's the good old-fashioned flouting of the seventh commandment? Where? People expect it of us!'

'So?' Heavily.

Matthew put down the can, stepped over the fence and plucked a leaf off a fern. He presented it with a flourish, but when he spoke, his words were soft: 'Come and live with me, Jen.'

She dropped down from her perch and faced him next to the warm brown bark of the rata tree. White paint slid back down the brush towards his fingers. 'I love you, Matthew Fleming...' He waited. '...but I'm not going to come and live with you.'

Matthew turned slowly and resumed painting.

'Look at me,' she demanded. He glanced sideways as he applied the brush. 'You're still afraid. I can see it. You only want me with you because you're afraid. That's the wrong reason, Matthew. I can't.'

He dipped his brush and slapped it erratically on an already coated paling. His wrist was unsteady.

'It's all a trap, isn't it?' Jennifer pursued. 'The healing, the teachings, your bloody mystery woman in the forest ... You won't admit it to yourself, but it's all a trap and it's going to close on us!'

He spun, furiously, a swathe of spotted white streaming across her shirt and across the warm bark of the rata. He shouted at her. 'If you believe that, then why are you still here! Why are you still in Waiata?' He slashed at the fence with his brush.

Again, the special intercessionary prayer for Amelia Crocker united the hearts of the church. But when that was over, the invisible ether that had long held the Sunday services together dried up and crumbled away. The congregation felt it. The minister felt it. He tried to halt the decay; he put his utmost into the sermon. He delivered an ingenious attack on the Sanctuary, using a previously untried sequence of scripture-based logic. But to no avail. If anything, it had the opposite effect. It was as if his sermon freed scores of thoughts that, once liberated, hunted the spaces, guilty in their freedom, seeking rest and seeking it in vain. The change was intangible but unmistakable. And soon, even while the sermon was still in progress, the movements began and the whispers ran. There were self-conscious, sidelong glances, hand-screened asides. Heads swayed and turned.

The old guard, the ones who had never doubted and never would, were agitated but not really surprised. After last week's sermon they had sent a deputation to the minister, independent of the elders, pleading with him either to demand that the two-timers leave God's house or to confront them with their shame. Then, he had given no answer. But now, they thought, now it was clearly inevitable. The poison had taken its grip and must be purged at once. He must — he certainly would — come down from the pulpit into his people and single out the transgressors one by one, proclaiming their sin and the certainty of God's wrath if they did not repent.

But he didn't.

Bewildered, Colin Richardson, Wayne Slater, Elaine Drury, Evan Paget and others looked around for some kind of reassurance from the elders. But the mayor, Peter Thorn and Paul Marsen were as disturbed and angry as anyone. Next to Gordon Crocker, Jimmy sat unhearing, gazing sightlessly ahead.

After the service, groups gathered on the lawn. The mayor

and Peter Thorn went to find the minister to arrange an urgent session of the elders.

It was held that same evening. And it was a fiasco.

While they waited for the last arrival, the minister rested his bearded chin on his thumbs, looked out from under his iron-grey, hedgerow eyebrows and said nothing.

Last to come was John Fleming. He greeted no one when he limped into the vestry. He sat hunched in his place, looking only at the table top. The moment the prayer was over, he laid a small white envelope down, thanked them all for putting up with him for so long and limped back towards the door. Peter Thorn glanced, incredulous, at the still mute minister; then he snapped at John that he was just handing another victory to his son. But John just shook his head wearily. He used his walking stick to lever the door open and went out into the night without looking at his long-time friend at the head of the table. The minister said nothing. And the normal courtesy and protocol of session were stripped to a thin veneer as the business began.

'Robert. We are concerned, deeply concerned, with the state of Waiata. It seems more than obvious that it could have been avoided.' Norman White felt the strangeness of using such a tone to the man he had respected and admired for three decades.

'Oh, yes,' Robert said evenly.

'We have inquired as to the state of your health, and you say —'

'My health is perfect.' Just as even.

'Then . . .' — the mayor almost growled the word, afraid of losing the upper hand — '. . . some explanation is in order. You must admit that you have been, uh, indecisive, to say the least.'

'You are incorrect.'

Peter Thorn broke in in disbelief. 'Do you deny that —'

'Hardly the appropriate language,' Gordon Crocker snapped. 'This isn't a formal inquiry.'

Peter was well aware that the minister could be dragged through every clause of the modern *Book of Order* and come up smelling of roses in front of presbytery nostrils. The thought only increased his anger. Why had it taken so long to confront the man? Blind respect, that was the culprit. Unreasoning, entrenched veneration. He glared across the table at Gordon Crocker. 'I take back the word "deny", but it doesn't change a thing. We all know he actively *encourages* them to come to church and sit with decent, god-fearing folk! Not content with that, he neglects to even *notice* when his congregation is falling apart before his eyes! On top —'

'I object! I object!' Alan Bailey was blinking rapidly. 'Robert is proven as this nation's finest minister. What right have we —'

'Scores of them, bringing the smell of the pit right in —'

'This is deplorable! Preposterous! I demand —'

In the midst of it all, the session clerk's voice pleaded, in a single, inarticulate sound, for them to slow down or indicate what she should and shouldn't write. The only response she got was from the minister, whose fleeting glance said that under the circumstances it had better not be he who instructed her what to put on the official record. Norman White overrode the bickering and informed Robert that in the opinion of the parish, he appeared to have lost his grip on the situation at the worst possible time.

'I am aware of that interpretation,' the minister said grimly. 'I must say I am grateful to you for not telling me the *other* interpretation in circulation: that I am in the first stages of senility!' He regarded their discomfort. 'Very well. I own that you deserve an explanation, and it was remiss of me not to have explained myself before this. It's just that I can no longer preach to sinners instead of people.'

Five faces showed puzzlement, three of them suspicious puzzlement.

'Put it this way: a doctor might get away with treating the condition rather than the patient, but I cannot. If I treat only the sin, I am less likely to cure the soul. Furthermore, no sin is so heinous that the whole man must be cut off from the saving grace that is his right in his Father's house. That is nothing but an act of wanton cruelty.'

'That's it? That's your explanation?' Peter Thorn spluttered. 'You're just playing with words. The analogy is false. We are born in sin. That's our nature. It's not a condition like a cold in the head!'

'You're so busy saving individual trees, you can't see that the whole forest is collapsing around you.' Norman White.

'I still object to this tone. It's quite intolerable that Robert —'

'The morale of this parish is at an all-time low. The situation calls for a return to clear direction and strong leadership.'

The minister leaned forward. His voice was icy. 'If the direction I offer has insufficient clarity, then I suggest you ask that I resign as John has just done.'

The significance of this sank in immediately. Thorn, Bailey, Marsen and Crocker, all looked as if they had been struck. They had gone too far and they knew it. They'd allowed themselves to be carried away by their frustration. There was, of course, no question of asking for Robert's resignation. To do so now, to the man who had been the spiritual heart of the peninsula for thirty years, would be to destroy what was left of the parish. And they'd never replace him. Not these days. In the modern, decadent world, he was still the best there was and they would have to make the best of him.

'But Robert...' Paul Marsen looked like a man swimming upwards, trying to find the surface. 'You *told* us, yourself, that Fleming's Pit was the greatest test we could possibly face. But now you seem to have chosen the worst possible time to... to pull your punch. This timid, namby-pamby psychology — it's weakened you, Robert.'

'I will tell you what weakness is, gentlemen. Weakness is fighting for the Lord with one *skerrick* less than the highest possible principles He has seen fit to grant us. Would you have me sacrifice principle to win the battle, knowing that to do so must lose us the war? It is impossible. I warn you now, that even if *every single parishioner* were to visit that hell hole, even if I have to preach the gospel to an empty church, I will *not* sacrifice principle!'

'I don't like the slur on *our* principles.'

'Hah! I suppose we should have trounced Hitler without using our guns? Our ex-service boys are going to love that one!'

'I think we should listen to him. Maybe it's —'

'A clever way to justify...'

When it all lost momentum, Chester Farnsworth spoke for the first time. They had ignored him until now, because they knew he didn't have the stomach for unpleasantness. He surprised them. He looked each of them in the eye as he said what was on his mind.

'That Paget boy was right. We condemn the Sanctuary and not one of us has ever been inside or heard a single word —'

Two minutes later, amidst the hubbub, Chester resigned. He walked out, assured them that the written resignation would be in the post the next day. No one tried to stop him. The clerk shut her eyes, knowing that if anyone so much as looked at her, she would burst into tears. Peter Thorn muttered that he for one wasn't going to stand by and let the Lord's work be sabotaged by histrionics, defeatism and inaction when there were people more than willing to do something positive. Norman White looked at him thoughtfully, and their glances met.

SEVENTEEN

The Sanctuary phone went dead the next day. At the post office, Matthew was told that it might take a while to locate the fault. The electricity went off the following morning. The supply office manager looked up the records then apologised: the number had been disconnected by mistake. And, unfortunately, the electrician had a heavy schedule over at Okains Bay. It might be a day or two...

On Tuesday morning, the mailman delivered a letter from the county engineer, Colin Richardson. It was a very long letter, quoting at length from the Town and Country Planning Act (1927), the Health Act (1942), and Buildings By-law NZSS1900, Chapter Five. It referred to such things as residential zones, conditional usages and places of public assembly. It boiled down to the fact that if two more toilets, a fire extinguisher, a hose reel, another exterior exit from the largest room, and parking spaces sufficient for ninety-three vehicles were not quickly forthcoming, the owner would face prosecution under all the aforementioned Acts.

That night, the dream returned for the last time.

The fingers of the hand that came out of the murk were clawed with intent. There was something familiar about the hand and the fear that he might recognise it nearly paralysed him. His flight, his struggle to rise from his hands and knees was slowed to almost imperceptible movement by the clocks at the end of the universe. Perpetually falling, he came up against a huge obstacle. It was the former source of light, the dead stone, now a giant boulder.

The hand, and the arm that came out of the fog, now also grew. It became enormous, with fingers as long and thick as his legs. But it did not reach for him. It reached instead for the boulder, plucked it off the ground and raised it high over him.

251

The terror was choking him. But even now, he knew he must not recognise the hand.

The boulder began its descent. It was almost on him now. But just as it neared his naked body, he caught sight of the monstrous thumb curled around it.

It was misshapen, squat and bulbous. And it was bleeding.

He woke. He was bolt upright in bed, back arched, hands clawed, and his scream echoing through the old mansion. He sat in the dark for a long time and listened to the nor'-west wind keening in the bush out the back.

EIGHTEEN

With the electricity off, the only light came from the fire and the candles. In more than a dozen places, improvised stands held extra candles, adding to those already mounted higher up the walls. Tonight there were so many small, shimmering flames that the entire assembly might have been gathered high on a hilltop, on a still, warm night, surrounded by a sky brilliant with stars.

The Sanctuary was packed: the chairs and floor cushions all taken, the bare floor scarcely visible. People stood against the walls, sitting when they tired and then rising again after a rest. Others remained in the alcoves, with curtains pulled aside. A few even stood in the hallway. The sea of bodies was never quite still: a leg adjusted position, an arm straightened, stiff shoulders and elbows flexed. A pair of crutches was raised and lowered to a more convenient place.

As each healing came to an end, Tommy Ransley turned to explain some point to a first-timer next to him. Beryl Digby and another farmer's wife from Okains Bay whispered to each other. Two city reporters sat against the wall near the dais. They were bored at first, and irritated at not having secured seats. But when a six-month-old baby suddenly stopped screaming and chuckled and gurgled under the healers' hands, the newsmen began to take an interest. In the breaks between healings, one or two of the locals winked at Chester Farnsworth, who had taken the seat in the back row of the corner furthest from the alcove. The kidding was good-natured, even respectful: they knew his decision to come must have taken courage. But the former church elder was more troubled by the silence of the proceedings than anything else. He wished someone would explain what they were doing, to counter the only explanation he knew.

The room warmed so quickly that the fire was soon left

unstoked. When the last flame curtsied and dipped, D'Arcy struggled to his feet and went to gaze glumly at the ashes. He waited for someone to remedy the situation, whiffling impatiently in his throat. No one did. A healing had just been completed, so the audience allowed itself suppressed amusement as the old sheepdog whinged crossly and creaked back to his mat and his dreams.

The healings ended. Matthew mounted the dais, sat in the empty chair, closed his eyes. Nathaniel rose to his feet and began to teach. Every now and then he would take a couple of casual steps along the dais, his hands motioning smoothly as he elaborated on some point. His expressions, his gestures, his black eyes were his own, no longer to be confused with those of his host.

The questions began.

'If God is so just and everything,' said an Aylmers Valley farm girl, 'how come He's going to let a little seven-year-old girl die of leukaemia?'

'If you believe in a single "one-chance" life span,' Nathaniel replied, 'then you make your God into a cruel tyrant dealing out arbitrary, indiscriminate justice.'

Someone from the city called out helpfully to the farm girl, that she should get the parents to bring the child to the Sanctuary, a suggestion that provoked muttering from the locals. One called back that the child's daddy wouldn't be too keen on selling his daughter's soul to Beelzebub.

Nathaniel said nothing.

Well back in the audience, a thin, dapper-looking man darted a look loaded with significance to the woman next to him. He wore a cord-thin tie and a shiny navy-blue jacket. She, as plump as he was thin, gripped a Bible in her lap as she returned the glance in full measure.

Many hands were in the air. The robed arm pointed from the dais.

'Even if we have more lives to balance things up, why all the suffering?'

'Suffering is a refining crucible of the soul.'

'It's all very well my soul getting rayfeened, but if I have to keep coming back time after time for the suffering, it's not much cop for me, is it?' The questioner gave a little bow to the sardonic applause.

'You don't come back time after time,' Nathaniel said.

'But you just implied reincarnation.'

'I did. But when you separate yourself from your greater being the way you did, the answer is different. The you that you know is almost never born again, as is. But your greater self does reincarnate again and again, always choosing the fragment of itself most suited to the challenge it wants to experience.'

'So the fragment is absorbed afterwards, right? That seems like death to me.'

'Is the song of the flute lost in the symphony?'

'No, but —'

'Picture your world as a stage upon which you act out the drama of your life. From curtain rise to curtain fall, you *are* the character you portray. But when the play is ended, you recall the greater existence and eagerly anticipate the next play.'

'If we have lived before, why don't we remember?'

'It is necessary not to remember, but to forget. Imagine that you are a rich man who sincerely wants to experience what it is like to be poor. There is little value in dressing in rags in a tin shack if you remember what you can return to. But suppose it were possible to take a fragment of yourself and give it a gentle push into the waiting body of a baby which grows inside a woman in rags. Suppose it were possible for the baby to forget you and to be left to its own free will.'

The fat woman prodded her thin companion urgently. But he shook his head. Not yet.

The next questioner was a woman whose nasal voice made people wince. 'This world is an illusion then, isn't it?'

'Your eastern mystics have been misquoted. For all that the world is a stage, it *is* real, and so are the players. The illusion is to imagine that your world is all there is to life.'

'Do you live in a time? With a date?'

'No. Time and space are two planks of your particular stage.'

'If time doesn't exist, how can we have lives in past times?' This was greeted by a chorus of groans, but Nathaniel held up his hand.

'There are two disconnected wings to your question, so it is worth sprinkling salt on its tail. Here you play a life "game" in which a rule of play is sequential time and at the boundary of the playing field I see you have hammered up a sign with

255

a date stamp. But up in the grandstand, I can also see other playing fields with signs that say, for instance, A.D. 2030, A.D. 1906, 50 000 B.C. and so on. I can see other games *in progress* and other fragments of your greater self pursuing the ball.' He smiled broadly at the bewildered shaking of heads.

A voice called, 'Can you see if I've been sent off for a foul anywhere?'

'I can indeed. But it was not for a foul. Your team mates dispatched you for denying the existence of the Referee. You might say it was a warm send-off,' he added, and the questioner stopped laughing to look at the fireplace.

The thin, dapper man had been coiled for too long. Snatching the Bible from his companion's lap, he held it like a shield as he leapt to his feet. His eyes bulged with fiery zeal and his free hand stabbed the air between himself and Nathaniel.

'It's easy for you to mock and belittle what is sacred, isn't it? And make it sound all sweetness and light! But you don't fool all of us with your serpent's tongue. You'd like to destroy Christ's work, wouldn't you?'

'Hey!' a voice shouted, 'you're supposed to be out at the gate.'

But the man was not to be put off so easily. He turned to the assembly around him. Grinning faces, uncomfortable faces. He pointed again at Nathaniel and demanded, 'Look at the cunning in his eyes. Just look at it! Can't you see how he's laughing at you suckers? This one belongs to Satan, I'm telling you. Just watch his eyes when he tries to deny it!' To his obvious satisfaction, many glances flickered to Nathaniel, who said nothing. The accusing voice rose above the noise. 'Don't you see, you've all been conned, good and proper? This is exactly what the Bible warns us about: *"For even Satan disguises himself as an angel of light"*! Look at him! See the evil in his eyes!'

Most of the audience were shaking their heads uncomfortably. Some were laughing; and this caused the man's voice to rise to such a passionate pitch that it subdued the humour. His words were heard clearly by everyone in the room.

'Holy Father in heaven,' the zealot implored, 'I beseech Thee to strike the blindness from the eyes of these foolish sinners. Send them a sign, Lord. I entreat Thee to send them a sign.' And he turned his face upwards as if he suspected that the appropriate cure for blindness was a bolt of lightning.

'You will see what you want to see,' Nathaniel said to no one in particular.

There was a rattling sound from beyond the alcove. The tops of the curtains thrust apart, then a tall, powerfully-built man was through and blinking, glaring balefully about him at the assembly. It was Jimmy Crocker, and Amelia was in his arms, wrapped in a blanket.

The candlelight layered Jimmy's gaunt, scarred face with a multitude of tiny, overlapping shadows, scales of dark light that cried his desperation, fear and hatred in unsparing detail. He located Nathaniel on the platform, but, before moving, glanced down at the child in his arms, his pleading and grief interwoven in silence. She was fully conscious in a body too lethargic and too weakened to stir even against discomfort. Her gaze fixed intently on the dispersed points of light, but her head was tilted back over her father's arm, mouth open. Her cheeks were almost translucent. Her hair poured straight down from the end of the blanket in a wheat-gold mist.

Jimmy. Amelia. The two names pattered swiftly about the room. The Aylmers Valley farm girl stopped herself from crying by biting the ends of her fingers. Locals forgot that townies were outsiders and whispered essential information to them: Amelia, the girl dying of leukaemia: the doctors said she had six more months. But was it too late? Had it been left too long? And Jimmy Crocker, here! Jimmy, who despised anyone who had anything to do with the Sanctuary!

Throughout the entire audience, the word 'sign' was not uttered once, but it flew silently on furtive glances. If Jimmy's arrival with his daughter was indeed the sign requested of the Almighty, then no one knew where it pointed. At least not yet.

On the dais, the robed figure sat down on the chair. The head sank, stopped, rose.

Jimmy stumbled forward. People scrambled clear of him, because he didn't know where his feet were treading. At the end of the dais, he halted, breathing heavily, staring fearfully at the one in the chair. He gestured with his burden, raising Amelia a few inches, then lowering her gently. Anguish clipped the ends of his words, but his voice was strong and clear as he made his simple proposition.

'Make her well, and take me instead, when I die.'

Amelia made a sound like sigh. Her head rolled back on her father's arms. A voice came out of the crowd, telling her father that he'd got it all wrong, that it wasn't like that at all. But other voices hushed and shushed until there was silence again. The one in the chair seemed not to have heard Jimmy's proposition, so it was repeated: this time more forcefully:

'Make her well! Take me instead of her!'

The one on the dais stood. He moved the chair back and pointed to the boards where the chair had been. Three more robed figures rose and began to tack forward.

'Wait! Do you agree? Is it a deal? Will you take me instead?'

'This is Matthew you're talking to. No one is after your soul or hers.'

'Don't try to snow me!' Jimmy snarled. 'You can have mine. I'm the one who deserves to lose it. I'm the sinner. She doesn't belong to you. If you don't promise, I'll take her away. You won't get either of us.' Spittle formed in the corner of his mouth and he had no free hand with which to wipe it away.

Matthew looked down at the child's face. He hesitated. Jennifer, now close to the dais, saw uncertainty cross his face. Easy enough, Jennifer thought. Make the promise: the main thing was to give healing to Amelia. Even if it only brought her temporary relief, it would be better than nothing.

'I promise,' Matthew said. 'In front of all these people, I promise that this child's soul will not be taken.'

Jimmy came on to the dais and laid Amelia out on the boards, straightening her legs, tenderly lowering the back of her head until it lay on a swirl of hair on the hard wood. He spun on the people immediately behind him and hissed for a cushion. Half a dozen were promptly offered. He snatched one, glaring at its owner; then he knelt again to place it under Amelia's head.

'We need a minute to prepare,' Matthew said.

Jimmy backed away to stand on the floor. He folded his arms, preventing tired shoulders from sagging further. After a last look of suspicion at Matthew, he fixed his eyes on his daughter and kept them on her. Amelia's chest rose and fell steadily.

Soon, the four healers were seated in a circle of chairs brought to the back of the platform. The attunement meditation began.

All whispering and rustling ceased. For a full ten minutes, 250 people waited, their wills more united for this healing than for any that had gone before it. Even first-timers from the city clasped their hands together and prayed silently for Amelia in their own way. The heads of the two reporters went up and down as they looked, strained to listen, and wrote on their pads.

The meditation ended. The four knelt beside the girl. Matthew murmured. Four pairs of hands hovered over the girl, head to foot, two or three inches up. Jimmy's arms unfolded; his hands clasped together, fingers crushing fingers.

Amelia's expression began to change immediately. It drifted smoothly from detached interest to mild surprise. She continued to look up past the hands, and it seemed as if she were about to smile. In the audience, hand sought hand: friend to friend, husband to wife, brother to sister. It was working. It was going to work. The alcove curtains shivered and Gordon Crocker was there, breathing hard and staring. On the dais, Amelia's eyes suddenly moved. They focused on something in mid air, that no one else could see. She smiled and the assembly breathed in with one breath. Undoubtedly, this was going to be the most spectacular healing of all.

'Daddy.' The whisper was audible only to the very nearest.

Jimmy was beside her, fumbling for her hand. But he caught only a few of the words. '... to take me away,' she breathed. The smile faded, leaving the serenity like an empty shell on the sand. And then she was gone.

NINETEEN

Jimmy's feet moved as automatons: not fast, not slow, but relentlessly, as they carried him of their own accord along the dark waterfront. He had eyes only for the dead child cradled in his arms and for the cluster of lights on the hillside at the south end of Waiata. Of the noise and confusion and movement about him, he saw nothing and heard nothing. Six months. Gone. Six months. Gone. His mind tried to grapple with the concept — as impossible for him as imagining a universe which did not exist. Six months. Stolen. Six months. Stolen. Stolen, stolen, stolen...

The crowd had begun to stream from the Sanctuary five minutes ago, deeply shocked, stricken with remorse, many openly weeping. Now, as Jimmy moved steadily down the middle of the road, the remnants of the crowd were still around him: hurrying, often running away to their homes, urging horses quickly into the darkness, slamming car doors, revving engines. People stared, white-faced, as they steered clear of him. Sometimes they called out. One car stopped beside him; a young man leaped out, ran to him, clutched at him and cried out, 'Jesus, man, I'm sorry. I'm really sorry.' But Jimmy didn't hear him. Nor did he hear his father behind him, plucking at his sleeve, asking where he was going.

He trod on past the shops, past the wharf, until he came to the empty old cottage that had once been home to him and Amelia and Angela. It had been left alone, neglected in the years since Angela had gone away. Dead leaves and old moss spilled over ragged guttering. Dry rot swelled under crazed, peeling, weatherboard paint and wisteria creepers grew across the windows. Light from the street lamp penetrated to cobwebs and dust and empty rooms. He had allowed no one here in five years.

Gordon would have opened the door for his son, but Jimmy

just backed into it. The rotten wood around the lock gave way with a rending cough and the hinges whined as the door swung back. He went on in, then turned as his father tried to follow.

'Get out,' Jimmy's lips shaped.

Gordon backed fast down the front steps. Peter Thorn and Paul Marsen caught hold of him on the path and steadied him. They went back to the road, Gordon with his fists to his temples.

Through the window they saw Jimmy go into the lounge, his feet leaving clear imprints in the dust. He laid Amelia's body out on the floor with her grey face in the patch of street light. He straightened her, placed her hands over her chest, touched and lowered both eyelids at once. With care not to disturb the film of dust around her, he tidied the blanket so that it lay evenly over her torso and was neatly folded at the sides. Then he sat on the cold hearth beside her and began to rock backwards and forwards. And after a while his lips moved with thoughts that were not sounds.

He was still there the next morning.

Doctor Pringle tried to speak to him from the lounge doorway. But he, too, beat a retreat when Jimmy left his hearth with swift, flowing menace. Margaret Crocker brought a mug of steaming hot coffee and a cushion, but Gordon forbade her to take it in and she went slowly away to the Mercedes parked close by. One of the city photographers stole to the window and took three snapshots. But he made the mistake of allowing his leather camera housing to swing and tick against the glass. Jimmy came towards the window with such speed and ferocity that the photographer tripped in the wisteria in his haste to get away. Two local men on the road looked at each other, then grabbed the camera and threw it into the sea. They told the outraged man that if they could still see him in two minutes they would help him off the end of the wharf to look for it.

Half of Waiata came by to look through the window from the street. The policeman came. And the minister and the mayor. There was a conference. Robert McKay went warily to the lounge door to try to reason with Jimmy. Jimmy seemed to know who was speaking to him, because he stayed where he was on the hearth. But he didn't look up from his child's face. He didn't indicate that he heard anything being said, not even when the minister told him that Amelia's mortal remains must be dignified

261

with a decent burial, which must, at the latest, be held the next morning. Robert pulled out his walkabout Bible and made to move into the room, but a single swift look from Jimmy froze him in his tracks. He placed the Bible on the floor and backed slowly away, while Jimmy resumed rocking back and forth.

There was another conference. Better to leave well alone, they decided. He must tire soon.

The few shops that had opened were all closed by mid afternoon. The rest of Waiata's people came by during the remainder of the afternoon. Once seen, the sight through the window became an image that clung, rocking endlessly in the minds of young and old wherever they went. The vision was so mesmerising that the mood of the village stayed curiously unresolved, as if it had been forced into temporary suspension. Even when people passed the Sanctuary, they would stop, stare, and then continue without a word.

In the late afternoon, the minister went back to the cottage and looked in the lounge doorway. Jimmy looked different. He was no longer rocking. He still gazed at his daughter's face, but now he was nodding to something within himself. He was smiling. And it was a smile so devoid of human warmth that it stopped Robert McKay from attempting any kind of contact. He left, though not before noticing that his walkabout Bible now lay beside Jimmy, open.

By mid evening it was clear that Jimmy was going to stay put for another night. Throughout Waiata, tempers began to wear thin. Incredibly it seemed that there were a few people who still had something good to say about the Sanctuary. But, even so, by some unspoken understanding, no one discussed what was going to be done, about the Sanctuary or about those who had hastened Amelia Crocker's death. Something would be done, of course. Everyone knew that.

TWENTY

Lou Crawford left the engine running and loped inside. In the kitchen, his wife Nancy was hastily rattling cups and saucers on to the bench, but he shook his head and went straight to the phone. While the operator was putting him through to City Central he ran his eye over the morning newspaper on the sideboard. The article, the photograph of Amelia and the inset map locating Waiata, took up the top half of the front page.

CHILD DIES AT SECT 'HEALING' RITUAL

'She died before her time.'
That today from the heart-
broken grandparents of seven-
year-old Amelia Crocker who
died suddenly...

The control senior sergeant had also read the paper and heard the radio bulletins. 'It'd make you puke, wouldn't it? Seven! Weirdos like that oughter be strung up. What'd they do to the kid, anyway...? Okay, okay, hold your fire. I'll put you through to Dickybird.'

Chief Inspector Richard Sparrow was more to the point. 'How many men do you need?'

'Twenty, sir.'

'Twenty! What the devil for?'

'I'm going to have real trouble on my hands if I don't get a show of uniform smartish, sir. The locals are really stirred up. They're talking of burning this spiritualist place down.'

'Talk's cheap. What else?'

'I've got two mobs gathering outside the place now. One lot's toting petrol, and the other lot says it's going to stop them. I'd have a go at jugging the ringleaders, but I can't get near them. They're all cooperating. Shops are closed down. Sir, I know these people, and they've never been worked up like this before. Already, I've got women tearing each other's hair out on the street. Fathers and sons beating the hell out of each other. I've even got old codgers wading into young fellas with their walking sticks — '

'All right, all right, you've got a little problem; why didn't you say so in the first place? But I'm damned if I'm going to have the commissioner breathing down my neck about police overreaction. Hang on . . . '

Lou heard the hum of an intercom, a crackle of quick exchange. He ran his fingers through his thin sandy hair. Blasted city career men, always thought country cops were out of *Noddy and Big Ears*. Nancy placed a cup in front of him. The chief inspector came back on the line. ' . . . On the way in five minutes. I can spare you half a dozen.'

'Half a . . . But these people aren't just — '

'Your two mobs aren't fighting now, are they?'

'No sir, still arriving.'

'And the local doctor signed the death certificate?'

'Yes, but — '

'Then skedaddle and tell those petrol-happy idiots that the doc says "natural causes".'

'That's half the problem, sir. His daughter is one of the spiritualists who're supposed to have done in the little girl. Two-thirds of the town think he's covering for murder.'

'Bloody hell. Nobody laid a finger on the kid! The medic association over here says it's a load of baloney. Tell 'em that . . . all right, all right, so they won't take any notice? So go pump up the girl's father to tell 'em about violence besmirching his kid's memory.'

'He's gone bush.'

'What!'

'Went home after the funeral and then took off into the trees. There's a search party out looking for him now. But he knows the bush; they won't — '

'Christ, what kind of people are you breeding over there, Crawford? Look, I can't do your thinking for you. You know the scene, so play it. Wait a minute, haven't you got some hot-shot dog-collar artist over there that everyone listens to? Shovel him in front of them. Thou shalt not burn and all that. Use

264

your head, man. If you can't defuse a village squabble, you shouldn't be wearing the uniform. You are wearing it, I hope. What are you waiting for? Get down there.'

Lou heard the distant click of the receiver, then slammed his own down. He uttered a loud two-word opinion of Chief Inspector Sparrow, ground his teeth together, then called the mayor's house. Dorothy White told him that Norman had just left town to visit his brother, Trevor, in Pigeon Bay and would be there all day, and, no, there wasn't a phone. Convenient, Lou thought. He swore again. It would have to be the minister. He lifted the receiver again and asked for the manse. The conversation was brief. Lou took a scalding gulp of tea and ran back to the car, barely hearing his wife's plea to take care.

In less than a minute, he was parked outside the house between the Sanctuary and the church. He stood beside his car, carefully evaluating the scene before him. No mistakes, Lou boy, he breathed to himself. This time, no mistakes.

On the road were 250 people, with more coming. They were spread from the Sanctuary fence to the sea wall and fifty yards in each direction. Their faces were bitter and determined. They were restless, but mostly silent. Waiting. Lou scrutinised faces and movements. Half of them would initiate it, he decided, and the other half would follow; he could almost see the dividing line. Close to the front ranks were the most dangerous ones, those who had seen Amelia Crocker die and were tortured by their own guilt. He could pick them out by their expressions. And there were the ringleaders: Sidney Irwin, Murray Smart, Tom and Alan Glubb, watching him as carefully as he was watching them. There were the cans of petrol, four of them now, five. Sticks in hands. Rocks and stones lay in little piles built by small boys. Lou clenched his fist. Some people didn't deserve kids, bringing them here as if it was some sort of picnic. He made himself relax the fist. He had to keep his cool; he would make no mistakes. He had never forgotten how this town had run all over him when the vigilantes took off for Pudding Flat that night twelve years ago. They might have forgotten, but not him. He'd been nothing but a greenhorn then, fresh off the beat. But he wasn't a greenhorn now, by heaven.

Inside the gate were just over thirty people, under the trees, on the lawns and driveway, mostly young, mostly male. Nearly all were locals, Lou noticed: Bill Paget, Tommy Ransley, Beryl and Trevor Digby... and Alex Drury, of all the unlikely people to fall for that spirit crap — the only halfway decent fullback on the peninsula. There were only a few strangers on that side of the fence, townies buying trouble. A few women watched from back by the Sanctuary building. Of the four responsible for the whole mess, there was no sign.

It was interesting, Lou decided, that the two sides were not yet yelling at each other. None of the training files at Trentham had covered this kind of thing, as far as he could remember. There seemed to be some kind of undeclared agreement between the sides that nothing would happen until all the ranks had been drawn up. He reached for the microphone and the public address system, but then changed his mind. He'd tried that already, and had gained nothing but egg on his face. If the 'unlawful assembly' angle didn't impress *this* lot, nothing would. And it was no good talking about reinforcements: the hotheads would just speed up the action. He turned, looking at the manse. Shapes moved in the study window. He turned back. No, not yet. It was dangerous waiting this long, he knew, but the minister was too much of an unknown quantity now. Better to delay as long as possible. Timing. Timing. Every minute brought the reinforcement squad a mile closer.

There were three hundred on the road now. People were coming in from the bays.

'Hey!' a voice shouted across the fence to those in the Sanctuary grounds. 'Why don't you lot buzz off? It's not you we're after.'

No response.

Nor was there any follow-up. Lou relaxed his muscles.

The sun edged past mid afternoon. Still there was no sign of action. Perhaps they were going to wait for dark, he thought; the old wooden building would make quite a bonfire. But the reinforcements must be close now. Lou was hungry; he hadn't eaten since breakfast. He thought of calling up Nancy on the radio telephone and getting her to bring down a few chicken sandwiches, but he left the microphone alone.

Another voice shouted. 'Hey, Lou. Why don't you go home? You know the law can't touch them. Go home and let us do the job.'

He seethed inwardly, but forced himself not to show it. Let them think he was helpless, for now. But then the random movements on the waterfront suddenly took on purpose and meaning. Separate individuals now seemed invisibly connected: individuals within groups, groups within bigger groups. It was like the behaviour of the organisms he had once seen in a microscope. It had started. Without looking at the manse, he walked around to the other side of the car.

Inside the manse, Alan Bailey and Paul Marsen both turned from the study window at the same moment and nodded. Chester Farnsworth, standing gloomily in the corner, turned noticeably gloomier. Peter Thorn eyed the minister with grim satisfaction. Robert McKay was rising to his feet just as Alan Bailey gasped:

'Too late! They've set fire to the fence!'

McKay went down the stairs two at a time, but without running. He walked all the way out the driveway and along the waterfront, firm of step, back straight, head erect. Ahead of him, red flame rushed into black smoke along the fence line. The sea breeze pushed the smoke so that it leaned over the Sanctuary grounds, up towards the top of the sequoia tree. The defenders were scooping sodden leaf mould out of the shrubbery and throwing it on the fire, but with little effect. Their movements and the crackling of the flames were the only sounds. The crowd on the road watched, fascinated.

Robert McKay walked along the fence line between the two sides, as if he were walking down the aisle to the pulpit. He transferred his grandfather's gold fob-watch from his jacket to his waistcoat as he went. When he reached the first flames, he shrugged off the jacket and used it to beat at them. Now the people on both sides of the fence watched, even more fascinated. The flames began to die away, partly because of the jacket and mostly because the petrol was burning out. When the flames were gone, the minister folded the ruined jacket as if it were going into a suitcase and laid it over the charred, smoking pickets. He faced the mob on the road. For some reason, it occurred to him that this was the first time he had ever been seen in town without a jacket.

'Are you blind?' he addressed them. 'Are your wits so befuddled that you can't see what this pit has done to you?'

'We saw what it did to Amelia!'

267

'No!' He shouted. 'Divide and conquer. That's how he works. What you're doing now is *exactly* what the deceiver wants you to do. Look at yourselves. *Look* at yourselves: you Pagets, Drurys, Tomlinsons, you Glubbs...' His hands moved quickly, pointing out fathers, sons, daughters, families, split by the blackened fence. 'You've played right into the deceiver's hands.'

'So what do we do? Let 'em kill more little kids?'

'They *are* blind!' The sound came from behind the minister. He turned his head. It was Alex Drury, speaking from the front of the group in the Sanctuary grounds. The young man appealed passionately to the people across the fence. 'Why can't you see? That was beautiful what was done for Amelia! Some of you helped to do it! We *all* — '

A storm of abuse drowned his words. 'Euthanasia service for little children!' screamed a woman back by the sea wall. She threw a stone over the crowd so that it tumbled past Alex's head. He backed away. More enraged abuse followed him. Robert McKay found himself yelling, trying to override the noise, but his efforts now only seemed to fuel the anger.

'Go home, Mr McKay. This isn't the place for you.'

'McKay! If you'd done your job right, Amelia would be alive today!'

So intense was the exchange that only the boys on push bikes back by the railing noticed the plain grey car pulling up. And even then, they didn't see who was in it, until the dark blue uniforms were clambering out. 'Cops!' the boys screeched, each one imagining the long arm of the law descending on his father's collar.

In an instant, rocks and stones tumbled to the ground, sticks and petrol containers seemed suddenly not to belong to anyone in particular. Even boxes of matches and a couple of cigarette lighters sat innocent of human hand inside a rapidly expanding semi-circle of people. Somehow Sidney Irwin, Murray Smart and the two Glubb brothers were now on the outside fringes of the crowd, on the far side from the police squad. The squad walked into the fast-emptying space in the middle and looked about for Lou, who was pushing his way through from the railings.

Abruptly, the crowd stopped retreating. There were only six policemen. Seven, counting Lou. Heads craned to see. Any more? Surely there were more. No, only seven.

The uniformed men glanced about them uncertainly. They looked expectantly at Lou, who had reached the debris in the middle. But, at this moment, he appeared not to be aware of his colleagues. He was staring at two milk bottles standing in the gutter, and he was cold with rage. Each of the milk bottles was filled with petrol, topped with a tight wad of cotton wool around a cloth wick. His narrowed eyes sought Sean O'Brien in the crowd, but Sean was nowhere to be seen. The country policeman scanned the faces closest to him, but detected no surprise. At the same time, low-toned, urgent conversation started in the back of the crowd and spread quickly. Lou picked up the two milk bottles, looked at the waiting squad and jerked his head. In a trice, everything containing petrol was on its way to Lou's car.

Shouts rose from the rear of the mob, urging fast action. But it was too late. The petrol went into the boot of the car and the boot slammed down, locked. They couldn't burn the Sanctuary without fuel. It was either overwhelm these seven policemen, or go home for more petrol. The front ranks wavered, thought about it.

While they dithered, Lou and the squad scooped up sticks and other improvised cudgels. Howls of frustration rose from the midst of the crowd: they had allowed themselves to be castrated with hardly a murmur. Cries of abuse were directed at the squad, and at Lou in particular. He spoke to his new team. The two cars came to life and rolled forward in front of the fire-damaged fence. The seven men then lined up on the street side of the cars and folded their arms. Each wore the standard-issue short baton.

The crowd held an impromptu conference. The largest groups gathered around Irwin, Smart and the Glubbs. At first there were loud arguments. Then the decibels plummeted, as one idea took hold and held sway. There was a muttering back and forth, agreement on detail, decision. There were sidelong looks at the tiny, nervous police contingent. Then the mob broke up, moving away along the waterfront in both directions. Most, particularly the older ones, avoided looking at the men in uniform.

Robert McKay didn't move as the crowd jostled past him. He watched them one by one as they streamed by, searching the faces that had once held respect for him. They avoided his eyes now or simply ignored him. After a while he looked at the policemen instead. They were gathered around Lou Crawford and seemed to be angry with him. But Lou was even angrier, explaining something to them with emphatic gestures. They looked less angry, but no happier. They looked grimly at their watches and shook their heads. Lou sent one of them off to the nearest house at the double. A call for more reinforcements.

The minister felt a hand on his sleeve.

'Mr McKay?'

He turned. Karen Drury. She was both tearful and angry. The whole world, it seemed, was angry. He looked at her, absently wondering why she wasn't in the Sanctuary grounds, just as absently remembering that she was expecting a baby. What did she want? He didn't want to speak to her. He wished she would go away.

'Mr McKay, you know why all this is happening, don't you? Who was it taught them all about a sense of sin? You did it really well, Mr McKay. Really well.'

'That's not right,' he snapped at her. 'You're distorting...' But she was already walking away from him.

TWENTY-ONE

Dusk.

The new moon rose high above, a gleaming sickle embracing the faint full ghost of its greater self. Silver light danced in the harbour, down a shimmering path that narrowed as the water calmed for the night. High tide. In the lamplit streets of Waiata, cherry and kowhai blossoms hung their twilight fragrances about them and veiled their colours. Bellbirds chimed their nightfall song and flitted to the bush. Dogs sounded in Aylmers Valley, then settled. Crows cawed their last caw across the cold hillsides.

The trawlers alongside the wharf were silent under the lamps, unattended. There were no engines pulsing in the harbour, no cars droning in the streets, no squeak of harness or clop of hooves on clay and stone. No one walked the sea wall under the stars. No one moved outside at all. Window curtains parted and closed stealthily. Slim vertical columns of light appeared in front doorways, then thinned to vanishing point.

As dusk turned to dark, a figure stole out of the bush, slipped across an unlit section of Rue Lavalle and into the shadows at the back of the waterfront shops.

On the waterfront, the policemen stood around Lou Crawford's car as he sent out a call on the radio telephone. The only answer was the hiss and crackle of atmospherics. He dropped the microphone through the window on to the seat, then looked, yet again, into the Sanctuary grounds. Here and there, a shape moved amongst the tree trunks, shadows against the faintly moonlit mansion. The building was without lights, its windows like black holes. The waiting alone was hard enough on Lou's men without that eerie, ghostly bulk looming at them. The youngest asked him why they didn't just take everyone out of the building and move them to the station. He had looked his contempt at the suggestion and nothing more had been said. They accepted his authority now, respecting the implacable, grim determination that had emerged from his rage.

Uneasily, he eyed the bush behind. Too much cover. He should have men out the back and down the side fences. But what could he do with six men? Divided, they'd lose what little strength they had. Together... One of the men was drumming his fingers on the hood of the car.

'Lay off!' Lou snapped. The sound ceased.

'Why don't we pick up the ringleaders from their homes?' another said. For answer, Lou pointed to the houses on both sides of the Sanctuary grounds: in one, a triangular chink of light, on the front porch of the other, the firefly glow of a cigarette.

Together... Yes, keep together. Even the hotheads were in this for their righteous bloody principles: they'd come the front way. But so many of them, so many! He had to find a way to stall them. Think! He peered in both directions along the waterfront. It was as dark now as it was going to get. Why weren't they coming? They must know he had called for more reinforcements.

He walked down the length of the fence, looking at the shrubbery, the trees, the long stretch of lawns, and the spectral mansion behind. He stopped still, frowning at the building. He went to another position, then another, and yet another, inside the grounds. Then he went back to the waiting squad. First, he got one of his men on to the RT in the city car to call his own vehicle. He kept the receiver volume low. Yes, working well. He sketched a quick diagram on paper, laid it down on the surface of the road and gathered the squad around him. With the help of a torch, he began to explain.

Somewhere, a telephone rang.

Jack Sullivan and Emily Nisbet descended the front steps of the Sanctuary. The elderly couple were in their everyday clothes: he in corduroys and mountain shirt, she in brown cardigan and a sober floral skirt that had seen twenty careful summers. It was so dark under the trees that only Emily's white hair showed up clearly. They couldn't see each other's faces in detail, and they were glad of that because they found themselves needing to walk arm crooked in arm and such a thing had never happened before.

272

Without hurrying, they wandered, seeking out the few people in the grounds. To each they gave the message that Nathaniel was speaking in the small lounge. Most went inside immediately. One or two elected to stay where they were.

Then the couple wandered further. They went out as far as the shrubbery by the front fence and stopped near the street light to watch the huddle of police bent over something in the road. Torchlight shone on a piece of paper. There were explanations, questions, grunts. Fists rubbed against palms, protesting the chill night. From somewhere they heard a telephone, a short needle of sound.

Even before that sound died, there was another: running feet. The circle of bent heads jerked up. Uniformed backs tensed. But there was only one runner coming along the sea wall. It was Roger Slattery, the owner of the chemist shop. He planted himself in front of Lou Crawford, talking agitatedly between gasps for breath. He kept pointing back towards the shopping end of the waterfront and seemed to want Lou to go with him. But Lou waved an irritated, negating arm. The chemist persisted. Lou grew angry and sent the man packing in the direction he had come.

Jack and Emily glanced at each other puzzled; neither had caught the gist of it.

'What the hell!' Lou had caught sight of them. He trod briskly across to the fence. 'I told you four to keep out of sight. Are you asking for more trouble or something?' The couple turned sheepishly away. 'Hang on. You've got fire extinguishers organised?' Nods. 'Everyone downstairs? All doors unlocked? O.K., now get back inside, I've got enough trouble without you making it worse.'

They went, hearing the policeman informing his squad that the world was chocker with idiots. When they reached the porch, they heard one engine, then another. The two police cars were moving, swinging into the Sanctuary driveway, without lights. They came in, turned in a wide semi-circle and came to rest facing the road, close to the front fence, but in the shadows the street light cast from the shrubbery. The engines switched off. Then, nothing. Jack and Emily went inside, feeling their way through the pitch-black corridor.

The small lounge was both elegant and comfortable, with

soft furnishings, wooden panelling, and a tiled fireplace set into the wall. The lighting was subdued: just four candles set along the mantelpiece. Half a dozen people were coming away from the window, one pulling the blind down after him. Both the Drurys. Tommy Ransley. The city couple who always sat in the lotus position were doing so now. There were less than two dozen in all. Some were troubled, some apprehensive, some looked to be almost daydreaming, gazing into the fire. A city youth in a motorbike jacket made for the door, volunteering to get more wood from the shed. On the hearth rug, D'Arcy stirred. His old head shifted restlessly from between his front paws to across his right foreleg. Jennifer was on the settee next to Nathaniel. They were both in everyday clothes, paired by jeans and T-shirts. But she was drawn imperceptibly away from him, an unconscious shifting in response to the change from Matthew to Nathaniel. In her lap rested the large hardcover book into which all the teachings were duly written. On top of that, her pad, the top page already well filled with shorthand.

She turned the page.

Nathaniel's piercing black eyes were focused on a young man reclining on the carpet. 'No one learns by words alone. If my words alone could teach, then this house would not be in darkness now and the police would not be preparing to defend it. Understand: *the total situation is your lesson.* Whoever — and whatever — you encounter tonight and at any other time, *they* are your teachers.' The flames from the fireplace reflected in Nathaniel's eyes as tiny twins, dancing in black velvet in perfect unison.

By the back wall, Jack Sullivan was frowning. There was an odd undertone to Nathaniel's voice tonight. He had heard it before and wished he could think where. Feet tramped in the hallway. The three who had stayed out in the grounds came in. They said that Lou Crawford had ordered them inside and that they were all to keep the blinds down and stop attracting attention to the room. The youth with the motorbike jacket returned with a couple of logs of wood. He crossed to the fireplace and set them. The flames swallowed and grew.

'Funny smell in the woodshed,' he commented.

'You're in the country now, boyo,' Bill Paget informed him.

Another question to Nathaniel. Another answer.

274

Jack rubbed his chin stubble. He left his place and picked his way to the window, pulled the blind half an inch to the side and peered through the gap. The police cars were difficult to see in the shadows. Still there was no one out on the road. Wait! Yes: one lone figure, out on the sea wall, moving into view. Rubber necking? Or a scout? Jack looked back into the room and shrugged at the questioning looks.

'...You may choose to ignore the lesson,' Nathaniel was saying, 'but the lesson will not ignore you. It will wait for you at the next turning in a different form...'

Karen Drury pointed towards the street. 'What's this one about then? What's going to happen?'

'You mean you want to sneak a look at the answers in the back of the book?' Nathaniel inquired.

Jennifer remembered something. She pointed to the small leather sleeve hanging from Nathaniel's belt. 'Matthew wanted me to ask if you'll tell him who it is who found his knife and uses his place in the bush.'

'A travelling companion,' Nathaniel answered. 'He and his companion have shared many lives.'

'You going to tell us who it is?'

Nathaniel's eyes sparkled. 'Only that Matthew's unknown companion is another apprentice to the Weaver. Just as each of you is an apprentice. Some life hence, as you work on your own tapestry, you will realise that, at the same time, you yourself are a thread in a much bigger tapestry; look over your shoulder and see *its* weaver, much older than yourself. And he, in his turn, is a living thread in an even bigger tapestry, woven by an even *older* weaver. And so on, without end. *All is consciousness; part within part within part.*'

Jack pursed his lips. There it was again, that undertone, that hint of... of finality. Then it came to him, and for a brief moment he was back by a fire on his own farm, watching helpless as Matthew screamed and collapsed, as Nathaniel went into oblivion and as the villagers rushed them all. A needle of ice pierced his stomach. Emily glanced across the room and he saw that she too was aware of it. She then looked swiftly at Nathaniel, and Jack could see a trembling in her throat. She looked intently at the presence distorting Matthew's face, and it did not return her look. Slowly, she leaned her head back against the wall, the muscles on her face giving way to age and despair. The coldness within Jack grew. He straightened, standing away from his corner. He wanted to leap forward and take Nathaniel by the throat and shout, *Who are you? Who are you? Who are you?* He felt a snarl rise in his throat. But a soft, thudding sound came from outside. His grasp crumpled the edge of the blind as his face went to the window. Police shapes were running, spreading out in line with the two cars, facing the road.

'... No one *needs* to recognise the lessons,' Nathaniel's voice went on. 'You will learn them anyway, eventually. Progress is not restricted to those who join churches or find gurus or...'

Four, no, five cops were standing at the ready, the other two still in the cars. No lights. Jack turned. Jennifer was looking at him.

'... Throughout your history men have hunted for the Truth. Knights sought the Holy Grail, pilgrims travelled to Mecca, adventurers sought Shangri-la, countless journeys have been undertaken to find holy men, secret brotherhoods and mystery schools. But such journeys are not the only way...'

Jack's feet moved in a curious dance of indecision. He was torn between the immediate danger and the overwhelming desire to take hold of Nathaniel, put his hands around his throat and scream the question. No. Out on the waterfront, two masses of people were closing together from left to right: two centipedes with many feet and many heads. A planned, orchestrated meeting. Again the voice came behind him, maddening now, with its seductive offer of riches...

'... but the best teacher of all is within you now. The greatest place of learning of them all, the one best suited to your needs, is about you at this moment, composed of everything you see and much more that you do not see. The lesson you most need is being presented to you right now.' The voice dropped and softened. 'And so it should be, for you are creators, growing up to be like your Creator. I salute you.' The eyelids grew heavy. The head sank, then rose, and he was gone.

With a cry of impotent rage, Jack whirled, leapt forward, stopped. By then, everyone was on their feet. The need to see what was happening outside gripped the room. There was a rush to the next room where the blind could be raised without lights showing.

Only the four healers remained, and D'Arcy, who clambered stiffly to his feet and looked from one to another.

On the waterfront, the two centipedes had become one. A single mass of people faced the Sanctuary grounds from one end of the fence to the other. Jack strained to hear the distant murmur of voices. Emily went to stand beside him, her wrinkled face sagging and tired. Matthew stood listlessly in front of the dying fire and Jennifer took his hand and pressed her face to it.

'He didn't say goodbye,' she said.

'He didn't go anywhere,' Matthew said, unconvincingly. He took his hand away, laid his fists on the mantel between the candles and tensed them until they drained of blood. He released them with an explosion of breath and then roamed the room with hands in pockets, unsettled, unpredictable in his movements. Each time he came near the hearth rug, D'Arcy thrust a wet, concerned nose at him. Jennifer watched, knowing that it was not the time to communicate with him. When all this was over, she would hold him close, closer than they had ever been. She would tell him that she had made up her mind: she would live with him and be with him always, whatever happened. She shivered. The room was cold.

The sound of a police loud-hailer made them jump. It was high pitched and penetrating, though the words were distorted beyond recognition by distance and the wall. Jack was peering through the small space between blind and window frame. 'Crawford is playing them with psychology. He can see them, but they can't see him ...' The amplified voice ceased. '... It's working. So far. They're just standing there.'

Emily came to Jack's side and passed an arm through his. Jennifer rubbed warmth into her arms. Matthew paced the floor, aimlessly, distractedly.

A pause.

'... Still nattering about it,' Jack said.

'Why don't they hurry up and decide?' Matthew snarled. Jennifer looked at him anxiously; fear growing in her, as if by contagion.

Another minute. The murmur from the road carried clearly in the still air. Absurdly, they heard the flippant *peep peep peep peep* of a kingfisher in the bush.

'They're not moving!' Jack said. 'Just standing there.'

'Shit!' Matthew struck the wall with his fist.

'Matthew?' Jennifer was bewildered by his increasingly frenzied behaviour. Her own teeth were chattering. He stared at her suddenly, as if noticing her existence for the first time, then touched the goosebumps on her arms with his fingertips.

'I'll get some wood.' He flung open the door.

'No, not *now*, Matthew! For heaven's sake not *now*!' But he was already on his way, the door slamming shut behind him. D'Arcy whined, padded across the carpet and scratched at the door.

At the window, Jack froze. 'Oh, God,' he said softly. 'Here they come.'

Jennifer bounded to her feet, swept the four candles off the ledges and stamped on the flames. Then she was beside Jack, yanking at the blind, releasing it with a rush and a clatter to give them full view.

The attackers were pouring over the fence, black dots bobbing against the moonlit harbour. But none of them reached the police line. Almost as they began to pour through the gaps in the shrubbery, two car engines roared to life. Five hand-held police torches switched on, and the cars were reversing rapidly towards the Sanctuary, five men running at top speed beside them, lighting the way.

'Back-door time,' Jennifer cried out, her voice high with fright.

'No. Wait.' Jack sounded puzzled. 'The cops aren't running away. It's too organised . . . '

The wave of noise from the street was a single angry surge of sound. It broke over Matthew as he went through the moon-lit doorway of the woodshed. Adrenalin racing, he snatched blindly at a couple of pieces of wood. He had to get back. What was he doing here?

Something rough and hard crashed across his temple. He went down, dazed. There was a scrabbling sound. A grunt. A pungent smell. His heart hammered high and hard in his chest. Then someone was on top of him. A hand wrapped in a wet cloth slammed down on his face, forcing the back of his head down into the tumbled wood. An acrid, heavy vapour invaded him. He couldn't breathe, couldn't even cry out; terror was a blinding, transfixing white bolt. He tried to kick, snarling in his throat, ripping and tearing at the hand behind the cloth. The cloth lifted. A fist plunged into his stomach. The cloth came back.

Two cars halted abruptly, their bumper bars just half a dozen paces from the building. The thin police line formed again, as it had been out by the fence. The car headlights switched on, full beam, raking across the lawns and through the trees at the advancing mob.

Puzzled, the mob slowed from a run to a walk. The shouting ceased. They came on cautiously, closing ranks, suspicious. All they could see were the dazzling glare of the headlights and the black bulk of the old mansion behind. The only sound was the snarl of a dog, echoing inside the building. They halted. A few began to edge towards where they might see behind the glare. But then Lou Crawford's voice was heard, speaking briskly, calmly. And not to them.

'Waiata police to one-oh-six. Are you receiving?'

His radio telephone replied. 'Reading you ten, Waiata.'

'Where are you? Over.'

'Wait one...' A pause. '...Coming down into, uh, Taka-matua. That how you say it? How's the little problem?'

'Just about to blow away, mate, soon as you get here. You all there?'

'Yep. Save some for us, won't yer?'

'...Pleasure. Waiata out.'

Heads turned in the direction of the Takamatua Saddle expectantly, as if police cars might come into view at any moment. A switch clicked behind the headlights. Lou Crawford's voice came again, this time booming at them from the loud-hailer. 'You're trespassing on private land with intent to commit a serious crime. Anyone still here in two minutes will be arrested and charged, and by God I'll throw the book at them!'

'It's a trick!' shouted Tom Glubb. 'The guy in the other car did it! The sound was too clean. It ain't never that clean with an easterly front comin' in!'

But the mob was stirring. People looked about them, especially behind at the distant front fence. If they were still here when reinforcements arrived, they'd be trapped. Inside the great black shadow, the dog was still snarling.

A tall, upright figure walked into view between the police and the mob. He stopped, faced the crowd. With the headlights behind him he was only a silhouette, but an unmistakable one. He raised his arms in desperate appeal. 'In the name of all that is good and holy, I implore you to turn aside from this madness!'

Every man and woman on the grounds froze to the spot. They looked at him. In the silence that followed, the crowd of individuals snatched itself back into a mob. The resentful silence became a muttering and Robert McKay reeled back as if pushed.

'Get him out of here!' Lou Crawford snapped. The nearest man leapt forward, grabbed the minister by the scruff of the neck, bustled him back and around the corner of the building and hissed at him furiously to stay out of the way.

But the damage had been done. The muttering became a growl, the growl, a howl of final decision and resolution. A light flared in the crowd, washing faces orange in defiance of the headlights. A small pool of liquid fire floated lazily over Lou Crawford's car. The bottle smashed on the concrete porch steps and with a soft whoomp, the steps were awash with fire. Then scores of people were running forward, towards the cars and to the side, around the house.

Lou scrambled out from behind the wheel.

His radio telephone spewed words.

He threw himself back in, snatched up the microphone and yelled into it. Kept on yelling.

On the porch, white clouds billowed out of extinguishers and down onto the blazing steps. Between the cars, policemen struggled, as knots of men tried to remove their batons. Down the sides of the building, lids rattled off petrol cans and petrol poured bubbling along the walls. Sean O'Brien stood by with another milk bottle, screaming at the pourers to hurry up and get out of the way.

Then the sound penetrated. The extinguishers kept gushing, but all other activity froze. Sirens were keening: many of them, soaring and swooping independently. Lights were sweeping down from Takamatua Saddle, scything the moist air on the outcurves and raking the bush on the incurves. Three, four, five, six cars, coming fast. The lead car was less than a minute away.

Only half the mob risked running back out the way they had come. The rest went over the side fences. And they kept going like that in both directions: through the church grounds, through backyards, behind the saddlery, behind the fire station, where the engine had broken down only that morning. By the time the first of the sirens was winding down outside the Sanctuary building, the fire on the front steps was out. Two policemen were circling the building on the run, checking that no one had remained to light a match in a quiet corner.

Jack put his extinguisher down on the steps and wiped a sleeve across his brow. In the light of the arriving cars, he saw that Lou Crawford was watching him. Both men eyed each other, but each man's thoughts were unfathomable to the other.

'Jack!' Jennifer was beside him, frantic. 'Where's Matthew? Have you seen Matthew?'

'No. Isn't he inside?'

Jennifer turned in panic and dashed back into the house, thrusting past people, stumbling through the dark corridor towards the back door. D'Arcy was there before them, looking at the closed door. His ears were laid back as he lifted his old head and howled. The thin, mournful sound threaded through the spaces of the mansion. It made the newly-arrived policemen out on the grounds falter and look about apprehensively. Chief Inspector Richard Sparrow broke off from giving orders and stared at the dark building. He muttered. 'Suffering Jesus. I hope that's a dog. Is that a dog in there?'

The men around him didn't know.

Four of them found Robert McKay standing dazed near a side fence. They had him spreadeagled against the palings for a search before they noticed his collar. They took him to the chief inspector, who called Lou Crawford. Finally, the minister was escorted to the street where he walked slowly away towards the church.

A light, cold rain started.

Jimmy's body ran with sweat as he climbed. The rain would cool him soon; it fell straight down, light but penetrating. The night was pitch-black now. He couldn't risk even a single flash of torch light being seen from below. But he knew every twist and turn of this track from his boyhood days. The way unwound slowly before him in his mind's eye; his feet picked out the path, step by step. One hand detected overhanging branches ahead.

281

The other held Matthew fast over one shoulder so that the head and arms swung free behind.

Stop, change shoulder, start again. Stop for a rest. Jimmy lowered his burden carefully until the head was down, then let the rest of Matthew flop into the sodden mush of the bush floor. He knelt, feeling for the side of Matthew's head. It was difficult to distinguish blood from water in the dark, but the wound didn't seem too bad. Repugnance at touching Matthew's flesh rose in him, but he overcame it. There were more important things to consider now than his own feelings.

The rest over, he knelt again, rolled Matthew, manoeuvred him on to a shoulder, forced himself up, then set off again. The track levelled out and turned south, following a contour around the basin, then along and across Aylmers Valley. The rain eased. The moon returned, now close to the hills. He speeded up: he must be clear of the track quickly, in case of a search party. He was so tired. It was so much harder than he had ever imagined to carry an unconscious man such a distance. And yet, how marvellous, how wondrous the flow of energy into his body, bringing vital strength to legs and shoulders. It wasn't *his* energy. He knew its source, and gave humble thanks out loud.

It took two hours to reach a patch of dense bush in Kaik Bay, a rocky harbour inlet along from Waiata. The moon set as he covered the last few hundred yards and he located the shelter itself entirely by feel and memory. He lowered Matthew to the ground, felt for a canvas rucksack waiting under the one-man shelter and rummaged in it. In a few seconds, a candle lit up the underside of the fernleaf frame and the surrounding dank, dripping bush. A weta waved its feelers at him from under a rotting branch. Supplejack vines looped down into the light, guiding water droplets from the bush canopy. Above, a wood pigeon warbled, disturbed by the sudden light. Moss, fresh and moist green, blanketed roots and branches and much of the ground. Matthew lay across a gnarled rata root, grotesquely splayed in the position in which he had fallen. His head lay in a young fern, sodden hair covered an eye and a cheek, and the candlelight made his pale face deathly white.

He made a sound. His hands curled against moss, his head stirred, then jerked convulsively as he vomited. Jimmy came out of the shelter in sudden concern. If he didn't do something,

Matthew might die of exposure. He hauled Matthew to the edge of the shelter, then rolled him on to the dry ferns underneath. He felt his chest: not bad, dryer than his own, anyway. Matthew's limbs moved weakly. He moaned.

Jimmy took out the ether bottle and looked at it. He didn't know how much was too much, but nor could he risk Matthew making a noise, not this close to Kaik Bay farm. He wet the cloth, squeezed it, held it on Matthew's mouth long enough for the inhalation to pull it inwards twice. In a few seconds there were no more movements. Jimmy dug an old singlet out of the black flap of the rucksack and carefully mopped the still face, taking care to dry gently over the eyelids. He smoothed the hair back with his fingers. Yes, sleeping like a baby now. The candle flame protested at a waft of air. Matthew's features seemed to flicker, reminding Jimmy of old cowboy movies. Then he remembered a time, long ago, when he had sat on Matthew's bed, and the Pringle girl had sat on the dresser, swinging her legs backwards and forwards like scissors. Matthew had seemed such an ordinary boy then.

Jimmy opened the front pocket of the rucksack and took out a plastic bag. He wiped his hand clean on the wet singlet, then removed a sealed envelope from inside. He inspected the carefully printed message on the outside, dipping his head in satisfaction. It said, 'Hammer, please take this letter to Mr McKay. Extremely urgent. Thank you. Yours faithfully, Jimmy Crocker.'

He returned the envelope to the plastic bag, and the bag to the rucksack. The letter mustn't get wet or marked in any way. Everything must go right. He poked his head out to check the patches of sky visible from the bush floor. Some stars, some clouds. Rain now didn't matter, but it had to be clear tomorrow. It had to be perfect tomorrow.

It would be.

Eleven o'clock. Three hours to wait.

He noticed the dozens of sodden bits of paper lying on the ground outside the other end of the shelter: there had been many rejects before he'd found just the right wording for the letter to Mr McKay. He went around the shelter and picked every bit up. It would hardly be a good start to tomorrow to leave litter lying around in the bush.

In the moist air, the torch beams were rods of light, following D'Arcy away from the woodshed like spotter beams. The sidelight made bizarre shadows cavort on the back walls of the Sanctuary. This time, D'Arcy didn't even bother to try for a scent. He padded stiffly straight to the same spot on the back fence, pushed through the two bottom wires, then tried to climb the six-foot bank to the bush. His old body failed him again. He stayed there, pinned by the torch beams, moaning to the trees and the night.

A constable wiped the fence wire with paper, but if there had been blood on it, the rain had long since washed it away. The chief inspector looked dourly at the edge of the dank bush. It returned his gaze bleakly out of two ovals of torchlight. He shook his head with final certainty.

'No. Not until first light tomorrow.' He looked hard at Jennifer. 'And don't you do anything stupid, Miss Pringle. If something happened to you up there, we'd have to divert men from looking for your friend.'

Emily led her inside. Jack climbed the fence and brought D'Arcy back. In the small lounge, they relit the fire and wrapped themselves in blankets to wait the night through.

Ellen found Robert in the church, sitting in the front pew. She hesitated, knowing that the news of Matthew's abduction could now only torment him further, also knowing that he would not thank her for keeping him in ignorance.

She came to him, sat with him. Told him. His head bowed further.

She went back to the manse and sat in her bedroom rocking-chair, prepared to wait up all night for him if necessary. Much of the time, she prayed. She asked forgiveness for the people who had so wronged him, forgiveness for the bitterness in her own heart, forgiveness for Matthew for what he had done to Waiata. But, knowing what single conviction lay like a sword across Robert's bowed shoulders, she prayed most of all for a sign: one sign, she begged, to show her husband that his life, devoted entirely to Him, the Father, had not been entirely in vain.

Water.

It surged rhythmically along his side, curling around knee,

hip, shoulder and head. He knew it was cold water, but he didn't feel cold. He didn't wonder why that was so. It didn't occur to him to wonder the why of anything. He was caught up in a wondrous drifting sensation, together with a marvellously sensitive, minutely detailed awareness of the things around him. He not only heard, but felt the bubbles passing by below and the occasional clumps of bead weed knocking on the clinkers. It even seemed that he could feel the miniscule shifting of the overlapping planks, one against the other. There was the stealthy plop, the creak of rowlocks and surge of movement, the swish of water. Plop, creak and surge, swish. Plop, creak and surge, swish. On each surge, the plank pulled against his cheek, and the water ran away, only to return in leisurely flat fingers. Sometimes, too, it seemed that his cheek was not in the boat at all, but a few inches away through the planks, where the tiny wavelets chattered against the side of the boat.

Plop, creak and surge, swish. Now, on each surge, a plastic object rolled against his face. Even though his eyes were closed, he knew exactly what it looked like. It was a detergent container with the bottom cut out. He knew that as surely as he knew that the person causing the steady rhythm was Jimmy Crocker. One piece of knowledge seemed neither more nor less important than another.

It was night.

He felt that the boat was very gradually turning, on the arc of a giant circle. And it was good: a sense of promise allowed him to ignore the wisp of fear floating loose-tendrilled somewhere out in the darkness. It was not his fear. It did not belong to him.

The wavelets were dying. They murmured more rapidly against the boat, but finally gave up with a sigh. The odour of trawlers, of engines and fish, crawled into his nostrils. The side of a trawler approached: he knew it as a mounting pressure on his forehead. The rowing stopped.

Clunk. The canvas under his cheek jerked, but stayed. Something had been removed from it. The planks under him rocked wildly, then lifted to ride high and still. Boots trod on the deck, going away. A click. A rustling. Another click. The boots came back and the planks rocked again. A surge sideways. The rhythm began again, more slowly now and with quiet care.

And stopped a second time.

Clunk. Another trawler. This time, there was something familiar about the pressure on his forehead. Jimmy departed, returned in seconds, and a thin hard object was forced under Matthew's side. A rope. A net strop. The planks bucked then rode high. Pain tightened around his chest and back and under his arms. He was being hauled up the side. He squirmed and groaned, protesting that the blackness had left him. It came back and he was grateful as it slid over him.

Click. Light seared his eyelids. The fear tendrils lifted out of the darkness towards him. That smell! Over the fish and oil odours, an acrid, heavy stench brought fear whipping around him, finally certain of its prey. He forced his eyelids open. At first Jimmy was only a fuzzy, hulking shape. He was standing, holding something, looking at it. A bottle. Matthew groaned and tried to raise his head, to cry out no, no, no, through the fog that was thick in his throat and mouth. There was a hesitation above him, then the bottle disappeared and so did Jimmy. Matthew's eyes rolled about. He recognised the hold of the *Phoenix*. He had stacked fish bins here, pumped bilge water, oiled the shaft. The last time he'd been aboard the *Phoenix* ... the last time ... the accident ... hospital ... Nathaniel ... Nathaniel ...

Jimmy returned with a length of oily hemp. Another hesitation, then he rolled Matthew on to his back on the plank beside the bilge trough. Down the middle of the trough, above the water, was the propeller shaft.

Sound forced a path. 'Wha ... ?'

Jimmy ignored him, pushed his arm under the two-inch shaft so that the elbow dipped in the bilge water, then passed the other arm over the top and tied two wrists together.

'Wha ... !?'

The hatch opened, closed, and Jimmy wasn't there anymore. Soon there was a whirr, a series of crisp explosions, slow, then faster. The *Phoenix* engine was starting up; the shaft was going to turn! He had to keep his arms clear. The strain of holding himself away pulled the blanket of blackness over him. His elbow rose and white pain exploded as the shaft began to move. He cried out, jerking his elbow down into the stinking water. The shaft sped up, the *Phoenix* reached cruising speed. He tried to keep the blackness at bay. He attempted to cut the hemp on the rusty, pitted surfaces of the shaft but then shrieked as it tore at his flesh. In a half-shadowed world, he drifted around the turning metal, sufficiently conscious to keep his skin clear and to know that his blood was dripping into the bilge water. How long, how unendurably long it went on — a forever in each turn of the shaft. He must not let go, must not.

The shaft stopped turning and he plunged deep into nothingness.

When he next awoke, it was with a start. His eyes jerked open, but in the darkness he could see no apparent reason for the sudden waking. The pain was familiar to him now, like a backdrop from which to view existence. Nothing more had been added to the backdrop, except, perhaps the pains in his side. He was lying on sharp stones. The sea was murmuring close by, water was lapping on rock. He frowned at a hazy, blue-white mushroom in front of his face. He shut his eyes and opened them again. It was still there. Faintly he heard bellbirds, then the mushroom sprang away to infinity and became dawn.

Dawn. The moist air tortured and cracked the acid desert that was his mouth and throat. Where was he? He tried to move and couldn't. His wrists were tied behind his back now, attached to his ankles, which were drawn up behind him. He pushed his head back, gasping as the stones opened a path for fresh blood through the old caking his cheek. In the new position, gravity seemed to be pulling him sideways, back away from the horizon. His stomach lurched as he realised he was looking straight upwards. Cliffs. He was lying at the foot of cliffs. Again, he shut his eyes, trying to make sense of it all, then opened them to a metallic sound. A figure was moving high above him, black on the grey face. It was Jimmy, climbing down something.

The quarry! He was across the harbour from Waiata, lying at the foot of the cliffs, on the track used to take the fossilised wood to the jetty. The sea was a few feet away. What was Jimmy doing up there? A whirring sound came down from above, as a power tool started up.

Six o'clock. Just before sunrise. Hammer Keegan rattled the manse door knocker. Ellen McKay opened it, looked at the message on the outside of the envelope and hurried across to the church. When she returned, Robert was behind her, grey with exhaustion and defeat. He held the envelope for some time, then opened it with leaden movements. There was just one page.

Dear Mr McKay,

The Lord has chosen me to be His hand of justice on earth. Come straight away and witness that it is carried out as He commands.

I am at the quarry. Please come in Hammer's boat, *Te Rau Tau*, because it has a loud-hailer on board. Bring your Bible with you. You'll need it.

Yours faithfully,

James Crocker

Robert stared at the page for much longer than was needed to read the message. He gave the paper to Ellen and, for the moment, ignored Hammer who was watching him with insolence masked by curiosity. He trod to the end of the porch to gaze across the harbour. The first edge of the sun was gilding the top of the quarry cliffs. Lord, Lord, what more do you ask of me? I have given you my best.

The chief inspector gave up and switched off the walkie-talkie savagely. He turned to Lou Crawford.

'Is Crocker armed?'

'The tone of the letter — '

'Bloody marvellous! Forty-one men in this two-shack dump and I'll probably have to bring in the armed offenders squad as well. What the two-tack blazes are we going to do? Twenty-five men chasing thin air in the hills. And sixteen on the Sanctuary is the bare minimum with the hotheads still loose!'

Lou said nothing. He knew what the decision would be: life before property.

The chief inspector made up his mind. 'I want two .303s. I want Crocker's old man with me. I want two boats: launches or trawlers.' He turned to his sergeant. 'Pick ten men, including the two best shots and get them down to the wharf.' Back to Lou. 'That'll leave you with half a dozen again, Crawford, but we scared the pants off them last night; chances are ... take that look off your dial, constable ... get me those boats before they're all gone. Get moving!'

It was ready. Everything had been checked and rechecked.

Jimmy walked to the edge of the quarry face: a ledge two hundred feet up the cliffs. He looked out across the water with deep satisfaction. Almost every vessel in Waiata was on its way. He raised the binoculars. What a sight they made. A long, loose string of beads on a braided belt. A convoy. A fleet. Coming to witness. And how they would rejoice when it was all done. All was going to plan. And the day! The day! It was as he had foreseen: a clear, blue sky, unmarred by even the slightest patch of cloud, the hills as proud and green as ever, and the harbour a breathless sheen.

He waited, square on the harbour, feet slightly spread, arms folded, patient. What vitality, what strength was in him now, though he had not slept for three days and nights. What power coursed through his veins, tingling in his fingers and hands and around his head. If he were not in such masterful control of his body, he might tremble for sheer happiness. That he, whose sin had condemned the soul of his only child, should be chosen for the task of delivering the world from its greatest evil. And when it was done, the Lord would stretch down His mighty hand and pluck Amelia from Satan's grasp forever.

He looked obliquely down the face of the cliff to the loading track by the water, where Matthew Fleming lay like an angular, upside-down question mark. Good, good, the sun was just coming on to Fleming now. Perfect timing. And he was lying with his face to the sea. That was a bonus: it seemed right that he should face the witnesses.

Jimmy raised the binoculars again. Yes, yes, yes, the leading boat was the *Te Rau Tau*. Now nothing could stop him. He watched intently as the leaders came within a quarter of a mile of the cliffs, then nodded eagerly to himself as they suddenly stopped. He had known they would see it from there. Now the others would catch up; they would talk it over and come ahead at reduced speed, behind the *Te Rau Tau*. He waited. Yes, here they came, idling cautiously forward. Closer, closer yet, he let them come. When the *Te Rau Tau* was 150 yards from the loading track, Jimmy put one hand warningly on the plunger beside him, and raised the quarry hailer to his mouth.

'That's far enough. I've plugged in everything in the store. A hundred and twenty sticks — it'll blow away half the cliff.'

He exulted at how quickly the white water leapt from their sterns. But then, puzzlement. He snatched at his binoculars. One of the latecomers wasn't heading this way at all. The *Anita*! She was pointed away somewhere past the next headland. Refusing to witness! Spurning the Lord's work! Suddenly, Jimmy was frightened. Nothing must be allowed to cast a slur on this day. The binoculars dropped, the hailer jerked up.

'Tell the *Anita* to come back, or I'll do it right now!'

In ten seconds, the *Anita* was rounding back towards the fleet.

In the wheelhouse of the *Sea Nymph*, Jack ran his binoculars over the scene for the third time: Jimmy beside the plunger, the hair-thin, black line, looping across the unworked quarry face and ending abruptly; and directly below that, Matthew. His eyes were open. He seemed to be looking directly down the binoculars back at him. His mouth was open. In pain? Thirst? Impossible to tell.

Jennifer knew Jack was monopolising the binoculars to spare her the sight. She placed a hand firmly on the glasses and he gave in. When she had finished, she sank back on the bunk and curled up, leaning against the wall in the foetal position, head in hands. After a while, she mumbled, 'If we go close, talk to Jimmy...' But she didn't finish. She knew that no one from this boat could talk to Jimmy.

D'Arcy touched his nose to her lap.

On board the *Sirius*, Chief Inspector Sparrow was called to the radio telephone. The caller was one of the eight policemen hidden on the *Anita*, checking whether there was any point in remaining below decks, now that their cover was blown. The chief inspector granted the request with barely veiled anger and replaced the microphone. Beside him in the wheelhouse, his remaining two men were unhappily loading the .303s. Gordon Crocker was watching them bleakly, his lips dry.

'Last resort, Mr Crocker,' the policeman reassured, crisply. 'We're depending on you to talk some sense into him. And I just hope that idiot minister of yours doesn't foul it up. Are you ready?'

Gordon swallowed. The policeman motioned to Peter Stewart, the owner of *Sirius*, and the vessel began to idle forward through the fleet. At the rear, the last boats were arriving, including the chastened *Anita*. On the cliff, the hailer blared.

'Ahoy, *Te Rau Tau*. Mr McKay, speak to me so I know you're there.'

Hammer Keegan held out the microphone and switched to deck address. For the minister, the moment had arrived as a leaden yoke. He pressed the button and spoke, but uselessly: he was unfamiliar with such devices and held it too far from his mouth. The cliff voice came again, edged with fear, demanding that he reply immediately. He tried again, and this time succeeded.

'I'm here, Jimmy.' Around the fleet, dozens of pairs of binoculars registered the change in Jimmy's posture. Relief.

'All right. Open your Bible now, Mr McKay. Open it to...' The sound cut off abruptly. A pause, a quick shuffle of hailer and binoculars, then the hailer was redirected at *Sirius*, now idling level with *Te Rau Tau*, further along. 'Sirius. You're too far forward. Get back.'

The chief inspector gave a terse command. Slow down. Peter Stewart complied, sweating. The vessel crept forward. The policeman nodded to Gordon, who stepped out onto the foredeck, raising the police hailer. The two riflemen slid Perspex windows aside and laid barrels on the sills.

'Jimmy? This is Dad. You're making a mistake, lad.'

'You're interrupting. Go away.'

On another command, the *Sirius* drifted in neutral. The chief inspector snapped an inquiring look at the two riflemen. They shook their heads and he swore. On deck, Gordon tried again.

'Jimmy, why don't you come down, lad? And we can have a good —'

'You dare interrupt the Lord's work? Get out. Get back right now!' The voice was vibrant with anger.

Gordon glanced in panic towards the wheelhouse. It was the policeman's turn to swallow. He ordered slow forward. The fisherman at the helm shook his head. The order was repeated furiously.

But Jimmy spoke again, and this time the sound was high and brittle, crackling with sibilants. 'You've got five seconds to start moving to the back of the fleet. One! Two!...' His sunlit figure stepped close to the plunger. Peter Stewart slammed the *Sirius* into full reverse. Water rumbled beneath as she slid back, and the chief inspector's expletives reverberated in the wheelhouse. As Stewart spun the wheel and headed his trawler back and around the fleet, he replied, surprising even himself with the extent of his normally unused fisherman's vocabulary. Chief Inspector Sparrow stormed from the wheelhouse. The two reluctant riflemen laid down their weapons, nodded gratefully to the fisherman and also went out on deck. Jimmy noticed the uniforms for the first time. He declared from above, 'Man's justice cannot prevail over God's.'

Silence. It was high tide, and still no breath of wind disturbed the harbour. Most engines had been switched off. Forty vessels waited, set in glass. Two hundred people watched the man on the skyline.

'Mr McKay.'

'I'm here, Jimmy.' Robert sensed Hammer Keegan turning to look at something.

'Open your Bible to Leviticus, chapter twenty, verse twenty-seven.'

Hammer left his side; but the minister was concentrating on the pages. His hands fumbled. Leviticus. Leviticus. One. Fifteen. Nineteen. Twenty. Over the page. Verse twenty-seven. He stared fixedly at the words, paling, even though Jimmy's intention had been obvious from the start.

'Have you found it?'

'Yes. Yes . . . I've found it,' Robert said into the microphone. Now Hammer was at his side, holding his arm, pointing behind. He turned. A plume of smoke was rising from the other side of the harbour, behind the only tree large enough to be visible at such a distance. The sequoia. The Sanctuary was burning. Robert turned his head away from the sight and pressed his forehead against the glass of the window. Burning. Burning. Something was burning in his mind. And in that instant, his own flame sprang fiercely into focus. It wasn't over! He had not yet failed the challenge. If he had failed it, he would not be here now. In spite of all, it lay ahead. It was now!

Jimmy had seen the smoke plume. His voice soared in triumphant delight. 'See! See! The pit is burning. Look, the pit is burning. The hand of the Lord has begun to strike evil from the land. It's time, Mr McKay. Read it out so everyone can hear.'

The minister's legs were trembling. No, this was no time

292

for weakness. But what was it he had to do? What *was* the challenge? He needed time to think. Delay. Delay.

'I . . . I . . . can't, Jimmy. Jimmy, this is . . . '

'Read it, Mr McKay! God is giving you a chance to make up for your weakness.'

Dear Father, what must I do? What do You want of me?

The voice came again, impatient, but sorrowful. 'All right then, I'll do it. You could have been perfect too, Mr McKay, the way you used to be.' The hailer dipped, paused, and rose. An arm rose with it, as if, incongruously, in benediction. 'Leviticus chapter twenty, verse twenty-seven: "A man . . . that hath a familiar spirit shall surely be put to death: they shall stone them with stones; their blood shall be upon them." ' The upraised arm fell to his side. The loud-hailer descended, then dropped to the ledge. The clash of metal on stone reached the boats a second later. Jimmy leaned over the plunger.

On *Sirius*, the chief inspector shook his head and passed a finger under his chin. On the *Sea Nymph*, Jennifer buried her face in Jack's shoulder and her fingers dug into his flesh. He didn't feel it. On the *Te Rau Tau*, the minister screamed at the flame in his mind, demanding that it show him the solution. But it licked on, burning. Delay. Delay.

'There's a mistake, Jimmy. It's not perfect this way.'

For a moment, man and plunger seemed frozen together. Then they separated. Jimmy wavered between the plunger and the cast-off hailer. The hailer won.

'Of course it's perfect. What are you talking about?'

'I want you to do God's work, Jimmy, but God's word says Matthew has to be stoned to death. He can't be stoned to death if he's already dead.'

The loud-hailer moved about erratically. The man behind it took the steps to the brink of the ledge and looked down. He stepped back, then forward. Looked again.

'Move, Fleming,' the hailer blared.

No movement.

'Move. You're alive.'

Matthew's form was still.

'Wake up! I looked after you. You're alive.'

'Let me check. Let me look at him,' Robert said to his microphone.

'No! No, you can't. No one is allowed near him.'

'But you'll be watching all the time.'

Silence. Jimmy's body performed a complicated movement of indecision and frustration. He tried several more times to cajole Matthew into making some movement, even a tiny movement of the head. But there was no response. The hailer lifted. The voice was frightened now. 'You'll tell me if he's alive, won't you, Mr McKay?' Yes. 'All right, hurry up. Land along at the jetty. Hurry.'

Robert looked at Hammer Keegan and nodded towards the wooden platform that lay as far to Jimmy's left as Matthew was to his right. Hammer returned the glance, dealing grudging respect, then kicked the *Te Rau Tau* into gear. She throbbed forward, sliding away from the silent field of vessels, spreading an unseemly wake on the blue-grey sheen.

By the time Robert stood on the jetty, he felt as though his head was being squeezed through a tube. Everything around him was hazy and out of focus. Even the beams under his feet seemed insubstantial and unreal. He set out along the track, stumbling on the unseen, uneven stones. Only the still, small human form, a hundred yards away was clear and vital . . . that, and the flame twisting in his mind. There was something he had to remember. Something terribly important that would explain the riddle and reveal the challenge. If only he could remember, the great challenge could be met even now.

What was required of him? Save Matthew's life by deception? Claim that he was dead? Perhaps he really was dead. But if he was alive, the deception might not convince Jimmy. What then? There was no shelter to drag Matthew to. No overhang. The face was sheer.

The voice beat down the rock face at him, suspicious now. 'It's only because I want to know, Mr McKay. He's got to be stoned anyway, even if he's dead. So you have to tell me the truth.'

Dried blood. It caked Matthew's wrists and forearms and matted his hair. The limbs were slack, the mouth open. The face was bloodless, the eyes closed. Robert knelt, putting one knee and one hand on the sharp stones.

'Matthew?'

The eyelids flickered and lifted. The eyes moved slowly to

294

look at him. Unbelievably, they were at peace. They were contented.

'Is he alive?'

Robert stared, leaned further forward to Matthew. 'No, no,' he protested. 'You must be afraid. You must be afraid!'

The throat strained, white lips framed the whisper.

'It's dawn. You can turn out the light now.'

'You try to teach me? Even now?' Robert pushed back on his heel trembling. Remember? Remember? But how could he remember when the very air around him was a haze throbbing with strange, distant voices.

'Is he alive?' Booming down the rock face.

Robert turned his face up to the top of the cliffs. Made a trumpet of his hands. 'I don't know yet! It's hard to tell!'

'Well, hurry up. Check his pulse. Quickly.'

The minister knelt again, reaching a hand over to the wrist free of encrusted blood. Then he froze. His heart lurched as his gaze fixed on a small bright object hanging from Matthew's belt. The leather sleeve had torn free leaving the miniature pocket knife exposed. The engraving of the puma was unmistakable.

'You!' Robert's breath sobbed in his lungs. With one hand he wrenched the knife free of the belt and brandished it in Matthew's face. 'You!'

Even now, Matthew was not beyond shock. His eyes and mouth widened and his throat rattled. 'You,' his lips mirrored.

Robert heard the gritting of sandals on sand, the scrape of earthenware. He looked up. There was a small boy beside him, wearing a djellaba and carrying two pitchers on a wooden yoke. The boy was looking at him with frank curiosity and something about the expression reminded Robert of Matthew.

Then Robert McKay remembered. Lives he had lived before came to him like shafts of light into a box of shadows. He remembered writing love sonnets long, long ago. Now he remembered himself as a woman, stealing the fur seal killed by her son. Now a man, running naked for a laurel wreath, while his greatest opponent sulked in the arena seats. He ate maize porridge from his mother's little finger; watched enraged as his daughter wheel-danced with commoners; strutted while his priestess prophesied his chieftainship over cracks in the bones of a wolf. All his memories wove around himself and *one* other.

295

'Have you done it? His pulse? Is he alive?'

The sound jolted Robert. He swayed, confused.

Faintly, there came the sound of a splash, then a voice called urgently. Reluctantly, he forced himself to look out across the water. A twin ripple was spreading in front of the fleet, like an enormous arrowhead, pointed at himself and Matthew. At the tip of the arrow was a bobbing black dot.

Matthew's neck muscles contorted. His head rolled. His mouth whispered, 'D'Arcy hates to be left out.'

'He's alive! I saw it!' Exhilaration. 'Get out of the way, Mr McKay.'

Robert smiled out over the water. The sea was so beautiful, so clear and deep and welcoming. He looked down at the knife in his hand, fumbled with the blade until it slid out with a smooth snick, leaned over Matthew.

'What are you waiting for? Get out of the way.'

He sawed at the wrist ropes.

'What are you doing? Mr McKay! Stop that!'

The ropes parted.

'Don't make me do it to you, Mr McKay! Don't make me!' The pleading, screaming voice was amplified to grotesque distortion.

Very slowly, Robert placed the knife in a pocket of his fire-ruined jacket, the one in which he kept his gold fob-watch. With his last reserves of strength, he rolled Matthew on to his back with the arms loose by the sides, sat next to him facing the head and finally slipped an arm under Matthew's neck, lifting his upper body into a half-sitting position.

'You made me do it to you! You made me do it!'

Matthew's arms could not return the embrace, but as the top half of the cliff turned to boulders and tumbled slowly down to them, they were both smiling.

'Time to go home,' Robert whispered.

'And after that,' Matthew's lips framed. 'What shall we do after that?'

When the dust was only beginning to settle, a dog crawled out of the sea. He had not had to swim the full distance, because the great jumble of rocks had spread into the harbour. He crept, battered and bleeding, on to the nearest of these rocks, up on

296

to the next one, then slipped back, falling heavily. He struggled to his feet, tried again, succeeded, and kept on going. When the boats came, the searchers found D'Arcy's body wedged between two rocks near the top of the pile.

Across the harbour, a straggle of men watched the last beam collapse into the ruins of the Sanctuary. Behind the licking flames they saw an old woman in a black shawl. Under the shawl, the hair was pure white, the face lined beyond the count of years. The eyes gazed sightlessly into the ashes.